Thanks for the talk
Terry.
. I hope you enjoy
this little story
of Pana and the lake.

David

MUSIC
OF
THE
LAKE

a novel
by
David Mohrmann

LastWord Books

Printed and bound in
The United States of America

Library of Congress
Cataloging-in-Publication Data

Music Of The Lake
A novel by David Mohrmann

ISBN 978-0-9969922-4-4

Front and Back Cover Paintings
by David Mohrmann
Cover design by David Mohrmann
and Rich McCutchan

ACKNOWLEDGMENTS

From my first visit almost 50 years ago, Lake Atitlán has felt like home. I was there in 1976 during the massive earthquake. I've returned often since then, nearly every year, for months at a time, and always find it difficult to leave. And yes, like Hank I've been longing to write a novel about how much I love its water, volcanos, and amazing people.

I feel lucky to have Lee, my dear wife and sometimes harshest critic, for her constant support. And good friends Nancy Carlson-Paige and Douglas Kline, always ready with thoughtful notes and needed encouragement to keep working.

I'm also grateful for my weekly writer's group (Pete Springer, Wanda Naylor, Bob Morse and Jeff Wright) for their kind yet ruthless honesty

An ongoing thanks, as well, to my long-time editor, John Heckel, for all of his great questions and advice about this story—a story that, in certain essential ways, did not want any direction whatsoever.

I dedicate the novel to my old buddies from Pana, Anando le Boef and Alan Rosenblum, whose loving carefree spirits often inspired me as I wrote.

And a special hug to my good friend, Rich McCutchan, for his generous help with the novel's cover.

"All humans ever needed
for proof of God
was music."

-Bokonon, during the last days of the world

Panajachel, Guatemala
Sunday, December 1, 2019

1
Every Day

Hank has lived at Lago Atitlán for forty years. He knows this place as well as any gringo could, which means hardly at all, and has no problem admitting his ample ignorance.

Still, he longs to write a novel about what, if anything, he's learned. Thinks the hard work might quell his urge to drink.

Thinks about it every day.

It's a twenty-minute walk to his favorite swimming spot. Each morning it seems like he's being led. Being called. Not by God—Hank's not religious—but by something he can't name. Plainly put, he goes because he has to. That's how it feels. Booze used to have a similar magnetic pull, then held him squirming in its sticky grip, trapped and inconsolable. This calling, though, makes him feel hopeful—better able to face the world and maybe...just maybe...find some peace.

While barely eight o'clock, the air is already warm. Halfway down the beach he drops his pack, strips to his skivvies, goes to the same large flat rock where he always sits. Plops his feet into the clear cold water. The resulting ripple, a sight and sound Hank loves, could never truly be described. He glances around, then focuses on his arms—on the bronzed and finely wrinkled skin that hangs from his once taut biceps. Can't really describe that either, or the rest of his long-lived, ever-so-slowly deteriorating body. Hank gives himself a playful smirk. Truth is, he's doing good for 70. Or at least damn good enough.

Across the way, edging the far shore, a crease of liquid sunlight stretches out and shimmers. The lake now mirrors the deep blue sky, and skimming over it, like massive greenish arrowheads, are reflections of Atitlán's three magnificent volcanoes. Hank knows one thing for sure: how grateful he is, *every day,* to be a part of this.

He squeezes the worn edges of his rock, feels safe and snug, bedazzled by the splendid morning and curious about whatever might happen next.

From behind him, sunshine arcs over the eastern hillside. The swirl of prismatic rays is so intense that he must look away, down at the shaded sand. His eyes follow along the shoreline, a hundred yards, to the steep cliff of massive boulders. An egret, atop a protruding ledge, flaps its sleek white wings, takes off and flies toward him. Hank watches closely, enthralled by the creature's graceful flow, when out of nowhere some airborne insect ambushes his right ear, beats and buzzes up inside, a loud frenetic scramble as if burrowing to his brain.

"Well, you little motherfucker!"

Shocked by the tenacious, unrelenting attack, impressive were it not so overwhelmingly unwelcome, he pokes and prods, crushes the pesky thing and scrapes its mangled body out.

Whoa, he thinks, *if only I had that kind of spunk!*

Hank shakes his head from side to side, his curly white hair flying, takes several deep breaths and struggles to relax, reconnect with the harmony all around him. A dragonfly lands on his knee like they're the best of friends. A fish splashes in the shallows close to shore. A bird trills out its morning song, again and again and again.

Then sunshine finds the pebbled beach. Makes it glisten.

Quick to counter the instant heat, a breeze whispers from the south, the first tremble of what is coming, a wind the Maya call *Xocomil.* By late afternoon, on most days throughout the year, the lake's ripples turn to waves, lapping the sandy shore like thirsty tongues.

Hank stands, closes his eyes, nods to the waiting water and feels its ancient spirit, something beyond his ability to fathom, a depth impossible to reach. He treasures the feeling, offers a slight yet reverent bow, then dives in and opens up to the translucent turquoise blue. The lake is its usual frigid self, on warm days like this more soothing than a psalm. Ten feet beneath the surface, stroking through the mystery like a happy frog, he's aware that Fiona would love to be here with him. Had he the gumption to ever actually write a novel, she would be his main character. He'd show her knee-deep in the shallows, unable to take the leap. "It's freezing!" she'd shout as Hank pretended to lose his patience. Then, as it happened every time in real life, Fiona would dive in, and be thankful, even joyful, for the few minutes she could tolerate the cold.

Hank swims till he's good and tired, stops, then sees—in the near distance—a *cayuco* fisherman tossing out his net. It appears to be the friendly young guy he met a few months ago.

Yes, it could be Juan, and he'd love to go say hello, though this is no time to distract him—the fisherman busy fishing, and Hank, as usual, busy doing nothing.

He looks across the lake, acknowledges the volcanoes of San Pedro, Tolimán, and Atitlán. The enormity of each makes him feel small, and when considered as a trio, like giant guardians of this wild majestic place, he further shrinks, well aware of his relative insignificance.

This is when, like every day he comes, Hank feels awed, *immensely awed,* by the mighty lake. A thousand feet deep! Beyond his imagination! Its sheer profundity fascinates and at times, especially when the wind is blowing, can unnerve him. As a boy, in Arizona, he remembers how easy it was to touch the bottom of a pool. In Atitlán, even fairly close to shore, a person can't find the bottom without scuba gear. Weird that its depth never used to matter. He would swim for half an hour, past the rocky point to a sulphur spring on the other side, sit in a bubbling pool and soak in the morning's glow. Hank no longer has the strength to go that far, and happily accepts that, amazed to be here at all, thrilled to feel so at home in this blessed water.

But he's been out long enough. The eerie thought of such vast dark space below makes him anxious. He takes a calming breath and slowly heads for land.

Then, from around the point, a jet ski roars in his direction like a wild beast.

Shit. Hank stops and faces the damn monstrosity. *Ah yes, it's Sunday.* Since he comes most every morning, the particularity of each day sometimes eludes him. Weekends, he should not forget, bring rich *ladinos* from Guatemala City. They luxuriate in age-old family mansions along the shore, called *chalets,* and unleash their demonic toys, like this jet ski, on an otherwise tranquil paradise.

And—*FUCKING A!*—it's coming straight at him!

He waves his arms until the hellish thing veers off.

Safe, yet viscerally rattled, he gulps in air and swims hard for the beach.

Some minutes later, while Hank is drying off, the cayuco fisherman rows his way. Yes, it's Juan. Must have seen his encounter with the jet ski. *"Buenos días!"* the young guy calls out, paddling his tiny rough-hewn wooden boat, cruising through the rippled water with total ease.

As usual, he looks happy as can be. "Good morning!" says Hank, also speaking Spanish, "any fish today?"

"Maybe," says Juan. He frowns, lifts up his empty net. "Only none for me."

"I bet that jet ski didn't help."

They've joked before about the obnoxiously loud and disruptive mechanical bugs. "No! Makes the fish go hide!"

Hank laughs. "Which makes your job even harder!"

"Así es," Juan says—a common Spanish phrase that basically means *Just the way things are...nothing to be done.*

4

It's a tried-and-true banality which most folks never question: a lighthearted surrender to forces beyond one's control.

And in principle that makes sense. Hank agrees that natural disasters, like droughts or fires or floods, are best accepted because they can't be stopped. No argument there. But to tolerate man-made contraptions like a jet ski, in a place like this, is another thing altogether! *Nothing to be done, my ass!* "Those damn things are a real problem." He smiles, tries to look less angry than he feels. "Surely *something can be done.*"

Juan seems confused by what that might mean.

Yeah, so is Hank. Still, he can't resist this chance to vent. **"Así Es!** That's what I'll call it if I ever write a novel."

"A what?"

The young guy is from Santa Catarina, has probably never gone to school. "A novel," says Hank, "is a kind of book."

"Oh. Like at the library in Pana?"

"No." Hank can't help but chuckle. "A book of mine would not be wanted by any library. No, it's just a story I might make up, stuff I think is true, that I'd like to say. I want to write about what I see happening here, how some people are causing problems. A novel about the lake and how to protect it."

"Protect? Protect from what?"

Oh, c'mon, Juan's at least sixteen, can't be that clueless. Or, if he is, should give his world a closer look. "Well, amigo, you know better than me. For one thing, the noise and pollution of a jet ski close to shore. The danger to swimmers and the trouble it makes for you cayuco fishermen. I just think some things need to change. If nothing else, rich *chaleteros* should understand how local people are affected."

He sees what looks like sadness in Juan's eyes. It seems a familiar sadness, a sense of hopelessness—something the young man has learned to live with.

Then Hank looks deeper, and inwardly winces. At himself. How can he, a First Worlder, possibly know how a Guatemalan feels? Where does he get off advising a native fisherman about the lake? Yeah, life gets harder every year, what else is new?

Juan won't go to City Hall and complain. It has always been useless, and sometimes dangerous, even fatal, for the Maya to make a fuss.

The sadness, if that's what Hank's seeing, is probably meant for him. Juan must have heard his kind of naive lament before. He knows this foreigner does not understand the truth. *Así es.* The young man turns away, gazes out at the water, and looks concerned, or maybe worried—as some *Indígena* worry every day —of somehow getting into trouble. Might even wonder if Hank can be trusted. They barely know each other, and this sort of conversation, if shared with the wrong people, could be a problem. The last thing he would want is to be in some righteous gringo's novel! "Hey, I'm only joking."

Juan looks at him and smiles. "Joking?"

"I'm not writing any novel. Never have and never will."

Juan shrugs. *"Pues, no me importa,"* he says, like he truly does not care, then glances up at the sun. "Sorry, amigo, I can't stay. Have things to do."

Hank feels awkward, and embarrassed. Decides to make a joke. "Like catch some fish?"

Juan laughs. "No, no, I give up. Better to go home early, my son's first birthday."

Hank beams, grateful for the change of subject. "Well, hey," he says, "congratulations!"

"Thank you, Enrique, yes, we are very happy!"

"As you should be!"

True, thinks Hank, because infant mortality remains extremely high among indigenous Guatemalans. To survive the first year is worthy of celebration. The child will likely be mired in poverty all his life, complete with the various dangers that entails, but Juan smiles anyway, and looks hopeful as he rows away. It makes no sense for the Maya to fear what may be coming. Insecurity is expected, and not a whole lot ever really changes.

Hank smiles too, and shakes his head, finds it almost funny that, in spite of his obvious privilege, he also feels insecure. Life never has been easy.

Luckily for him, *and also worthy of celebration,* things have changed now that he's helping out Fiona. It truly feels like an honor. Also a final chance. He needs to do this right, and is aware that he could learn some things from Juan. Like how to be more patient, more accepting of unwanted realities, more able to find goodness, no matter what.

He truly is intrigued by this young guy. Would love to know about his daily life, the strength and courage it must take to go out each cold morning, in his wobbly little boat, and, more often than not, catch no fish. Wow, what a novel it would be if he could learn, first hand, those kinds of details!

But no, he won't dare ask, afraid Juan might think he's prying, or maybe somehow trying to use him. He'd never take the chance of destroying this valued friendship.

So yeah, Hank tells himself, *it's damn good that you won't ever write a novel about the lake!*

However, even if he did—if by some freakish turn of destiny that should happen—no big deal. Because of course he'd change Juan's name. And, because telling the truth might also cause trouble for him and Fiona, he'd change their names too. He'd change everybody's name, and would be certain to make it seem, from beginning to end, that none of the characters or situations or ongoing problems described are real —that his entire story, every bit of it, is fiction.

2
Uh-huh

The other regular morning swimmers, Ingrid and Analu, arrived while he was talking to Juan. As usual, they went farther down the beach. Always give Hank lots of space. "So you can concentrate," Analu once flippantly tossed out, referring to the notes he's often scribbling in his notebook.

"We know you have much need to *think,*" Ingrid added in her sketchy English—as if *thinking* were, itself, a problem, a wretched habit he could not kick.

Analu has a separate reason for keeping distant. Something to do with Fiona, an ongoing spat between them about who the hell knows what? A conflict Hank wants no part of.

8

Ready for some shade, he moves away from the shoreline, up beneath the caña, and looks over at the women. What a marvel they are! Like family he loves but rarely speaks to. Both are avid swimmers, which over the years has forged a lasting bond. They come early for their daily workout, are usually in the lake when Hank arrives, each going off in a different direction. Today, as is her normal practice, Analu heads toward the middle, will continue until she's almost out of sight. Ingrid likes to go around the far point. She'll get back first, her friend still at least ten minutes away.

For Analu, raised on a mountain lake in Argentina, the strenuous exercise is like breathing. Something that must be done. After her long swim she'll look totally spent, then shake off the apparent exhaustion and do ten pushups before lying down on her towel.

Both women have jobs that start in the late morning. Ingrid owns a boutique in Pana with one of her German friends. Analu works at the expat school, AMA, as some sort of an advisor. Once warm and rested they generally leave together, a way to extend their visit. They will wave good-bye to Hank and walk off chatting.

He'll stay longer. Since Fiona does not expect him till late in the afternoon, he sometimes waits for the Xocomil to arrive. Should the wind hold off and the air get too hot, the cold water is right there. He might stay in the shade for hours, jot down thoughts about the novel he'll never write. Or, as more locals show up at the beach, he'll hang out with some he knows. One great thing about people on the lake, Guatemalans and foreigners alike, is that they're friendly to whoever comes along, and always have something to discuss.

Yesterday he found a typical bunch of expats. Typical in how similar they are in spite of obvious differences. In other words, like him, quite certain of their opinions.

Federico, a computer geek from Mexico City, works with most businesses in Pana, and prides himself on *being in the know*. Carolina is from London, an accomplished abstract painter—

and talker—who, though ignorant about most things, does not hesitate to speak her mind. Peter, from Tennessee, got rich selling acid and mushrooms in the 80's, and has bribed enough officials to have learned, if necessary, how to slip around or through the porous legal system.

Yesterday's topic was Panajachel's new mayor, a former lawyer, Miguel Reñado. Unfamiliar with the man, Hank didn't have much to say. Not like the others, who are more connected to the social scene, astute observers of Pana politics. Each had strong opinions of Reñado. None of them were good. All agreed that he is corrupt in "slightly different ways" than the former mayor. The distinctions were too subtle for Hank to follow, which was one reason he kept quiet. Also because, in his opinion, they purposefully missed the point, and would not want to hear that from him. He'd learned, at the risk of being further dismissed as a pain in the ass, not to speak his truth too plainly. Yes, there was some serious talk about the lake. This mayor, like all others, would do nothing to protect it. About that they spoke in dark, disapproving tones, like the first notes of some tragic opera, then said how futile it is, as foreigners, to complain. But, same as Hank, they are included in this mess. Everyone plays a role in the coming tragedy. None of them are innocent.

Today, Ingrid does not leave with Analu. She now walks up from the shoreline, clearly wants to spend time with Hank. And he knows why. On occasion—presumably because he's so old and, therefore, will not create any sexual tension—she tells him about her troubled love life. Does he simply provide a way for her to vent? No, she must do plenty of that with Analu, who can be counted on to give lots of stern advice, and harsh rebukes should her friend not follow it. Hank, on the other hand, is never the least bit judgmental. He wants no serious involvement in Ingrid's perpetual melodrama.

Luckily, his tiny part is not difficult. Or important. He'll be supportive, on her side, come whatever may. The only thing she really wants from him is kindness.

"Is it a time where we can talk a minute, Hank?"

"Yes, yes, of course."

"Am I not interrupting?"

"No, my dear. Never."

A tall ravishing redhead in her early thirties, she blushes a rosy pink. Hank cannot deny, in spite of feeling somewhat used, the pure pleasure of having Ingrid close. She sits down, cross-legged in her short shorts, leans toward him and starts to talk, her freckled face lit up, her hazel eyes gazing into his, her expressive hands soon to be slapping his thigh or squeezing his knee for emphasis—her wild emotion like a puppy's, and impossible to tame.

While all of this is very nice, his main attraction is to Ingrid's strong German accent and uniquely husky tone, an enticing combination that holds him captive. Yes, Hank is infatuated with her voice. Music he adores. There is a quirky, inexplicable lilt to it, a heavy yet buoyant timbre that somehow stays in tune with her lithe, athletic body. She is talking, as expected, about her Brazilian boyfriend, Paulo, *a real dick,* who once again must have proven it. Though trying to pay attention, Hank is distracted by the grieving, almost moaning sound of her, a strangely haunting chant beneath her words, like a requiem for the girl's tormented soul. Now Ingrid sighs, a soft yet piercing note in perfect harmony with her sad and troubled eyes. He thinks of Fiona, how her song of him was probably much the same. Maybe, instead of what he'd planned, he should write a science-fiction novel about a stunning female alien—a cross between these two gorgeous women—who roams the Earth in search of selfish men.

"There I tell you," Ingrid says, "this stupid shit I cannot take!" And she goes on. Something about Paulo's druggy friends. Something about religion. Something about her divorced parents in Berlin.

Though it's the alien's incredible beauty which first attracts the selfish men, they're soon mesmerized by her deep throaty voice. Not aware she is speaking an unknown language, they scoot in close, like ants to honey, and try to read her luscious lips. That's when she whispers something, a nearly breathless mantra—irresistibly sweet—and, as if it were their idea, the men completely change, stop thinking only about themselves and begin to behave like good, or at least decent, human beings.

"Hank, you will be proud for me."

"Hey, already am."

Ingrid slaps his knee and frowns. "No, I mean *really,*" she says, then bursts into a triumphant grin. "Paulo, that damn asshole, is moved out!"

"Oh," he says, "good!"

"Yes, yes, I...I wake up happy every day. My breakfast is more tasty to me, you know?"

"Yeah, uh-huh, I do."

Ingrid grimaces. "No, I...I do not maybe always like he's gone, but things they have to change!"

Clearly, she needs to get her sadness out. Again. Several silent seconds pass as Hank ponders, based on their last conversation, a month or so ago, how little things have changed. *Didn't Paulo also move out then?* He tries to remember the number of times a split has happened during the last five years. Too bad there's no kind way to say how bored he has become with this futile mess. Oh yes, he's certain Paulo will be back.

She should be talking to Fiona.

Ingrid wrinkles her brow and gives his thigh a gentle tap. "You know what I am meaning, yes?"

"Yes," Hank says, aware that she's not ready to hear the truth. Maybe some day, but for now he'll try not to hurt her feelings. To his relief she keeps on talking, and in empathy with her sadness he says "Uh-huh" a lot. Comfort, at this moment, is more helpful than good advice.

In the end, Ingrid gives him a tender hug, then kisses both his cheeks, a European custom Hank likes very much.

"I cannot choose to stay," she says with a lovely frown, her soft pink lips like some exotic fruit.

12

Hank would once have thirsted for those lips, and is glad that time has passed. She gives another loving squeeze and leaves.

A few minutes later he also decides to go. Once packed up, however, Hank stands there feeling empty, feeling lost. And anxious. This has little to do with Ingrid, but her leaving somehow triggered it...the sense of disconnection from the world, from other people, that he's suffered with his whole life.

Then he thinks of Fiona, imagines her close, sees her looking at him, and smiling. Hank knows how lucky he is to have her back in his life. Also that he must be careful...not fuck up.

He gazes out at the lake. Maybe it will calm him. When it doesn't, his mind kicks in, pushes aside his lame resistance and, with great authority, insists it's time to talk—*seriously*—with himself. *I mean it. Seriously. Do you hear?*

Hank sighs.

None of your damn joking around, okay?

"Uh-huh," Hank says aloud, gives his head a weary shake, sits back down and laughs. A somewhat nervous laugh. There's no pretending he hasn't done this—and quite *seriously*, same as Ingrid—so many times before.

3
A Curious Little Tune

The serious talk ends where it began, in the familiar zone of discombobulation—a word Hank learned from his Uncle Abe. Good word, *discombobulation,* because it feels much the way it sounds, like he's missed out on important information, has taken a wrong turn, or maybe the wrong train, with no idea where he's going. Hank should be used to these moments of inner turmoil, has never had a plan for life and doesn't need one now.

He shuts his eyes. Focuses on each breath. Waits until his scattered mind resettles in his body, then smiles and looks out at the lake. The beach has emptied out, its people gone, perhaps scared off by his heavy thinking. He stays put and feels grounded. There's no place he'd rather be.

Around noon the breeze turns fierce. Instead of the expected Xocomil, blowing in from the south, the wind has shifted to a quickly mounting *Norte,* rattling the shoreline reeds, charging across the lake.

A Norte can get vicious. One never knows, but it's wise to expect the worst. Before leaving the beach he picks up trash: candy wrappers, tiny bits of this and that. The least one should do in honor of the lake.

There are a couple of routes back into town. His favorite is the way he came, on the path above the shore. Several small powerboats, called *lanchas,* are out on the water—the taxi service to lakeside villages. They throttle on, obliged to battle the sudden turbulence. Today their roar is swallowed by the swelling wind. Hank used to dread *El Norte,* but for the last several years has felt energized by its raw, unharnessed power, its gusty challenge. It tests an old man's physical endurance and mental fortitude. Or at least his stubborn willingness to keep going. He steels himself, bends into the resistance, his shoulder-length white hair blowing behind him like a tattered flag. In fusion with swaying branches and lapping waves, there is a sacred hush intoned by the mighty wind. For him it is a profound, enigmatic sound: a brief diminishment of humans, of human behavior and human noise. At moments like this, when the unknown takes control, Hank often thinks of Uncle Abe.

Were it not for that dear man he would not be here.

From the time Hank was a small child, then called Henry, his uncle would visit their home in Phoenix. It only happened once a year, during winter, because Abe suffered from a severe heart condition, could not endure the otherwise excessive heat. Or much activity. He would stay for a couple of months. Never strayed far from the house. But in spite of his physical fragility, Abe was a spirited soul. He loved to play and joke with Henry, called him "a curious little tune."

The toddler, while not knowing what that meant, heard the nickname as a term of deep affection. Uncle Abe would follow him around, watch everything he did. Even at three years old, Henry was amazed by the strangest things. He might stare for many minutes, glossy-eyed, at a cobweb. Uncle Abe would ask, with genuine interest, "Hey there, buddy, what is it you see?"

Though puzzled by the question, the child somehow understood that no answer was expected. He could feel his uncle's constant encouragement to be baffled by the world.

As Henry grew older he got more baffled. At six he and Abe discussed, at length, the inexplicable mysteries of air, wind, and water. During much of his eighth year he stayed focused on the sun—where it came from, day after day, and could he be sure it would come tomorrow? Was not surprised to get no good answer. By ten he wondered, a lot, about things that he'd been taught, was supposed to know, which to him made no sense. Like why, when they ate dinner, his mother insisted on crossing herself and praying aloud to Jesus Christ. "Who is that?"

Abe had tried his damndest to explain, but the boy remained skeptical. He could at times be quite obstinate. Some things seemed "just plain stupid," and his uncle could only nod.

About religion they were largely in agreement.

On his eleventh birthday, Henry declared (whispered, most privately, to Abe) that "Stupid Thinking" was a good name for ideas based on unprovable beliefs.

Abe also agreed with that. "Conversely," he suggested, "certain observations, if undeniable—like the beauty of a flower, the coldness of an ice cube, the sourness of a lemon— are not worth mentioning at all." Abe frowned. "From now on," he said, "we shall term such senseless utterances *Indubitable*." The boy nodded, in full accord, and his uncle felt inspired, it seemed, to further clarify his meaning. "Stating the obvious," he said, "means losing sight of the mysterious."

Henry squinted at him and showed a mischievous smile. "You mean like that?"

"Yes, yes, exactly," said Abe, pleased by the mild rebuke. "Forgive me, I shall not mention it again."

Though on occasion very serious, most of their time was spent having fun. They might watch for many minutes the random meanderings of a single ant, or puzzle over the simplest words, like *pillow*. They'd repeat it, faster and faster and faster (*"pilllowpillowpillowpillow"*) and break into peals of laughter.

His mother liked to say, "Abe and Henry are thick as thieves." Something else the boy did not understand. "It means that you're good friends."

He loved how happy she was when his uncle came to visit. But Bill (Abe's brother, Henry's father) at some point became conflicted, did not like his son called "a curious little tune."

One morning at breakfast, when Abe said it again, Bill finally got downright angry. "C'mon, could you please knock that off."

"That?" Abe glanced at the table, then looked under his plate. He was known for goofing around. Especially with words. His physical malady, which meant a necessarily subdued life, had turned him into something of a bookworm. As a young man he'd dreamt of being a writer—dreamt it until, to earn a living, he ended up a bored, over-qualified accountant. Did Abe have a strange way of seeing life? Yes, oh yes, and he'd admit it, but claimed it was not his fault, that he'd been victimized by too many worthless, mind-boggling novels. He set down the plate. "To which *that,* precisely, are you referring?"

The frivolous deflection, Henry knew, was sure to piss his father off. "You know what I mean, don't—"

"Sorry, I…I simply fail to grasp why you're so upset."

Henry was twelve, and curious what might happen next.

"Shit," said his red-faced father. While a normally self-contained man, Henry was aware of his inner rage, which at times he could not control. According to his mother, Bill had been a WWII marine, had witnessed numerous atrocities, had developed a basic distrust of human beings. "I swear to God," the boy once overheard him shout at her, "I'll do whatever the hell it takes to protect my family from the fucked-up world." One of his basic precepts was to never show vulnerability. Sure, he knew Abe meant well, but to call Henry *a curious little tune* just seemed very wrong. "I'm sorry," he said, "it just sounds weak."

"No," said Abe, "he's not weak. But the kid is definitely different. In a good way, I mean."

"I think it's sweet," his mother said.

"Way too damn *sweet* for me," his father said. He stood up, as if to give someone an order, then sat back down, looked at Abe and started saying things that everyone already knew. Bill owned a construction business. He'd taken it over from their father, and expected his son to take it over from him. Which meant the boy had to "toughen up. Or at least not get any softer." His face was flushed with brewing anger. He stood up again, strong and tall next to pale and skinny Abe, who was three years his elder—who Bill had watched over and protected, because of Abe's illness, the whole time they were growing up. He loved his brother, hated to confront him, but must have felt he had no choice. "Am I making myself clear? Do you understand?"

Abe slowly rose and gave Bill a tender hug. "I understand."

It was the only time Henry saw his father hugged by another man. He rarely allowed any physical contact, even from his wife. And, just like that, the argument was over, the subject never raised again.

Abe later told Henry, in no uncertain terms, to never stop being curious. "My brother does not know how to deal with your sensitivity." That was his main point. "Your dad is a good man," he said, "and also, I'm afraid, emotionally injured. That's the war's fault, son, not his. And certainly not yours."

Sure, Henry wondered what had happened to him, and knew he'd never know. Not something Bill wanted to remember, or would ever discuss.

In part out of heartfelt sympathy for his father, Henry tried hard to please him. With no clue of what else to do, the teenage boy followed his lead for many years. He took wood-shop in high school. Then, instead of going to college, he went to work for him. It was 1968. Henry was eighteen. Though the Vietnam War was in full swing, the odds of getting drafted were only 1 in 10. He didn't worry—if necessary would go to Canada, and his father agreed. No son of his would be forced to kill other human beings.

Henry learned a lot of good things as a carpenter, like how geometry applied to the real world, and how to use power tools, and how to build a house. He was a decent worker, but not as dedicated as the older men. For him it was just a job, and each day he looked forward to its end. He liked hanging out with friends and smoking pot—or occasionally dropping acid, taking what they called "star walks" through the desert. From time to time, after being up till two or three in the morning, he was late getting to the job site. Or would fall asleep at lunchtime. The older guys gave him shit, an ongoing joke.

His father noticed and didn't like it. Then, on one of those late nights, he stood his ground, planted himself in front of his son's bedroom door—would not let Henry in. "Damn it, boy, you can't live like this!"

He sighed at being called a boy and given, although quite vaguely, another order.

Then his father got specific. "I'm sick and tired of your attitude at work! You have to shape up, is that understood?"

"Yes, sir, very understood."

The sarcasm must have been apparent. "I don't think it is."

"No, no, it is," Henry said, then channeled his Uncle Abe. "Understood, only disagreed with."

His father pushed him against the hallway wall. The two exchanged blows as a vase of flowers, a family photo, and then Henry went crashing to the floor. It took his mother's hysterical screams to stop the fight. As she tended to her son's bloody nose, his father hovered over him. "For chrissakes, boy, I'm trying to teach you how to survive in this goddamned world, how to be a man!"

The next morning Bill went early to the job site. There was a deadline, and work always took precedence over any family squabble. Henry's mother, a devout Catholic and blind defender of both God and her volatile husband, made her wayward son a hearty breakfast. She didn't have much to say, only that his

19

father loved him dearly, worked hard to give them a good life, "did what he did for the best of reasons, and must be forgiven."

Well, yes, of course, and Henry did forgive, yet the chasm between them widened. While well-intentioned, his father's righteous guidance was at odds with Henry's nature. The young man felt unseen. He managed to get through each work day, which was not easy. His father ignored him, hell-bent on finishing the house.

The morning after their supposed deadline, with everyone's nerves on edge, and especially Bill's, Henry shattered a plate-glass window by forcing a slightly oversized piece of trim.

"Take care of your fucking mess!" his father hollered. "Then try to do something right!"

Henry did what he was told. After cleaning up the shards of broken glass, vacuuming the floor of every sliver, he dropped his tool belt and walked away for good.

That was impossible for his father to accept. "Do what you need to do," he said before kicking him out of the house, "only somewhere else."

So Henry went to live with Abe in Santa Cruz, California. His uncle welcomed him with open arms. He'd never married, had always felt obligated—because of the chronic illness—to live alone. For Abe and his otherwise constant loneliness, what a joy to have Henry near!

But the young man was deeply troubled. While thankful for the friendly refuge, he kept ruminating on what his father said. "Do what you need to do."

The problem was, he had no idea.

Abe tried to engage him in conversation. Got nowhere. There was nothing Henry wanted to talk about, far too embarrassed by what he saw as his childish confusion and stupid choices. For months he moped around, took long walks by himself, usually to the ocean, where he would sit on a cliff for hours, drink beer or smoke pot, and stare at the breaking waves.

Every morning, before heading out, he did whatever needed to be done—like vacuum, wash the dishes, mow the lawn.

His uncle always thanked him, and once in awhile asked, "Are you okay, buddy?" Though he wanted a real answer, Henry still didn't have one. He'd just nod, and Abe would sadly, with remarkable patience, let him go.

After a couple of months, the money Henry had earned as a carpenter was running out. Soon he would need to find some sort of job. An unwelcome, unacceptable realization. So he stopped drinking or buying pot—and, even harder, stopped eating lunch at the Harvest Cafe where he'd hoped a pretty waitress named Hope might someday notice him. Even if she did, then what? He couldn't afford to take her on a date.

One night Henry returned home around 2 a.m. He'd gotten stoned again, what he'd promised himself was "the last time," while watching the full moon reflect on the ocean.

Abe was in the living room pretending to read a novel. He sighed, noticeably relieved, then asked, somewhat shyly, "See anything worth mentioning?"

Henry smiled, reminded of his early childhood. "Full moon shining on the water."

"Wow," said Abe, as if seeing it himself. "Lucky you."

They said no more, but the next night Henry fired up Abe's old Buick and took him to the ocean so they could watch the moon together. That's when their talk turned *serious*.

At times the young man cried. For the most part, though, it was a clear-eyed conversation, and went on for many days, about what Henry might *do* with his life.

His uncle had no advice, only implored the gods that he not become an accountant! Abe laughed and slapped his forehead. "Worked for me," he said, "because I'm a home-bound gimp with no imagination. That's why I was always intrigued by you."

"A curious little tune," Henry said. "Too bad that's all I got."

"Hey, it's a quality most folks are sadly lacking. They go after the damndest things without ever wondering why. At least you know what doesn't matter."

21

"Yep, no problem there."

Abe clapped his young nephew on the shoulder. "All you need is time to find your way. And time is in no hurry."

Their conversation led to Henry attending Cabrillo Junior College. He took all kinds of classes over the next two years, only nothing to do with business or hard science. Not enough space in those subjects for his mind to move around. He studied hard, got straight A's, and remained unsettled. While interested in everything, the idea of "majoring" in any specific area felt wrong, like some kind of trap.

Once again (that is, *as usual*) he had no idea what to do.

Abe sat him down on the couch. "Seems we've learned that schooling is not for you."

"Maybe nothing is."

"Yeah, could be." His uncle must have seen this moment coming. "In my opinion, buddy, you're not meant for a normal life. Best to accept it and move on."

Henry laughed. "Sure don't sound like *good news*, Uncle Abe."

"Well, depends on how you hear it. Hell, who knows, you might be a poet."

"I'm not wise enough for that."

"Whoa," said Abe, "I didn't say a *good poet.*"

"Hah!"

"Listen," said Abe with a ticklish grin, "here's a deal you can't refuse." He reached into his pocket and pulled out a stack of bills. Two hundred dollars. "One thing I could not take is you being drafted. I say, get out of this damn country! Go wherever you want. I'll Western-Union two-hundred bucks a month for you to live on."

"*Huh?* No, I...I couldn't, I—"

"Yes, you damn well could, and I insist. Look, I've made some good investments. I can afford it and want to do this. All I ask is that you send me a letter once in a while, saying where you are and what you're up to. And, of course, a line or two of bad poetry, or whatever—just some *curious little tune.*"

22

"Sounds like a dream."

"Better yet, a dream come true! Why not? Adieu, get lost, see where you end up!"

Abe was serious. Hank remembers that moment well, how challenged he'd felt by such an outrageously generous offer. Did he deserve it? No, hell no, but he would not disappoint his uncle. "For how long?"

"Until you find your place, I guess, or I stop sending money." Abe stuffed the bills into Henry's shirt pocket, then grabbed his hand and shook it. "Deal?"

"Okay," said Henry, holding back a well of tears, so astonished he could barely speak, "deal."

On the corner of Salpores Street, Hank goes into the tiny La Gloria grocery store to exchange a *"Buenos días"* with its owner, Diego. Having known each other for over twenty years, they take some time to chat. First about the blustery Norte. Then about Diego's daughter, Manuela, who Hank met when she was just a baby. He once paid for her elementary school supplies. Diego, a proud and hard-working guy, never asked again, which is why the two men continue to be friends.

Hank says good bye and keeps walking, enters the large forested area along the lake. Here, each weekend, busloads of Guatemalan evangelicals come from villages far and wide to be baptized in the holy water. Along the path are make-shift wooden stalls where vendors pray that supplicants (before and after sermons, confessionals, ceremonial dunkings) will eat and drink from their food carts. Other vendors hope they'll be tempted to buy a trinket. One can find the traditional Maya *artesanía,* some of it expensive—the same hand-woven fabrics they've been selling for fifty years. But the majority of stuff is meant to entice poor villagers. Some of them travel for many hours, packed into crowded buses, and perhaps, after wailing out their love for *Jesús Cristo,* might want a small memento of that devotion. One can purchase a Lago Atitlán cap, a Lago Atitlán tee-shirt, or a variety of Lago Atitlán knick-knacks—an array of trashy souvenirs meant to provide cheap proof that a person made it to this amazing place and was blessed by their heavenly father. Turns out even the poorest villagers look for something to bring home. Not guaranteed to ever see the lake again, they zealously haggle prices down. These are not just impassioned believers but also savvy consumers. Each vendor, as is the accepted custom, takes whatever he can get.

Hank moves along the crowded pathway, past loud devotional music, competing sermons, and, of course, dogs— scruffy mongrels asleep under the tables or in the shade of towering pine and jacaranda trees. He assumes, based on much experience, they've been out carousing all night long. Must be exhausted. Several crack open their bleary eyes and watch him wander by.

As he exits the woods, the path drops down to the river basin, a wide and rocky flat kept mostly unusable by the rainy season's flooding waters. Hank hears the clanking shovels of men at work upstream. Some of them are laughing.

He wonders what might be funny. Maybe it's the fact, hard to believe, that they get paid to create more problems. All week long, from dawn till dusk, they separate sand from gravel, both ingredients used to make concrete block. The block is then used to make more houses, hotels and restaurants, which are certain to bring more people, more noise and pollution to the lake.

Hank smiles at himself. *No, that's just my way of seeing it. They don't think like me.*

Coming up the path, a Maya woman balances a basket of bananas on her head while carrying an infant on her back. He and she make eye contact and nod at each other, a pleasant hello between sentient beings who live as if on different planets.

He gets to the San Francisco River. What a stench! Like a creek this time of year, it spews a steady flow of muddy water into the lake. The color comes from dirt dislodged by the sand and gravel diggers. Also from liquid waste, the *desecho* of many sources, including pesticides and human sewage, the seeping residue of every creek along the river's twisting journey through the mountains.

Two small boys, undeterred by the foul odor, stand knee-deep in the roiling shallows. They laugh and splash each other, clearly having fun.

Hank sighs at their innocent joy and shakes his head. *So,* he imagines some of his expat friends asking, *why the hell would you keep swimming in the lake?*

Were he attempting a fair answer to an open-minded person, he'd explain what they refuse to understand: that the river's contamination is a mile from where he gets in.

But his friends would laugh if he ever said it. Far from open-minded, most people here believe swimmers are half-crazy, in a risky state of dangerous denial. *Au contraire*, as Uncle Abe might say. Thanks to the three volcanoes, and itself an ancient volcanic crater, the lake is composed of a strong alkaline solution, a natural disinfectant that keeps it clean. In addition, he might insist, one must factor in its incredible depth, plus the powerful daily winds that churn the surface and filter pollutants downward. Which is why (or so Hank's rationalization goes) there's no reason for him to worry.

He grins, a private joke, because he'd never actually bother to explain. Non-swimmer friends could never understand.

The thing is, with or without a defensible reason, he cherishes the lake and needs, every day, to get into it, feel it all around him and hear its music—each time a sacred anthem. As with Stravinsky's Rite of Spring, music Hank also loves, his draw to the lake defies logical explanation.

He steps over the stinky river on a rickety wooden plank, crosses the wide flat and passes the landing spot for Pana's famous para-gliders. There are none today. The strong but predictable Xocomil is required for that adventure. This Norte would push them out over the lake to who knows where, an adventure no one is dumb enough to try.

The normal flight, led by trained guides, lasts thirty or forty minutes and costs 100 U.S. dollars—far more than most Guatemalans could afford. On Xocomil afternoons the sky is adorned with these colorful contraptions. Though at first an amazing spectacle to behold, for Hank the sight has gotten boring—just a pretty version of the invasive human spirit. Far more offensive, however, are the helicopters in transit between Guatemala City and ladino chalets along the shoreline. So, yeah, he should be less critical of the gliders. At least they're quiet. And maybe the people they carry understand their privilege.

Just maybe, while drifting through space with God-like vision, they are inspired, or possibly troubled (if that's what it takes) by an urge to save the endangered lake.

Beyond the flat basin, about twenty feet above it, is a road, and on the road a long string of hotels and restaurants. They are empty much of the time, awaiting the weekend rush of ladino tourists from Antigua and Guatemala City. Though many of these patrons are evangelical, religion is not why they come. For them, this is a vacation spot. Not rich enough to own a house by the water, they stay in one of the cheap places, eat fish and drink, make merry in any way affordable.

The restaurants' many waiters, young bright-eyed men, hang out on the street like brothers-in-arms, fellow soldiers in the daily battle to earn a living. Better here, they must think, than out all day working in the fields or gravel pits. Each is clad in the same starched uniform: black trousers, shiny black shoes and a clean white shirt. All hold menus, and are assigned to coax in potential customers for overpriced, mediocre food. If lucky, they'll get rewarded with some tips. True, tipping is not a custom in Guatemala, and with ladino tourists rarely ever happens. Still, the waiters laugh amongst themselves—ever hopeful, against heavy odds, that this might be their day.

Hank gives a friendly nod as he passes, knowing none of them will waste energy on him.

A few minutes later he arrives at the roadside stall of Josefina, steps inside the small concrete enclosure and says in Spanish what he always says. "How lucky I am to find this amazing place!"

Josefina speaks no English, nor Hank her native Cakchiquel. She laughs and shakes his hand. As a kind of joke, since they've known each other many years, today she welcomes him with mock formality. *"Bienvenidos, Señor Enrique!"*

He long ago became "Enrique" to his Maya friends. "Hank," the way they pronounce it, comes out "Honk." Sounds too much like a car horn, or sometimes a flustered goose.

"Gracias, Señora Josefina."

Middle-aged, short and stocky, she has a pretty face and kind brown eyes. "So, you had a *good* swim?"

Josefina knows Hank goes swimming every day, and she is thankful whenever he comes to eat at her stall. *"Good* enough," he says, his standard reply, "which made me *good* and hungry."

"Good, good, very *good,"* she says, enjoying the bit of word play. "And you want *The Same,* yes?"

Hank might simply nod and take a seat. Instead, he shows a quizzical look, as if *The Same* might be something to reconsider.

Josefina, as usual, expects his pretend suspicion, and mimes it back at him. Plainly having fun, she puts her hands on her hips and shrugs. "Well?"

"Well, all right, okay," he says like a surrender.

The Same consists of a bony chunk of grilled chicken, served with rice and beans, guacamole and corn tortillas. All for twenty-five *quetzales,* or about three dollars. In the past, he'd usually add a beer for another buck. Unfortunately, those days are over. Needed to be over.

Some expat friends, of course, would think him nuts for eating here, at an "Indian stall."

So he doesn't tell them. One of many things they don't need to know about his life. Their assumption is that all street food makes you sick, a subtle form of prejudice he won't bother to address. That kind of ignorance feels corrosive to his mind, confounds the music in his heart, and used to make him fighting mad. He's learned to just ignore it.

Hank sits at the end of the wood-plank table. From here he can see the lake. Sure, there are electric wires in the way, and a couple of metal power poles. *No problema.* Hank doesn't need the panoramic vista he'd get at the lakeside tourist restaurants.

Though it's lunchtime, there's no one else in this little *comedor.* Josefina glances down at the walkway that leads to the lake, hoping for customers. Other than Hank, she's told him, there are rarely any foreigners, or many ladino tourists either. While on vacation they prefer the better view, the well-dressed waiters and fancier food. The bulk of her business comes from local

Maya laborers, who stop their work trucks on the street, ten feet from her grill, and order food to go.

She brings Hank his meal. It includes, on the side, a bowl of salsa and a plate of jalapeño peppers.

"No beer today, Enrique?"

She's aware that he's stopped drinking, yet still asks—knows to never presume a thing. "No, Josefina, thanks."

She smiles, goes back to stirring beans and flipping meat on the grill. Every few minutes she sings out, like a little jingle, to people passing on the street: "Chicken, beef, pork, fish, or whatever else you want!"

Her tone always bothers Hank, makes her sound pitiful, like an undeserving waif begging for stale bread. In the not too distant past this kind of groveling was presupposed. Indigenous people, once the Spaniard's slaves, were still treated like lowly servants by the ladino gentry, expected to be grateful for any given kindness. Though things have changed a lot in the past fifty years, many Maya people remain on guard, traumatized by their long history of abuse.

Hank is tempted to stand, make an announcement, tell any tourist within shouting distance what a great cook Josefina is, as if a gringo's testimonial might be the hook to reel one in.

If he really thought it might, Hank would, but he worries it could embarrass her. Not a chance worth taking.

He calms himself, re-settles in his seat, and listens to the steady percussive clatter, the hodgepodge matrix of tin-roofed stalls being rattled by the wind. It's not beyond an ardent Norte to send a rooftop flying. People have been seriously injured, some even killed. He gazes out at tempestuous whitecaps. In days gone by, Hank would be drinking beer and taking notes for his someday novel. While now determined to never write it, he still feels the same compulsion to voice his feelings, his deepening sense of dread. He'd learned not to do it out loud in bars. But, he used to think, why not in a book?

Well, cabrón, he tells himself, again, *because someone might actually read the damn thing—feel offended, or maybe even threatened—and nothing in this town ever remains a secret!*

He looks across at the Tolimán Volcano. Close to its verdant shoreline, eighty feet underwater, is a small sunken island and the remnants of an ancient Maya village. For him, though an unexplained geological occurrence, it is a symbol of the lake's historic, and ongoing, desecration. Known as "Samabaj," the village was discovered in 1980. He's seen photos of the two thousand-year-old site, and many of its artifacts. There are conflicting theories about what caused the island to submerge. A massive earthquake? Years of endless rain? Or, as some evangelicals suspect, a curse from God!

Hank sips from his bottle of water and ponders the fact that no one knows.

Then it hits him, strong as a blast of wind. *Of course,* he thinks, astounded, this may be it: *a novel about the lake that won't get me into trouble!* Instead of a sourpuss griper, he might simply be dismissed as a hopeless fool, a guy who plays around with words. Nothing to get upset about.

Based on the mystery of Samabaj, his story could comment, metaphorically, on what is happening here and now.

Though not the novel he'd want to write, it would be far less risky: a sci-fi satire, an outlandishly absurd tale of some mythical lake on some mythical planet.

The planet, of course, would be strikingly similar to Earth, and the lake strikingly similar to Atitlán.

He gobbles down some beans.

Yes, it must read as farce, yet on some level reflect the truth. What immediately comes to mind is this: The fictional planet, in a galaxy far beyond the Milky Way, is a living, conscious organism. The fictional lake, therefore, is mindfully aware of its dysfunctional, self-centered inhabitants. Most of them live, and create havoc, on its gorgeous tropical island, as if nothing matters but what they want…and want…and want.

Finally fed up with their constantly unconscious disrespect of nature, the lake swallows the island whole with one galactic gulp. *Yes! Yes! Yes!*

He will call the novel *Underwater World*. Inhabitants of the island, who look and act much like the people who live at Lake Atitlán, have no clue what has happened. No one seems to notice that the air has turned to water. Non-plussed by the sudden sogginess, they continue to carry on from day to day—doing, as usual, whatever the hell they want. Lots of it will be non-sensical—an intentionally cynical comment about what happens on planet Earth. He'll have buff young aliens sputtering their big motorcycles in the mud, unaware they are getting nowhere. Others are confused why the fish are flying. At last, no longer able to pretend that all is well, and deathly worried, these aliens do the same as earthly humans during times of stressful change, they get religious! Each prays to some vision of an all-powerful God. While everyone agrees they must have sinned, no one is certain how. And by now, holy shit, what does that matter? The only thing they want is to be saved!

Uncle Abe would have loved this novel, and for a few moments Hank feels encouraged to actually write it. Then he puts down his piece of chicken, bows his head and sighs. A terrible feeling has come over him. He senses it as a warning. It's not that the story seems too weird. Given his experience on planet Earth, the weirder the better.

The problem is, it seems too aimed at being funny.

Satire, yeah—*uh-huh, hah-hah*—but the last thing he wants is laughter. He worries that to joke about something so serious is...well...he isn't sure but it just feels wrong, like it might somehow make things even worse.

Whoa, Hank tells himself, alarmed by his emotional volatility, *damn good thing you stopped drinking.*

31

5
The Promenade

Hank pays Josefina, then leaves her stall. Before checking on Fiona, needing a few more minutes by the water, he meanders down to the promenade, what was once a rocky hillside above the shoreline. Though valuable land, no one dared build here because of the lake's reputation, it's capricious will to rise or fall for no apparent reason. Changes cannot be predicted. An especially wet rainy season might see its level drop a foot. Then, during a drought, it might climb two. While there are various geological theories of why this happens, no one really knows. Some say, since it once was a volcano, there is a "diaphragm" down below that, for whatever reason, sometimes "flexes in or out." Others say something else, and Hank has no idea. Not long ago, during a three-year span, it rose ten feet. Houses built close to shore in the 80's (by wealthy and clueless foreigners) were submerged. Perhaps they should have taken notice of Maya villages, all constructed high above the water. Whoever put them there must have known of Atitlán's willful spirit.

Hank goes to his favorite boulder—preferred because it stands alone, like a monument to the past, in the one remaining natural area by the docks. He sits, leans back against its warm flat surface. To his right are concrete walkways, and, because of the weekend tourists, plenty of people passing by.

It feels good to be off by himself. That's been true for the past ten years, at first in Thailand, then all through India. At some point, convinced he needed a more spiritual life, Hank tried an ashram in Rishikesh, studied yoga and meditation. But, being far too restless, he went back to wandering, bought camping gear and spent long periods of time wherever he could get away from people, be out in nature, all alone.

Hank was thirty when he first came to Panajachel. January, 1979. His hair was long and curly, his beard short and scruffy, his eyes intense and full of wonder. He'd leaned against this same boulder, looked out at the deep blue lake, and felt at home. What was it that made him feel so at home?

The next morning, intent on finding out, he climbed aboard the daily mailboat with his backpack. The plan was to visit every village, but on the hour-long journey to Santiago he changed his mind. It was not the villages that called him. No, it was the lake, and how it changed from place to place. He needed to walk the shoreline, see every nook and cranny. The captain said that would be possible from the next town, San Pedro, which meant staying aboard in Santiago.

But the engine had problems, needed parts, and much of the day was spent fixing it. Then something else held them up. Then something else. The sun had set by the time they landed in San Pedro.

Hank hurried from the dock, searching for a place to camp, not easily found because this was the edge of town and even at dusk there were children playing, men fishing from the shoreline, people moving all about. He must have looked lost to the young boy, maybe eight years old, who was watching him.

Hank smiled. *"Hola."*

"Hola," the boy answered, and shyly signaled him to follow.

33

A few minutes later they entered a small adobe house. Inside, standing on the dirt floor, was a woman, presumably the boy's mother. She looked at Hank, plainly flustered, and he guessed why. Because there was no place to put him. The woman smiled at her naturally generous son, then re-focused on the stranger, concern returning to her face.

She pointed at her chest. "Elena."

Hank pointed at his. "Enrique."

The boy at his. "Manuel."

All three nodded at each other, pleased by such an excellent beginning. From there, because neither mother nor son spoke Spanish, they tried to communicate in their native *Tz'utujil*. Hank had no idea what they were saying. After many blank stares between them, Elena looked deep into his eyes, pretended to hold something with her fingers, then to eat it.

Thinking they might be hungry, Hank opened up his pack, showed them his nuts, raisins, oatmeal, instant rice and dehydrated beans.

Elena raised her eyebrows, then went into a corner of the small room. Came back with an egg.

"Oh. Oh, yes," Hank said, now nodding with unmistakable gusto, *"por favor."*

She built a fire in their tiny earthen stove. Along with soft-boiled eggs, cooked in a pot, she fried tortillas on a *comal*. The sky had turned dark gray. Elena lit a candle and set it on their wood-plank table. After they'd finished eating, she leaned forward, got Hank's attention, let her eyelids droop, gave a dramatic sigh and bent her head over sideways.

Manuel made a little gasp, and a funny face. He mimicked what his mother had done and added in some raucous snores.

They all laughed.

Hank nodded. *"Sí. Por favor."*

He slept on their dirt floor. Mother and son were in the only other room. At sunrise, as he left, Elena handed him a large stack of cold tortillas. He tried to pay but she would not accept any money. She patted Hank on the back and sent Manuel along

34

as a guide. The boy took him to the other edge of town, to a path that led to the next village.

"Gracias," Hank said.

Manuel smiled, shook his hand and ran off.

Over the following three days, Hank slowly made his way along the shore, below the villages of San Juan and San Pablo, through fields of corn and beans. Late each afternoon he camped out on a beach. Cooked on his kerosene stove. He sometimes built a fire and always stayed up late, then slept beneath the stars.

In the morning, after a short swim in the chilling water, he moved on, passing village farmers as they went to work on their crops. Many waved and greeted him in their strange language. They seemed surprised, must have wondered who he was, what he was doing, where he was going.

Sure, and so did Hank. That was the wonder of it. He stopped often to swim and marvel at his surroundings: the terraced slopes of corn on every hillside; the Maya people tending their *milpas*. And, of course, the water. It was always in his sight, his mind, his heart, like he'd stepped into some magic spell, a time that lingered on, day after day like uninterrupted grace…until, late afternoon, his supplies ran out. *Huh?*

Hank emptied out the pack, certain there was, at the very least, another bag of instant rice. No. *Oh shit.* He hadn't eaten since last night. His fixation on the lake, and avoidance of towns, had blinded him, made him stupid.

Okay, now what?

He could not bear the thought of backtracking to San Pablo, a poor indigenous village high above the shore. Even more isolated than San Pedro, there would be nowhere he could buy food, and he didn't speak the language, would look ridiculous miming that he was hungry. He hated the thought of that, of seeming desperate in the eyes of these noble people. In his heart, Hank did not consider himself a foreigner. He felt a special connection to this place, and a vague assurance—though beyond his understanding—that he belonged here.

So, with Uncle Abe's constant company and encouragement, he pushed on, tired and famished but strangely hopeful. Perhaps too hopeful. After a few hours he felt weak. Felt dizzy.

He struggled up a final hill. Stopped and stared. Straight ahead, above some shoreline crops of corn and beans, he saw mangos, papayas, avocados. Beyond that there were enormous trees. Ceibas? Hank didn't know. Didn't really care. He sat down and took several deep breaths, overwhelmed, convinced he'd found his home.

With a sudden burst of energy he hurried along the narrow path, atop a shoreline wall of boulders and up into that dense forest of massive trunks and overhanging branches. Interspersed beneath their protective canopy were coffee plants. Hank wandered aimlessly among the red-berried bushes, and met no one, like being alone in his own dreamt-up jungle.

Then the path got wider. He followed it to a section of town below the main village—what someone told him was San Marcos. He found a collection of adobe huts, and a woman selling fruit. Hank pointed at what he wanted. First of all, bananas. She handed him a bunch. Unable to resist, he ripped one off, peeled and gobbled it down.

She laughed, said something in her native tongue, handed him another and insisted that he eat it.

He thanked her, bought five mangos, and the biggest bunch of bananas. That would last him until tomorrow. In the meantime, for tonight, he had to find someplace to sleep. He mimed the gesture of being tired, Elena-style.

The woman laughed again, then pointed to a trail.

Hank took it and soon found the lake.

There, sitting on the beach, was a middle-aged man with a friendly face. A foreigner. Looked like a happy little elf. Turned out he was from Paris, and owned this bit of shoreline. "I am Henrí," he said in English with a strong Parisian accent. "Please, *Monsieur*, forgive my French."

Hank laughed. They shook hands and he introduced himself.

"So," Henrí said, "in *Español* we are both of us Enrique!"

Hank liked this guy, the laugh lines all around his eyes. "Seems you've been here awhile."

"Oh, yes," Henrí said. "I come here in 1960, just before they start killing Indians."

He was referring, Hank knew, to what some historians call "Guatemala's Civil War." To be more accurate, it was an attempted genocide of certain Maya groups, like the Ixil, who had finally organized and rebelled against having their land stolen, for centuries, first by the Spaniards, then the Guatemalan government, then the United Fruit Company of *Los Estados Unidos*. "I know they're fighting in the northeast," said Hank, "but not around here, right?"

"Not on the lake. Bad for business. Or anywhere tourists are." Henrí shook his head. "Not yet. I will leave before that happens, young man, and you should be leaving too."

"Nope," said Hank, "I'm here to stay."

"Why, because it is so beautiful?"

Hank could not explain his deep attraction to the lake. That was beyond words. But Henrí, having found it and stayed so long, must know what he was feeling. "Yes."

"Do not be fooled, my friend. This place, like all beautiful places, will be ruined."

Hank was far too idealistic to believe it. As a young man, sitting on the shore of Lake Atitlán, the most beautiful place he'd ever seen, *idealistic* seemed the perfect way to be.

Which was also, it turned out, perfect for Henrí. He showed Hank his small custom-built adobe house. It had terracotta floors, handmade doors and stained-glass windows. "I do this all myself," he said, and led him around the property, complete with a small pond, banana bushes, mango and avocado trees.

"Wow," said Hank.

"Yes," said Henrí, "wow. Too bad I have to sell it."

"No! Why?"

"Oh," Henrí said, "a very long sad story. But I do. A realtor from Pana says he can get me twenty thousand dollars." The Frenchman frowns. "He is now certain for almost, I think, two years, but no one buys. He blames the war. May be he is right, I do not know. Only that I must sell it. Lucky for you, my friend, I have to make a special discount. What about fifteen?"

Hank was stunned. Yes, of course he'd buy it, but didn't have that kind of money. And wouldn't dare ask Abe. His uncle, helping all he could, had decided, because his sickness was getting worse, to formalize their "deal" into a trust fund. The monthly stipend was now three hundred dollars, and would go up from year to year, eventually to a thousand. He told Henrí all that, and offered to make payments.

"Sorry, no, I have to get all I can, and soon. At this lower price, I hope it can sell fast."

"I'm sure it will," said Hank, who would not find out till much later that even this "lower price" was far too high.

"Until then," Henrí said, "I think you can rent it."

"What?"

"Yes, of course. You see, I need to get back to France."

He asked for fifty dollars a month. To pie-eyed Hank that sounded like a gift, which must have been evident to Henrí.

"Yes, yes, a good price," he said. "*Very good* because I have to go. If possible, tomorrow. But I need six months in advance. Three hundred dollars. You know, in case it does not sell soon."

Hank once again felt defeated. How could this possibly work? He had only half of that with him, and the next bank transfer would not come for a week. The whole thing seemed way too sketchy. What if it came late, as sometimes happened?

Henrí patted his arm, perhaps thought Hank did not trust him. "Do not worry, my friend. If I am lucky, if it sells fast, you will get your money back."

"No, it's not that."

"Tell me," said Henrí.

So he explained, then pulled the cash from his pack and counted it. More than he'd expected, nearly two hundred dollars in quetzales. Hank thought fast, how little it might cost, if living in this hut, until the next check came through.

The Frenchman watched him closely. "What?"

He felt desperate, like he was begging. "I could give you a hundred and fifty?"

Henrí sighed, shrugged, smiled and shook his hand.

Hank leans back against his boulder, gazes in the direction of San Marcos, not visible from here, and remembers those four years in his little house by the shore. Oh yes, of course, he'd thought of Walden Pond. That's when he first imagined a novel about the lake.

Shit, what time is it?

He pulls the flip-phone from his pack, see's it's after three o'clock—tries to figure out if, while daydreaming, he'd missed a call from Fiona. No, Hank doesn't think so. A luddite *par excellence,* he's still learning how to use the damn thing. Only doing it for her.

He walks to the upper path. At this busy hour it's like a Maya dime store. Vendors, most of them wearing traditional *traje,* peddle jewelry, hats, nuts, knives, pirated CD's, DVD's, and whatever else they can think to sell. After countless years of seeing Hank, they smile, nod hello and go about their business, smart to ignore him and the other low-budget travelers who must puzzle them no end. Even the poorest *estranjero* is, in their minds, rich. Obviously, these vagabond-types have money. Plenty of money. *So,* the vendors must ponder every day, *why not give a bit of it to them?*

Hank wishes he could afford to be more generous. Like many other expats, he's learned to not spend money on things he does not need. Today will be the usual exception. Ahead of him sits Dolores, who sells flowers. Lately, because he knows how much Fiona loves them, Hank has been buying lots of flowers. The teenage girl lights up when she sees him.

Dolores comes across the lake each day from Santiago. She's at her normal spot, in the shade, on a bench by the back entry to plush Hotel Don Rodrigo. The two of them have a system and both know to keep it secret. If other vendors see Hank buying, they will swarm him.

As he moves past she hands over three red roses. Though they cost twelve quetzales, Hank slips her a twenty and keeps walking. The promenade ends at a large wooden platform that looks out on the lake. Hank goes to the rail above the water and takes it in, a fond farewell before heading home.

He climbs the steps to the foot path at the bottom of Santander, Panajachel's main tourist street. Here, beneath towering trees, are clothing and souvenir stalls. Though constructed of simple wooden frames and tarp roofs, these are established spots, spaces rented on a monthly basis. As in the market areas of other lakeside villages, Hank is amazed by the array of vibrant things, hung out each day, which rarely, if ever, get sold. Unlike vendors on the promenade, many of them children, these are grown men and women with families to support. Their cheerful greetings seem so hopeless. He kindly shakes his head, again and again. *"No gracias."*

He doesn't need or want any of it. To pretend otherwise would feel wrong, like some kind of condescension. He respects these resilient people and will not treat them falsely.

Still, Hank's sense of privilege haunts him.

That must be why he always feels so helpless along this stretch, why the hubbub of Santander—its constant bustle and distracting noise—comes as a relief.

But today his sadness cannot be escaped.

Again he feels worried about Fiona.

"Adiós, Hank," she'd said that morning like a gentle order, "enjoy your day." For him a mixed message. While clearly meaning it, she was also ready to be alone, to have lots of time *alone*. Fine, but he's been gone long enough.

He takes the little c*allejón* called Los Quenún, backtracks to Rancho Grande, hurries up the busy street and turns onto Calle Frutal, now just minutes from her house.

She would be bothered by his sudden worry.

Yes, she'd say, something's wrong—and has been for some time—but she's "dealing with it." That's how she wants him to think as well. And, Hank must admit, usually he can.

Fiona, at sixty-one, continues to be the most beautiful woman he's ever known. Her long dark curly hair is turning silver-gray. It hangs down over tanned and still well-toned shoulders. The wrinkles in her face seem to enhance its lovely features, especially her eyes, as blue and bright as ever.

In other words, most days she does not look sick at all. Stomach pains come from time to time and then, like magic, disappear. A strange illness. Doctors in the states had supposed it to be some sort of auto-immune disease, nothing they were able to diagnose in spite of all their tests—an endless run of expensive tests, until she finally gave up on modern medicine, started doing "alternative therapies" of her own.

That was years ago, and for a long time she felt better.

Lately, though, the pain has gotten worse. Plus she lacks her usual energy. Once a social butterfly, Fiona now rarely leaves the house, is steadily turning inward, and doesn't eat enough.

So how can he not worry?

Two months ago he talked her into letting him move in, just until she feels better, an "arrangement" she was not eager to accept. To make it work, Hank must remember how independent this woman is, must give her the space she needs, must never assume he knows what's in her best interest.

And at times he crosses that red-hot line. "Don't piss me off!" she might say with a jesting sneer, an impish sort of warning that he *not be so damn nice!*

He gets to their wooden gate. The little bell Fiona hooked up tinkles as he enters, a welcome for whoever has come to visit. No, she's not afraid of being exposed to unwelcome people. Will not allow that kind of thinking. Naive and maybe foolish, in Hank's opinion, Fiona insists on "staying open" in whatever way she can, convinced that is essential for her healing.

Along the brick path are flowers she grew from seed. He sees they've begun to bloom. Yellow, her favorite color! He kneels down and fingers the dirt. Wet. That means she watered them this morning, which is good. Hank gauges her well-being by the time she puts into gardening. If the plants look happy, chances are so is she. He chuckles to himself. If only it were so simple. Fiona is a complicated person, difficult to read, and sometimes impossible. It's been over twenty years since they shared a house. Back then, of course, sex had been included. Happier days for sure.

"Hi, honey," she says as he comes through the front door. Fiona sits up on the mattress, supports her back against the wall.

"Everything okay?"

"Yeah, yeah, sure. Just took a little nap."

She'd been sleeping out here for months before he moved in. Likes the extra light from the garden window, her plants just a glance away. Hank sleeps on a foam pad in what used to be her bedroom. The separation was a "key condition" of their "arrangement." One of their few but essential "laws."

In addition, they don't have a television or a radio. Neither of them want the invasive noise. Hank is especially thankful for the calming silence, has stopped paying attention to what others call "The News." The corruption in Guatemalan politics is bad enough, but Trump getting elected seemed like proof of the world's collapse, and he would not let it fall on him!

Pretending they'd slipped his mind, he hands over the roses. "From Dolores, our *angel de Santiago.*"

It's what he always says, which always makes her smile. How she maintains this mysterious glow, even when feeling shitty, is for him a daily marvel. As expected, she wants to know about his day at the lake. Hank says what he can, just shy of gossip, about the lengthy chat with Ingrid.

"That girl adores you."

"Must have lacked an over-indulgent father."

"Or," says Fiona, "like most women, a decent partner. I bet she wishes you were younger."

He shows a suspicious smile, could remind her of how indecent he used to be. "I must admit, my dear, that sounds to me like a compliment. I don't know what to say."

"Good, because I doubt I'd want to hear it."

Hank bends over and kisses her forehead. "I see you're feeling better."

"I am, I really am. It's been hours since I've wanted to be run over by a truck."

"Excellent!"

"Yes!" She hands him back the roses.

He puts them in the vase with those from yesterday. "So, when did the barking stop?"

Fiona feigns confusion. "Did it?"

Hank cocks his head to the side and cups an ear, leans toward the open field beyond their garden wall. Lately, sometimes from dusk til way past dawn, dogs congregate to bark and howl and fight about who knows what. When he'd left for the lake they were still at it. "All quiet on the southern front."

"Poor babies must be tuckered out." Fiona winces, squirms a bit, trying to get comfortable.

"Anything I can do?"

"No." She re-adjusts the pillows, then looks at him and sighs.

"What?"

"There is something, Hank. I suppose it's only fair that you be warned."

"Wait." In the hope she's still fooling around he straightens up, crosses his arms in front of his chest and stiffens his body, like preparing for a collision. "All right, I'm ready."

"I'm not joking."

Hank's heart begins to pound. He sits down and takes a breath. "Okay."

Fiona rubs her eyes, a *tell* that she's feeling pain. "Vicente came by while you were gone."

"Oh. Why?"

She looks nervous. Looks exhausted. "He thinks we need another ceremony."

Vicente is a Maya shaman, someone Fiona has known for a long time. Her first "ceremony" came after she and Hank split up twenty years ago, while she was suffering from depression, searching for peace of mind, a different way of living in this world. And Vicente helped. Hank is aware of that, has heard some of the story, though most of it she withheld.

The shaman now consults about her illness. Hank thinks that's a bad idea. Sure, he understands her distrust of modern medicine, but why give such credence to a witch doctor? Aside from advice, Vicente provides salves, poultices, potions and tinctures. A couple of years ago they did a ceremony by the lake. Hank was there. A lot of *copal* incense, a lot of Maya mumbo jumbo. According to the shaman, Fiona suffers from "a malady of the soul." But he told her not to worry. "Things like this can happen," he said, "to the very best of people."

44

Yes, Hank feels certain that is true. About the rest of Vicente's ideas, however, such as the chance she's been cursed by some *brujo,* he remains extremely skeptical. Never says so, but she knows. Also knows he'll support her wishes, no matter what. They've always joked about their differences. Never lacked material. Now, though, he must be careful, because Fiona really believes this stuff. In her mind, without Vicente's help she'd be long gone. And that could be true. Belief, whether justified or not, can be potent medicine. *So...another ceremony? Hell yeah, sure, why not?* "Same as before, by the lake?"

"No," she says, "here. He thinks there might be an evil spirit in this house."

"Whoa. Not me, I hope."

She laughs, thinks he must be joking, which he isn't. While Hank does not believe in evil spirits, it's also true he has no proof they don't exist. There have been moments, flustered by how horribly people treat themselves and others, he worries that they might, and that one could be hiding inside of him. His past fuckups refuse to be forgotten, much less forgiven. At times they truly dominate his thoughts.

Has that darkness found a way to leak out? Is it now haunting Fiona's house? Haunting her?

"No," she says, as if reading his mind, "Vicente says it's affecting both of us, may have been here long before I moved in. He won't know for sure without a ceremony."

Hank takes a breath and nods, thankful for the reprieve.

"Look," Fiona says, "I'm not asking for permission. This is my place. But you live here, too, at least for now, so I'm hoping you're okay that I said yes."

"What, to have a ceremony?" As usual, when in any doubt, he surrenders. That's his conscious practice. Makes everything much easier for her. "Sure, sweetheart, whatever you think might help. Speaking of which, how about something to eat?"

"No, I'm fine. I had a banana."

Great chance to change the subject. "Just one banana?"

"It was a big banana, Hank."

"Must have been enormous."

"Bigger than you could ever imagine."

"Ah." He gets the sexual reference. *"Que suerte para ti."*

"Yes. And luck has nothing to do with it. The thing is, *sweetheart,* that one banana is all I want."

In other words, pal, *gimme some freakin' space!*

Hank smiles, playfully flips her off and saunters into the kitchen. Sits at the table. Wonders how he became such a hovering caretaker. Because he loves her, that's how, whether she likes it or not! *Hmmm.* The question is, how much love can he get away with before she kicks him out? Most of it she doesn't seem to mind. The only real rub is when he sometimes feels the urgent need to give advice. *Like now.* Fiona has gotten too damn thin. This slow starvation can't become a habit!

He steels himself for combat, then goes into the living room with a look of nonchalance, knowing she'll see right through it, hoping she'll find him funny and, perhaps, correct.

"Okay," Hank says, like nothing could be more natural, "no bananas." He pauses for effect. "How 'bout a salad?"

She fixes him with those impenetrable blue eyes.

"Um, no thanks," he interprets.

"Got it?"

"Oh yeah, I got it." Though truly grateful for his help, Fiona remains fiercely self-reliant, a New York City girl of Irish heritage. Dangerous combination. "Sorry, won't ask again."

She smiles, what seems an apology for her gruffness, then lies down and closes her eyes.

Hank goes back to the kitchen for some water. When he returns she seems to already be asleep. He sits on the old beige couch, sips from his glass and tries to quiet his mind. He imagines copal smoke filling up the room. A ceremony here? *Ugh.* Will have to psyche himself up for that. He closes his eyes, too, is about to doze off in the quiet, warm, lazy afternoon.

Then, softly slipping through the silence, Fiona whispers, "Tell me, how was the lake today?"

46

Like everyone who loves Lago Atitlán, she worries about the invasive cyanobacteria. What used to be an oddity now comes every year. She fears that the noxious blooms might someday never leave. "Really wet," Hank says.

"C'mon, please, tell me."

Before describing the water he tells her about the egret, which gets a gentle "Ah," and then his heroic conquest of the savage demonic bug that wanted to eat his brain. Fiona grins. Thus inspired to get her laughing, he explains how his rattled nerves could only be calmed by the ice-cold lake.

She shivers, perhaps remembering. Her eyes get big. "It's still clear, right?"

"Clear," he says, "as a bell from heaven."

The Christian reference (Hank being so irreligious) finally makes her laugh—a joyful release of tension shared between them. Because she knows he means it. Knows, having experienced it herself, there is no better way to describe the water. A tear drips down her face.

He goes and sits on the bed. "I swear, it was like a love song from another world."

"Yes," Fiona says, wiping at her eyes.

"And today, like every day I'm there, I felt you close." He knows he's pushing it but can't stop. "Like our best times. Just us, alone, dancing to cool clear music." Hank sees she is overwhelmed, but in a good way. Too emotional for words. "We're out there treading, holding hands, our toes dangling beneath us, like playing on the grandest of pianos. Then, like deep sea divers, we let go, let ourselves sink—down, way way down—to where there's only that quiet hum."

Fiona's eyes have closed. He takes a long deep breath.

"Please," she whispers, "tell me more."

So Hank does, his voice now even softer. Goes on and on until he hears her begin to snore.

While Fiona sleeps, Hank checks what's in the fridge. He still has plenty of stuff to eat, but for her it looks pretty bleak: just gooey pastes and liquid concoctions made by Vicente. And the cupboard shelves don't look much better. There is, of course, her ubiquitous stash of bananas, all different varieties, colors and sizes, some fast approaching rotten.

Yep, no doubt about it, time to do some shopping. Hank checks the living room clock. Nearly five p.m.

He empties his pack of beach gear and slips out of the house. From where they live, on the river side of Pana, it's a ten minute walk to the main part of town. He crosses Rancho Grande, which at this hour is terrorized by traffic: mostly trucks, whirring *tuk-tuks* and speeding motorcycles. To avoid that raucous clatter he takes the back way, a twisty matrix of narrow alleys that lead to the dirt soccer field. Not a place to be when the wind is blowing hard. Thankfully, it's calmed down.

Hank walks alongside the field, where kids are often playing pick-up games, or maybe just out practicing their moves. Today it's empty, a strange sight. Must have been scared off by El Norte. Up in the bleachers, though, a boy and girl are making out. Hank pretends not to notice. He keeps his head down, gets to the callejón beyond the field and follows it to the upper end of Santander. This longer route means another ten minutes to the town's fruit and vegetable market. No big deal. The reward is that he gets to see María.

The old woman sits cross-legged on the other side of the street, tucked into a tiny corner next to an electric pole. She's been given permission to set up there. Whereas most vendors pay for a spot to sell, María is an exception. No one bothers her about money, or anything else, perhaps because she looks so frail, or maybe—as some say—because she is a saint. Hank doubts that, but would not be surprised to find out it's true.

All he knows for sure is how his spirit brightens whenever they're together.

She stands about four feet tall, but is usually sitting, receiving guests. Two young indigenous men are with her now. They lean down to say hello. María looks up with her loving eyes and, like always, thanks them for the visit. She holds and squeezes their hands, says a few words under her breath. Grateful for that short moment in her presence, they smile, bow, and move away. This, Hank knows, has been going on, with minor breaks, all day long. The poor woman must be exhausted. People bring her food and water, or whatever she might need. At night she's given a room for free and a thin foam pad to sleep on.

María is from the village of Nahualá. She goes there each Monday morning, stays a few days to check on her daughter. Clara, raped by government soldiers during the war, suffers from extreme trauma and will not leave the yard. Now sixty-five, she has no idea how old her mother is. At least eighty, she'd told Hank. Maybe ninety. The two live in a one-room adobe hut with no windows, but spend most of their time outside. A few chickens run around the tiny yard. They cook under the overhang of a rusty sheet-metal shed. Aside from eggs, beans and tortillas, or a chicken if one dies, they eat whatever people bring.

Hank once spent several days sleeping beside them on their dirt floor. He'd gone to fix the hut's leaky roof, but a wall also had to be replaced. Hank would have stayed longer, done more, except María felt the need to make some money. That means each weekend coming to work in Pana. It's a fifty-minute ride over steep and curvy mountain roads on an always crowded bus.

She takes her neighbors' weavings, gets a cut for whatever she sells, which isn't much.

When seeing Hank, María twitters with delight—a sound unlike any other, the song of a mystical little bird.

"Querido Enrique!"

"Querida María!"

From their first meeting, more than thirty years ago, she has treated Hank like a long-lost son. Her eyes are barely visible through the thick surrounding wrinkles. The old woman takes hold of his hands, pulls him close, and quite methodically, almost ceremoniously, kisses both his cheeks. She speaks very little Spanish. A low whisper comes in Cakchiquel, soft into his ear, some Maya blessing he does not understand. Then she backs away and her face turns somber. *"Y Fiona?"*

María has known her as long as she's known him. The three of them used to huddle on this curb and gaze out on the passing world. That ended after Fiona split from Hank, but she'd show up alone for visits. A few months ago she stopped coming, and María is worried, asks about her every time Hank comes by. *"No bueno,"* he says.

She reaches out to gently touch his cheek. Then the two of them sit close. For the next few minutes, lacking a shared language, they communicate with simple sounds and gestures. Words are not important. Or, at least, not normally required.

To Hank, their meetings feel like a family reunion: a rite of honored history, deep connection and mutual love. Though different in almost every way, they're happy for any chance to be together. But today he senses something else, leans over and looks into her eyes. *"Qué pasa?"*

María shakes her head.

"Por favor, amiga, qué?"

The old woman shrugs, squeezes her eyes shut with obvious discomfort. An almost inaudible groan escapes from her pursed lips. She pulls up the end of her full-length skirt and points at her bandaged ankle. *"Perros."* Dogs.

"Perros?" he repeats, to make sure he heard her right.

She sighs and nods.

Given Hank's recent exposure to riotous howling, he's sensitive to the danger dogs present. Whenever possible he avoids them, especially late at night as the air cools, as the homeless flea-bitten mongrels rouse themselves. Having slept all day, and hungry, they sometimes roam around in packs, a damn rowdy, grouchy lot. Not a time to get in their way. Hank can't stand the thought of María faced with that. Her sad eyes are fixed on him. He holds up one finger, then two, then five, an obvious question on his face. *How many?*

She furrows her brow and throws up both hands at once. Hank takes the gesture to mean she doesn't know. Must have been caught off guard. María touches her ankle, then her chest, looks at him and winces. *"Duele,"* she says. *Hurts.* She wags her finger like a disapproving parent. *"Perros, perros, perros!"* she scolds, as if her pain should be a lesson to those nasty beasts.

He nods his head in full agreement. *"Malo!"*

María blinks, as if confused. Her expression calms and her eyes relax. To his amazement, she shows a gentle grin with her few remaining teeth. *"No."*

"No?"

"No," she repeats, and slowly shakes her head. It seems a sign of reluctant resignation. *"Amor."*

Love? Hank has no idea what that means.

María growls like an angry dog—her idea of a joke—and makes a funny face, perhaps also questioning her odd choice of words, her inability to clarify what she wants to say. This kind of misunderstanding does sometimes happen. How can it not, since their language and ways of seeing the world are so vastly different? Hank scratches his head and shrugs, meaning it's okay, meaning it doesn't matter, and he hugs her.

She giggles into his chest like a young embarrassed girl.

Irma, the woman María stays with in Pana, comes from across the street. A large and gregarious person, far more nimble than would seem possible from her wide and heavy frame, she'd befriended María many years ago, and does whatever she can to help. It is customary in Guatemala for the elders to be honored. The men are called *Tata,* the women *Nan.* People believe that these old souls deserve utmost respect. María, whose grace is so apparent, tends to get special treatment on that front, too. She seems aware of her bestowed privilege, and, like a true saint, is at times unwilling to accept it. Should the kindness go on too long she makes a sour face. Hank thinks that might be what's happening now. María frowns at her friend's approach, slumps over as she kneels down at her feet.

Irma looks up into the old woman's rheumy eyes.

"Ütz awäch, Nan?" It's one of the few Cakchiquel phrases Hank understands. *Are you okay?*

María squeezes Irma's hands. *"Ütz matyox, amiga."* *Yes, my friend, I'm fine.* The two women lean forward and touch foreheads, a sign of love and fealty.

Irma turns to Hank. "Don't worry, it's all right." They have also been friends for years, so she knows he's concerned. Her explanation comes in slow and steady Spanish, to make sure María can follow, does not feel left out. "Doctor Palacios looked at the wound. He said there's no infection."

"She was attacked by dogs?"

"Yes. Last night. Lucky there were just two."

María slaps Hank's knee, gets his attention and nods, holds up two fingers.

"Well," he says, "two is bad enough."

"And only bit by one," Irma says. "They were having sex and she got in the way."

"Got in the way?" He cannot picture it. "How?"

María sees his bewilderment, leans into him again and giggles. *"Amor."*

Irma laughs and gently slaps María's knee. "Love, oh yes, *love.* Or, as she said last night, 'The macho was fucking the bitch, who was not happy.' It happened while she was packing up for the day. She felt sorry for the girl, so went over and threw a rock, hit the boy in the head!"

Hank pulls back and cringes. "Oh, no."

"Yes," says Irma, "and he lunged at her."

Hank gasps, imagines her terror in that moment.

"Sí, Nan?" Irma mimes throwing the rock, then tosses back her head, like getting hit. *"Así?"*

María blushes, makes a little squeak and covers her mouth, as if abashed by her foolish act.

Irma shows a fierce scowl. *"Pinche hombres, verdad!"*

Yes, Hank thinks, so much trouble caused by *fucking men!* He turns to María. *"Pinche hombres,"* he repeats, certain she has understood and confident she'll agree. *"Muy malo."*

María squints at him like before, sighs and makes a sad face. *"No, Enrique, no. Pobrecitos."*

Poor things? Huh?

Irma lets out a chortle and gently slaps María's thigh. "No, she does not blame men, thinks they are pitiful creatures who cannot help themselves." Irma looks at the old woman. *"Pobrecitos hombres, sí?"*

María mumbles a few words in Cakchiquel, rolls her eyes, lifts up her tiny wrinkled hands.

"She says men are born that way, have no choice but to be bad." María pats Hank's knee, apparently sympathetic with his plight. "After the bastard lunged at her," says Irma, "she pretended to reach down for another rock. That's when she got bit. By the bitch!"

"No!" Hank turns to María. "It was the girl?"

She looks up at him and pretends to wipe her eyes. "Yes," she says in her shaky Spanish, *"the girl."* Then, as before, she puts a hand over her chest and frowns. "Hurts me here."

"The girl's betrayal hurts her heart," says Irma.

"Ah," Hank says, and kisses his old friend's forehead. *"Pobrecita María."*

She smiles at him, says "Sí," and all three share a laugh.

8
Unwritten Novels

A few vendors are still selling at Pana's large *Mercado*. Hank buys onions, carrots, tomatoes and avocados. His pack almost full, he tops it off with a bunch of greenish bananas and two mangos. Then he goes to Chalo's, their favorite grocery store, for honey, yogurt, and eggs. Puts that in a separate bag. On his way home, still having a bit more space, he stops at Ana's *Tres Tiempos* for a dozen hot-off-the-griddle corn tortillas. Smells to him like heaven. Ah, what joy fresh food can bring! His mouth waters all the way to their gate, where he feels welcomed by the tinkling bell.

Fiona's in the living room on the bed. In the hope it might make her hungry, Hank shows off a mango and a well-endowed banana. "Well, girl, whatcha say?"

She shows a reluctant grin, sighs and goes out to the garden table, has taken the laptop with her. He guesses she'll write her sister, who lives in Chicago, who she has tried to write for days. Keeps giving up. The two never got along. Hank stealthily watches through the living room window. Fiona looks away from the computer screen, gazes at the flowering vines that cover their adobe walls, all cared for as if they were her children. She looks upset. What, has he forgotten to water them? It being the dry season, that means nearly every day.

She looks back at the computer screen, then lets out an angry *huff,* slams the laptop closed, turns and stares at the largest vine, a mighty bougainvillea that starts at one side of the wooden gate and grows over to form a high sweeping arc above it.   The plant's fallen magenta petals spread over the entry like a carpet.

Hank goes to the open doorway. "You all right?"

She shakes her head, then lunges forward with surprising force and pushes the laptop to the far end of the table. "I can't do this anymore."

"Do what?"

"Pretend."

"Pretend?"

"I know she won't want to come."

He walks over, puts his hand on her shoulder.

"And if she did, I wouldn't like it."   Fiona shuts her eyes, starts sobbing.

Hank leans over and holds her. There's nothing he can say. Nothing she needs to hear.

After awhile she pulls free, looks up at him and smiles through her tears. "Quite a deal, this dying stuff. Way damn harder than I thought."

Hank feels upended. It's the first time she's ever said that, and definitely not what he wants to hear. "No, c'mon, Fiona, you're not dying."

"I don't know, Hank.   Facing that possibility might be the only way to hold it off."

As if on cue, some dog out on the road lets out a mournful howl. They both laugh, for the moment distracted from what neither wants to think about. She shivers. The sun has dropped beyond the western wall.   He gives her shoulders a gentle squeeze. "You want a sweater?"

"No, I'm coming in."   She pushes back the chair, gets to her feet, grabs the computer. He follows her to the house. At the doorway Fiona stops, turns to him and says, "Know what?"

"What?"

"I'd love a mango."

"Yeah? Okay."

Hank gets one. Fiona settles on the couch and eats the whole messy thing. He goes for a damp rag. She smacks her lips, cleans her hands, looks satisfied, even happy, and then suddenly pinches her eyes closed. "Oh shit," she says, "here… it…fucking…comes."

"Anything I can do?"

"No, I…I need to…" She hurries to the bathroom and locks the door. He hears her vomiting. Finally, the toilet flushes. Water from the sink runs for a long time. She comes out and goes to the kitchen, gets some of Vicente's elixir from the fridge and gulps it down. Hank knows it will do no good. She lies on her stomach. He rubs her back. Before long she says, "No more," turns over and scoots up to a sitting position. Looks miserable. "Would you mind reading to me?"

He wasn't expecting that. "Not at all, but…what?"

"Anything."

"Anything?"

"No," Fiona says, "bad idea. How about something to make me laugh."

"Laugh?" Hank sees she means it. *Okay, laugh.* He looks through the bookshelf, hopes that something he doesn't know about snuck in by mistake. The shelves are stocked with guides on health and well-being, new-age philosophies, vegan cookbooks, and various depressing histories of Guatemala's bloody civil war. Nothing even remotely humorous. The one novel is *Beloved* by Toni Morrison, not exactly a pack of giggles. *"Behold,"* he says, "here are some quotes from Shakespeare."

She flashes an ironic grin. "To be or not to be!"

"Good punchline, yeah, but not what I'd call funny. Where did you get this?"

"Helen brought it over years ago, along with a memoir of her Tibetan Rinpoche."

Helen owns the used bookstore, and is a Buddhist. Thinks everyone should be. "Hey," he says, "that could be hilarious."

Fiona laughs, then her face goes blank. She looks exhausted. "What I probably need is something mindless. You know, so I can sleep." He senses a joke coming, and probably aimed at him. "How about one of those silly novels you never wrote?"

"Ah, yes, excellent choice. Anything in particular?"

"I don't remember. You decide."

"Hmmm." He sits beside her on the bed, props a pillow against the wall and leans against it. "My favorite would have been called *Wackadoodle World*. Favorite because there isn't much to tell. It's about this planet in a far-off galaxy—a planet that greatly resembles earth."

"Of course."

"Of course." He can see she's already feeling better. "Wackadoodle is where all other planets in that galaxy send their crazies. It's like one huge insane asylum, only lacking doctors or any semblance of supervision. More like a leper colony than a hospital."

"What is it that makes them crazy?"

"No one understands," he says, "they just are. Some kind of pestilent mutation."

"No," Fiona says, "I mean how do the sane ones decide? How do they determine who is—?"

"Crazy? Oh, that's easy. The crazy ones act *human:* totally self-possessed, simple-minded and impulsive. The word 'human' means 'abnormal' on every planet except for earth. 'Wackadoodle' is a slang term meaning 'people.' That's what crazies are called in the rest of the universe."

"Sounds a bit too complex."

"Nah. In fact, like the rest of my stories, almost brainless. Would have been a very short novel."

"Shame you never wrote it." Another joke. Good. "So... um...what others have I missed?"

"Sorry," he says, "most of them I've forgotten too. I was, however, inspired again last night."

"Yeah?"

"Or, I should say, in the wee wee hours of the morning. I would call it *Planet Of The Dogs*.

"So original!"

"Thanks," says Hank, proudly nodding, pretending she meant it as a compliment.

"One might guess it takes place in Panajachel."

"Yes, one might." Hank sees he's got her interest, that she's distracted from the pain. "This story does occur on earth, and in a town quite similar to ours, only far, far away. Like Pana, it has strong indigenous roots. And plenty of poverty. Each poor villager, as a means of protecting his few valuables from other poor villagers, has a dog that barks at night to discourage potential robbers. But the people are so impoverished they can't afford to feed the dogs. Can barely feed themselves. So the beasts roam around at night in packs and cause a ruckus. Especially the males, fighting each other to determine who will *stick it to*—I mean *court*—the females."

"Hearing this will help me sleep?"

"Well, no. But it might prepare you for the rampage coming again tonight. You know, some historical perspective."

She grins.

Hank hasn't thought this through but can see he should keep going. "Since the place is so damn beautiful, many foreigners travel there to live. Some buy local handicrafts *for almost nothing* and sell them in first-world countries *for way too much*. They start a variety of tourist businesses and employ poor native people, who are grateful—no matter what the pay—for any kind of work. As more and more tourists come, and spend their money, everyone's life improves."

Fiona smiles, fully aware he is speaking, in part, of her, since she had a small export business in Pana and employed local people. "That would appear to be a happy story."

"Yes," says Hank, "it would. But appearances, as we both know, can be deceptive. Turns out that locals soon earn enough to fix their crumbling houses, send their kids to decent schools, and, thanks to the high-interest loans from local banks, treat themselves to some real expensive stuff, like televisions and cell phones and motorcycles. Which means, as you might imagine, to protect their increased bounty everyone gets more dogs."

"I sense a vicious circle."

"You sense right." Hank sighs, not sure how he can possibly make this funny. "Alas, most cultural advances have their drawbacks. Modern life, for these poor people, means high monthly payments to the bank. They have to work longer hours, must prioritize their needs and make sacrifices, like choosing not to properly feed their dogs, who once again must go scavenge on the street."

"So damn sad."

Hank takes a breath. "Yeah, so damn sad. But the novel would have a silver lining."

She does not look hopeful. "Uh-huh, what?"

"Good-hearted foreigners get involved, sponsor veterinary clinics where poor people can have their females spayed for free." Fiona knows this, too, because she helped organize such clinics. "They also want to castrate males," he says. "Sure, why not? The local men, however, veto that idea, insisting it's not the machos who make the babies."

Fiona winks. "My bet is they must somehow be involved."

"Not what men want to hear, so they don't listen."

"Yep," she says, "that sounds like men."

"Yep. An age-old problem. And, damn sad to say, because of them even the spaying fails."

"Ooh, let me guess," says Fiona. "Women are not *allowed* to bring the females to the clinics."

"Nope."

"Because their husbands, thinking only of themselves, fear that one thing might lead to another."

"Bingo!" Hank lets out a mighty sigh. "So, with the spaying option gone, the town's good-hearted people do the next best thing, they set up feeding stations for the starving dogs."

She sighs. "A sweet idea, you must admit."

59

"Yes," he says, "I do. A noble effort that leads to happier, healthier dogs, who live much longer and have more puppies, most of whom end up—"

"On the street, hungry, carousing all night long."

"Así es," says Hank. "Etcetera *y* etcetera."

Fiona sniggers, leans back against her bank of pillows. "Dear God, that story sounds way too real! What I need is a little fiction, something hopeful, okay—something to help me sleep!"

She pretends to be kidding, but isn't. Hank thinks fast, remembers his glorious morning at the lake. "Lucky for you, today I had a wonderful new idea."

She knits her brows, looks doubtful.

"No," he says, "I mean it. Something sweet, and truly inspirational."

"Truly?"

"Yes!" Hank smiles, then shrugs. "The problem is, as usual, I would not know how to write it."

"What's the plot?"

"It doesn't have one, just a title: *Music Of The Lake.*"

"Well," she says, "sounds to me like a good beginning."

Sounds good because that's what Fiona named the store she'd opened five years ago. It's goal: to protect the lake. At the time, algae blooms were huge. People had come to fear cyanobacteria as a dangerous long-term threat. A group of environmental types, with Fiona in charge, decided to start a non-profit business. She'd found a place where artists and crafts people, locals and foreigners alike, could sell their merchandise. Musicians as well, but this was much more than a music store.

"Caring for the lake, that is our music," the mission statement read, "and everyone is welcome." Half the proceeds went to a Maya activist group, *"Amigos Del Lago."*

Fiona and others, including Hank, volunteered to run the store. The small space filled up with CD's, paintings, pottery, weavings and other handicrafts. Many artisans, however, while in favor of the idea, decided they could not afford to lose so much profit. Others, while never saying a negative word, thought the whole thing far too "idealistic." The business lasted less than three years. Fiona had hoped some rich benefactor might emerge to help finance it. That never happened.

"The problem," he says, "mine being an *investigative novel,* is how tempted I would be, against my better judgment, to include some ugly truths about why the lake is dying."

"As you should."

"As perhaps I should. But which would, I fear, fill our life with trouble we do not need."

"What trouble?" She shows her most impish grin. "No one in Pana cares what you think."

"Got me there." Hank sees she's into this. "Still, best I watch my P's and Q's—you know, like not name actual people, or businesses, or any of their senseless destructive habits."

Fiona nods agreement. "Yeah, best not."

"Shit no one wants to notice."

Fiona yawns, her eyes at half mast.

"However," he says, "for someone needing sleep, the story might work well as a sedative."

She leans over to kiss his cheek. "Boredom can at times be such a blessing."

Hank smiles, wants to end this on a positive note. "Most of the novel, I swear, would have nothing to do with humans. I'd keep my focus on the lake, its cool and deep expanse, its endless sky, how every day its harmony mutes our pitiful little squeaks."

"You'd write that?"

"You bet," he says. "Except, you know, nothing ever actually gets written."

She closes her eyes, is fading fast. "Ah, yes, I forgot."

9

To Do Or Not To Do

This is far worse than last night. It's two in the morning and Hank feels like a target, that his griping about dogs has made them furious, made them crazy, all their chaotic energy harnessed and aimed his way in order for him to understand, without any doubt, the life of a wretched animal.

There are at least twenty angry beasts just beyond the garden wall, on a large piece of land that's in the process of being split into separate lots. It's bordered on three sides by the concrete walls of existing properties. Enclosing it to the west is an old stone wall running along a callejón, and in the middle of that wall is a metal gate.

During the past few weeks, as the doggy din increased, Hank has looked at that gate every day on his way to the lake. Hanging there is a sign:

12 Lots For Sale: Call 502-6181-7478.

What most grabs his attention, however, is the gap beneath the bottom rail, the obvious spot where dogs have been gaining entry. He's once or twice kicked dirt into the gap, and every night they dig it out.

Though Hank has no desire to own land, he must consider buying the lot that abuts Fiona's garden. He'd build his own concrete walls along its outer boundary. That would at least create a buffer zone, a way to push the animal racket farther from the house. The thought, though he'll never act on it, provides a needed sense of hope.

"Planet of the dogs!" Fiona shouts from the other room.

He's been checking on her from time to time. Not long ago she was mumbling and squirming around in bed, tortured by some nightmare, her troubled face slick with perspiration.

"My fault," Hank calls back.

"Yes, my dear, agreed. Tell me how the story ends."

"Believe me, *hon,* you don't wanna know."

He imagines that gets her smiling. A feeble consolation.

Naked, Hank goes out into the garden. The full moon looks like a gaping hole, an open mouth in the cloudless sky. A muted scream. But the north wind wails, as if in sympathy with the frenzied dogs. Pine tree branches shake, their cones rattling like the percussion section of some demonic band. He throws a handful of gravel over into the black abyss. There comes a second of scurrying beasts, then a reprise of the horrific pandemonium, louder and more vicious than before.

Hank knows there's nothing he can do. Best not to make things worse by getting all amped up, which would only stress Fiona. He goes inside the house and shuts the door.

She sits up. "Rocks won't do it, *hon.* How 'bout a cluster bomb?"

"Why didn't I think of that?"

"Oh, well, never mind," she says, "seems there'll be no sleep again tonight."

He sits on the couch. "Nope."

"So, like responsible human beings, perhaps we should make use of the extra time."

"Absolutely. Perhaps memorize some pithy Shakespearean quotes?"

Fiona drops down, prone, and rolls over to her side. "O, prithee, anything but that."

Ten minutes later, the mongrels still barking up a storm, she's in a dream, her eyebrows twitching.

The clamor continued well into the night, but Hank wakes at dawn to utter silence. The dogs must be back out on the street, carousing until the sun's heat saps their last ounce of strength.

Fiona snores in the other room.

Hank dresses and slips away, knows exactly what to do, and it has to happen before the work day starts. He hurries to the callejón that goes to the metal gate, looks at the phone number on the sign. He'll call it later. Buying property could take weeks. To build other walls a month. He doesn't have that kind of time, needs to stop these hounds today.

Farther down, by the corner of the river road, are remnants of an old stone wall. Hank sorts through the rubble, finds a piece of rusty pipe and several hefty rocks. He carries them, and the pipe, back to the gate. Before starting, he looks around. Already regarded by some people as a troublemaker, he can't be seen messing with someone's property. His reason, no matter how defensible, would not be well received.

Confident he's alone, Hank takes the pipe and scrapes out a slot beneath the gate about four inches deep, about six feet long. He jams the rocks into the slot. Twelve in all. Each requires adjustments, a bit more digging, but perfection is not necessary and time is of the essence. Still, the line is a bit too loose. Hank remembers some pieces of broken glass by the old wall, goes and gets them, returns to the gate and shoves them, sharp edges up, between and around the line of stones. He covers the gruesome trap with a few inches of dirt. Even the most determined dog could not dig out the heavy rocks, and trying would be a bloody mess. Sorry, yes, he's sorry, but too bad.

Satisfied with his work, he tosses the pipe back where he found it and goes home for some coffee. Fiona is awake, a steaming cup of tea beside her on the end-table, the computer opened up on her lap. She seems startled at the sight of him, must have thought he was sleeping. "Where have you been?"

"For a walk."

"Yeah, bright eyes, but where?"

"For now," Hank says, feeling slightly guilty for what he's done, and not certain it's going to work, "I'll keep that secret."

"Why?"

"Because I love surprises?"

"Ah." She shrugs, does not really seem to care, re-focuses on whatever it is she's looking at.

Hank changes into shorts and a tee-shirt. "Off to the lake."

"So early?"

"After last night, I need some peace and quiet. Then I'll go see Aakesh."

"Oh, good. How's he doing?"

Fiona doesn't know Aakesh well, but cares. She and Hank officially got together at one of his parties. She used to be grateful for that. She also knows how hard he tried to keep them from falling apart, occasionally pushing Hank to straighten out his life. At the time, of course, that was a lost cause, but the guy's sincere effort created a warm place for him in her heart.

"I don't know," he says, "it's been a while."

Hank feels bad and it must show. He normally sees his old friend every week, but Aakesh was in the hospital. Fiona has no idea. Hank didn't either until Analu, Aakesh's nearby neighbor, mentioned it several days ago.

What the fuck! Why the hell would Aakesh tell her and not him? So, feeling neglected, Hank has intentionally stayed away, and keeps waiting for a call, an explanation that never comes.

"Shame on you," says Fiona. Aakesh, who this year turned 85, has become reclusive in his old age. She knows that, and thinks Hank should be a better friend. Which pisses him off. She doesn't really understand what's going on. But it's true, Hank needs to get over feeling hurt. "Poor guy," she says, "he must be wondering where you've been."

This is no time for a difficult conversation. He grabs his pack, kisses her forehead, gets out the gate and beyond the tinkling bell, glad to be leaving.

It's barely seven o'clock. The sky is gray, the beach completely vacant, the lake like a vast sheet of liquid steel. Hank walks up and down the shoreline, feeling rattled. Cannot calm his restless mind. Is he worried about Aakesh? No, Analu said he's home and doing fine. Of course Fiona is a worry, nothing new in that, but this is different. Some nebulous fear he cannot name.

Ah, the hell with it! He drops his pack a few feet from the water, strips and dives in.

The instant cold slaps his face, drags his tingling body straight into the present moment. Here he is, all by himself, and for these few seconds there is nothing else, just him and this endless void he's swimming through, fluid as a fish. Then he sees it. Cyanobacteria. A flurry of almost invisible strands flow by. He looks harder, sees more, and his heart sinks, his arms feel weak and his breath comes hard.

Hank surfaces, stares up at the empty sky. There's nothing he can do, no way to make it go away, that's what he must accept. And Fiona would agree. She knows plenty about things beyond control.

He gets out of the water, shivering. He dries off, dresses, sits on the beach and looks across the lake as daylight, lowering like a veil, slowly descends the dark volcanos. At last it crests the eastern hill behind him. Still cold, he moves up the shoreline and gets to the sun's first rays. They cover him like a blanket, but the warmth does not bring his normal peace of mind. Again he starts to shiver. Then, like an alarm, he hears a loud and insistent honk.

Hank looks out at the water. A group of ducks paddle by the nearby reeds with their unassuming quacks. Nope, not them.

HONK! HONK!

He glances back, beyond the caña, to the twelve foot concrete wall that stands above it. There are no geese on the

66

lake, so the sound must be coming from that lakeside *chalet*, from someone's captured pet—the poor thing clipped to make sure it never flies again. Damn good reason to be honking!

Hank doesn't like it, no, but this is also music of the lake, a noise that also represents his home, a racket he must accept. Like the speedboat that now whizzes across the water, leaves behind its disgusting diesel scent. Or some damned helicopter, not yet arrived—a shocking, calamitous thunder, chopping its way over the southern mountains, shattering the placid air. The monstrous thing will be carrying some rich ladino, some self-made demigod who can't be bothered with normal travel. Like a fabled mythic beast, it will rumble out a warning, then gobble the peaceful silence, whir to a loud cyclonic landing and deliver its precious cargo to the paid-for adoration of his servants.

Just more music of the lake!

Hank picks up a handful of sand, flings it at the water, wonders why he's getting so damn worked up. He's not some innocent witness of the lake's daily desecration. While blaming others, he should not forget himself. He lives here too, can't dodge his part in this—doesn't have a helicopter, no, but takes a *lancha* across the lake whenever he damn well pleases, or a smoke-belching bus to the city. And what about the soap from his showers, or washing his clothes or dishes, or the toilets he flushes every day, where does he think all that *desecho* goes? Turns out that humans, him included, are damn difficult for the natural world to live with! Just ask that crippled goose!

But to admit his guilt feels no better, which might explain why he seldom does. Why so few people ever do. Hank closes his eyes, tries to calm his mind and let this darkness go, because it's true: there is nothing, not a damn thing to be done. *Así es.* Yeah, uh-huh, if only it were that simple.

Like a door has swung open in his heart, Hank thinks of Aakesh, and misses him. He takes a breath and smiles.

Yes, it will help to go see his friend.

10
Aakesh

Hank goes to the nearest trash can, dumps the litter he's collected, then continues along the shoreline toward his old friend's house. He stops at the base of Salpores Street, now five minutes away, leans against a wall and wonders how to best voice his hurt feelings.

Oh, come on, what the hell's my problem?

With Aakesh this will work out, it always does! Neither of them quit until a problem's solved. Or, more often, until agreed that it's not, in fact, a problem, or is a problem that's unsolvable, that there is nothing more to say, which means they can laugh and then together enjoy the silence.

Hank pauses at the gate. Pictures his old friend. Aakesh, 85, once stout and strong, these days walks with a heavy limp, his back severely bowed, his spindly legs shuffling beneath, struggling to maintain balance. Nevertheless, as always, his blue eyes shine. So does his bald head.

Born in New York City as Arnold Müller, he changed his identity in the sixties after going to India and becoming a Sannyasin: a follower of Bhagwan Shree Rajneesh—aka Osho.

In spite of his guru's many problems, including a spate of denunciations from other former devotees, Aakesh kept his Indian name, which means "Lord Of The Sky."

He doesn't care about its meaning, or about his guru's critics. "When telling the truth," he once told Hank, "you can count on being criticized."

Aakesh decided long ago to leave the past behind—to stay focused, as Osho once advised, on the eternal here and now. But today Hank won't let him do that. No fucking way. He's still upset at not being told about the illness. In this eternal moment, that's the issue. He opens the gate and steps into the garden. "Surprise, asshole, guess who?"

"Chill out, I'm on the pot!"

Hank goes to the tiny cobblestone patio. There are two wooden chairs next to a wooden table. He sits, breathes in the fragrant air, looks up at the copper arbor and its canopy of vines. They grow up the surrounding stucco walls as well. Most noticeable among the blooming plants are two of Aakesh's copper sculptures. One is a small version of Da Vinci's famous "David," but with the head of a fierce gorilla. The other is a life-size naked figure, with gorgeous female breasts, arched backwards over a tiny goldfish pond. Extending vertically from its groin is a penis-like copper shaft that supports a copper birdbath. His friend has always been an iconoclast, does whatever the hell he wants without any need to explain.

Hank never used to have a problem with that.

Aakesh comes out of the house with two cups of tea, hands one to Hank and sits down with his. The sun has risen above the eastern wall. It filters down through the lush purple bougainvillea. Aakesh shows an ironic smile, seems aware that something's wrong. "So," he says, *qué pasa?*"

Hank sets his cup down on the table. *"Qué pasa is what the fuck?* Why was I never told you were in the hospital?"

"Oh shit, *that.*" When he feels pressured, like now, his Brooklyn accent gets much stronger. "Hey, man, no one was more surprised than me. I had no clue what was happening."

"But why didn't you call? I don't get it. Is there some problem between us?"

"Us?"

"Yeah. Did I do something to piss you off?"

"No more than usual."

"Come on, Aakesh."

He sets down his cup. "No, Hank, no, we're fine." He sighs, smiles, scrunches up his face as if deadly serious. "The problem was with me. Why would I bother you?"

"Bother?"

"Worry you, I mean. For what? Truth is, like it or not, I didn't want anyone, *you included,* to interrupt me. Selfish, yeah, so be it. I was doing some personal research, a most private investigation."

"About?"

"About why I'm still hanging around. At my troublesome age, a damn good question."

Huh, this is something to joke about?

Hank feels ignored, blown off, like his feelings don't much matter, then suddenly realizes, as he probably should have all along, that he's the one being selfish, that his friend's joking is just a coverup, that he must have been truly frightened.

"What was it, the dizziness again?"

Aakesh sighs, apparently resigned to the fact that something more must be said. "Yeah. This time got real bad. I let Fernando, my taxi guy, take me to the hospital in Guate. Doctors said I might've passed out and fallen—even died—if I hadn't gone."

"Died?"

"Well, who knows, but yeah, that's what they said. So I guess it's good I went. Time for me to do some thinking, figure out what's going on."

"Did the doctors know?"

"Wasn't them I needed to consult." Aakesh shrugs. "Sure, they had opinions. Always do. Said there might be something wrong with my brain." He laughs. "Hell, man, *psh,* that's no big surprise. Same shit you've been telling me for years."

Hank smiles, also wants to keep things light, but can't. "So, there's some way they can help?"

"Naw."

"You mean there aren't more tests or—"

"No," says Aakesh, "no more damn tests! I can't afford it. With all the needles they stuck in me, the MRI's and other different scans, it was hundreds of bucks a day. Was draining my account."

"Hey, come on, at least they saved your life."

"No, man, you missed the point. They did nothing I could not do myself."

"Which means?"

"I'm telling you, it was up to me. My choice to live or die. I woke up one day knowing there was a decision to be made." He lifts his hands in front of his chest, puts his palms together and aims his fingers outward, straight at Hank.

It seems a well-contemplated moment, a gesture thoughtfully constructed. Hank appreciates that. At last he feels noticed and included. Whatever these pointing fingers mean, his friend is trying to explain, to share some personal discovery.

Seeing Hank's piqued attention, Aakesh swings his bonded line of fingers slightly to the left. "Life." He pauses a second there, then swings it slightly to the right. "Death." He drops his hands back into his lap and frowns, clearly not pleased with either direction. "Those were my only options, life or death. Life, of course, would be much more of a hassle." He laughs. "Would cost more, I mean, and keep costing me, too. But I could choose that if I wanted."

Hank grins. "And, turns out, you did."

"I did."

"Why?"

"Why…yeah…why?" Aakesh shows his own sly grin. "Like I said, a damn good question." He sighs and sips his tea, as if

71

there's nothing more to say. Then, to confirm it, he points off to the side. "Did you see my new cactus?"

Hank doesn't look.

"Over there, man, by the goldfish. Analu got it for me. A homecoming gift. Nice, huh? She thinks it can handle our rains but I really—"

"So what's the answer?"

"Answer?" Aakesh knits his brows, looks confused, like Hank is speaking a different language.

"To the damn good question."

His friend simpers. "Ah, yes, *the answer.*" He puts on another wise-guy smile. "If I knew that, lad, I certainly would tell you. Might even write a fucking book."

Hank knows he's supposed to laugh, but doesn't. There is something not being said. Again he feels left out, disregarded and pissed off. "You mean it doesn't matter why you live?"

"In my case, maybe not."

"Bullshit."

"Come on, Hank, let's just forget it. Can't we talk about something pleasant?"

"No."

"No, okay, no." He shrugs. "Which must mean, I assume, you want to hear the whole ugly truth?"

"That would be nice."

"Don't bet on it," says Aakesh. "Sad to admit, I chose to live because I don't know any better."

"Yeah, right."

"I'm serious."

"No, asshole, you're not!" Hank still feels left out, deprived of some essential information. He slaps the table. "You come on with the big theatrics, set me up with that 'live or die' thing." Poker-faced, he mimes Aakesh's hand gesture, swivels his fingers left, then right. "Such a dramatic moment—-*Wow*—and then," he throws his hands in the air, "you just let it go. *Ho hum, la dee da,* like it was nothing."

His friend's face has stiffened. "Yeah, okay, it wasn't."

"Of course it wasn't."

"It was worse."

"Worse?"

"Shit." Aakesh looks off toward the house, takes a breath and shakes his head. "It's, it's not easy to make sense of, that's why I…" Several seconds pass, he's thinking hard. "I don't know, I…" Then he fixes his eyes on Hank. "The truth is, it's embarrassing. Too goddamn *woo woo* to admit."

"To me?"

"Yeah, especially you. Like I'm making shit up."

"What kind of shit?"

Again Aakesh looks away, at once restless and ill at ease. One thing about Sanyassans, they pride themselves on being honest. Never mind that up till now he's been purposefully misleading. Which must be why he looks so sheepish and ashamed. But Osho, it seems, is finally breaking through. "You're gonna think I'm nuts."

"Already do."

"Okay, fine, so here's the proof. This damn idea came into my head, and would not leave, telling me I'm not finished, telling me there's something I need to do."

"Do?"

"Listen," says Aakesh, obviously shaken, "it's not as bad as it sounds. Not like I'm hearing *GOD* or some such crap. But yeah, it was fucking weird. I swear, I could feel it in my bones."

"Something to do." Hank shrugs, says, "Yeah, well, what's wrong with—?"

"Wrong?" His old friend stares at him, determined to get this over with. "No, nothing *wrong,* I suppose, but for me it makes no sense! Was like an order, you know. A fact I can't avoid. There's some reason I need to live, that's what I was told, but with no instructions given. I got no fucking clue. Damn it, man, I'm 85, what the hell else can there be to do? *Nothing.* But now, every day, I think there might be, when deep down I know there isn't. So I do *nothing,* which is how I like it, because that's what feels good. Real damn good! I mean look at where we are, out in this garden with all these flowers, all this…" He pauses, sucks in air and blows it out, his eyes watering, "the fresh air and blue sky and…and birds, can you believe all the fucking birds!"

"Not so bad, huh?"

"No, man, not so bad."

Hank picks up his cup and smiles. "So fuck it, pal, I'm with you. Let's just both do nothing!"

They clink their cups together.

"At least nothing that really matters!" crows Aakesh, his energy renewed. "Here's to whatever happens without forced, unwanted effort! Here's to us, a couple of useless farts, and whatever the hell comes next!"

"Which certainly will be me…finishing my tea."

"Or, who knows, maybe not! I mean, we can't possibly know for sure, right?"

"Right." Hank drinks it all, sets it down on the table. "Or, in this case, wrong."

"Well, I'll be fucked! Wrong again!" Aakesh laughs, then gently slaps his forehead. "But, right or wrong, I had no idea until it happened. Surprise, surprise! And now here I am as usual, ignorant as a babe."

"Exactly," says Hank. "You have no clue what I'll *do* next."

"Nope," says Aakesh with an air of acquiescence. Several seconds pass. "Okay, asshole, what?"

Hank stands. "I need to go see Fiona."

"Ah, I shoulda known. Beats the crap out of hanging with me. So, uh, how's she doing?"

"Definitely not good." He puts his palms together again, swivels the pointed fingers left, then right. "Changes from day to day. She asked about you and sends her love."

"Please send her mine."

"Yeah, of course," say Hank. He grabs his pack and smiles down at his friend. *"Will do."*

74

11
Pain

While walking home he has another long talk with himself. This time a truly serious talk. A necessary and painful talk. Never mind Aakesh, Hank's got his own shit to consider. Such as all the time he wastes imagining would-be novels. A damn distraction, that's what it is: a way to avoid realities he doesn't want to face. Like Fiona dying.

Even before she got sick he knew his flights of fancy were a problem. So what if his stories tell the truth: find funny ways to show how people, even with good intentions, can't stop from fucking up the planet.

Yeah, okay, big deal! Is any of that worth making into a novel?

Worthy, perhaps…but not worth what it would take to sit at a computer, day after day, for years, trying to flesh one out. Yes, he could do it, of course—but why? That would only prove how disconnected from reality he's become.

And, much more important, he'd miss time with Fiona.

Hell, what the else is there to say? That's the main reason he'll never write a novel.

Hank stops, clenches his fists and lets out an angry growl, because what he does instead just might be worse. "So damn self-indulgent!" he spits out at his feet.

Standing on the tuk-tuk bridge, he glances down at the river, at the many sand and gravel diggers, all busy with actual work while he, like some village idiot, talks to himself about things that only exist in his muddled head.

Hank blinks away sudden tears, genuinely concerned, afraid he can't stop the "creative" thoughts from coming. It's like an addiction, how he welcomes in these strange ideas, lets them lead him on for days, away from normal, everyday concerns, and at times against his better interests, because deep down he believes there is a reason for his fictions, something he might discover, a truth that might be worth recording.

Even crazier, he imagines his discovery will be easy for others to understand. That's his secret hope. That's the dream he's hooked on. That's what keeps him searching, believing it must be hiding somewhere inside him: a story so true to life, and necessary, it will practically write itself.

"Bullshit, bullshit, bullshit!"

Several of of the diggers look up at him.

One calls out, *"Oye, amigo, está hablándonos?" You talking to us?*

"No," Hank says in Spanish, "only to myself!"

They laugh, go back to work, except for the one who had spoken, who keeps looking at the gringo. They share a few seconds of silence.

At last the man says, *"Cuidate." Take care of yourself.*

"Gracias," Hank says, *"y tú también."*

He waves good-bye and continues walking. The man's friendliness has soothed him. Encouraged him. *Hell, c'mon, you can do this.* He was able to stop drinking, right? Getting high, and not caring a damn about a thing, was far more addictive than concocting silly stories. But Hank quit that for Fiona, to prove he could be trusted, and now, for the same reason, he has to stop losing valuable time on senseless crap.

He thinks of her, how she occasionally likes to hear his silly stories. What about that? She might some day need one to distract her from the pain. Well, sure, if that happens, of course he'll make something up. No, his little fictions are not the issue,

76

it's where they come from—his endlessly questioning mind, his lost and wandering self in search of some truth he'll never find. That's the real problem. And Fiona sees it, too, knows that's the reason he had such trouble with drink and drugs. For years she had to deal with his self-deception.

Well, all right, enough. She needs to see he's past all that. The last thing he wants is her worrying about him.

When Hank arrives he finds her doubled over on the bed, gripping her knees. Lydia, the eight-year-old daughter of their good friend, Concepción, is there. She has brought them a plastic bag of eggs. The girl looks at Hank, terrified. *"Seño Fiona no está bien."*

"No, she doesn't feel well today," he says in Spanish. Hank drops his pack, gets on the bed and puts his arms around Fiona. "I'll stay with her now, Lydia, you can go."

"Should I bring my mother?"

"No, sweetheart, we're all right, but thank you."

The girl heads for the door, then stops, comes back and sets the eggs on the edge of the mattress. "I hope you feel better."

Her head still down, Fiona raises one hand as a good bye.

Lydia hurries off. Fiona moans.

Hank says, "Real bad, huh?" She nods. "Anything I can do?"

She pushes herself upright and faces him. "No, I…it'll pass." She shows an unconvincing smile.

"What's it like?"

"A stomach cramp with teeth."

"Ugh."

"Yeah." Fiona gets off the bed and goes into the bathroom. The water runs for a couple of minutes. Hank is on his way in when she rushes past him, goes out to the garden. She looks up at the sky, down at the ground, then just walks back and forth along the path, massaging her stomach.

He fills his water bottle and drinks it down, fills the bottle again, goes to the couch and waits, keeps taking sips from time to time, like medicine for his aching sense of helplessness. Ten minutes later she comes in, sits next to him and sighs. He waits for her to speak. She doesn't. "Gone?"

Fiona stares up at the ceiling, takes a breath and flashes a sardonic grin. "Almost."

"Good."

"Yeah," she says, "good." Then tears leap into her eyes, drip down her cheeks. "I...I have to..."

The sudden change startles him. "What, honey, what?"

"I don't know," Fiona says, "I, I..." She's trying to tell him something, but her crying and constant wincing keep getting in the way. "I'm sorry, Hank, I...I..."

"It's okay. Take your time."

"I messed up."

It sounds like a planned confession, like she's relieved to get it out. "How? What's going on?"

She gasps, then takes some long deep breaths. "You know Ernie, the guy who deals drugs from his motorcycle."

"Yeah, sure, I know who he is." Hank knows because for years he bought stuff (pot, cocaine, and downers) from the guy. A real low-life. It's been a long time since he's had to give him a thought. No reason to think of him anymore, and Hank doesn't want to, but here the guy fucking is, floating around their living room like a ghost. Ernie sells drugs to tourists, waits as they get off the bus in Pana. Amazing that he's never been arrested. "Wish I didn't," Hank says. "Why?"

"He came here."

"What?" The thought of Ernie, his smug face and high-pitched voice, makes Hank feel dirty. That's how it always felt while dealing with him, a filth he could not clean off. "When?"

"This morning, when you were gone."

"That fucker was in our house?"

"No, not here."

Hank shakes his head, confused. "I don't understand."

"I mean he never came inside, he...someone told him about me being sick."

"Someone? Told him what? Who the hell would—?"

"I don't know." Fiona is breathing hard, her face pinched, her lips quivering. "I was sitting in the garden. He poked his head inside the gate, said he was sorry to disturb me, said he'd heard I was in pain and that he could help."

"Yeah, right. You know that guy's an asshole."

"Sure, I know, but today he was very nice."

"Nice?"

"I mean respectful. He only stayed a minute, to say he could get me something. I can't remember what. Said it would take away this kind of pain, said he could get it soon."

Hank stomps his right foot. "No!" Fiona looks rattled. "I'm sorry, but..." He slows his breathing. "Not from Ernie, we want nothing to do with him."

Her face turns red with fury. "Not *we*, all right, we're talking about *me!*"

Hank flinches. No, okay, he didn't say it right, regrets his irate reaction, but he has to make her understand. "That's not what I—"

"This has nothing, not a *goddamn thing* to do with you!"

"Yeah, all right."

"Sometimes this shit gets bad, Hank. You need to know that! More than I can take!"

"All right. Okay. I'm just saying that guy is trouble. Not someone you want to deal with."

"It's not about what I want!" She closes her eyes. "What I want is for the pain to go away, but Vicente's medicine isn't strong enough. When this gets really bad, nothing helps."

"I'll go to the pharmacy right now. I can get Tramadol over the counter."

"Already did."

"Huh?"

She gives him a sad look. "I didn't want to tell you, Hank. Didn't want you to worry."

Worry? That's what Aakesh said, too. Why is everyone so damned worried about him worrying? Is she afraid he might start drinking again? Did she keep Tramadol a secret in case he might be tempted? What, does she still not trust him? "Who's been buying it?"

"Me, of course, who else?" She blows out air. "I'm not an invalid. I can't always depend on you."

"I thought you were finished going into town."

"Yeah, except when I really need to. I bought it one morning while you were at the lake. It helped, but…not enough."

"I know a pharmacist who can get whatever you need."

Fiona shakes her head. "I might need something stronger than a pharmacist can sell."

He leans her way and stares. "How do you know?"

She stares back. "I've asked around, I—"

"When?"

"When?" She scowls at him, seems to think that an unfair question. "I don't know when."

She's dodging him, she's lying. "Who did you ask?"

Fiona slaps the couch. "Go fuck yourself!" She looks close to tears. "Why are you—?"

"Sorry." Hank sees he's gone too far, like he used to do when he'd been drinking, would get all burned up about some stupid damn thing that didn't matter. But this matters a lot, and he can't stop. "Asked Ernie, right?"

"Look, I don't like him either, but the guy understands what I'm going through, I could tell, so I listened when he told me what was out there."

"Please," Hank says. He feels cold. His hands are trembling. He stands up, then sits down. "Please, all right, let me go see the pharmacist, let me—"

"Damn it, I messed up." She presses her eyes shut. "I'm sorry, I should've thought this through, should've waited till you got back."

"It's okay, Fiona."

"No, it's not. I said you'd meet him."

"Huh?" Hank feels caught off guard. He laughs. "You're kidding, right?"

"No," she says. "I'm sorry."

Hank shakes his head and looks away. Ernie, for him, is like living, breathing slime. Must be because he used to need that arrogant piece of shit, used to chase him around town and pay for his fucking slime.

"At the Palapa," she says. "Tonight at eight."

What the fuck! "I'm not doing that."

"I said you would. I promised!" She lets out a little whimper. "He told me what it costs, and I said yes."

Hank feels lightheaded, cannot think. Doesn't know what to say. He looks down and watches his fingers fidget.

"A thousand dollars."

"Huh? No." He squints at Fiona. "No, that can't be right."

"That's what he said. Said it would last for as long as I needed it. Said he could get it by tomorrow, and I said yes."

"You paid him?"

"No, not yet. Not till tonight."

"What the hell could possibly cost—"

"I don't know, I...I was stupid, was in a lot of pain, okay, I couldn't...think, I couldn't...but soon as he left I felt so scared. It's not the money, it's..." She wipes a stream of tears from her face. "I can't do it. I just can't!" Her whole body is trembling. "You have to tell him, Hank, tell him *no,* that I can't do it, that... that it costs too much or, or—"

"Don't worry, honey." Hank holds her close. "I'm going to fix this, okay?"

She squeezes Hank tight. "Okay," she sobs. "Okay."

He helps Fiona get to bed, pulls the covers up to her chin.

She looks at him with wet and swollen eyes. "Thank you."

He kisses her forehead, tries to look calm as his mind spins and his stomach churns.

81

12
Slimeballs

To fix things with Ernie he has to first buy Fiona pain meds. Something strong. Though Hank is hungry and tired, this must get done. He goes to his room, moves his sleeping bag and pad, lifts up the old throw carpet and flips it over. In one corner of the black lining is a piece of black duct tape covering a slit. A poor man's safe. He pulls off the tape, reaches in and retrieves two envelopes. One has Guatemalan quetzales, the other American dollars. An emergency stash he's never had to use. Combined, there is close to five hundred dollars. Aware that the meds might be expensive, and uncertain what currency the pharmacist will want, he takes everything: dollars in his right pants pocket, quetzales in his left. This should be enough. *It better be.* He can't afford more until his check comes in on Monday, three days away.

Hank gets a banana from the kitchen and heads for the door. "Gonna check the pharmacy."

"Good luck," she says with a frown and painful sigh, "you're gonna need it."

"I'll use all my charm."

"Yeah, that's what I mean."

On his way to town he gobbles down the fruit, tries not to think, trudges along in a kind of mind fog—passes buildings, people, dogs—and feels estranged from everything.

He turns down Santander, the pharmacy less than a block away. Almost there, his focus sharpens at the sight of Ernie straight ahead, astride his dusty black motorcycle. Dirty blond hair drips down behind his faded Yankees cap. His slightly hunched back, covered by a red, paint-stained sweatshirt, sticks out like a stop sign.

But Hank won't let this jerk get to him. Defiant, he keeps walking. Hey, c'mon, it's a drug-dealer's job to hang out on the tourist drag, forever on the hunt for customers. Around town he's known as "E" by those who buy his shit. Hank used to call him Ernest, knowing he didn't like it. The guy's jovial high-pitched tone would set his teeth on edge, like upbeat music coming from a haunted house.

Ernie's strangely handsome face—always a bizarre surprise—comes into profile, its prominent chin thick with graying stubble. Somewhere in his late forties, tall and lean, he's rolling a cigarette, blue eyes focused and on task.

Seems a perfect chance for Hank to slip by unseen. He moves to the far side of the stone-paved road, somewhat hidden behind a gaggle of prattling tourists.

"Yo, brother!"

That's Ernie's standard greeting whenever he spots a customer on the street. In this guy's mind, though it's been five years since they've done business, they'll always be like family. Hank pretends he doesn't hear, is lost in thought, head bent toward the road, but the tourists enter a souvenir stall, leaving him exposed.

"Yo there, my brother!"

Hank gives him a sideways glance.

The guy smiles. "Turns out all is good."

Which means he's bought Fiona's stuff and is ready to close the deal. Hank feels Ernie's eyes like cold sharp teeth against his neck. To pretend ignorance would show weakness. He nods.

"Palapa at eight," Ernie states like an undisputed fact.

There are too many people around. Not the place for a confrontation. "Okay."

The slimeball licks the waiting cigarette, smug as hell, like he's done his humane duty, is some sort of blessed savior, can now enjoy a smoke and let the day go by.

Hank keeps walking. Struggles to relax. He'll figure this out later, how to make Ernie accept that Fiona has changed her mind. It won't be easy. He went through the same sort of thing with him five years ago, but in reverse. Hank's check had gotten held up in the system, was being "processed" by the bank. For over a month he'd owed Ernie three hundred dollars, and then needed to borrow more, for more cocaine. The guy grinned when he groveled to ask the favor. "Sorry, man, no can do."

Hank, far too strung out, slightly drunk and brimming with animosity, felt that as a betrayal. He took a swing at the slimeball's head, missed by a foot, lost his balance and fell.

There were lots of people watching. Ernie just laughed and walked away.

A few weeks later, after many days and nights of severe withdrawal, at times almost more than he could bear, Hank found Ernie and paid his debt.

The guy said, "Cool, my brother, very cool. I say bygones be banished. Want some blow?"

"Fuck yourself," said Hank.

"Yeah, okay, whatever," Ernie said, and did not look bothered, like he knew Hank would be back, like he accepted the stressful moment as a cost of doing business.

Since that harsh encounter he's often waved to Hank on the street, smiled his sleazy smile and asked, like a dear friend, if there was anything he needed. Did it again just a couple of days ago. Hank, as usual, ignored him, and he dreads having to face the guy tonight. But their meeting should not take long. To make damn sure, Fiona must get what she needs.

He turns off for the pharmacy. It's located in an alcove off the street. Ernie may be watching, may even be guessing what he's up to. Hank doesn't care. Wow, quite a shift from the days when he used to hang out on Santander, sometimes for hours, until the slimeball showed up. He's so glad that shit is over. In a weird upside-down way he's grateful to Ernie, and does feel somewhat bonded. Not like a brother, no, but it was this jerk who'd ended up forcing Hank to get straight.

He enters the tiny store. Not much to it. Mainly just a space to stand in front of a long glass counter. Below, on a set of shelves behind a glass partition, are medical supplies only accessible from the other side. In a darkened room behind the counter he sees the flickering light of a television. Then hears a woman moan. Not the sound of pain, more like a coming orgasm. He has heard that this guy also sells pornography. "Hello!" Hank shouts in Spanish. "Anyone here?"

The moaning ends as the flickering light goes off.

The pharmacist comes out in a clean white lab coat. "Good day," he says. All business. The tag on his coat reads Porfirio Gonzales. He is short, with silvery gray hair, and has grown a silvery mustache since Hank last saw him. "Can I help you?"

"I've been here a few times before. To buy Tramadol."

"Yes, I…I remember. Many years ago."

"Yes. And you told me, if things got bad, I could also get Oxycontin."

Gonzales gives him a close look, then shakes his head. "No, you must have misunderstood."

The guy is lying. Seems Hank will have to play the game. He wrinkles his brows and looks confused.

The pharmacist shows an empathetic smile and shakes his head. "Oxycontin," he says, "is an opiate. A dangerous drug if not carefully monitored. To make sure of that, you must have a doctor's prescription."

Hank had not expected such resistance. "I know, I…look, I have cash with me. I have dollars." Assuming the price will be negotiable, he goes into his right pocket and lifts out the thin stack of money. A fifty dollar bill is visible on top. Hank makes sure Gonzales sees it.

The pharmacist sighs, looks uncertain about the best way to proceed. "I don't know what to tell you. This medication is not something I can—"

"Please, my wife is very sick. She's in a lot of pain."

"If I could help, Señor, I would."

"It's an emergency."

"You should take her to a hospital."

"No, not in Sololá. The only decent place is in Guatemala City. We can't afford it."

The pharmacist holds his gaze. Nods. "Yes, I understand."

"If it gets worse there'll be no choice, but for now we have to stop the pain."

Again Gonzales nods. "I sympathize, Señor. The problem is, Oxycontin is hard to find, and illegal to sell without a physician's order. I could go to jail."

"Oh, no, I…" Hank puts the money in his pocket. "Forgive me, Señor Gonzales, I don't want to cause you any trouble. I remembered you helping me before. I had to try."

The pharmacist appears thankful for the apology. He puts his hands on the counter and leans toward Hank. "Look, my friend, I don't know any doctor here who would prescribe it, and getting an appointment in the city could take weeks to arrange."

Hank takes a long deep breath to show his desperation. "There's really no other way?"

Gonzales frowns and sighs, what appears to Hank quite practiced. "I'm not sure, there might be." Again the man pauses, the picture of deep concern. "It's sold illegally on the street in Chimaltenango. Not cheap. For a month's dose, I think, it could be as much as one hundred dollars."

Much more than it should cost, even on the street, but a lot better than a thousand. Never mind a negotiation, best not to quibble. Hell, if he has to deal with a slimeball, he'd rather it be this one instead of Ernie. "That's all right, I'll pay."

"I know someone there," Gonzales says. "At least I can call and ask."

"You need the money in advance?"

"No," he says, and takes a breath. The man looks noticeably uncomfortable, perhaps not sure this gringo can be trusted. "Don't get your hopes up, Señor, I do not know if this is possible. I will try. Can you come by here tomorrow?"

"Yes, what time?"

"At 6pm, when I close."

"Okay."

"Okay," says Gonzales, who looks so damn sincere, so genuinely kind. "God willing, I can help."

Hank shakes his moist hand, makes sure to show a grateful smile. "Thank you," he says, and gets free from the lingering grip, wishes he could smash this fucker in the face. "I'll see you tomorrow evening."

"I'll be waiting," says Gonzales, and returns to his dark room.

13
Peanuts

Hank leaves, turns left on Santander and heads straight for the lake. He passes through the final section of vendors, nods a few friendly greetings, steps down to the wooden platform and walks to the metal railing. Still feeling rattled, he gazes out at the water. The Norte has ended, the Xocomil now in full control, the lake again it's gentler wind-blown self. Hank needs this clean fresh air. He breathes it in, feels soothed by the soft yet persistent power.

It's a busy time for the *lancheros*, carrying folks to and from the various lakeside villages. Each passenger is on a different journey, with a personal share of painful things to deal with. Hank's problems are mild compared to what others face every day. Thankful for a mostly peaceful life, he goes looking for Dolores. Instantly feels hopeful. Yes, that's all he needs right now: flowers for Fiona! And what a blessing when he finds the teenage girl where she always is, smiling as she sees him coming.

Sometimes life is just so simple.

Dolores picks up three red roses, as usual, and awaits their expected handoff.

Hank, however, slows way down, suddenly befuddled. *Shit,* he doesn't have the twenty quetzales to pay her! Obsessively focused on the pain pills he'd hoped to buy, he had not considered flowers. He halts in front of Dolores, pulls the stash of Guatemalan money from his left pocket and shuffles through it, finds nothing but one-hundred quetzal notes.

Hank looks at the girl. She sees the money, his troubled expression, and seems equally perplexed.

He reaches out with a hundred. "Do you have change?"

Dolores blinks, apparently startled by the wad of cash he's holding, and blinks again, might never seen so much all at once. "*No, Señor, no tengo.*"

Making matters worse, a small boy steps up beside him and gapes at her. He giggles, looks at Hank, shrugs and smiles. In his right hand is a large plastic bag of peanuts. A poor indigenous kid, he's probably carried that bag all day with few if any sales. Intrigued by this strange diversion, the boy shifts closer to Dolores. Both of them now stare at the gringo.

Hank feels embarrassed, perhaps should walk away, but really wants those flowers. It's stupid, yeah, he knows it's stupid, but after being hassled by fucking Ernie, then forced to schmooze that slimeball pharmacist, he needs something to go right— some way to appease Fiona when he gets home without the Oxycontin. Seeing no better course of action, Hank hands her the hundred-quetzal note and reaches for the flowers.

Dolores holds them to her chest. "No, Señor," she says, glancing at the bill, "that is too much."

"No problem," he says, and shoves the remaining money in his pocket.

"You can have more," Dolores says.

The girl seems genuinely disturbed. Does she worry this might be a sexual advance? Such things do sometimes happen to poor women in Guatemala. "Yes, all right," he says, "more flowers."

She smiles, the problem apparently solved, and counts out fifteen more roses, wraps them all in a piece of newspaper and hands them over. Hank thanks her again and hurries off. It's not clear he's being followed until a child's voice calls out in Spanish, "Please, Señor, maybe you want peanuts?"

Pretending he didn't hear, when both of them know he did, Hank keeps walking along the promenade, his rudeness meant as an answer—a common ploy among tourists in Guatemala.

The boy, undaunted, runs up next to him on the path and shakes his bag of peanuts.

Hank knows from plenty of past experience that the kid will not give up, that quitting is not an option. Assuming Hank to be a rich tourist not careful with his money, the little pest will suck at his patience (like a mosquito would his blood) until there's no other choice but to swat him down.

Not actually hit him, of course, though that's often how it feels. Hank might say "No" a dozen times, might wave the child away, which always seems unfair, like a vulgar first-world privilege, an entitlement undeserved.

"Señor," the boy says, keeping pace as he shakes his bag of peanuts, "a very good price."

Hank glares at him and shakes his head. "Thank you, amigo, not today."

"A special bargain for you, Señor."

He stops, looks down into the boy's dark brown eyes. "Sorry, I have lots of these at home."

"Only five quetzales."

While the average kid would by now feel rejected and give up, some—like this one—are aware that they're being pests, use it to their advantage, and will carry on until finally paid a few quetzal coins to go away. Hank hates being put in this awkward position, does not approve of these petty extortions, worries that one surrender might mark him as a target. Today, though, to escape this kid, he'd be glad to hand over the ransom. The problem is, he has no coins. "Yes," he says, "a very good price," and kneels, gets face to face with the boy. He must make this end as soon as possible, does not want to draw attention. "I promise, next time I'll buy from you."

The boy looks disappointed, well acquainted with that line. "No one bought anything today."

Hank has heard it a hundred times. "You'll have better luck tomorrow."

"Please, Señor, I'm hungry."

Hank knows it's probably true, and is certain, because he'd shown how poorly he manages money, the boy will keep trying to get a big quetzal note for himself. This is why you should never leave the house without a few coins in your pocket. It's like a rule for every traveler in Guatemala—a rule, due to his obsession with the pain meds, Hank forgot. *Damn!* A quetzal or two, the equivalent of twenty cents, would be good enough for this kid, but to get nothing is unacceptable.

"Very hungry," the boy says with pleading eyes.

Hank stands up. "Okay, come with me."

"Where?"

Hank turns and starts walking. "To eat."

"No, Señor, wait."

But Hank does not wait, and the boy follows him as he walks to the end of the promenade, along the final path and into Josefina's stall. She looks surprised, smiles big and says, "Ah, Enrique, you brought me flowers!"

"No." He hides them behind his back like a shy lover and points at the boy. "Only a new customer."

"Even better!" Josefina bends down, shakes the kid's hand and speaks softly in Cakchiquel. They have a short conversation, nothing Hank can understand, except she keeps looking at him, probably saying nice things about the old gringo. The boy does not look impressed. "Orlando thinks you're rich," she says in Spanish. "He does not want to eat, only wants to sell you peanuts."

Hank looks at the boy, who must be anticipating a few tortillas, his normal meal. *Just this foreigner's way to buy me off,* that must be what he's thinking. "Orlando, that's your name?"

He nods.

"Okay, Orlando, listen."

He nods again, this time with a hint of trepidation.

"The money I have is to buy medicine for my sick friend. Very expensive medicine."

Orlando blinks, then his eyes get wide. "And flowers."

Hank smiles at the witty comeback. This kid is smart, and damn determined to sell his peanuts. "Flowers for my friend, and I have no smaller bills, okay?"

"Okay," Orlando says. It's one of the few English words that all Guatemalans know.

"So," says Hank, "it's hard to spend money on anything else. But, because you said you're *very hungry*, I thought I'd buy you lunch. Is that a bad idea?"

Orlando stares at him, looks caught in his self-made trap.

"No," Josefina says, "it is a *very good idea*. If not for Orlando, then for me."

She and Hank both laugh. That gets the boy laughing too.

"Okay," Hank says to him, "You hungry or not?"

Orlando nods.

"Good." Hank looks at Josefina.

"Two of *The Same?* she says.

"*Perfecto.*" He and the boy sit at the wood plank table. Hank holds out his hand. "*Yo soy Enrique.*"

Orlando shakes it. "*Mucho gusto, Señor.*"

"*El gusto es mio,*" he says, thus completing the typical exchange. That formality taken care of, a few seconds of awkward silence pass between them. Hank can't think of what to ask, except the obvious. "You live in Pana?"

"Yes," Orlando says. He sighs and looks out the lake.

"You sell at the promenade every day?"

"Yes," the boy says, his bored eyes still on the water. Then he looks at Hank, perhaps suspicious of the questions. For all Orlando knows, some sort of answers are required as payment for the food. "Not every day," he says, and pauses, wondering what more must be said. "Not when I'm in school."

That pleases Hank. Some Maya kids don't have the time or money to go to school. But this small boy looks far too young. "How old are you?"

"Nine."

Nine? Hank would have guessed six or seven. "You go to the public school on Santander?"

"Yes. When I can. Most days I have to sell."

"What about your parents, where do they work?"

The boy hesitates. His face turns grave and Hank feels like a clueless gringo. Could be he has crossed a cultural line, become too personal and, perhaps from this kid's view, judgmental. He's about to apologize when Orlando says, "Not my father, he just drinks. My mother sells fruit on the street. And does laundry. Cleans houses. Maybe she can clean your house."

So, the kid is back to doing business. "I clean it myself."

The boy squints, as if doubting that could be true for any foreigner. Again he gazes out at the lake.

Hank does too: at the whitecaps, the volcanos, the gathering clouds. He's asked a fair but not excessive number of questions, feels no need to keep a conversation going.

When Josefina brings the food, Orlando stares at his full plate like at a miracle. He closes his eyes, his lips moving without a sound. Some kind of prayer. Finished, he looks at Hank. *"Buen provecho, Señor."*

Another common saying, a wish for Hank to enjoy his meal. Like *"Bon appétit"* in French. But to him it always feels like more than that. *Provecho* comes from the verb *aprovechar,* which means "to take advantage." That's the key. In Guatemala, its history marred by violence, insecurity and dire poverty, the chance to eat is never guaranteed. One must, therefore, be grateful whenever fed, must take advantage of this wonderful opportunity.

Hank nods at Orlando. *"Buen provecho a usted, Señor."*

The kid grins at being addressed with such respect, then grabs hold of his drumstick, takes a bite and chews, his eyes glazing over with obvious satisfaction.

"You want a drink?"

Orlando swallows and looks hopeful. "Coca cola?"

"Sure," Hank says. Exhausted from another night's lack of sleep, he gets one also.

While eating they don't talk. Josefina comes by with more tortillas. The boy says, *"Gracias, Señora."* That makes her smile, and as he eats she keeps bringing more. Brings extra beans and rice as well. At last finished eating, Orlando thanks her for the meal. *"Muy sabroso!"* *Very tasty!*

"Well," she says, "thank you *very much* for coming to eat it," and they laugh.

Hank pays with one of his hundred-quetzal notes, gets a couple of twenties in return. *"Hasta pronto,"* he says to Josefina.

"Hasta pronto," she says, first to him and then the boy.

Orlando picks up his bag of peanuts, Hank his roses, and they move down the narrow walkway toward the promenade. Though Hank likes this kid, it's time to be free of him. He's worried about Fiona's pain—this damn hang up with the pharmacist—and tonight's meeting with Ernie.

He stops at the pathway leading to Rancho Grande. "Adiós, amigo, I need to go home."

"What about your sick friend's medicine?"

"They don't have what she needs until tomorrow."

"Oh," says the boy, and sighs. "Well, she will like the flowers. I hope she feels better."

"Thank you."

Hank shakes Orlando's hand and turns to leave.

"Señor Enrique?"

Hank looks back as he walks.

"Maybe she would like some peanuts."

Hank stops, turns around and stares at the kid, cannot believe he's still on the hustle. "Really?"

Orlando shows him a shy grin and walks away, a clear sign that he's joking.

14
Concepción

When Hank gets home he finds the front door open. Stops outside and looks in. Their good friend, Concepción, is sitting on the bed, next to Fiona, holding her hand. She speaks softly. Something about the grace of God.

"La Gracia," she repeats, as if Fiona has a problem with her hearing. The moment being so intense, they must have missed the gate bell's little tinkle, do not know that Hank is there.

He steps back into the shadows. It's been a couple of weeks since she's come to visit. The women had a squabble one day while he was at the lake. "I can't stand it when she gets preachy." That was Fiona's abridged version of the fight. Anyway, Hank is glad to see Concepción, and wishes he could make out what she's saying. Her Spanish, a slow melodic flow, sounds to him like a lullaby, like she is patiently, *oh so patiently,* singing a child to sleep.

But Fiona is wide awake, her left hand with a stranglehold on the blanket, her face stiff with resistance. They've known each other for almost forty years. This short, stout *indigena* woman was an infant when Fiona met her. The gringa had just settled in Panajachel. She stayed at the small hotel owned by the young girl's parents, studied Spanish with a private teacher, met a lot of Maya artisans and started what would turn out to be a small yet successful export business.

Over the years she remained close with the García family. Concepción, her favorite, became a trusted employee at seventeen. Now, at thirty-nine, she's like a sister, and takes that role to heart. Hank sees the glowing sympathy in those large unflinching eyes. Fiona appears frozen beneath her caring gaze.

Because the two are always frank with each other, some conversations are difficult. This is definitely one of those, and for the moment seems one-sided, Concepción going on and on, her tone now turning less melodic, even somewhat strident.

Fiona nods. And nods again. "I'm all right," she blurts out, loud enough for Hank to hear.

"No, you're not!" says Concepción, her words a staccato blast, like a high-pitched flute.

Fiona looks ready to explode. Hank steps into the house and tries to look surprised. "Oh, hello."

Concepción looks down and clasps her hands. "I should go."

"No," he says, "please, amiga, stay. We've missed you."

Fiona stares at him, an obvious plea that he not be so damn polite. She seems to need a break from her friend's well-intentioned counsel. Hank knows how much she admires Concepción, would hate to lash out, and is fighting back the urge. Yes, she's sick, her body hurts, but what bothers Fiona most is hearing other people's opinions about how to live her life. Or, far worse, to feel pitied in any way. That could be the crux of this. She does not want her relationships clouded by sorrow, especially with the few she dearly loves. That would be more troublesome than the pain.

Poor Concepción. Not kept informed about the sickness, she has no idea what Fiona has gone through, the many adjustments she's made, day after day, to be "all right" with this terrible malady trying to end her life.

He pulls the roses out from behind his back.

Fiona shows a coy smile. "What, for me?" she says, still speaking Spanish.

"Sure, why not?" He also speaks in Spanish, doesn't want Concepción to feel left out.

"Wow, Hank, thank you. I do deserve them, of course, but why so many?"

"Long story." He puts the new flowers in their vase, relieved that no one asks him to explain.

"I already feel better," says Fiona. "A kind thought is all I really needed."

Concepción takes that in and glowers. "What you need is to see a doctor."

Fiona groans. From the look on her face, like a brittle plastic mask about to crack, Hank guesses things could turn ugly fast. "I also got your medicine," he lies.

"Oh," she says, "good," and eyes Concepción. "Prescribed by a doctor in the city."

"You saw a doctor?"

"Yes."

"And what is the medicine for?"

"My occasional pain."

"Fine. Good. But what does this doctor say is wrong?"

"He doesn't know," says Fiona, "which is why I didn't tell you. Some things I keep secret because it's easier. Because it makes me sad when you worry, amiga, it really does. *All right?*"

The tacked-on question sounds like a warning. She does not want any further interrogation, does not need her friend's sensible opinions or good advice.

Concepción sighs, shrugs, lets go of Fiona's hand. "Bueno." She gets off the bed and stands, her abrupt movement a trumpeted complaint that she knows there's more to this, a whole lot more, and is upset to not be trusted with the truth. "I'll check on you in the morning. *All right?*"

The mimicked question is, as well, a warning: that she's coming no matter what.

Fiona smiles. "Okay, amiga, *bueno.*"

She lies down and closes her eyes.

Concepción leans over and kisses her cheek. "Bitch," she says, one of her only English words, which sounds like "Beech."

That gets a snicker from Fiona. "Beech," she says back.

Heading for the door, Concepción gives Hank's sleeve a gentle tug. He gets the hint and follows her out, beyond the gate. She closes it. "Please, tell me what's going on."

He wishes there were some way to calm her fears. It would not be lying, Hank decides, to give a generic version of the only truth he knows. "Doctors in the states did a lot of tests, said it's some kind of auto-immune disease."

"Some *what?*"

"An illness they don't know much about. They're not sure what this is, so neither is Fiona. That's why she won't talk about it. Not with me and not with you."

"She's going for more tests?"

"Yes." A lie, like Fiona's lies to her, that can't be helped.

"When?"

"Soon. First, before all that, she wants to have a ceremony with Vicente."

"Him again?" This Evangelical Christian woman has no tolerance for Maya shamans. *"Ay, Dios."*

"Yeah," says Hank, no fan of any religion, hers included.

"Okay," says Concepción—at last resigned, for now, that there is nothing to be done. She gives him a tender look. "It's good you are here to help her, Enrique, but she also needs other people."

He mugs a frown. "Smarter ones, you mean."

"Well, that too," she quips, then hones in with those big brown eyes. "No, I mean friends and family. Her sister in Chicago, why doesn't she come?"

"Fiona wouldn't want that."

"Why?"

"Her family isn't close like yours."

"Yes, I understand, but this…this is different."

"No. You met Elise, right?"

"She came once, many years ago. Very nice."

"Yes, very nice. But nothing like Fiona."

"Lots of makeup."

"Lots of fancy makeup. And she has other city needs. She's always thought Fiona crazy for living here. Sure, she'd come, like some kind of duty, which would only make things harder."

"Very sad," says Concepción.

"Yes," he says, "very sad."

"What about her friends in Pana?"

"Fiona avoids seeing them these days, has always been private with personal matters."

Concepción lowers her head. "Oh yes, I know."

"Hey," he says softly, and waits until their eyes meet, "she is closer to you than anyone."

"So why keep this such a secret?"

"I'm not sure. I guess she's afraid of being pitied."

"Pitied?" The word seems to have hit a nerve. "By me?" Concepción's lower lip begins to quiver and her huge eyes fill with tears. "This is not pity, it's…my whole family, we love Fiona, we want to help." She wipes her eyes. "We don't know what to do."

"Nothing. Just be her friend. Be patient."

"I will pray for her," she says like a holy vow.

Hank flinches. Oh god, no. Fiona, as much an atheist as him, would rather die than submit herself to that. The two women have had long arguments about religion. He leans in and whispers, like the punchline to a joke, "I think it best, amiga, to keep your prayers *a secret.*"

Concepción laughs, clearly gets his humor, a few more tears spilling down her face. "Yes, I think you're right." She glances behind her and to both sides, as if to verify they're alone. "I best keep this to myself. God would not understand, does not approve of people who refuse to see the truth."

Hank says, "I promise not to tell."

"Gracias, amigo. And don't worry, Enrique, I'll be praying for you too." She kisses his cheek and leaves.

He returns to the yard, closes the gate, sits at the garden table. "Can you please come here." It's Fiona, who sounds desperate, and right away Hank knows what she wants: the painkillers he doesn't have.

Shit. He goes into the house and explains what happened at the pharmacy. Not all the sordid details, just the short "facts-only" version.

She huffs, shakes her head and throws up her hands. "Why did you lie?"

"I thought it might ease things with Concepción."

"Ease things with her? What about me?"

"Yeah, sorry, big mistake."

"Gee, ya think?"

"No one ever said I had good judgment."

"This isn't funny, Hank." She grimaces and her hands begin to shake. "Fuck!"

Fiona gets out of bed, stomps into the kitchen. He follows. She gets a glass of water, then goes to the drawer that contains the fancy spices, the drawer he never opens, and lifts out a vial that looks like all the others. Inside are a bunch of pills. She pops one into her mouth, gulps it down with the water, shows no apparent interest that he's watching.

"That's Tramadol?"

She glares at him. "Yes."

"How often do you take it?"

"Whenever I damn well need to."

"Yeah, okay," he says, "I'm only asking because—"

"Sorry, I can't talk now. I need to try and sleep." She goes to the living room and gets back into bed, lies down, turns her head away.

"Fiona, please, I tried." She doesn't move. "Fiona?"

She flips around. "Yeah, okay, I get it. Not easy to find stuff in this town."

"I'll get Oxycontin tomorrow."

"Can't guarantee that, can you?"

He hesitates, aware it's true. "No."

"No. Which is why there's a guy like Ernie."

"A guy we definitely don't need in our lives."

Fiona sits up and glares. "There's that damn *we* again! Not *we*, Hank, it's just *me!*"

He's pissed too, is struggling to stay calm. "Hey, come on, I'm the one who has to deal with him."

"No, you don't! That's not what I'm saying! We're not buying *shit* from Ernie!"

"Oh, I…I thought you meant—"

"No, do you hear me, no!" Fiona closes her eyes. A few seconds of blaring silence pass. "I'm sorry, Hank, for…please forgive me. Like I said, I messed up."

"I'm confused. You mean I don't have to—?"

"No. I mean yes, you have to meet with him tonight." Her voice is resolute but the tone has softened. "Just this once, to tell him I can't do it." She sighs, sits up, gazes out the garden window. The sun has dipped beyond the western wall. "Can you do that for me, please."

"Of course."

Fiona turns to him. Her eyes have softened too. "Look, I know how hard this is for you. Just say I can't afford it. Say it's all my fault. I don't care what you say."

"Don't worry, I'll take care of it."

She smiles, close to tears. "Thank you, Hank."

He holds her hand and gently squeezes.

Fiona nods, flops back and stretches out on the bed. "I need to sleep."

He pulls the blanket up to her chest, then goes out to the garden. The air is cool. He gratefully breathes it in. Except for the upper pine branches behind the house, everything is in shadow. He sits at the table and gazes at the violet clouds.

Dogs are barking out on the road, beginning to gather for the night. He hopes, by luck, they'll end up somewhere far away, will let him and Fiona sleep. Should he go check his work on the metal gate, make sure they haven't dug another hole?

No, he has no energy for that. He goes to his room, lies down on the pad, closes his eyes. A short nap before Ernie, that's all he needs. *God damn fucking Ernie.*

He stares up at the water stains on the ceiling. They look like clouds, how clouds change shape, start to look like other things. Hank gets lost in the changing clouds, sees a flock of birds, watches them fly over the lake, their reflection moving across the still blue water until the room gets too dark, the image fades, and all he can make out are those formless stains.

15
The Deal

"Hank." He sees a boat on the lake being tossed about by the wind, hears his name again, tries to open his eyes but can't. It's Fiona shaking him. "Hank, wake up."

Her anxious face says something is very wrong.

"What," he says, "the pain?"

"No." She shows a sour smile. "Worse. It's time to go meet with Ernie."

He shuts his eyes. "Shit."

"But there is good news," she announces, her tone dramatically upbeat: a sarcastic warning that he will not agree. She gives his shoulder another shake. "Hank?"

"Uh-huh."

"Vicente called while you were sleeping."

"Ah." Why tell him now, to get his mind off Ernie? Good luck with that. He opens his eyes and stands up, not yet awake enough to hide his aggravation. "And?"

"Yeah, I thought you'd be excited."

God, he feels so selfish.

"I'm sorry, Fiona, I'm tired is all, I'm—"

"Hey, no problem." She steps forward and pats his shoulder. "I have to say, you really are a sport."

Hank manages a wry smile.

"He's coming at noon this Sunday."

Okay, that gives a day and a half to prepare. "No sweat, dear, I'll behave." Already dressed, Hank slips into his flip flops. She's still standing there, watching him, chewing on her lip. Not a good sign. "Something else?"

Fiona reaches into her pocket, pulls out several one-hundred dollar bills. "Here."

"What's that for?"

"Look, I'm sure the bad pain will come back." He sees she's thought this conversation through, many times, and is determined to get her way. "Even if you can buy stuff from the pharmacy, it won't be half as strong as what Ernie has."

"Sure, I guess that's true, but—"

"So it makes sense," she says, as if nothing could be more obvious, "in case I need the option."

Option? Hank wants to scream. He thought this was decided, is pissed off that she's changed her mind, which means—for him—a much tougher time with Ernie. "Wait, I..." He stops and shakes his head, doesn't know what to say.

Fiona groans. "Why is this so damn hard?" She sighs, holds out the bills. "Tell him I can't pay it all at once. Here's three hundred dollars. Ask him if—"

"Okay. Fine." He waves it away. "I don't need your money." A thousand dollars is what the guy is going to want, way more than they have, which Fiona seems unwilling to understand. She looks so hopeful, has no idea how Ernie thinks, or what he might do, and there's no point getting into that. Maybe it's the pain but right now she won't listen. Not a chance. She'd say *Who knows, it might work out.* Oblivious as a child. "I'll deal with this, all right?"

"My deal, Hank, not yours."

He walks past her, heads for the front door.

She follows close behind. "Come on, please, I—"

Hank wheels around. "No! I said no!" Fiona stops cold and her face goes blank. Looks scared. He feels bad but…but she's making things so damn hard! "I'm doing this, goddamn it, so let me fucking do it!"

He turns and gets past the door, slamming it behind him.

Ernie is in The Palapa when he arrives, at a table by the far wall. The bar is named for its appearance: a large open-air space under a bamboo frond thatched roof, a favorite ex-pat hangout where Hank used to spend lots of time. He doesn't remember ever making trouble here. True "dives" were more his style. His lack of certainty, however, is disturbing. The long U-shaped bar is crowded, mostly with men watching American football on the large flatscreen TV. Some, when they see him passing, nod. Others turn away.

Hank sits and faces Ernie. The guy points at his nearly empty bottle of beer. "I'm getting another. Want one?"

"No. Thanks."

Ernie shrugs and saunters to the bar. A woman turns and gives Hank a steely gaze. Must think he's there to do a deal. Fuck her. He looks away, watches the two musicians who have shown up with guitars. They'll soon be playing on the small stage. Hank knows how packed this place can get and is determined to be gone before that happens. Ernie comes back to the table with his beer. "So, man, you got the thousand?"

"No."

Ernie squints. "No?"

"Fiona did not understand what she was doing."

Ernie takes a drink. "Oh yeah, she understood."

"A thousand dollars?" says Hank. "What the hell costs a thousand dollars?"

"What she ordered, that's what."

"Which is?"

"Twenty grams of Fentanyl," Ernie says in a low voice. "And not the standard powder, that wasn't good enough for her. I explained what I could get, okay, and she wanted the most expensive stuff, which comes in pills. Eighty nice little shiny pills. Has other additives, almost as strong but with a softer touch. Special made, real boutique shit, like a good aged wine. " He shows a surly grin. "Comes in two brown plastic vials, with fake labels. You know, looks like a prescription, like she's taking medicine instead of some filthy drug. That's what she wanted."

Ernie comes off so damn self-assured.

"It costs too much," says Hank.

"Agreed."

"So, she changed her mind."

"Too late. She ordered it and I bought it. Now it's hers."

"Not unless I pay you."

"Yeah," says Ernie, "which you will."

"A thousand dollars? No. Sell me half of it, for five hundred, and next month, if it works for her, I'll buy the rest."

"No can do," Ernie says with the same obnoxious sneer he showed five years ago. It's like nothing has changed—his oddly handsome face, as always, mysteriously diabolical. Like Clint Eastwood's evil twin. Yes, that's how he sees himself—some dangerous outlaw hero in this Third World wild west. He smiles. Yeah, oh yeah, he remembers their fight on the street and is intent on reminding Hank, on rubbing his nose in it.

Hank shrugs. "My best and final offer."

Ernie snickers and takes another drink. Puts down his bottle. "Man, oh man, I swear...dealing with burnt-out hippies."

Though not liking the dig, Hank sees it might be used to his advantage. "True enough," he says, trying for some humor, "our enlightened minds do, at times, surprise."

"Am I supposed to think that's funny?" Ernie's voice has climbed to its regular high pitch. He shakes his head, then rivets his eyes on Hank. "You have any clue what it took to score her stuff? I had to make lots of calls, could only find it in the city. Spent fifty bucks getting it delivered. And no extra charge to you, okay?" He takes another drink. "No, my friend, it was my utmost pleasure. Whatever I can do to bring your girlfriend peace of mind."

"Fiona's not my girlfriend. And doesn't need twenty grams."

"According to her, she does."

"No, that's what I mean, the pain is sometimes bad, sometimes catches her off-guard. She must've been confused when you came by."

"Confused?" Ernie blinks, then stares at him. "She said you're living with her."

"Yeah, I am."

"So, uh, you two ever talk?"

"Look," says Hank, not wanting a conversation with this asshole, especially about his relationship with Fiona, "I'm here to make a deal, okay? I've got five hundred dollars if you want it, yes or no?"

"Hmmm." Ernie scratches his graying whiskered chin, pretends to give it serious thought. "No, I guess I'll pass."

"You'd rather get nothing?"

"That would not be my choice. You owe me the whole thousand, now."

"Impossible."

"Impossible? Well, brother, in that case we've got ourselves a problem. Thing is, I can't sell these pricey pills to anyone else."

Hank sees he means it. Though certain he won't budge, it's worth one last try. "Please, all right, I've got five hundred now, can pay the rest in a couple of months."

"Of course," says Ernie, laughing, "like you are someone I can trust."

"C'mon, man, I paid you before. Everything I owed."

"No, man, you didn't."

"What?"

"For me it's not just the money."

Hank leans back in his chair, has no idea what Ernie means.

"I'm saying you owed more. Owed me for that stunt you pulled on the street." His voice sounds strained, like he's reliving the hurtful moment. "I let it go back then because you were so fucking pitiful. But yeah, for sure, you owed me for that stupid swing at my face, for bringing attention I did not want. Remember?"

"I remember."

"Good. So. I never got an apology."

"Okay, all right, I guess…guess I should've—"

"No, never mind, brother, too late for guessing. I won't waste more time on you. What matters is, I got what Fiona wants and now you need to pay me."

Hank feels trapped. He turns toward the bar, stares at the TV, at the football game that looks like every football game he's ever seen. He's breathing hard and his hands are sweating. There's nothing left to say. Nothing to be done. No way to fix this. He should get up and leave, tell Fiona the deal is off, but for some reason cannot move.

Ernie laughs. "Wow, so strange to see."

"What?"

"How she's got you all tied up in knots."

"You know nothing about us."

"Well, I know she lies to you."

"That's it," Hank says, getting to his feet, "we're finished."

"Nah, not by a long shot. I mean, how? How is it she's fooled you all this time?"

"Shut your fucking mouth."

"Geez," Ernie says, and grimaces, holds up his hands as if to protect himself. A few people from the bar have glanced their way. "Cool down, brother."

"I'm not your *brother.*"

"Okay, okay, chill." He picks up his bottle and takes a long slow swig. "C'mon, man, sit down so we can talk."

Huh? More talk? Why is that even a question? *Why am I still here?* Hank takes a breath. Though desperate to go, he senses a change in Ernie, can see the guy wants him to stay. Sure, because he needs money, as much as he can get, which means there might be a chance for them to work something out. And no, this won't be easy. He's still pissed about that fight they had on the street. Fair enough, he needs more time to vent. Hank sits down. "Look," he says, "I know I screwed up before. I'm sorry, all right, so maybe we can start over, find a way to—"

"Hold your horses." Ernie smiles. "Can we, uh, cut the crap and just be honest?"

He's lost his cool smugness, seems to mean it, and Hank feels slightly hopeful. "Yeah, okay."

"You won't like what I have to say."

Hank is not surprised. No big deal, he'll put up with this guy's bullshit for Fiona. "Okay, man, what's your problem?"

"No, man, it's not mine." Ernie leans in. "You don't know that she's a junky?"

Hank's heart begins to pound. The asshole's face is right in front of him. He fights the strong urge to punch it, does not want to cause a scene.

"Sorry, man, I see you don't."

Hank just sits there like he's frozen. *What the fuck? Why listen to Ernie's lies?* Then suddenly he sees it, peeking out from somewhere in his mind. It's because of those pills, that's why. He blinks. It's because she lied about the pills that he can't be sure what's true.

"I figured you must know," the asshole says. He sounds sympathetic. "She's been using for at least two years. Mostly drugstore stuff, I guess, but she's bought Vike from my boys on the street. And Perk. More than once."

Hank admits to himself it's possible.

"You didn't know any of that?"

Hank sighs, uncertain what to believe. "I know the pain has gotten worse, that's all."

"No, this...this isn't about pain. That's not why she wants the Fentanyl."

"What?"

Ernie's face softens. "From what she told me, my guess is she plans to off herself."

The words bolt into Hank's mind, bounce around but will not stick. The space around him shrinks. His head shakes back and forth by itself. "No, that's...that's fucking crazy."

The guy looks away while Hank struggles to calm his mind. Ernie eyes him again, looks almost sad, seems to understand how hard this is to hear. Actually seems to care. "I don't know, man, maybe not as crazy as you think. Maybe she's thought this through and—"

"Fiona told you that?"

"What, her planning to...?" He sighs. "No, she only hinted. Wondered how much Fentanyl it would take." He rubs a hand across his face, perhaps uncomfortable with the turn of this conversation. "That's how we got to the twenty grams. A guaranteed amount. I wasn't pushing, all right, it was only because she asked. You know, if the pain ever gets unbearable. Said it might be good to have the option."

Option? Yeah, that's the word she used, but this couldn't be what she meant.

"Look," says Ernie, "I've helped others who really need it. Not my place to judge."

Hank stares down at his hands. The guy sounds so convincing with his lies—lying to get more money, keep his hooks into Fiona. If there was a gun on the table he'd shoot the fucker dead. Swear to God, he would, and he's frightened by that impulse, the murderous rage coursing through his body.

"You know," Ernie says, "she didn't have to get you involved. Know what I'm saying?"

Hank doesn't know and doesn't care. Is he actually going to need a gun?

"I mean why now?" Ernie says. "Could've kept it secret, right? Seems to me she wants your help on this." The slimeball sips his beer. "Hey, man, never mind that we don't get along. What matters is I'm trying to help Fiona, get her what she—"

Hank slams his fists on the table. "Stay the hell away from her!" he says in a vicious whisper. "Is that plain enough?" He glares at him, gets no response. "You hear me?"

Ernie purses his lips, defiant, and glances over at the bar. He smiles at that same nosy woman, who again is eyeing them. Smiles at her like a stare-down until she turns away. Then he faces Hank, looks deadly serious. "Oh yeah, I hear you. No problem, brother, pay me and I'll stay away."

Hank stands up, determined to say no more.

"Pay me," says Ernie, "or I won't."

"Leave us alone or I…I swear that you'll regret it. I'll make sure the police know all about you."

"Already do," Ernie says with a knowing grin. "Pay them and they don't care."

16
The Circus

Feeling dazed, his thoughts jumbled and feet unsteady, Hank steps out onto Calle Principal. It's a busy Friday evening, full of automobiles and dogs and people, a world of bright lights, random noise and commotion, all of it unaware of him, unconcerned with his growing fear, oblivious in a way that helps him breathe a little easier. He can't go home yet, is not ready to face Fiona. But where else? *Where?* For a second his mind goes fuzzy. Then an orange and green "chicken bus" thunders by, just a few feet away. He jumps back, stunned. The damn machine blows black smoke in his face.

Hank takes the warning. One must be careful on this town's streets. Always. To his left is a traffic light, one of Pana's three, which glows red, a signal for him to hurry, get across to relative safety. That's when he decides to stay in town. Just for awhile, till his nerves calm down.

He turns up the sharply angled *Calle De Los Árboles. Street Of Trees.* A strange name because there are no trees, all of them chopped down during the 1980's, replaced by a hodgepodge of small commercial buildings.

Being close to the bus stop, this grew into a prominent tourist area. Various shops and restaurants competed for the new influx of money. Over time there came the present row of sleazy discotheques, but the most renowned place—and his favorite—has always been the Circus Bar.

Opened in 1983 by two former members of the European-based Sarrasoni Circus, it's still going strong. And in all these years has never changed. Inside the stretched-out cave-like space are white-washed stucco walls plastered with yellow-tinged circus posters: lots of tightrope walkers, lots of clowns. It has the only decent pizza in Panajachel and is the likeliest spot to find good music.

That's what Hank is looking for tonight. Music. Pleasant sounds to fill him up, flush Ernie from his mind.

The saloon-type swinging doors allow him to see inside. The place is packed. Its long-time bouncer, Felipe, greets people before they enter. The burly man now rubs his eyes as if they're trying to deceive him. "Enrique, is that you?"

"More or less."

"It's been quite a while, cabrón."

"Five years. Am I allowed?"

"Of course, amigo, come in, come in."

Though they don't know each other well, it is the custom in Guatemala, in casual settings like this, to call everyone amigo. Even strangers. All people are treated as friends unless one learns they're not.

Encouraged by the wave of Felipe's hand, Hank pushes through the doors. It's like a scene out of the Wild West, except instead of cowboys he sees expats, men and women from all around the world. To his left is the bar, every stool taken. To the right of that, against the wall, is a tiny stage, where musicians are playing. Two latino men. They strum guitars and sing in Spanish, some love song with a dramatic flamenco flair. Many in the crowd sip at their drinks and listen. The rest are either eating or making an attempt, in spite of the music and multiple layers of ambient noise, to carry on a conversation.

In other words, as usual, the Circus Bar is loud, exactly what Hank needs. So loud he cannot think.

It's odd to feel like an outsider in this place where he'd spent two or three nights a week for many years. In some inexplicable way, everything seems foreign. He looks above the table to his right, at the same exact poster that's always been there: the glass-framed drawing of a white-faced clown with a big red nose, standing atop a dark blue horse while juggling numerous multi-colored balls. Incredible, as if he's seeing that magical image for the first time. Hank glances at other posters and feels equally astounded. The whole scene is so strange, like a circus coming to life all around him. And he's delighted by every bit of it! He looks down at the floor, aware that he's never really looked before. And why would he? It's just old red and whitish tiles faded by decades of shuffling feet. Not in any way remarkable. Then he looks closer, sees within each tile thousands of tiny cracks, an undecipherable record of this place's peculiar history.

"Enrique!" Armando, one of his favorite waiters, carrying two large pizzas, has come over to say hello. "Good to see you!"

"Thanks."

"There's a table back by the bathrooms."

"That's okay, I only came for a minute, to hear some music."

Armando looks at the crowded bar. "No place to sit."

"No problem, amigo, I'm fine right here."

"We'll talk later," says Armando, and hurries off.

The latin love song ends and the crowd applauds. The musicians announce they'll take a break. One holds out his hat, a hint that he'll be coming by for tips.

A tourist at the bar, perhaps to save a few quetzales, decides this is a perfect time to leave. *Good riddance.* Hank sits down on the abandoned stool, nods at the approaching musician and drops a ten quetzal bill in his hat. Luis, the main bartender, smiles and says, "The usual?"

Wow, after all these years he remembers? "No, Luis, I don't drink anymore."

Luis looks unconvinced. "Oh, okay. How about everything but the booze?"

"Por favor."

Luis brings him a glass of ice and pours in tonic water. Hank remembers how good it tastes with the added gin. That's why he's here, to get a bit of that goodness back, have a few peaceful moments. How great it used to be when he could drink "the usual" and enjoy it. It was The Circus where he finally learned how to hold his temper. While not the best of times, things were better than when Fiona had first left him. That blow knocked him for a loop and he went down fast. Seemed like he was always drunk, always getting into arguments, or sometimes actual fights. Hank knew things had to change, and here, because he liked it and needed a place to heal, here he'd made a real effort. After years of being a jerk, he learned to avoid certain people. Bloodying noses, he'd figured out, could not heal his broken heart, and only added to his self-hatred. He stopped taking things personally. It was sort of a surrender, a passive version of self-forgiveness, and in time Hank also forgave others. If someone riled him up, he smiled and backed off. No longer felt defensive or judgmental. Problematic humans, once difficult to stomach, were suddenly quite amusing.

Sure, after too much booze, he might get playfully sarcastic, but it was rare that anyone took offense. People knew Hank meant no harm, knew all he needed was a way avoid his pain. And The Circus gave him that. Rather than speak his troubled mind, he joked. A lot. Sometimes, late at night, after the musicians and dinner crowd were gone and only the drinkers stayed, he'd go on stage and wave his hands to get attention. "Like it or not," he'd announce, "for your minimal entertainment, I'm going to bore you with my most recent unwritten novel."

The meager crowd, inspired by too much booze, hooted and applauded, pleased by his senseless bullshit.

It was like a clown show. Everyone urged him on, stomped their feet, laughed at the silly made-up stories and clapped again, or let out jaunty groans, when his act was over.

"No tips required," he'd say.

"None deserved!" they'd shout back.

Hank's success at playing the fool earned him a free gin and tonic from Luis. One of his routine jokes was to pretend he'd lost his place in a story, could not remember what happened next. He'd throw up his hands, smile and say, "The End."

For that he got a round of dismissive boos. Like music to his ears. The more people pissed and moaned, the more he liked it.

"*Oye*, Enrique," says Luis, "you got a new story for us?"

"No, amigo, I'm finished with stories, too."

"*Que lastima!*" *What a pity!*

"*Sí, pues,*" Hank says, a catch-all phrase intended to change the subject, in this case meaning: *Yeah, well, if you remember, amigo, I could not always behave myself back then.*

Luis makes a sad face, then tends to another customer.

Hank sips his drink and absorbs the surrounding chatter. Unconcerned with what's being said, it is an anthem of warm white noise, pure and soothing. He used to love how it cleared his mind, how it allowed him to forget. That's what is needed now. Hank remembers being at peace in this wacky place. He told some stories, got some laughs. Life was simple.

He sighs, drinks more tonic, and feels the temptation, that familiar urge to get high. Maybe just a bit. *Yeah, come on, why not?*

And the answer is right in front of him.

Five years ago, Hank's last time at the bar, he totally lost his shit with the dumb fucker walking toward him now. For some reason, he's not sure why, this one guy, Bret, had made him go ballistic, made him realize how angry and out of control he truly was…that he'd been faking it with the clown act…that he needed to stop drinking and stay the hell away from bars.

"Hey there, Hankers, how ya doin'?" says Bret in his twangy Texas English. He's one of the few people who had never liked Hank's stories and always made sure to tell him. The guy's big fat face is red from years of boozing, plus whatever he's had tonight. And he looks pissed off.

Now that Hank thinks of it, this guy had usually looked pissed off. "I'm doin' okay, Bret. You?"

"Truth is, man, I'm not so good. Seein' you in here kinda gets me bothered."

Hank takes a breath. "Listen, man, I don't want any trouble."

"Nah, you never did. Just liked stirrin' it up in others."

"Never my intention."

"Right," says Bret. "Same as you always said."

"Yeah, well, if I stirred it up in you, I'm truly sorry."

"Yeah? *Truly?*"

"Truly," Hank says with a slight twang of his own. "For me, them stirrin' days are over."

"Glad to hear it," says Bret, and smiles, reaches over and claps him on the shoulder like they're old buddies. "Hey, how 'bout I buy you one for old times? Bury the rusty hatchet."

He must have heard that Hank stopped drinking, would otherwise not have made the offer. "No...thanks."

"No?" Bret nods, not in a friendly way, like he's taken Hank's refusal as a personal rejection. Looks more pissed off than before. "Suit yourself," he says, and stares off to the side, his fat red face in profile. The musicians are getting ready to play again, but that's not what Bret is looking at. Hank sees the vacancy of his stare and feels pretty sure what's coming. "Just wanted to ask," the fool says, turning to him, "you remember that last fight we had?"

"Nope."

"Nope? No clue at all?"

Hank shows him a crooked smile and slowly shakes his head, a message for Bret to please back off, leave well enough alone, because yeah, sure, Hank remembers the whole damn thing, this guy getting all bent out of shape after hearing one of his silly stories. And Hank also recalls the story, which he'd called "Leaky Brains": a tale of disturbed people who believe crazy shit for no understandable reason. In addition to his regular jokes about religion, he improvised a critique, sharp and flippant, of even more screwed-up conspiracy theories—like those of 9/11.

Well, turned out that Bret was a big proponent of that crap. Before the fight began, he'd said to Hank, "It's you, not us, who's got the leaky brain!" Then he went on and on about "The Rothchilds" and "The Illuminati" and how Kennedy was murdered by the CIA. According to Bret, so were Marilyn Monroe and John Lennon! Maybe even Elvis!

Hank doesn't know why he'd snapped, why he told the fool to go fuck himself. Or why—when the guy got in his face—he said, "Look, Bret, I admit my stories are dumb, okay, *but*…the thing is…at least I'm smart enough to not believe them."

When the idiot blinked and shut his drunken trap, Hank thought he'd settled things—made clear that they were both pathetic losers. For a second there appeared to be a truce, a brittle peace between them. Then Bret's big beefy hand reached out, took hold of Hank's throat, and squeezed.

While shocked by the assault, that did not stop him from bashing the asshole's face, knocking Bret to the floor, getting on top and pounding till he had to be dragged away.

That fight, in a nutshell, typified his sorted past. A time he would just as soon forget. *Oh well.* Hank sighs, dead certain from Bret's goopy, bloodshot eyes that he also remembers (is hellbent on remembering) the whole damn thing.

"Nope," Hank repeats, "no clue at all."

"Was about you callin' me dumb," Bret says.

"Could be," says Hank, hoping his disgust with this dumb fucker, strong as ever, is not too obvious.

"Called me dumb for knowin' shit you don't."

"Uh-huh."

"Uh-huh," Bret says, and sniffs with his bulbous nose. "So, you uh, learned anything since then?"

It would be best for Hank to leave right now. That would be the reasonable thing to do. He stays put because he's not feeling reasonable. Not one damn bit. That battle with Ernie broke down some barrier in his mind, let loose an urgent need to not be bullied, not ever again! "What I learned," he says, "is that humans are, by nature, full of shit."

"Oh? Yeah? You included?"

"Me included, Bret, though less so for admitting it."

"What's that supposed to mean?"

"Nothing you'd understand."

118

Bret sticks out his finger and points between Hank's eyes. "Fucking A, man, there you go again!"

Felipe steps up, separates them with his extended arms. "Everything okay here?"

"Hell," says Bret, "never was and never will be."

"No problem," says Hank, "I'm going."

"Better make it fast," says Bret.

Hank bites his lip, considers grabbing this jerk's throat the way he once did to him.

Bret, like he's expecting it, inches forward, juts out his head, neck easily within reach, then grins and locks eyes with Hank, coaxing him to try.

"Back off," Felipe says to the fat obnoxious fuck, "or I'll make sure you never come here again."

"Buncha shit," grumbles Bret. He shakes his head at the bouncer, turns and walks away.

"Sorry for the trouble, Enrique."

Hank smiles and shrugs. *"Sí, pues."*

Felipe pats his shoulder. "Come back any time."

"Thanks."

Hank leaves drink money on the bar, returns to the treeless street and starts walking toward the Catholic Church, far out of his way. Has no idea why. He stops, wonders what the hell he's doing, looks up at the full and beaming moon. "Yeah, okay."

Though not wanting to go home, that's where he needs to be.

17

Getting It Over With

On his way back to the house, a twenty-minute walk, Hank's mind keeps replaying what Ernie said, that Fiona might want to kill herself. No, he can't believe it.

Still, he feels confused, somehow betrayed and taken advantage of. To be evasive about the street drugs is understandable. He was the same. Sure, Hank gets that, a secret to keep from others. *But damn it, I'm not others!* After all they've been through, why can't she tell him the truth?

He opens the gate, steps inside and slams it closed. *No,* he thinks, angry at himself for being angry, *this won't help.* The problem is, he doesn't know how to help. The living room light is on. Fiona is waiting up, must be wondering how it went with Ernie. Or is she just jonesing for the drug? Hank regrets the thought, pauses at the door, calms himself and goes in. She's sitting on the bed, upright against the wall. Looks anxious and worn out.

"Hey," she says with a tone of true concern, "you okay?"

"Tired."

"I was worried, Hank. Was there a problem?"

He flops onto the couch and stares up at the ceiling.

"Oh, shit," she says, "you didn't get it."

"No."

"Why not?"

"I tried, okay, but Ernie won't sell just part, wants the whole thousand dollars."

Fiona sighs, takes a long deep breath. "Yeah, all right, I…it's my own damn fault. I ordered those pills, it's only fair I pay."

"You're saying you want all of it?"

"No, but…oh, hell, let's get this over with. I have four hundred here, and more than seven in the bank. I'll deal with it, Hank, no worries."

Her nonchalance makes him wince. "No worries? Really?"

"Look, we'll never have to mess with that jerk again."

"C'mon, Fiona, why didn't you tell me?"

"Tell you?"

Hank can't hold back his exasperation, blows out air and throws up his hands. "According to him, you've been buying from his guys."

"A few times, yeah. So?"

"So…so…you think maybe that's why he came here the other day?"

She shrugs with obvious irritation. "I don't know."

"To find out what other stuff you might want?"

"Not *stuff*, it's not *stuff*, okay, it's medicine for the pain."

Hank stands and stares down at her. "That's all?"

"Wait, why are you—?"

"He said it's more than that, said—"

"Who cares what Ernie said? Since when do you give a shit what Ernie says?"

"I don't, I…I'm confused. *Confused* why he would—"

"Damn it, this is not helping!" She gets up and hurries past him to the bathroom. Shuts the door, turns on the faucet. After a few minutes she comes back, gets into bed, pulls the blanket over her lap.

Hank's had enough. "Got medicine in there too?"

"Yeah, okay, I do."

"Yeah, okay, *what?*"

"Vicodin in the bathroom," Fiona says, her look and tone defiant, "Tramadol and Percocet in the kitchen. They help, but not enough. Which is why I need something stronger."

"No, you need to see a doctor."

"Already did."

"I don't mean back in the states, I mean—"

121

"Look, Hank, I know you're trying to help. *I know.* But doctors cannot fix this."

"How can you be sure?"

"Because over a year ago, way before you moved in, I went to see a specialist in the city."

"Huh? Why didn't you say something? Why would you...?"

"Lie?"

"Not what I was going to—"

"Good. Because I didn't lie. I didn't tell you, or anyone else, because I didn't want to. My choice. An ugly little truth I decided not to share."

"Uh-huh, well," he says, his frustration uncontrollable, "I'm just wondering, can you bother to share it now?"

Fiona holds his livid gaze. Hank expects retaliation, or at least some self-defense. To his surprise, she lowers her eyes and fidgets with the blanket. "Sorry I left you out." She looks at him. "I didn't mean to hurt you, I..." She takes a few seconds to gather herself. "I stayed at the Herrera Hospital for three days, found out I have cancer. Stomach cancer. Stage four."

For a second his mind goes blank. The news is shocking, but that's not what's most disturbing. Hank just stares at her, like he's uncertain who she is. Like she's a stranger. Then, all of a sudden, he can't escape it: this person loves him, yeah, but does not really trust him, and feels the need to keep her distance.

"That's what this is," she says. Fiona sounds resolved, her voice calm and matter-of-fact. "The doctor is certain, and said it's terminal. Too late for surgery."

"No. No, c'mon, you can't...who is this doctor? It's one opinion, nothing else."

Fiona shakes her head, blocks a laugh with her right palm. "Geez, honey, you're as bad as me!" She takes a breath, turns serious again. "The thing is, I checked him out before I went. Best damn doc around. A real whiz. He trained in Switzerland and the United States, worked at the Mayo Clinic in Minnesota. After blood tests, an ultrasound and two MRI's, he—"

"I don't care. We should go see someone else."

"No, Hank, no. I'm convinced he's right, okay? But wrong that I had less than a year to live. Said with radiation and chemo I could extend it. I refused, went to Vicente, and right away started feeling better. Even began believing he might cure me." Fiona sighs. "Well, okay, I've changed my mind on that." She makes a playfully penitent face, like a kid who knows she's eaten too much candy. "Can't let myself get all carried away."

Hank does not appreciate the humor. "Vicente agrees?"

"Yes." Again she's serious. "Says this is much more than a sickness in my stomach. The cancer is real, but we both know there's something else, something causing it, sucking away my spirit. Says I have to find the truth. That's why I'm still around, he says, because I'm trying."

Hank slowly nods, sees she believes it, pushes away his doubt, knows he needs to be supportive. What matters is that she's finally being honest. He goes to the bed, sits down, reaches out and holds her hand. "I wish you'd told me."

"About the cancer?"

"About everything."

"Yeah," Fiona says with a loving smile, "me too."

He looks into her clear blue eyes. This is not someone who wants to die. "Anything I can do?"

"No, just let me...I've got lots more time, I feel it. I'm trying to be strong, be brave, and it's not easy. There's only one thing I know for sure, I can't stand the frigging pain!"

"You're feeling better after—?"

"Yes. For awhile. This stuff I've got doesn't last too long. At the most five hours."

"I'll get Oxycontin tomorrow. If that doesn't do it, I'll go deal with fucking Ernie."

"Fair enough. Thank you."

Hank holds both her hands and gives them a gentle squeeze. "We should try to sleep."

"Yeah."

While she gets settled, he refills her glass of water, puts it on the table by her bed.

She smiles at him. "Good night."

"Good night." He heads for his room, stops and turns back to her. "I love you."

"Love you too."

Hank can't sleep, his breathing difficult, like there's an anvil on his chest. *Cancer.* She's got *cancer.* It seems impossible. He lies in the darkness like there is nothing else. Nothing but the awful truth. Hank shuts his eyes, shuts them tight, tries to make his mind go blank and can't, can't stop the fear, chasing down an alley, around a corner into another alley, finally catching him and shaking him and will not let him go.

His eyes snap open. He stares up at the stained ceiling, stares at the door. He looks at his phone and sees it's after eight.

Huh? How did he sleep so long? Unheard of. Wow, his dog barricade must have worked! Or maybe, from sheer exhaustion, he'd somehow missed a night of cranky beasts. Either way, the bright and quiet morning has, for the moment, lessened his strangling grief. For Fiona's sake he has stay like this, has to try and keep things light. Knows that's what she wants.

He gets up, changes into his beach gear, grabs his pack and goes into the living room.

She's sitting up in bed, sipping tea, looking almost happy. "Oh," she says, "good morning, sleepy head."

Her genuine smile is a relief. "No dogs last night?"

"Not a single howl!"

Hank raises his hands into the air and sticks out his chest. "Well, though you know how much I hate to brag, it's me you need to thank."

He describes the gate adventure in minute detail.

She seems amused by his long-winded specificity, and also a tad impressed. "My hero."

"A temporary fix," Hank says, and mentions his hope to buy the nearby lot.

Now Fiona looks incredulous. "Yeah, uh-huh."

"I'm serious."

"I'm sure you are," she says, obviously not believing him. "And I appreciate the thought."

It's been awhile since he's seen such brightness in her eyes. "Damn good thinking, right?"

"Absolutely brilliant. I guess I'm forced to say it, Hank, you're really not so bad."

It's like a tender kiss on his forehead. He pretends to blush. "Ah, shucks."

"Should've known you'd take that wrong."

"Could not resist."

"Cool down, big boy. You need to go soak your head."

"Yeah, but don't you fret none, darlin', I'll be back."

"No," she says, "please take your time."

He frowns as if she'd hurt his feelings.

"No, I...I'm serious, Hank. Concepción will be coming in awhile. Best you're gone for that, we need some hours alone to talk. I'm going to tell her everything."

"Good for you."

"Yeah. Thanks."

Hank immediately feels better, can't wait to jump in the lake. He walks out through the garden, the gate bell once again sounding sweet. First things first, he stops at the entrance to the vacant lots, sees his barricade undisturbed, and is certain that won't last for long.

He gets out his phone, calls the number on the sign.

A man answers, confirms that he owns the land and asks how he can help. Hank explains the situation, that he wants to expand his garden, buy the lot on the other side of his existing wall. The man, Eduardo, not clear about which lot he means, says, "Most of them are unsold. I can be there at one o'clock to show you what's available."

"Perfect," says Hank. "I'll see you then."

Buying the lot won't cut out all the dog noise, but at least will hush it down. He'll do whatever it takes to help. His step feels lighter, his body stronger as he continues to the lake. He turns onto the river path and sees the water, like a sheet of glass. The sky is clear and the air is warm. In twenty minutes he's at his favorite beach. As expected, it's rather empty, only a few *artisanos* playing guitars. Hank waves and walks past them, far down the shoreline to his rock. He senses Fiona smiling inside him, and feels grateful there are now no secrets between them, that they can face this frightening time together. He takes off his flip flops, strips to his skivvies, sits on the rock, eyes closed, and flops his feet into the water.

In spite of his deep sadness, the world feels full of goodness.

Then something brushes against his leg. It's a tiny tan-colored puppy, a street dog breed, gazing up at him with big brown eyes. Poor thing looks way too pleased, like at last he's found his master.

"No," Hank says in a most solemn tone, "no fucking way."

The dog, a male, nuzzles his elbow with its nose.

"Sorry, pal, I ain't your human."

The pooch nudges his leg. Getting no response, it sits at his side like a loyal guardian and looks out at the lake. Hank is impressed by the mutt's tranquility. Laughs and pets its head. The soft brown fur feels soft and silky. He loves puppies, just not what they turn into. "When a fully-grown and disgruntled beast," he whispers like a hypnotist, "you will remember my show of kindness, will cut me a bit of slack, will encourage your mongrel buddies to torment someone else."

The puppy's ears perk up. He looks down the shore at some other dogs, then scampers off.

Hank wishes the little guy had stuck around. The contact made him feel, well, kind of blessed, like he'd been judged worthy, accepted as a part of this sacred place. Such flashes of inclusion are indescribable. And, like this one, fleeting.

He thinks again of Fiona, is overwhelmed by sorrow, and dives into the water, his splash a perfect tone that echoes out in all directions. The cold envelops him, holds him, and he senses, strong and vibrant, a lasting joy. Feels Fiona near.

"Have no fear," she happily whispers in his head, "I'll always be around to give you shit."

He smiles at her. *Yeah, uh-huh.*

"There you go," she says, "that's better."

Though seeing strands of cyanobacteria, Hank will not let that ruin this precious time.

Later, as he lies in the caña shade, taking in the deep blue sky and a band of passing clouds, Analu and Ingrid walk his way and say hello. Both look beautiful and strong. Especially Analu, who's short-cropped salt and pepper hair glistens in the sunshine, her brown skin glowing like some exotic wood. The women's hugs are warm, their voices soft and comforting. The three chat for a few minutes about unimportant matters. Then Analu's face turns serious. "How is Fiona?"

Hank pauses, surprised to hear the question but knows to keep her secret. "Doing good."

"I'm glad to hear it," says Ingrid. She gazes out at the water, seems ready to move on.

But Analu's dark brown eyes stay glued on Hank. "Really, doing good?" She narrows her gaze, enough to clarify her suspicion. "Does that mean I can visit?"

"Well, um, no. She's not quite ready to be social."

"Social?"

Her puzzled face tells him she took that wrong. She and Fiona used to be good friends. From the little Fiona told Hank, he's guessing Analu got too strong with her opinions, her constant good advice. Fiona did not like being told how to take care of herself, and said so.

Unlike Concepción, however, Analu made no attempt to mend things. This is the first time she's shown any sign of that.

Hank says, "You know Fiona needs her privacy."

Analu freezes him with a flinty stare. His fragile sense of peace is fading fast.

Ingrid seems to feel the tension, which is anathema to her nature. "I need to swim before it's windy," she says, waves a quick good bye and hurries off.

"Privacy from me? " Analu says.

"That's not what I meant."

"Then what?"

Now he feels boxed in, and a bit pissed off. "Tell me, Analu, what is it you want to hear?"

"How about the truth?"

He sees she will not give up. Maybe she feels bad for letting the conflict with her friend go on so long. Or maybe she wonders why Fiona never comes to the beach, which used to be a favorite place. To avoid her? Anyway, whatever's driving this powerful woman, Hank can't avoid it, his thin veil of serenity gone, his resistance overwhelmed. Truth is, he's so damn sick of secrets! No more fucking secrets! "She has stomach cancer."

Analu's mouth gapes open. "No!"

Immediately he regrets it. "Please, we have to…Fiona would not want this to get around."

She doesn't seem to hear him. "No, no, who told her that?"

"A doctor from the city. A specialist. He did a lot of tests, and says it's terminal. Says there's nothing to be done."

Analu studies his face, must see how hard it is for him to agree with that dark prognosis. She takes another breath, exhales and slowly nods.

Both gaze out at the lake. The volcanos stand tall, distant, and exempt from human sorrow. Faced by their indifference, Hank puts an arm around his friend. Analu looks at him with tearful eyes. She cries into his chest for several seconds, then gently pulls away. "Can I please help?"

"Yes, but…not yet, I…" There seems no easy way to say what can't be known. The silence is unbearable. "A shaman is coming tomorrow, to bless her house and…and whatever else he does. Beyond that, we'll see what she wants to do."

Analu gives his hands a squeeze, then walks off toward Ingrid. She stops and looks back at him. "Don't worry, Hank, I promise to keep this secret."

18
A Lot

Hank leaves the beach.   Though hungry, on his way to
Josefina's for a meal, he stops for a couple of minutes to watch
various groups of evangelicals spread out along the shore. Each
has its own pastor, and a few of them preach with microphones.
The largest gathering also has a band. It will play at the pastor's
signal, a chance for him to catch a breath.   His throng of
followers, like the other separate throngs, praise the
righteousness of Jesus and beg God to forgive their sins. They
have come in smoke-belching buses to be baptized. This water
is seen as holy, the Lord's creation, a proof of His endless glory
and meant for them to use, which every week they do.

Hank sighs, continues walking, crosses over the narrow
tainted river on its rickety plank bridge. After climbing the hill
beyond the basin, he passes the fancy tourist restaurants and
arrives at Josefina's stall. "Wow," he exclaims, glancing around
the tiny alcove as if never having been there, "how lucky I am to
find this amazing place!"

"*Ah, Enrique!*"

"*Ah, Josefina!*"

"So, you want *The Same?*"

"Sure," Hank says in a dramatic tone, "why not?"

He sits and gazes at the water. Below her stall is a row of docks. This is where people find public lanchas to Santiago, largest of the eleven villages on the lake. Boats motor in and out. Perhaps a hundred trips per day. Being tourist season, there are also many private speedboats, and on weekends come the jet skis, and huge party ships that cruise around blasting music, a steady stream of obnoxious sound, along with toxic chemicals leaked into the lake.

Josefina brings his regular plate of food. Hank is thankful to have his bad thoughts interrupted. She comes back with a basket of hot tortillas. "Orlando came by this morning."

"Really?" Hank feels suspicious. "Why?"

"To ask if I want peanuts."

"Oh."

"I told him no," she says, "but he insisted." Hank shakes his head and Josefina eyes him with annoyance. "You don't understand. He *gave me* a small bag. 'Just to try,' he said. 'No charge.' I think he wanted to show thanks for yesterday."

"I hope that's all it was."

"He's really had it rough, Enrique—a bit of a pest, maybe, but I like him."

Hank feels bad, has let himself get distracted by Fiona's sickness. She would not approve of his negativity. Not the kid's fault for being poor. "He told me his father drinks."

"Yes," she says. "His name is Fidel."

"You know him? Why didn't you say anything when—"

"I didn't want to embarrass Orlando. Fidel has a drinking problem, but he's a good man. And, from what I hear, a great carpenter when he's sober. He used to come here for lunch with the other workers. Now no one will hire him."

"Triste," says Hank. *Sad.*

"Sí," she says, then hurries to stir her pot of beans.

Hank finishes his meal. It's a quarter till one, time to go see about the lot. He grabs his pack and leaves his payment on the table. "Adiós, Josefina."

"Que le vaya bién," she says, the common wish that—*no matter what he's doing*—all goes well.

It's a ten minute walk to the property. The gate is open. Parked inside is a Toyota pickup. A man sticks his head out the window as he approaches. "Enrique?"

"Sí."

He gets out of the truck and shakes Hank's hand. "I am Eduardo Sanchez." Somewhere in his fifties, he is short and stocky. Along with blue jeans and a plaid shirt, he wears a cowboy hat and boots, not the normal Ladino look. "Please, Señor, show me which lot you mean."

The man seems hurried, somehow distracted, which at first puts Hank off. But as they head down the long driveway, Eduardo shares that he's new at selling land, that he manages a ranch in Antigua—his regular job—and is more comfortable with cows than he is with people. The driveway is much longer than Hank imagined. Eduardo, a real talker for a guy who prefers to hang out with cows, explains that he's got a back problem, which is why he felt the need to find other work. "I am part owner of this property. For me it's not an easy job."

Hank's mind has changed. He likes Eduardo, his friendly eyes and simple, straight-forward ways. If this is going to happen, it would be good to deal with such a guy. He hopes. Of course he must be careful, not let his hopeful thinking become a problem. That advice seems to come from Fiona, well aware of how impulsive he can be.

"So," Hank says, "how many lots do you have?"

"Fifteen. Some are already sold. The one I think you want is in the northeastern corner."

At the end of the road, about a hundred yards from the gate, sits a small white stucco house. In the yard out front are a bunch of bustling chickens. Hank looks at an open area off to the left, the north, and spots Fiona's bougainvillea. "There, that's our property."

"Ah, yes," says Eduardo, "that's what I was thinking. It's next to my smallest lot, which is still for sale."

The parcel is mostly devoid of vegetation, but has one mature mango tree. A huge plus! On the east side, abutting Fiona's property, is the outer wall of someone else's land, and on the ground—one to the south, one to the west—are lines of sticks. Hank points. "Those are the other boundaries?"

"Yes." Eduardo gestures to the western line. "And the owner on this side will soon build a wall."

"Good," says Hank. *Then I'd only have one to pay for.*

"So," says Eduardo, "you want to buy it?"

The question catches Hank off guard. Strange that until this very second he hasn't considered what it might cost. *Idiot!* His mind begins to churn, unsure what he can afford, and his hesitation seems to dampen Eduardo's spirit. The man sighs, perhaps worried, after his long drive from Antigua, that the gringo is having second thoughts. Hank also sighs, then suddenly senses the doubt between them as potentially advantageous, that it might help him haggle down the price. Alarming how instinctive this machination feels. "I do," he says, "but, well, I need some time to—"

"Sorry," says Eduardo, "I must know today." He seems sad, even apologetic, as if embarrassed by his ultimatum. "As I said, I do not own this property myself. I have three partners, and all of us owe money to the bank." He sighs again. "This work may look easy, but it's not. I never used to have so many worries, so much happening all at once. The thing is, if I can't make a deal today, my partners have ideas of their own."

Hank feels stunned by the sudden pressure. Could it be he's getting worked?

"Sad," says Eduardo, "because I think you would be perfect to buy this lot."

"Why?"

"If I heard right on the phone, you said it was to extend your garden, yes?"

"Yes, that's right, that's all I want."

"So, you do not plan to build a house?"

"Definitely not."

"Well, then," says Eduardo, who has clearly thought the whole thing through, "I think a deal may be possible. You see, my partners and I, we…we have a problem."

"What kind of problem?"

Eduardo points straight ahead. "The owner of that house, Señor Mocún, grew up here, on this land. His family owned three *manzanas*. You understand that measurement?"

"No."

"About five acres."

"Wow."

"Yes, a big piece of property. But otherwise they were poor. Lived in a little bamboo shack, had a goat and a bunch of chickens. On the rest of the land they grew corn and beans. For Indios, of course, they were doing well, but times were changing. As foreigners kept coming to the lake, land around here kept increasing in value. Others were selling theirs, but his father refused. Everyone, including the old man's wife and four children, thought him stupid. His father didn't care. When he died, ten years ago, it belonged to Señor Mocún as the eldest son. And right away he sold it. All but his one piece. After sharing the profits with his siblings, the señor only had enough to build this small house for him and his aging mother. He'd imagined, I suppose, that the land would stay as it always had, with maybe a few more families. He is an intelligent man, but not familiar with how things work. You understand?"

"Yes," says Hank, far too damn familiar with how things work, "I do."

"The man who bought the land split it into these fifteen lots. A year ago we bought the property from him. It seemed a great investment at the time. Now I'm not so sure."

"Why?"

"Oh, so many problems. I won't bore you with the details. Worst of all, Señor Mocún is angry with what has happened, he feels cheated, and is trying to make sure we can't sell your lot!"

"He can do that?"

"Maybe, yes." Eduardo groans. "It is true, the land was not properly divided. Your lot does not have legal access across his. How that is possible I do not know, the plan should never have been approved. To change it now, however, seems unlikely. My partners want to sue the city government. I tell them no, a big mistake, would cost a lot of time and money, and cause trouble. Could make us some powerful enemies."

The man seems genuinely vexed. Though he might be making all this up, it sounds plausible to Hank, who has known of similar land fiascos around the lake.

"To avoid those many headaches," says Eduardo, "we offered Mocún eight thousand quetzales—a thousand dollars—for an easement. He said no. The road would have to go right in front of his living room window. That is his main complaint, and I understand, I really do. So we offered him the lot itself. For cheap. Only enough to break even. But the Señor still says no. He is aware, I am sure, that without a road we cannot sell it." Eduardo wipes his sweaty brow. "Some problems seem impossible to solve."

Strange that Eduardo is now smiling. *Why would he be...?* Then Hank understands. *Oh.*

"You see?" Eduardo has read his mind, and lets out a nervous laugh. "Amazing, isn't it, that my problem might turn into good news for you!"

"Because we don't need a road?"

"Exactly!" says Eduardo, his eyes opening wide. "If you agree to that one condition, I can sell it for the same price we offered Mocún."

Hank's sunken hope resurfaces. "Yes, all right, how much?"

"Four thousand dollars."

Hank blinks at the number, far higher than he'd expected. He's got less than half of that. Again he feels deflated.

"Not much to pay for a lot these days," says Eduardo.

"A lot without a road?"

"With a road it would be ten."

Hank stares at him, aware that it could be true. With no interest since San Marcos in buying land, he's paid no attention to the rising prices. "I guess I've gotten too damn old. Still living in the past."

"What were you expecting?"

"I really had no idea. Was hoping about two."

"Two thousand?" Eduardo looks incredulous. "No, amigo, I can't go that low."

The man seems sadly certain. It's plain he will not budge, and Hank feels like a fool. "Sorry, amigo, to waste your time." He shakes his hand and turns to go.

"Wait." Eduardo looks cautiously optimistic. "You have the money now?"

Hank explains how his trust fund works: that a thousand dollars comes, guaranteed, each month.

"My problem," says Eduardo, "is I need at least two thousand by next week. Is that possible?"

Hank thinks fast, subtracts the monthly cost of living, the coming Oxycontin, then mitigates the loss with the thousand Fiona was going to pay Ernie.

He is confident she'll agree. "Yes."

Eduardo nods and takes a breath. "Okay, so, how about we do this." He proposes a deal where Hank would put two thousand down, then pay the other two within six months, thus making it possible to construct the needed wall and close the lot away from dogs. "Does that work for you?"

Hank feels shocked this is really happening, "Yes."

"I am glad," says Eduardo. "For both of us." They shake hands, agree to legalize the deal on Tuesday at his lawyer's office.

Hank hurries back to the house, excited to share his news, and finds Fiona sobbing on the couch. Concepción, sitting next to her, looks outraged.

He kneels down by them. "What's wrong?"

Tears pour from Fiona's eyes. "Ernie."

"Ernie?"

"He was here," says Concepción.

Fiona nods, though seems unable to speak.

Concepción points an angry finger at the gate. "He just now roared off on his *pinche* motorcycle." She grabs both of Hank's hands and squeezes. "I know about that man, the whole town knows. He is evil," she says, as might a pastor quoting scripture, "like the devil himself!"

"He says," blurts out Fiona, "says that..." But she can't finish, her crying now like a convulsion. She rushes off into the bathroom, shuts and locks the door.

"He wants money," says Concepción. "A thousand dollars, he says, or else!"

Hank's hands are trembling.

"When Fiona told him no, he kept threatening, said not to try and cheat him, said bad things are going to happen if she does."

"What things?"

"I don't know. He didn't say. But she'd regret not paying up. For some pills, he said. What is he talking about, Enrique?"

"She ordered pain pills from him, then changed her mind."

"Oh," says Concepción, whose expression shifts from confusion to something darker. Must be upset that Fiona got involved with such a terrible person. "It doesn't matter. He can't threaten her like that. I told him so, told him to get out, to leave us be. He laughed, so I threw a rock."

"Threw a rock?"

"It missed, and he laughed again. Left before I could throw another. Said he would be back."

"I'll kill him," Hank says, then shudders, realizes what he said. "No, I don't mean that, I—"

"Don't you worry," she says, eyes blazing as she turns and rushes off. "I'll make sure he won't."

19

What Needs To Happen

Fiona comes out of the bathroom, climbs into bed. Hank asks if she wants to talk, thinking that might help. "I'm too tired," she says, and turns away. In a few minutes she's asleep.

Hank lies down on his pad, stares at the water stain on the ceiling. *Fuck!* He gets up and heads for town. Has to find, and deal with, Ernie. At Rancho Grande he turns toward the lake, then follows the promenade to where it ends at the bottom of Santander. One of Ernie's guys is usually stationed on the wooden landing by the water, right where tourists tend to gather. And, as expected, there he is. Alto.

Hank knew this lanky teenager long before he got the nickname: *Tall.* Or, also, *high,* which he often is. Used to be a skinny little street kid selling Chiclets. *"Oye, Alto."*

"Qué onda, mano?" What's up, bro?

"I need to talk with Ernie," Hank says in Spanish.

"Sorry, I don't know where he is."

"When will you see him?"

137

"Quien sabe?" Who knows?

It's the standard response to any question lacking a definite answer—a throw-away line, a light-hearted comment on the unpredictable nature of human existence, and normally taken as a joke. Hank stares at the kid, not in a mood for joking. "Well, *mano,* when you do, tell him he was warned."

Alto stares back, seems stunned by the gringo's stark hostility.

"Just tell him," says Hank, and walks away, a bit surprised by his own bravado. *Yeah, okay, now what?* He doesn't know where Ernie lives. The guy moves around from year to year. Hank goes up Santander, again wondering how, if necessary, he might get a gun, and trembling at the thought.

At the end of the street, by the bus stop, is another of Ernie's guys. Chico, his right-hand man. His enforcer. Too scary-looking to be a hustler. About thirty years old, he is a short, compact ladino, with tightly muscled arms covered by tattoos. Unlike Alto, Chico cannot be intimidated. He signals Hank to come over. "You got the money?" he says in English.

"No."

"No?" He scratches his chin and shakes his shaved head. "Ernie won't be happy."

"I don't care."

The enforcer stiffens. Malice fills his eyes. "Too bad, *pendejo,* because you should."

The threat hits Hank between the eyes. *What the hell am I doing?* This guy is dangerous, so why provoke him? He spends most of his time in Guatemala City, only comes to Pana in order to deal with problems. Like Hank. That could be why he's here. Well, all right, but maybe—just maybe—there are things he doesn't know. Things worthy of his concern. "Careful," Hank says, his tone serious and, for Chico, hopefully alarming, "you're both being watched."

"Yeah?" He scoffs and looks around. "By who?"

"You'll find out," Hank bluffs, and walks away.

"Can't fucking wait!" calls Chico.

Hank keeps walking, trying to look self-confident. He rounds the corner onto Calle Principal, goes to La Palapa, checks for Ernie's motorcycle. Not there. Or anywhere up the street. In the hardware store by Calle Frutal, Hank buys two sets of hasps and a padlock. Also a machete. Though minimal protection, it's better than nothing till he can find a gun.

Back home, he hides the machete behind the house, then goes into the garden shed, lays the hasps on the counter and looks on his tool shelf for the Phillips screwdriver. Can't find it. *Fuck!* He goes to the house, tiptoes past the bed. Can't find it in his room, either, or in any of the kitchen drawers.

"You have a problem?" It's Fiona, standing in the doorway, eyes blazing.

He must have been too loud. "Sorry I woke you."

"What are you looking for?"

Hank flinches, needs to calm down, knows she's overwhelmed by this threat from Ernie. And scared. Though he wants to be sympathetic, Fiona's words and tone have added to his general irritation, made him feel like just another problem in her life. *Really, is that fair?* He throws his hands up into the empty space. "I can't find my fucking screwdriver!"

"What? All of a sudden you need a—?"

"Yes, I do!" He feels close to exploding. "Will you tell me, *please,* have you seen it?"

"No."

"Okay, sorry, never mind." Hank brushes past Fiona and sets off to re-check the shed.

As he reaches the front door she says, "Oh, um, wait."

Hank turns and looks at her.

"It might be on top of the cold-frame."

In other words, she used it, and did not return it to his tool shelf in the shed. They've had this kind of run-in many times. "Ah, on the cold-frame, of course, right where it belongs."

"Hank?"

"I don't say I need something if I don't! Why the hell can't you put things back?"

"Hank, I'm sorry." She's close to tears. "Please, forgive me."

They stand there staring at each other. Between them floats her sincere apology, and not about some damn screwdriver. Hank sighs, goes and holds her in his arms. "Please, don't... don't worry," he whispers. "None of this is your fault. I'll make sure that jerk won't bother you again."

She steps back, wipes her eyes and looks at him. "How?"

"I'd love to show you," he says, and smiles, "once I find my fucking screwdriver."

Fiona frowns. "A lock on the gate, right?"

"Right."

"I had the same idea."

"Geniuses think alike."

"Yeah," she says, and sighs, "when there's only one reasonable solution. Okay, can I help?"

"Absolutely." He sees she's not into this, has always hated locks on anything. Best to keep things light. "You can sit out in the garden, watch me work, and lie from time to time about how wonderful I am."

"You are." She kisses his cheek. "You really are."

"Yeah, yeah, thanks, good job."

It takes an hour, accompanied by Fiona's elaborate praise, to mount a hasp on each side of the gate. When it's locked—in addition to their eight foot concrete walls covered by thorny vines, including a thick patch arched over the entry—they'll be safe. Well, not completely. Which is why he got the machete, and needs a gun. Until then there seems nothing else to do.

There are two keys for the padlock. Hank hands one to Fiona, who hesitates before taking it. "We'll both have a key," he says, "in case we're gone at the same time."

"I don't plan on going out."

"Well...if by chance you ever do."

"Okay."

"If I leave and you're definitely staying home, I'll lock it from the outside."

"Okay."

"And if we're both here," he says, straightening up and speaking in a naively innocent voice, a playful *homage* to Mister Rogers, "we'll lock it from the inside."

Fiona shows a wry smile, like she's been forced into this nice agreement. "Okay…okay…okay."

"But?"

"But nothing. Unfortunately, I see no other choice."

"Unfortunately, yeah."

He shuts the gate and padlocks it. They walk arm in arm to the house. Fiona sighs again, wants to know when he'll be meeting the pharmacy guy.

"At six." He checks his watch. "It's three-twenty now. Do we have an alarm clock?"

"No," she says, "we have me. Go sleep, I'll wake you at five."

"Deal."

Hank goes to his room, lies on his pad and shuts his eyes. Imagines himself swimming in the lake. After awhile, without warning, the water slips away, drops out of sight, and he panics, lunges upward and looks ahead at a blank white wall. His watch says a quarter after five. *Huh?* He changes from shorts to pants, transfers the money to his pack and hurries to the living room. No Fiona. "Hello?"

"I'm in here," she calls from the kitchen. "Thought you might be hungry."

She's at the stove, stirring a pot of beans. "You're cooking?"

"Concepción brought these over. Someone has to eat them."

Hank loves that she remembers how he likes them: with a touch of soy sauce, a few cashews, sharp cheddar cheese and some strips of jalapeño pepper. He sits at the table, his mind wandering back to the long lost past, so many years ago, when this was a normal scene.

Fiona brings a plate of steaming food. "You want water?"

"Sure. Thanks." She fills two glasses, sits down and watches while he eats. Her focused attention makes him feel special, then slightly nervous. Maybe there's a problem. "You all right?"

141

"Yeah," Fiona says, "I'm good."

"Meaning you could be better?"

"Meaning I'm not in pain, which is good enough."

Hank mentions Aakesh, who, at eighty-five, likes to joke that "good enough" is as good as it ever gets.

Fiona laughs, she says, because it's "so damned unfunny."

He checks his phone. "I gotta go."

After locking the gate on the outside, he starts down the alley. A broad-chested man stands in the shadows, upright and vigilant like a sentry. At first Hank thinks of Ernie and feels spooked. Then he sees that it's Fernando, one of Concepción's brothers.

Hank walks up to him. "Don't worry, amigo, she'll be okay."

Fernando nods. "I'm here to make sure of that."

Hank shakes his hand, then hurries to Rancho Grande. It's the busy time of day, a lot of people on the move. He goes down the narrow callejón, Los Quenun, to Santander, makes his way to the pharmacy, arrives a few minutes before six.

Señor Gonzales is waiting behind the counter, a big smile on his face. "I have good news."

"You got the Oxycontin?"

He holds up two small plastic vials. "120 tablets. Enough for at least two months."

"Like I said, I can only afford one month."

"For that amount, I learned, it's quite a bit more expensive."

"How much?"

"A hundred and fifty dollars."

"No, wait, you told me—"

"Yes," the slimeball says, pretending to be upset, "I should not have guessed so low. Sorry. But for a two month supply there is a discount. Two hundred and thirty all together."

"Bulk deal, huh?"

"I suppose."

Never mind, just do this. Hank pulls out the money and hands it to Gonzales, who gives him the two vials. Hank puts them in the pack and hoists it to his back.

"Should your wife need more," the slimeball says, I—"

"Yes, yes, thank you."

Hank feels suddenly claustrophobic and rushes from the store. On the street he sighs, relieved to be finished with Gonzales, and checks his phone. It's only been twenty minutes. He's not ready to go home, goes up Santander to see María.

She sees him coming. *"Enrique, oh, Enrique!"*

They kiss each other on the cheek, sit together on the curb.

"How is your ankle?"

"Better." She pulls up her skirt and shows him. The wound has been re-bandaged. "Doctor Angelo says I should run."

"Run?"

"Races."

"Oh," says Hank. "Yes, I think you should!"

After a quick blush she plays serious, even stern. "I don't think you bet on me."

"Of course I will, María. All my money."

She giggles like a little kid.

Then, as is their custom, they get quiet and look out on the world. It's Saturday night and the one-way street is buzzing, bumper-to-bumper cars and motorcycles. People weave between the vehicles, are crowded together on either side along with kids riding bicycles, dogs begging for food, waiters waving menus. Tourists tromp by in crooked rows, speaking their foreign languages—English mostly, but also German, French, Italian, Swedish. Some are bunched up like herded cattle, the voluntary chattel of their paid guides. Others have come in pairs. Or are alone. Nevertheless, though in many ways disconnected, all now have one essential thing in common: It's time to eat! In spite of the packed street, the slow and bumpy progress, they seem driven, intent on finding a decent restaurant.

María lays her head against his shoulder, lets out an exaggerated sigh. *"Ay, Enrique, qué milagro."*

What a miracle, she said. It's one of their favorite jokes.

Such a crazy damn world we live in. That's what she really means, referring to all the noise and chaotic energy this time of day.

143

Horns, as if they might have some effect, honk. Motorcycle engines rev, awaiting their chance to roar. And people, in order to be heard, must shout above the din.

"*Ay, Enrique!*"

He knows, because María has often told him, how the loudness hurts her ears, and how the exhaust fumes burn her eyes. But this old woman, who has withstood so much suffering in her life, will not let these modern nuisances get her down. Would rather joke about things she can't control. Again she giggles, points at the busy street, and sort of swoons, pretending to be enchanted by the steadily roiling tangle of humanity.

"*Sí,*" says Hank with his normal sarcastic grin, "*qué milagro.*"

Then Ernie appears, cruising on his motorcycle. He doesn't mind the slow-going, is on the hunt for young tourists, or whoever might want to score some stuff. He calmly scans the street, then sees Hank and glares.

"Time for you is up!" he shouts in English.

Hank sighs, his blood boiling.

Ernie guns his engine as he crawls past. "I fucking mean it!"

María looks at Hank. She could not possibly have missed the venomous energy spewed in their direction. "What did he say?"

There really is no reason to explain it. Nothing she could do, so why make her worry?

"He says people like you make him very angry."

The old woman laughs, can probably not imagine anyone being mad at her. Hank gets a gentle elbow in the ribs. "Go on," she pokes again, ready for the punchline, "tell me why?"

"He says you are too beautiful for this world."

20
The Ceremony

When Hank gets home he finds Fernando still on guard, and looking tired. "I'm waiting for Diego to take over."

"Until when?"

"A few hours after dark. Sorry, that's all we can do."

"Hey, amigo, I...I truly thank you, but Fiona would feel bad that you're going to so much trouble. This can't go on forever."

"No," Fernando says. "Don't worry, my friend, it won't."

The two shake hands and say good night. Hank unlocks the gate, slips into the garden, locks it from inside. The sun has set beyond their western wall. "I'm over here," says Fiona. She's at the table, which is in shadow.

Hank hands her the bag of pills. "One, if necessary, every twelve hours."

She takes one and swallows it. "Let's hope that's enough."

"Yeah," he says, "let's hope."

He sits with her as the sky turns dark, as dogs gather in the empty lot and begin to howl. After a night of carousing elsewhere, they're back in force. Hank smiles to himself. Yeah, okay, his barricade didn't work, seems to have only made them crazier. But soon he'll be able to stop all that. Should he tell Fiona? His plan was to wait until the contract is signed and the lot becomes legally theirs. Yes, best he do that, because nothing is certain in Guatemala, especially with land deals, and if things go wrong it's better she doesn't know.

They go into the house, and try to read, but neither can concentrate with all the noise. Around nine they switch to cribbage. Hank wins almost every game.

At last she says, "I'm finished."

"With cribbage or the dogs?"

"Both."

Hank considers suggesting voodoo, but Fiona is in no joking mood, and might even take offense, might think he's demeaning tomorrow's ceremony with Vicente. He says good night, goes and lies down in his room. Surrender to the racket seems his only choice. He tries to hear the beastly brawl as heavy-metal love songs pounding him to sleep.

For many hours that does not work.

Hank wakes Sunday morning to pure silence. He stays prone until forced by the need to pee, and is careful not to disturb Fiona. Today he won't go swimming, needs to stay home, help prepare the house, and himself, for what—like it or not—is coming. First a strong cup of coffee. He's sipping it on the couch when Fiona starts mumbling in her sleep. She lets out a whimper and bolts upright, looks panicked, sees him sitting there. "What time is it?"

"Almost nine."

She picks up the vial of Oxycontin next to her bed and gives it a dirty look. "This can't be here." She takes and swallows another pill, then goes to the kitchen and puts the vial with the others in the spice drawer. "We have to…have to get things ready for Vicente."

"Yeah, okay. How?"

"I don't know!" She throws up her hands, walks back and forth through the room, like trapped inside some nightmare, then gestures in no particular direction. "Just make it clean."

"Got it."

"I'm sorry, I can't be inside." She goes out to the garden, begins watering the flowers.

Hank does the dishes, wipes down the counters, sweeps floors and washes windows. Meanwhile, she re-arranges pots on the front porch. He comes and sits by her. "Um, what else?"

Fiona hugs him. "Thanks, honey, you did great."

The medicine seems to have kicked in. "So, I take it you're feeling better?"

"Yeah."

"Which means the stuff I got is working?"

"Good enough."

"Yeah?"

"Well," Fiona says, eyes glinting as she walks off, "at least *good enough* to pull weeds."

He follows behind and helps her. After collecting an impressive pile, they prune the many vines and broom away cobwebs from the garden walls. Vicente won't notice any of their work. Not what this is about. Fiona needs to prepare her spirit to be "cleansed," which first means making sure that nothing else looks dirty. Who can say for sure where pesky demons might be hiding?

"Oh," she says, "I forgot. He'll need to use the fire pit."

Hank nods. "I'll clean it out."

Fiona takes his hand. "Ooh, what a treat, I want to help!"

Hank gets hopeful, feels them connected again, and wants to stretch out these lovely moments. *Sure, why not?* Like giving a weather report, he describes his meeting with Eduardo.

At first she thinks he's joking, telling one of his silly stories, and twice says, "Yeah, uh-huh." But when he outlines the actual deal she drops the trowel and stares at him. "You're messing with me, right?"

"No, Señorita, we sign the papers on Tuesday."

She lets out a happy little gasp, claps her hands and starts laughing. "Really?"

"Really."

"How? I mean, where did you get the money?"

Hank says he'll need some of her savings. "Is that all right?"

"Oh geez! Oh fucking yes!"

He takes the bucket of ashes and dumps it in the compost.

"Hey," she calls out to him, "you hungry?"

"Oh geez! Oh fucking yes!"

She nods and starts for the house, that long silver hair swishing down her back. *My god, what a gorgeous woman!* Hank shakes his head, amazed by how much she still turns him on. In the old days he could not resist, would follow her inside.

Oh geez! Oh fucking yes!

Though that time is long gone, he feels thankful for the memory. Not wanting to get emotional, Hank walks around the yard, admires the flowers, pulls a few more weeds and sweeps the walkway. Fiona comes out with a plate of eggs, beans, and plantains. Sets it on the table. "Here you go, Señor."

"You truly are a wonder."

"The wonder is to have you in my life."

Her obvious love, coming so fast and unexpected, shakes him up. Hank's about to lose it. "Yeah," he says, "I know. Like a daily lesson of what not to do."

"I'm serious."

"Oh." He has to clear his throat. "Well, um, thanks for saying that."

She's about to lose it too. "I'll get your coffee."

"Yeah, okay."

And the moment passes. Soon they're back to kidding around, giving each other shit. Fine with him. It means she's feeling good, his main concern.

He finishes eating and checks his phone, sees it's almost noon. "We ready for Vicente?"

"Yeah. I mean, I think so. You remember how the ceremony goes?"

"Am I supposed to?" He's glad to have forgotten the long and tedious ritual. "I only did it once."

"Truth is," she says, "I don't remember either."

"Well, let's hope I won't lose any blood." A jest with meaning. They both know that in ancient Maya culture there were occasional human sacrifices. "Any chance of that?"

"I think not."

Someone tries the locked gate, then knocks. *"Hola, Fiona, ya estoy."* It's Vicente.

"Just a second," Fiona calls out in Spanish. Hank hands her the key and she unlocks the gate.

The shaman, in his mid-fifties, wears traditional traje from Sololá—red pants and a white shirt, both ornately embroidered with Maya patterns and symbols. He carries a large burlap sack over his shoulder, smiles as he enters the garden. "Is there some reason you need protection?"

Did he notice one of the Garcías outside on guard? No, he's focused on the lock, humored by her newly installed security. Fiona looks at a loss. "My idea," says Hank. "I want to keep her a secret from the world."

"You know," the shaman says in well-enunciated Spanish, flashing a prankish grin, "a lock is a complicated thing. Both a defense and a possible trap."

"Exactly," says Hank with a knowing wink, "which is why I can use it on either side."

Vicente raises his thick dark eyebrows, no doubt aware that the non-sequitur was intentional. The two men share a smile. Though skeptical of his religion, Hank has always appreciated the shaman's sense of humor. He reaches out and shakes his hand. "Thank you for coming."

Vicente squeezes a bit too tight, perhaps also aware that Hank does not trust him. "My pleasure, Enrique."

Fiona claps her hands. "Okay, boys, time to get serious." She walks them to the emptied fire pit and points. "Will this work?"

"Much cleaner than I need," Vicente says. "Are you ready?"

"Sure," she says, and gives Hank a hopeful glance. "Yeah?"

"Oh yeah, absolutely."

"Please," says Vicente, "make yourselves comfortable."

They sit on the ground. He kneels and empties out his sack. There are lots of long thin candles and small square blocks of *copal* incense. He takes out a large round metal pan, places it down into the pit, and from a plastic bag starts pouring a white substance. The pan is soon marked by the sign of a white cross.

Hank doesn't remember this, and can't help wondering, "Is that sugar?"

"Yes. We Maya have always had a sweet tooth."

It seems a well-worn joke.

Vicente pours a circle of sugar around the cross, then a small arrow above each of the four points where the two shapes intersect. "The four elements of existence: *cielo, agua, tierra, aire.*" He lights a short stout candle and places it in the middle of the cross. "This is the center of existence, where all creation meets." He closes his eyes, says a few words in Cakchiquel, then surrounds the candle with copal incense and more sugar, sprinkles on some chunks of cacao and a handful of broken cookies. Around the outer circle Vicente layers some kind of dried green herb, says it represents human hair.

Or, rather, that's what Hank thinks he said. His mind had wandered off and he isn't sure, wants to ask but does not dare interrupt.

On top of all the rest, Vicente places several handfuls of those long slim candles. Then he closes his eyes. So does Fiona. And for several minutes the shaman mumbles to himself. Again he speaks in Cakchiquel, as if this part of the ceremony were meant to remain unknown to Hank and Fiona—secrets of existence, perhaps, only privy to Maya shamans.

When finished, he flicks water on the fire. "This cleanses us," he explains. "Lifts our eternal spirits into the sacred air." Vicente stands, gestures for Hank and Fiona to also rise. Together they breath in the lingering haze of incense, waft it toward themselves with their cupped hands. After a minute or two of that, Vicente bows to the waning fire, then looks at Fiona. "We are ready now to bless your house."

"Okay."

Vicente and Fiona go inside. Hank follows close behind.

The shaman stops in the center of the living room and scans the surrounding space. It seems he's on the lookout for something in particular. "Only the two of you live here?"

Fiona nods.

He sniffs the air. "I sense something very wrong."

She glances at Hank

He looks back with clear confusion. *What the hell?*

Vicente walks into his bedroom, steps past his sleeping pad, examines every wall and peeks into the closet. Several times he stops, closes his eyes and mumbles something in Cakchiquel. He comes out, and repeats the same process in other rooms of the house. In the kitchen he looks inside the refrigerator, where Fiona has carefully arranged the many potions and elixirs he'd provided. He opens the spice drawer and, as if perplexed, peruses the many vials. "What is all this?"

Fiona looks alarmed. "Spices."

"Spices? You mean for food?"

"Yes."

Vicente looks again, then nods and closes the drawer. He lights a stick of copal and walks through the entire house again, spends extra time in the kitchen and the bathroom, swirling the smoke about as he mumbles. Fiona follows him around while Hank waits on the couch. At last he stops in the living room. "I can feel them," the shaman says. His voice is soft and certain. "There are demons in your house."

Fiona had not expected that. "Really?"

"Really, yes. And there is nothing I can do."

"What?" Her face contorts, a mixture of confusion and mounting dread "Why?"

"Because you brought them here."

"No. No, I—"

"Yes," he says, raising his hand. "I'm sorry but…it was you who invited them to come."

"Please, Vicente…" She takes a breath. "Please, I promise you, that's not true."

151

"I am sorry, Fiona." The shaman bows to her respectfully, then walks out the door.

She stares at Hank, her eyes closed and lips quivering.

He goes outside.

Vicente is emptying the ceremonial ashes into the fire pit.

Hank kneels next to him, fighting the urge to slap his pious face. "You're making a mistake."

The shaman puts his round metal pan in the burlap sack, lifts it to his shoulder, gives Hank a long and caring look. "If that is true, it simply proves I cannot help her."

"You should go apologize."

"No," says Vicente, heading for the gate. "She knows where the demons are. And so do you."

"You mean the medicine?"

He stops. "Is that what you call it?"

"She's sick, Vicente. She's got cancer. Your potions don't stop the pain."

Vicente faces him, looks both sad and certain. "Some kinds of sickness kill the body. None can kill the spirit."

"God damn it!" Hank says in English. He takes a breath, touches the shaman's arm, says the rest in slow, insistent Spanish. "Please, you can't leave her like that."

"I am sorry, Enrique, I truly am."

He opens the unlocked gate and closes it behind him.

21
Nunca

Hank tries to comfort Fiona, but there's no way. She curls up on the bed and goes to sleep. Or pretends to. He lets her be, grabs his pack, locks the gate from outside. Pedro, the oldest García brother, is across the way, talking on a cell phone. They give each other a wave and Hank heads for the lake.

There is no one on the beach. It's nearly two o'clock. The windblown water greets him like a challenge. He strips down and dives in. The cold grips tight as he swims away from shore, out through the white-capped swells until suddenly he's exhausted. Something in him wants to just keep going. Hank stops, knows he's not thinking right, treads water and gasps for air. This panic is familiar, he's felt it out here before. Once, when a bit too drunk, and depressed, he'd almost drowned. Hank swore that would never happen again, so *what the fuck?* Slowly, with many calming breaks, he makes his way to shore.

A few minutes later, Hank splayed out on his back, something wet and kind of scratchy moves across his cheek. He opens his eyes to see he's being licked. It's the puppy from a couple of days ago. "Well," says Hank, sitting up to get clear of that busy tongue, "hello."

The dog runs in a tiny circle, like doing a trick he's been commanded to perform, then lies down next to Hank's leg, their bodies touching, and lets out a mighty sigh.

"Atta boy, just make yourself at home."

The pup looks at him, absolutely clueless.

Touched by such innocence, Hank smiles and pets its silly head. "What could be crazier," he says, "than me, the great hater of street dogs, having one?" Because that's surely what this feels like—like this little guy is his, like it's somehow been decided. *No, huh-uh, not by me.* He stops petting. The puppy raises its head for more. "Fine," says Hank, stroking the soft warm fur because, in fact, he needs a touch of comfort as much as his new friend. "But only here at the beach, understand?"

No, he thinks, don't let this get too chummy? Time to leave. Hank stands up, brushes off the sand, puts on his clothes.

The puppy waits. Still looks as if this gringo belongs to him.

Hank gazes down into its big brown eyes. *"Nunca."* Never. As in: Forget it, pal, because that will *never* happen. Ah, what a perfect name. "Adios, Nunca," he says, and walks off, has decided to go hang out with Aakesh.

But the dog follows right behind him.

Hank stops and looks back. "Sorry, you're not with me." Nunca perks up his ears, seems confused. "Go on, go on, *git!*"

Tail between his legs, the puppy sprints away. Hank walks on, hopes that's the end of it, but Nunca does not appear convinced. He lags twenty or thirty yards behind, from time to time distracted by some sound, smell, or another dog, then hurries to stay within shouting distance, perhaps hoping the mean old man might change his mind. Hank pretends not to notice. Walks faster. At Calle Salpores he turns and heads up the long cobblestone road toward Aakesh's house. Halfway there he glances back, sees three dogs come out of an alley. They corner Nunca against a concrete wall. At first things seem all right—a lot of butt sniffing, regular doggy stuff—but then the largest mutt tries to mount the pup.

Hank picks up a rock and rushes to the rescue.

Nunca shakes loose from his captor, scoots over to him, slides between his legs.

The three dogs all growl at the man, their hackles raised.

"Vaya!" Hank yells, and throws his rock against the wall. That causes them to flinch, and for a second freeze. Then they bark, snarl, and lunge in his direction. He reaches down for another rock. To his amazement, like in a movie made just for him, they howl and scramble back down the alley.

The puppy whines. Hank picks him up and that lightning tongue licks his face. "Yeah, yeah, okay." Not knowing what else to do, he carries Nunca up the street. As he reaches Aakesh's house an idea begins to form. He cracks open the metal gate and pokes his head inside. "It's me asshole!"

"What, you want a medal?"

Hank can tell his friend is somewhere in the garden. "Can you please come here."

"Why?"

"I've got a little surprise."

"Oh, sweet geezus!" A few seconds later Aakesh limps around the corner of the house, his back more bent than usual, his natural shortness further shortened. "Christ, you're a pain in the ass."

"Yeah, uh-huh."

"Yeah, uh-huh...so...hello...what's your fucking problem?"

Hank steps inside, brings Nunca into view. "Ta-da!"

"Oh, no, you finally lost your shit."

"He's not mine."

As if to disagree, the dog tries to lick his face.

"Coulda fooled me," says Aakesh.

"I was thinking," says Hank, "since you're here all alone, it might be good to have—"

"No!"

"No? You sure?"

"I'm sure."

"You mean...never?"

"Yeah, asshole, that's what I fucking mean. *Never.*"

155

"Perfect," says Hank. "That just happens to be his name."

Aakesh widens his eyes in mock surprise, which Hank sees as a possible opening. He holds the dog out toward his friend and the old man backs away, more nimble than he's been in years. "You really have gone crazy."

"More like desperate." Nunca whines, tries to lick Hank's face again, and again he blocks it. "Damn thing followed me from the beach. Is it okay if I put him down?"

"In my garden?"

"Just for a minute."

"He shits or pisses, you clean it up."

"Deal."

Hank sets the dog down. It sits between them, at attention, as if awaiting orders.

Aakesh kneels down and pats the puppy's head. "Nunca, it's a pleasure—*I hope*—to meet you. Welcome to my garden of delights. And if you mess with a single flower I'll cut your fucking head off."

He slowly rises and slumps away. Nunca and Hank follow. The three of them sit by the garden table. The dog lies down, his head on Hank's foot.

"Cute little guy," says Aakesh.

"See, I knew he'd grow on you."

Aakesh laughs. "No way, man, *nunca!*" The dog's ears perk up. "A smart one, too." The pup puts its head back on Hank's foot. "Yep, Hank, he's yours all right."

"Last damn thing I need."

"Well, maybe he's for Fiona."

"She doesn't like dogs any more than me."

"A regular street mutt, no, but this one seems kinda special. At least you can ask her, right?"

"I already know the answer."

"No, you don't. That's the point. Not until she tells you."

Hank sighs and looks away.

"Hey, man," says Aakesh, "stranger things have happened. Could turn out the best thing you ever did! Why not find out?

She says no, you bring it up to Sherrill's place. That woman takes any stray, and would love to get ahold of one so sweet."

"Yeah, I guess."

"So go on, let Fiona see this guy." Aakesh lets out a romantic sigh, puts a hand over his chest. "Laddie," he says in a romantic Scottish brogue, "this just might be what wins her heart."

"That I doubt."

"Yeah, me too."

They both laugh.

"Hey," says his friend, "how 'bout a cup of tea?"

"No, I uh…I gotta get back home."

"What, you just fucking got here!" Aakesh's gives him a flinty stare, must see that there's a problem. "Okay, what's up?"

Hank should have known he's here to talk. He tells about the cancer, about Ernie, about the García boys standing guard, and Fiona's hurtful moment with Vicente.

"Shit, man, yeah, you should go home."

Hank nods and stands.

Aakesh looks up at him. "Any way I can help?"

Hank smiles and glances down at the dog.

"Aside from that."

"Well," he says, "aside from that, I may need a gun."

"A gun?"

"I mean because of Ernie, if things get crazy."

"That's not going to happen."

"Maybe not, I don't know, I…I keep imagining the worst."

Aakesh stands and hugs Hank close. "Worst-case thinking won't help you, man."

"I know, I'm trying not to, but…"

"Okay." Aakesh steps back. "This may not be up to you."

"No."

"So, yeah, I know a guy with guns."

"Who?"

"No one you would like."

"I don't need to like him."

157

"Please, just go take care of Fiona. I'll talk to him. I'll tell you what he says."

"Thanks."

"Sure." Aakesh walks them to the gate, opens it, kneels down and shakes Nunca's paw. "Grow up fast, you little fucker, and keep my friends safe, you hear?" The dog licks his hand. "Okay, enough of that. Now both of you get out."

The sun has begun to set as Hank turns onto their alley. Pedro spots him and waves, so to be friendly he goes over, shows him the pup. Hank opens its mouth, points at its sharp little teeth and jokes that they now have a real guard.

"Good," says a smiling Pedro, "because I have to leave, was just waiting until you got back."

"Yeah, okay, no problem."

"Fernando says he'll be here in an hour."

"Bueno, amigo, y gracias. Hasta pronto."

They shake hands and Pedro hurries off. Hank, to his surprise, feels vulnerable with him gone. But his greatest worry is Fiona, that she'll go nuts about this dog. He'll tell her he's just keeping it overnight, tomorrow will take it to Sherrill's place. She should be okay with that. He unlocks the gate, opens it and slips inside, Nunca cradled against his chest.

"What the hell?" Fiona stares at them from the garden table.

Hank sighs. "I can explain."

She gets up and walks over. "A dog?"

"It followed me from the beach, was getting bullied by some mutts. I didn't know what to—"

"He's so adorable!" she says, and nuzzles her face against Nunca's head, gets a barrage of grateful whimpers and the usual spate of licks. "It is a boy, right?"

"Indeed it is."

Fiona takes Nunca into her arms like nothing could be more natural. "So, I can keep him?"

Huh, huh, what? "You want a dog?"

"Not really, no," she says. "But this town sure doesn't need another homeless one."

"Hey," says Hank, "we can always—"

"Bring him to Sherrill's."

"Yes."

"Okay, then, well...we'll give him one night, see how it goes."

"I named him Nunca."

Again she nuzzles his head. *"Nunca.* That's really sweet."

"As in, I *never* would have guessed, not in a million years, this would be happening."

"No," Fiona says, "me either," and sets the puppy down. Both watch as he looks around the yard. Fiona walks to the garden table. Nunca, still standing close to Hank, watches her every step. "Come, Nunca, come!" she says, and the dog does as he's told. She leans over and holds its head in her hands. "Oh, yes, look at you," she coos, "who's the smartest boy I know?"

As if on cue, Nunca does his little circular run again, like a dance of joy. Then he stops, squats on the path to take a shit.

"No, no, no!" shouts Fiona, but it's too late. A rush of liquid pale-brown excrement squirts out.

"Then there's that," says Hank.

She kneels down and pulls Nunca from the mess. "Poor guy. What he needs is some decent food. La Dispensa should be open. You go, I'll clean this up."

Without waiting for an answer she hurries to the shed, the puppy tucked under her arm, finds an old rag and lays him on his back, starts wiping that drippy butt like he's her baby.

Hank grabs his pack. "Need diapers, too?"

She smiles, flips him off and keeps wiping.

Hank wonders why she'd be so at ease after that ordeal with Vicente? Is she pretending it doesn't matter? Or, worse, shielding him from her grief? He doesn't know, and can't stand more secrets. "Fiona?"

"Yeah?"

"I'm sorry about what happened with—"

"He came back."

"What?"

Fiona puts down the dog and gives him her full attention. "Must have been something you said."

"That I doubt."

Nunca goes running off. "Anyway, he came back, about an hour after you left, and we talked a long time. About my pain. About Ernie. Vicente said he could feel his evil energy, could sense the pills in the spice drawer. Since I hadn't mentioned them, he assumed I was taking drugs."

"Yeah."

"Yeah, and I can't blame him. I told him we're done with Ernie. He seemed to understand, said he can't help much with the pain, but blessed me anyway. And the house."

"Oh, okay, good."

She winces. "So at least we got to a peaceful place."

"Hey, that's a lot."

"Oh," she says, "I meant to tell you, I called the bank."

"The bank?"

"For the money you're going to need. I talked to Abraham, made sure to sound real sick. He said you could come by tomorrow and sign my name for the thousand dollars."

"Wow, Fiona, thanks."

"No, thank you." Nunca runs back and starts chewing on her dress. She gently strokes his ears. "As for now, *por favor,* get this pooch some chow, and *pronto,* before he turns on me."

22
The Contract

Hank locks the gate behind him, walks over and shakes hands with Manuel, the latest García to stand guard, then hurries off for dog food. Also two plastic bowls. When he gets home, at six, Manuel says he can only stay two more hours. Hank wonders how the brothers manage to schedule all this time, the personal sacrifice it must take. He feels suddenly overwhelmed by their devotion to Fiona, and must harness his deep gratitude, knowing the Maya are not comfortable showing emotion.

Eye contact, genuine and fleeting, is what's needed. They shake hands—for Hank a consciously firmer handshake than before. The two men nod to each other and say good night.

As he opens the gate, Nunca comes running. Hank goes to the faucet by the porch and sets down the bowls, fills one with water, the other with food. Nunca plows his snout into the dry brown pellets and comes up munching. "Take it easy, son, don't hurt yourself." The pup ignores him, as expected, and goes for more. After emptying the bowl and licking it clean, he slurps some water. "Okay for now?"

Nunca wags his tail and runs into the house, Hank right behind him. Fiona is on her knees by the bed, making the dog a place to sleep, a couple of pillows covered with a blanket.

Nunca sniffs her work. She picks him up. "This should do while he's still small."

"Looks good to me."

She puts Nunca on the blanket and pats his head. "There, baby, whatcha think?"

The puppy whines, then charges outside, barking.

"Ye gods, oh no," says Hank, "I'd hoped he might've been spared that gene."

"Aaaw," Fiona croons, "already territorial. I think it's cute."

"Cute?"

"Kinda, yeah."

"Well, it won't be for long. We gotta snip that in the bud."

"Snip?"

He does the infamous scissors mime. "Soon as he's old enough, my dear. I'll talk to the vet."

Nunca comes running back inside, goes straight to Fiona, tail on full wag. She lifts him into her arms and sits down on the bed. "Don't you fret none, sweetie, I'll make sure he gets snipped first."

"Not a bad idea," says Hank. Getting his nuts whacked off might calm this daily longing for Fiona—a deep sensual desire that does him no damn good. It's not sex he wants, just touch, romantic touch, which is not about to happen. He walks to the pup and strokes the underside of his neck. "Tell you what, we'll get it done together." Nunca licks his hand. "In the meantime, pal, we need agreement on some rules."

Fiona leans her chin down onto the puppy's head. "Don't sign a thing."

"I mean just the basic stuff. Like…um…no damn barking unless it's *cute*."

"Yeah," she says, "I'm fine with that."

"Or whining without good reason."

"Agreed. Or shedding hair. Ever."

"Or getting fleas."

"Hell no!" She frowns. "That could never happen, right?"

"Not on my watch!" Feigning utmost dread, Hank points a finger between Nunca's eyes. "And no pooping anywhere I might see or smell it, understand? Which goes for pissing, too!"

The pup lets out a baleful whine.

"There he goes again," says Hank. "Does that sound reasonable to you?"

"Yes," she says, and snuggles Nunca closer. "But the old man's right, don't overdo it."

The puppy yawns, his eyes suddenly at half mast.

Poor little guy. Heck, after such a long day, all the running around, hassling with other dogs, then letting these two adopt him and told to follow their silly rules, he must be tuckered out. Fiona sets him on the blanket. He curls up and closes his eyes. "That's it, boy," she whispers, "take a nap. Then I'll point out all the places where you're banished in my garden."

"Such a good mama," says Hank. And he immediately regrets it. For them, a child did not happen, could never happen, because of him. Because of his selfishness, his troubling penchant for booze and drugs.

Though Fiona smiles, he sees sadness in her eyes. "You hungry?" she says, clearly needing to change the subject.

"Starving."

"How about a stir fry?"

"Sure, if you let me make it."

After her night pill, Fiona gets under the covers and within minutes she's asleep. Hank carries Nunca outside, to the back area of the house, a place that is rarely seen. Flashlight in hand, he shows him all the available space to do his business. "Anywhere you want." But as soon as the dog's feet hit the ground, he sprints off. Hank hurries to catch up, finds him out front, squatting in the exact same place where he'd crapped before. "No!" Grabbing Nunca by the scruff of his neck, he hauls him back behind the house and places him in the best of all possible locations: a patch of dirt between clumps of weeds. With a solemn scowl, crouched like a defensive tackle on a goal line stand, Hank hopes it's clear that this is the perfect spot. The frightened animal stares at him. Then, to the man's shock and disbelief, he takes a substantial and solid dump.

"Good boy!" Hank crows, proud as any father.

Nunca follows him to the shed to get a shovel, then watches as he scoops up the load and drops it by the concrete wall. Hank leaves the shovel there, kneels down and pets the puppy's head "Welcome to your domain. What a lucky boy you are!"

They return to the living room. In spite of all their commotion, Fiona is fast asleep. Nunca, as if tired of causing trouble, settles onto his blanket and shuts his eyes. Hey, maybe house-training this pooch will be easier than Hank imagined. The front door has been left open, a fact he made quite evident. He smiles at the sleeping pup and feels somewhat charmed, letting himself believe they just might make it through the night.

At one a.m. Hank is licked awake. He gets out of his sleeping bag, naked, and picks Nunca up. The pup probably needs a reminder of where to shit. Yeah, sure, that's to be expected, and Hank soon learns it's true, as leaving his bedroom he steps into a warm wet squishy pile.

Loudly cursing in his mind, hoping his muted rage is well-acknowledged by the dog, he gingerly tiptoes to the front door, opens it and goes outside. He sets down Nunca, who follows him to the side of the house, watches as he washes his foot off with the hose, then follows him to the shed, where Hank dries himself with a rag. He returns to the house, closing the door to keep the puppy out.

Nunca whines, but, thankfully, Fiona snores on. Must be the Oxycontin. He goes to their small hearth stove, grabs the small square scoop used for ashes, scrapes the stinking mess up from the floor, then takes it behind the house and dumps it against the wall, next to the mess already there. "See where this belongs?" he says to the pup, who seems to be paying close attention. *Yeah, right.*

Back in the living room, after cleaning the floor with a sponge and tossing it outside, Hank carries their troublesome orphan to his room. Shuts them in. "Sorry, pal, now you're stuck with me."

At six-thirty a.m. Hank gets up to pee. His door is open. The dog lies curled up by Fiona. How that happened he does not know, and at the moment does not care. It's Monday, he's got things to do, dresses and heads to town, first for some breakfast, a few cups of coffee, and then to be first in line at the bank, where, like some random miracle, it only takes an hour to get Fiona's thousand dollars.

The rest of the day goes by like a breeze.

Then Tuesday morning is upon him.

In a few hours, at some office by the Muni, he'll be signing papers for the lot. Sure, he dislikes lawyers, and hates all bureaucratic legalize, *but never mind, this has to happen.* He gets up at seven, puts on his beach gear, hides the cash he'll need in his pack and goes to the kitchen to make coffee.

Nunca is right there with him, squirming by his side, pawing at his bare legs, doing little butt twists and whining for attention. "Quiet, meathead, before you wake the queen."

"I heard that," calls Fiona.

Hank picks Nunca up and goes into the living room.

She looks puzzled. "I found him in your room again last night, whining to get out."

The pup leaps free, jumps to the bed, goes scurrying into Fiona's waiting arms.

"Wait," says Hank. "Sure you want to encourage this?"

"I'm afraid," she says with a little grin, "it's already been encouraged. Poor baby, isn't used to his new bed. I made clear to him, I did, it's just till he's settled in."

Nunca snuggles to her chest.

Looks pretty settled in to Hank, who is envious of the mutt. "I'm going for a swim. Then to meet Eduardo."

"Who?"

"The guy selling us the lot. It's not legally ours quite yet."

"Come here," she orders, and when Hank does, the puppy tucked between their chests, she gives him a loving peck on the lips. "Thank you, honey. For everything."

He smiles back, and gently pulls away, happy for the affection but not wanting to push his luck. "My pleasure." He goes to the kitchen, makes and drinks a cup of coffee, his every move supervised by Nunca. Hank grabs a banana for the road, then fills his water bottle and puts it in his pack. "Hey," he says, heading for the door, "I'll be right there by the market. Anything you need?"

"No, we're good."

Hank nods, glad she'll have Nunca with her while he's gone. The puppy follows him to the gate, watches him remove the padlock, then charges back to the house. His allegiance is plain, and comforting to Hank, who slips into the alley, locks the gate from outside. Across the way is yet another García brother, Cisco, standing guard. My god, what good friends they are! Hank goes and gives his hand a hearty shake.

The beach is empty. He looks out at the lake, lit by the morning sun, and sees Juan. The two wave at each other. Hank is ready to jump in when he remembers all that money. Twenty-one hundred dollars in quetzales. He's never been robbed at the beach, but has heard it sometimes happens. Can't take that chance. He hides the pack up by the chalet wall, in a dense stand of caña. That off his mind, he swims out by Juan, careful to stay far shy of the fisherman's net. "Everything good?"

"Yes, Enrique, perfect. Let's hope the fish agree."

"Did your boy enjoy his first birthday?"

"I don't think he noticed. But everyone else had fun."

"As they should!"

"Yes," says Juan, "which is what he needs to learn."

They both laugh.

"Pues, amigo, hasta pronto," says Hank, and swims off. Does not want to overstay his welcome. He breaststrokes toward the

point, entranced by the lake's deep silence. His most-beloved kind of music. A few minutes later, while swimming in to shore, he thinks of Aakesh. How blown-away his friend will be to hear he was right about the dog! *Qué milagro!* And, furthermore, that Hank, of all people, is buying a piece of land! *Qué loco, sí?* Plus, the crucial piece, that Fiona approves of everything he's done, that she even kissed him—sort of—on the lips! *Qué precioso!*

He gets to shore. First thing, though feeling like a fool, Hank checks his pack to make sure the money is still there. Yes, of course it is! He sighs at his paranoid self, lies down in the shade for a quick snooze and dozes off, dreams of who knows what, wakes in a sudden panic and checks his phone.

Twenty after ten, oh fuck!

He dries, dresses and rushes off, gets to the lawyer's office, his pits dripping with sweat.

It's a few minutes before eleven. Eduardo is out front.

They shake hands, go inside and wait. It turns out, though Eduardo had promised this would go quickly, there seems to be no one around to make that happen. A pretty young woman, perhaps the lawyer's secretary, who had politely said to take a seat, ignores them from behind a desk, perusing some sort of document—instructions, Hank imagines, on exactly how long a person can waste time, looking busy, before reasonable people get pissed off. Eduardo checks his watch, tells her they had an appointment, at eleven, with Señor De León. She says she's sorry, says he was called away on some sort of legal matter and "will be back any minute."

How conveniently vague, thinks Hank, as that minute keeps stretching out, like time taffy, to ten, fifteen, then twenty-five. He tries to relax, aware that this is common for Guatemala. Here, perhaps because it is so rare, legality seems to take its fucking time, is never in any hurry.

At last the young woman gets a text, rolls her eyes and motions them to her desk. "Señor De León will be delayed. He says I can begin the process." She then scrutinizes the contract, already prepared, in minute detail, by Eduardo, and takes it into an adjoining room. At least twenty more minutes pass before she returns. *"Todo bién,"* the young woman says. "Now we must wait for Señor De León."

Eduardo sighs. "It's nearly noon. Wait until when?"

"He'll be here at one o'clock."

Eduardo gives a disgruntled nod, leads Hank out to the street and throws up his hands. "I am sorry. The cost, I guess, of doing business in Panajachel. Can I buy you lunch?"

"Yes," says Hank, "if we can eat at my favorite restaurant."

Ten minutes later they enter Josefina's stall. "How lucky for us to find this amazing place!"

"Hola Enrique!"

"Hola, Josefina!" After introductions, he orders, for both of them, *"The Same."*

They sit down and look out at the bright blue lake.

"So beautiful," says Eduardo.

"Impossible to describe," says Hank, and means it.

Then they get quiet, both content to enjoy the warm air and glistening water. Josefina soon comes with their food. "Orlando brought me more peanuts."

Hank smiles and nods. "Good kid."

She laughs, apparently at herself. "This time I paid him."

"He deserves it."

"Yes." She pats Hank's shoulder and heads back to her grill.

They get to the lawyers office at precisely one o'clock. The door is locked. Five minutes later, the pretty secretary comes running up to let them in. "I am sorry," she says in breathless Spanish, the words blurred together like a passing gust of wind.

Some minutes after that, wearing a fancy light gray suit but looking like he just got out of bed, in comes Señor De León. He adjusts his yellow tie, then shakes Eduardo's hand.

"Please," he says, like a gentle order, "forgive my missing our appointment. Some things cannot be helped."

And so begins the arduous process, something else that apparently can't be helped, and at times beyond Hank's ability to follow, of printing out, perusing, and signing a pile of pages, then calling in an elderly man to "notarize the contract," then someone else—another pretty woman—to count the money and, by virtue of her numerous signatures, "certify the transaction" (all this necessary, explains De León, because "to verify the process, which normally takes three days, I must be positive that there are no mistakes, that nothing has been overlooked") before she takes Hank's money and hands him a receipt. The secretary then provides him with a copy of the contract's last two pages, including the lot's official description and his culminating signature.

He leaves the office rather shaken, feels lucky to have escaped without something going wrong.

"I was thinking," says Eduardo as they walk off, "since that mess is over with, and the land is now legally yours, maybe you want to meet Señor Mocún?"

It takes Hank a second to place the name. *Ah yes, my new neighbor.* "Sure, sounds like a great idea."

Eduardo grins with a telltale grimace. "Well," he says, "we can always hope."

Eduardo knocks on the door, then waits. Then knocks again. Nothing. "Maybe some other day." He turns to leave as it suddenly opens.

A Maya elder, in Pana traje, short and stout, stands there staring. Eduardo said this man is in his sixties, but he looks ninety. "Yes," he says in Spanish, his voice low and his eyes suspicious, "what do you want?"

"Buenos días, Señor Mocún." Eduardo speaks slowly and softly. "Do you remember me?"

"No."

"I am Eduardo Sanchez. My partners and I are—"

"Selling away my land, now I remember."

"Good," says Eduardo.

"Not for me."

"Well, I...I thought you might want to meet your new neighbor, Enrique Solter."

The man's eyes show no interest. "Why?"

His question does not seem to require an answer. Eduardo, however, pushes on. "He bought the lot in the back corner."

The Señor points to his right. "Over there, next to me?"

"Yes. I know we've been having problems, you've been against it and—"

Mocún shoots up his right hand, an aggressive motion that cuts Eduardo off. Now he looks at Hank. "There is no road to your land. You understand?"

"Yes."

The old man lifts his eyebrows. "What, are you stupid?"

"I don't think so. Just don't need a road."

"You cannot get to it through my property. Not ever."

"I don't need that either."

Mocún's face goes blank, like an old cracked wall, then his eyes brighten for a second, he lets loose a derisive laugh and slams the door.

Hank is resolved to solve the problem with his grouchy neighbor. Later. What matters now is that the land is officially theirs—a fact he can feel happy about, and proud.

But when Hank turns down their callejón, both happy and proud, there is no Cisco, nor any of his brothers. He panics, rushes to the gate. The lock is still there. A mild relief. He takes it off, goes inside and closes the gate behind him, leans against the solid wood. Nunca comes running, his tail wagging. "Hey, boy, what's up?" The puppy whines, turns and bolts toward the house. "Fiona?" Hank shouts, "where are you?"

"Here!" she yells, and he sees her, waving at him from the living room window."

He closes his eyes and takes a breath. *Okay.* Strange to have become so dependent on the Garcías, to feel like he's been abandoned. The sky, cloaked by its normal afternoon clouds, looks oppressive, and the shadowed garden ominous. He hopes Fiona did not see his frightened entrance. She'd never known that the Garcías were out there standing guard, and doesn't need to know. Today there will only be good news.

As he comes through the doorway, Fiona sits up in bed. Nunca is at her side. She smiles and waits, with strained patience, as Hank casually sets down his pack and sits on the couch. He knows she's about to burst, puts on his most serious face. "You'll never guess what happened."

Fiona leans forward, seems prepared to hear the worst. "Oh *gawd*, what?"

"The legal stuff was a breeze."

"Really?"

"No, was a total pain in the ass, but we got it done."

"You mean that lot is ours?"

He reaches into his pocket, pulls out and waves his copy of the contract. "Yes, I do."

Fiona lets out a little giggle. Her face glows. "Well I'll be damned, you truly are my hero."

"Yes, it seems I am."

She sits back and looks him in the eye. "This calls for a celebration."

"Absolutely!" In spite of his better judgment, Hank imagines them under the covers, cuddling like they used to. He shoves that vision from his head. "How?"

"Why don't we go to Guajimbos? You can have your regular *'Pollo, fofo y obeso'* and I can slurp some soup. Watcha think?"

Hank's next vision, with no García to protect them, is of Ernie. A most unwelcome sight. But they can't let that guy rule their lives. *Fuck him!* That's got to be his attitude from now on. Easier said than done, but he has to try. "Excellent idea!"

"So, what time is it?"

"A few minutes after three."

Fiona is still in her pajamas. "I guess it might be a bit early."

"Maybe just a bit. First, how about I take a nap?"

She frowns with genuine sympathy. "Oh, of course, it's been a long day for you."

"I only need an hour."

"Perfect. I'll take a bath and get ready."

172

He goes to his bedroom, closes the door, lies down on the pad. And not long after, like a dream, Fiona is kneeling beside him, smiling. "Oh," says Hank, "hello."

"*Buenas tardes, Señor.* It's after five."

"Already?" He rubs his tired eyes. "Yeah, okay." She's got on a silky black skirt, and a frilly silver blouse that matches her hair, now done up in one long braid. It's all he can do to not pull her down on top of him. "Geez, what a beauty you are."

She blushes. "Aw…thanks."

My oh my oh my, he thinks, marshaling his resistance.

Fiona frowns. "I don't feel like I'm up for walking, can we take a tuk-tuk?"

"Sure. Of course. You still have Gregorio's number?"

"Yeah. What time should I tell him?"

"Fifteen minutes?"

Fiona pats his chest and stands. "Okay." She hurries out.

Hank gets up, changes into his only pair of decent pants, his one nice shirt, puts on clean socks and a pair of lace-up shoes. He goes to the bathroom, brushes his teeth, and, with a quick sweep of his fingers, combs through his straggly hair.

Good enough.

"My," says Fiona, standing in the doorway, "don't you look handsome."

Hank is surprised by the playful flirting. Best he say something silly, but nothing comes. There is a second of awkward silence between them, erased by a honk out front.

"He's here," she says, and leaves.

Hank looks in the mirror. *Careful, boy. Nothing's going to happen and you know it.*

Fiona waits by the gate. Nunca, at her side, wags his tail at her obvious excitement, must be hoping it has something to do with him. She says, "No, big boy, you have to stay home and guard the house."

After taking off the lock, Hank picks up the dog.

Fiona opens the gate and rushes into the alley. "Gregorio!"

This used to be her regular driver. He's a middle-aged man, with a cherubic face, who has studied English for many years and always wants to practice.

"So happy," he says, "I am with you here again!"

Hank looks up and down the alley, as if Ernie might be hiding in the shadows.

"Come on, honey," says Fiona.

He sets Nunca inside the garden, kneels and points at his startled eyes. "You stay!" The command seems to freeze the pup in place, which allows Hank time step back and close the gate. He locks it, then climbs into the tuk-tuk and orders, like some clown colonel might, *"Ándale, amigo,* full speed ahead!"

Gregorio laughs, salutes Hank and hits the gas, starts put-putting up the alley.

"We are having a celebration!" Fiona tells him.

"Oh, really?" he says. "And it is why?"

"We bought the piece of land next door."

"You build another house?"

"No," says Hank. "We're going to make a bigger garden."

"Wonderful for you! Congratulations!"

She beams. "Thank you, Gregorio."

"My very real pleasure, Seño Fiona. And now, for this celebration, where is it I will I take you?"

"To Guajimbos, *por favor."*

Guajimbos, on Santander, is one of the most popular spots in town, well-known among expats as a "safe place to eat." Plus, every night with dinner, there is live music. Open to the street, the musicians play for anyone passing by.

They climb out of the tuk-tuk, pay Gregorio, and turn toward the restaurant. The sky shows a last fading tinge of blue. The coming darkness makes Hank feel a bit less visible. He wonders, slightly worried, how Fiona will deal with this exposure to the world.

He's relieved to see so many empty tables. With luck it will stay that way, they'll eat in peace and soon be heading home.

"Fiona!" It's Raul, the main waiter, who's been here for many years. He comes rushing toward her and they embrace. "I have worried so much about you!" he says in Spanish

"I know," she says, pointing at herself, "me too."

Raul shakes Hank's hand, gives him a curious look. "And where, Señor, have you been hiding?"

"I don't get out much these days."

"Well," he says in his most serious voice, "as history tells us, amigo, that may be good." Raul is famous for his dry sense of humor. Also for being the best waiter in Panajachel, able to single-handedly take care of this often crowded restaurant with ease and a constant smile.

"Any place okay?" Fiona asks.

"Wherever you like," he says, then hurries toward a troupe of arriving tourists.

She leads Hank to her favorite table, off in the corner by the street. It being a weekday, there is hardly any traffic. Cars, that is—though plenty of people are on the move. He's surprised that she has chosen to be so visible.

Raul seats the tourists and comes back, writes down their orders. "Anything to drink?"

"White wine for me," Fiona says, and looks at Hank. "A real celebration, right?"

"Right."

"And you, Enrique?"

"Just water, thanks."

The waiter nods and hurries off.

Fiona looks away, now gazing out at the street, a big smile on her face, as if its very existence gives her joy. Though groups of people are passing by, there is a quiet this time of day that the two of them always found magical. It's hard to believe, like a happy twist of fate, that here they are again! And he is certain Fiona feels the same. She looks at him. "I love it all."

Hank smiles and nods.

Raul comes with the wine and water, then rushes off. Fiona reaches over to squeeze Hank's hand. "Maybe we can get out once a week."

"Whenever you want."

"*Amiga!*"

They turn and see Analu in the street. She walks up to the table. Fiona stands and they embrace, hold onto each other for a long time. Both of them are crying.

"Oh my my," Analu says, "will you look at us." She stands back, tears still dripping down her face. "I've missed you way too much."

"Please," says Hank, "stay and have a drink."

"I can't. There's someplace I need to be."

"Come see me," says Fiona.

"When?"

"Any time would be great."

Analu hugs her again and leaves.

Fiona looks at Hank. "I'm finished hiding. I really am."

"Good."

"Yeah."

And, as if that simple decision were all it took, the next several minutes are full of people coming by to visit. People she hasn't seen for a year or more. Lots of expats, longtime friends, and also Guatemalans, some of whom worked with her at Music Of The Lake—local business people, artisans, and activists.

All and all, there are plenty of happy tears. Hank sees how much Pana has missed her being around. Most touching are the *indigena* Maya, *los naturales*, who still wear traje. Many recognize Fiona but do not really know her. Only her reputation, only how hard she worked to heal their beloved lake. They stand in the street, patiently wait their turn, then step forward, faces serious and respectful, to shake her hand. A few even bow and kiss it, and call her *Nan*.

Fiona looks overwhelmed, but also grateful. She and Hank are both choked up. Here, he thinks, is the ceremony she deserves. Not until their meal arrives are they left alone. She waves her last goodbye, then takes a long deep breath.

"Wow," says Hank.

No, that's not enough. He wants to say so much more, tell her how wonderful she is, how she has earned this appreciation. But he's distracted by Manuel and Cisco García. The brothers rush by, heading toward the lake. He's alarmed by their stern faces and sense of urgency.

Fiona turns her head and sees them pass. *"Oye, amigos!"*

But in their hurry they don't hear her, and soon are gone.

She looks at Hank. "You think something's wrong?"

"Could be," he says, and shrugs, does not want this lovely moment ruined. "Still, a person has to eat."

He's not being smug, just realistic. Truth is, there is always something "wrong" in Guatemala. Problems big and small on a daily basis. Expats who live here, since these problems do not normally include them, are accustomed to staying quiet, on the sidelines, accepting things they do not understand and cannot help with. While sometimes, like now, unsettling, it's an adjustment that must be made. Hank and Fiona know this, have learned to let these disturbing moments pass.

Trying to keep their spirits high, he spears a beet off his plate and serves it to his waiting mouth. Fiona takes her first spoonful of soup. Between them, at this very instant, everything seems so right, and both would prefer, for now, not to be brought down by whatever it is that's "wrong."

Raúl comes by. "Anything I can get you?"

"No," Fiona tells him, "everything is perfect."

Which is also true for Hank. Absolutely true.

A few minutes later, however, while they're eating, it all changes. Alto, Ernie's guy, comes running from the direction of the lake. He spots Hank and veers over. Panting, he gulps for breath. "Please, Señor, tell them I don't do it anymore." His eyes are pleading.

"What's wrong, Alto?"

"Please," the kid says, calling back as he runs up Santander, "you need to tell them!"

Fiona looks at Hank. "He works for Ernie, right?"

"Yeah."

Energy on the street has heightened. There are more people, all *naturales,* walking fast toward the lake. Raul goes out and stops someone he knows. The man is pointing that direction. Hank goes over and listens in. "A fire," the man says as he hurries off.

Hank is confused, at first imagining a fire on the lake. "What's he talking about?"

"Something burning," says Raul. "I don't know what."

The cook calls from the kitchen, points at a platter of meals, and Raul gets back to business.

Hank goes to Fiona. "I have to find out what's happening."

"Why?"

"I think it's about Ernie."

Fiona locks eyes with him, seems frightened. Seems certain, like Hank, that Ernie is out there, somewhere, causing trouble. "No, honey, please."

He hears her warning, and tries to show a calm resolve. "I need to see what—"

"No," she says, "you don't. That guy is not your problem!"

Yes, Hank thinks, *he is.*

More people rush down the street.

It feels like he has to go, like unless he does something terrible might happen. It's a feeling, a strong feeling, and there is no way to explain it.

He kisses Fiona's forehead. "I'll be right back."

24

Los Vigilantes

Hank follows a group of Maya men and women, some wearing traje, who follow others—all plainly anxious to find out what is burning. At the bottom of Santander, everyone turns right onto Calle Monterey. This street goes to the docks at Tzan Jujú, where lanchas embark numerous times each day for the different villages. Coming from that direction is a line of tuk-tuks, their drivers and patrons scowling. It must be around six o'clock. Maybe they missed the final boat? He keeps walking, and a third of a mile farther, on the long straightaway before the final turn to the docks, he sees the problem. A crowd has blocked the street. At least fifty people. Or, rather, a fire in the street has drawn their interest, bunched them all together. Orange flames leap above the onlookers, up into a graying sky.

Hank stops at the back of the crowd as others push in behind him. He is aware of being the only foreigner. People eye him and whisper among themselves. It's as if he's been lured to witness some private, sacred rite. Hank feels like an intruder. Even more alarming is his certainty, though wanting to turn and run, that he must stay.

"Get back!" someone yells. "Back! Back! Back!"

The crowd retreats a few steps. A second later comes a loud explosion. Flames burst into the sky and there's a collective gasp. Hank inches forward, can't leave until he knows what's going on. He squeezes past awestruck people, at last reaches the front row, faces the roaring fire that envelops Ernie's motorcycle. The seat and tires are already burned away. Paint sizzles on every metallic surface. Must have been the gas tank that exploded.

For a second he imagines it as a large dead beast, some mythic creature being sacrificed to the gods. Perhaps the gauzy smoke conjures that strange vision. Or perhaps it's the crowd's intense, mystifying chatter, all in Cakchiquel, which sounds like some sort of ancient incantation.

The woman next to him gently taps his elbow, looks into his eyes with apparent sympathy. "Sad, I know," she says in Spanish, "but sin must be *desfiado.*"

Desfiado?

He's not sure what that means. *Put to an end? Defied?*

"The time has come," says the man on his other side. "He has brought this upon himself."

Their words sound scriptural, like a reading from the Bible. Hank nods, agrees with what is happening, pleased that Ernie's motorcycle has paid the price for his bad behavior. Yeah, sure, fair enough. "Where is he?"

The man points ahead and to the right, at the concrete wall that borders the street. Beyond the fire Hank sees an opening, and what looks like a gate hanging by one hinge. "That is where he lives," the man says. "They went to bring him out."

They? "Who, the police?"

The man studies him for an instant. Hank has seen this look before: an acknowledgment of his First World naïveté. Despite having lived in Guatemala for forty years, there are things he still does not understand.

"En serio?" says the man (*Are you serious?*) and walks off.

Hank feels dismissed, racks his brain for what he's missing. *Oh, oh no, could these be vigilantes?*

The first time he saw this kind of scene was ten years ago, in 2009. A tourist bus on its way to Pana had been hijacked. Thirty people were robbed and the driver murdered. Such crimes, because of the mounting tourism, were now far too common, and the locals were fed up. Though the robbers were apprehended by police, and jailed, rumors soon spread that they would bribe their way to freedom. A reasonable assumption, a likely outcome, and something Pana's townspeople could not bear, so they demanded that the prisoners be given up to them.

When the police said no, their station was set on fire.

The robbers were then handed over, *pronto,* hauled away by the angry mob, beaten and later hanged in front of the Muni building. Vigilantes called this "The people's judgment." They insisted that crimes within the community be punished by the community, not by a vague, and often corrupt, judicial system. Three weeks later another thief was hung, his dead body set on fire. The vigilantes, all indigenous Guatemalans, were gaining power, now convinced this was their only hope of justice. Most native villagers, and some expats, were in agreement.

In 2011, however, a group of townspeople decided that Pana must be "cleansed of its immorality," and created a new type of vigilante. Men covered their faces with black masks and patrolled the streets after dark. Named *Los Encapuchados, The Hooded Ones,* they were on the lookout for any kind of bad behavior, including public intoxication. Local drunks, all Guatemalans, were beaten, and bars vandalized. The town's whorehouse was burned down. Expats, while unharmed, felt warned by the growing fervor. Many changed their ways, did their drinking and took their drugs in private. Ernie left town until the righteousness lost steam. Which eventually it did.

The municipal government, backed up by police, tourist agencies, bar and restaurant owners, outlawed *Los Encapuchados.* That did not stop the vigilante spirit, but helped control it.

Community leaders got involved. All preached the need for peace, and would not sanction "The people's judgement."

At least that's what they said, though Hank was not convinced. From time to time he'd hear rumors that someone had "disappeared." He made sure to ask no questions, did not want to get involved. That has not changed. Because of his general distrust of human beings, especially sanctimonious types *en masse,* he is against mobs taking the law into their own hands, the result often misguided and unnecessarily cruel.

Hank once asked Federico, a Maya friend, if the town had felt safer when the vigilantes were more active. His skepticism must have shown.

Federico sighed with undisguised disappointment. "Only a foreigner would ask that. Ever since the Spaniards came—and then later, of course, you gringos with your CIA—Guatemala has been a violent place. We Naturales know nothing else. For us, amigo, it's all the same."

"They got him!" someone yells.

All watch as a man backs out past the broken gate, pulling Ernie. A second man holds him from his other side. It's Fernando and Cisco García. Again the flames leap up. To Hank's far left, through a veil of smoke, he sees Diego, the youngest brother, throw branches on the fire. There beside him are Manuel and Concepción, each gathering wood.

Right then, swerving around the corner back down the street, come two police cars, sirens blaring. People move to the side, allowing the cars to drive up close. They screech to a halt and four officers emerge. One of them holds a pistol. "This gathering is illegal," he shouts in Spanish. It's the chief of police, Luis Aldamo, believed by many to be an honest man who tries, as best he can, to get rid of corrupt officers. Other townspeople claim he is their leader. "What is going on here?"

An old man steps toward him. He's short, slim, and looks sturdy as a nail. "Nothing that concerns you, Luis."

The chief flinches, seems uncertain what to do. "Please, Don Julio, we cannot allow this to happen, not again."

Hank recognizes Julio Perez. He owns a couple of party boats, runs a great deal of the lancha business on the lake, and is far more powerful, and trusted, than Aldamo.

The chief lowers his gun.

"This man is known by everyone," says Don Julio. "Has been selling drugs for a long time. There is proof, Luis, and we demand that he be punished."

"If you have proof," the chief says, "I will arrest him."

"The proof was under your nose for years!" someone yells.

"You know it and do nothing!" yells another.

"Please," says the chief, glancing around with a look of mounting fear, "I know about all the rumors, yes, but have never seen any proof."

"Here!" The crowd turns its attention to Pedro, the oldest García brother, who stands on the other side of the fire. He holds up a large plastic bag full of a whitish powder. "Here is your proof, Luis! Cocaine! I found this, and more drugs, hidden in his house."

Fernando and Cisco are next to their brother. Ernie is clamped between them, and looks petrified, his eyes like a frightened animal, watching as more wood is tossed on the fire.

"All right," says the chief, "let me examine the evidence, then I'll decide what to do."

"The decision has been made!" shouts Concepción. "God demands that we burn this devil!"

Hank is horrified by the hatred in her voice.

"No," says the chief, "I cannot allow it."

Don Julio puts his hand on Luis's shoulder. "With respect, *Jefe,* what happens here is not up to you."

"Please," screams Ernie, tears pouring down his face, "you can't just let them murder me!"

Hank looks across the fire at his enemy. It is not pity he feels, but disgust, revulsion that this degenerate could create such ugliness in good, life-loving people. They've put up with him, his crime, his vulgar behavior, his smug indifference, for too damn long. Hank understands and sympathizes with their rage. At the same time he also feels, in the depth of his heart, that to murder another human, *no matter why,* is wrong. Vengeance is not justice, it's a reckoning, and with it comes a curse, self-inflicted, a ghostly condemnation that punishes the innocent as much as it does the guilty. If that happens, he fears, these peaceful people will be haunted all their lives.

He looks across the fire at Concepción, her arms full of wood, her eyes on him, perhaps sensing his opposition. "Please, amiga, don't let that lowlife make you do this!"

It gets very quiet. Hank is conscious of being watched. By everyone. Many of these villagers know who he is. Because of his connection with Fiona, in honor of her, some seem willing to acknowledge what he says. But most appear suspicious, ill at ease with any foreigner telling them what to do. Especially one of Ernie's former clients. Why should his opinion matter?

He spots the man who had earlier dismissed him and walked away, who now peers down at the ground and shakes his head. Though Hank understands the man's distrust, it is misdirected. *This has nothing to do with me.* He takes a breath and looks at Pedro. "That guy is not worth killing, not worth the hell it would mean for all of you."

Pedro stares at Hank, both of them stiff as stones, and the crowd stays strangely hushed. The only sound is of Ernie whimpering. There is no way not to hear it, be repulsed by it.

Pedro blinks. His eyes soften and he steps forward, throws the bag of cocaine in the fire. "That is the poison this *cabrón* peddles, Luis, and there is more inside. If you come with me I'll show you."

"Yes," says the chief, "all right," and starts his way.

The crowd shifts and groans: some people with frustration, some with outrage, and some, it seems, with relief. Pedro, glancing around at the intense chaotic energy, points an angry finger at Luis. "Once you see the proof, you will lock him up?"

"I will."

"Yes, yes, we know!" someone shouts. "Then you'll get paid off and let him go!"

"That won't happen," says the chief. "I promise you all, I—"

"No!" Pedro shouts, "enough!" He pauses for several seconds, waits for the crowd to stop its grumbling and hear him out. "What matters is this," he says, and turns to Ernie, their noses almost touching. "If anyone ever sees you around the lake again, you're dead. *Comprende?*"

"Yes," sobs Ernie.

"Ever!" Pedro screams into his face, and Ernie cringes. "Or if you ever, in any way, bother Fiona or Enrique. You or anyone else, understand? *Tell me you understand!*"

Ernie cowers. "I understand."

"Bueno," says Pedro, and looks directly at Don Julio. "Are you all right with this, Tata?"

The trusted elder purses his lips, sighs, nods his head and turns to go. And with that, Hank feels this thing has ended. The crowd, as if ordered, follows Don Julio down the road.

Chief Aldamo tells his officers to stand by, then goes off with Pedro. Four men surround Ernie. It is evident, like an unwritten law, that no one, including the police, will take him anywhere without Pedro's permission.

Concepción steps up to Hank. "I'm telling you, Enrique, it's a mistake to let him live."

She seems angry. Also sad. And, above all, certain. He looks away from her dark resolve, toward Ernie, unable to see him because of the surrounding guards.

"That man," she says, "is evil."

One guard turns sideways and Ernie's face appears, gazing at Hank across the smoldering fire. His expression is inscrutable, some nightmarish mix of gratitude and contempt. "Yo," he calls out with an astonishingly steady voice, "I thank you!"

The words sound sincere, but Ernie's steely eyes tell a different story. The real message cannot be missed. He blames Hank for this evangelical persecution, for losing his motorcycle and his livelihood, and will some day, somehow, get revenge.

25

An Opening

When Hank returns to Guajimbos he learns the news is already out.   Everyone's yacking about the fire, the burnt motorcycle, and Ernie being arrested.   Most don't know his name, only that he's a drug dealer, and that some gringo saved him from getting murdered by the crowd.

Fiona, long ago finished with her soup, had his meal put in a take-out cardboard box. She looks exhausted.

He says to her, "You okay?"

"I need to go home."

"Yeah, me too."

He steps out into the street and hails a passing tuk-tuk. Fiona waves good-bye to Raul. The waiter, whose hands are full of plates, is limited to a smile and a quick nod.

Hank walks her to the tuk-tuk, is aware of being watched. People must have realized he's the gringo being discussed. He climbs in next to Fiona and they motor off. Assuming she'll want to know, he starts to tell what happened.

"No." Fiona closes her eyes and shakes her head. "Please, tell me tomorrow. All I want is a pill."

By nine o'clock Fiona is asleep. Hank carries Nunca into his room, shuts the door, feels duty-bound to keep him from waking her. They share his cold chicken dinner.   Street mutts on the lot next door howl from time to time, but are quieter than usual. Hank takes off his clothes, climbs into his sleeping bag, pulls Nunca to his side. They lie there in the darkness and he worries about Ernie—needs to know if the slimeball has, in fact, been jailed, and officially banned from any return to Pana. Until then he won't rest well.

He wakes at eight to a bright new morning, his little buddy gone. Hank goes into the living room, finds Nunca cuddled on the bed next to Fiona. She sips a cup of tea. "Another day."

"Another day."

"Yep, good enough, I'm ready."

Hank sits on the couch and tells all he can of last night. The incinerated motorcycle, the angry mob's desire that the drug dealer get burned too. He doesn't mention how much the Garcías were involved. Also, not wanting to disturb her, leaves out the threat he felt from Ernie.

"I'm glad you went," Fiona says.

"Really?"

"Hey, you helped get him arrested. That's good. If lucky, he'll get deported instead of hanged."

"Yeah." Hank sighs, relieved by her visible lack of worry. "Some people must think I should have let him burn, which may be true."

"No, Hank, no, it's not. You did the right thing."

"I hope."

"Hey, c'mon, enough of this, he's gone and won't dare come back to Pana." She smiles. "Can we now please talk about our new lot?" She gets out of bed and pulls on her robe. He puts on his jeans. Holding hands, they walk to the southern wall of the garden. Fiona looks both excited and perplexed. "So, um, where do you think we should make the opening?"

"Wherever *you* want it."

"Could it be here, to the left of the bougainvillea?"

"Perfect."

"Yeah, uh-huh, *perfect*, but who is going to do it?"

"Me."

Her brows furrow with obvious doubt. "How?"

"How else? With a great big hammer."

"No, Hank, I'm serious. That's gotta be damn hard work. Why not ask the García boys?"

"Those guys are always busy on some job." Not true, as proven by the many hours they've spent guarding Fiona. The real issue is in his head. In helping to save Ernie, Hank thinks he somehow betrayed them. Maybe even shamed them. Also problematic is their distrust of the police, their fair presumption that Ernie might bribe his way to freedom. Hank worries they could say something to Fiona, could make her feel unsafe. "First, please, let me give it a go."

She looks conflicted. "Well…all right."

Hurt by the lack of confidence, Hank goes inside the house, changes into shorts and grabs his pack. When he comes out, Fiona is at the garden table. "Going to the lake."

She looks sad, must sense his sunken spirit. "You okay?"

"Tired is all. I'll feel better once I take a swim."

"Hank?"

"Yeah?"

"Sorry if I—"

"No, sweetheart, no problem."

"Sure?"

"Sure. I need some space…you know…to think about the wall." He heads for the gate, stops and turns around. "I'm gonna keep it locked, okay?"

Fiona hesitates. Perhaps, with Ernie gone, that makes no sense. But she gives a reluctant nod.

Hank buys a stack of hot tortillas from the local stand, gobbles them as he walks, arrives at the lake a few minutes before ten. Analu is halfway back from her long swim. Ingrid is not in sight. He gets in the water and within seconds sees cyanobacteria, its tiny translucent threads more plentiful than last week. Most people would not notice the subtle change.

Hank does. He hurries out, dries off and dresses. Already in a sour mood, why not face what's really got him bothered?

On his way to the police station he stops by Josefina's stall.

"You're early," she says, and asks if he wants *The Same.*

"No thanks, I'm not here to eat."

She looks concerned. *"Todo bien, Enrique?"*

"Yes," he tells her, "everything is fine."

"Does this have to do with last night?"

Hank is always amazed by how quickly news travels around this town. "You heard."

"Everyone has heard."

"I guess most people think I was wrong."

"Yes, amigo, true, but I don't listen."

"Gracias, Josefina."

"You did not mean any harm. When they say bad things, like how you used to be a problem, I tell them you have changed, that you are a good man."

Hank knows he doesn't deserve the praise. "The reason I—"

"And good men," she continues, smiling, "to stay good, they need to eat good food!"

"No, I…I can't stay, I—"

"Oh, Enrique, do not worry. Only the stupid ones blame you. So many stupid people! They should know better, should know that—"

"Please," Hank says, and holds up his hands. "Please, amiga, listen. I came by because I'm guessing you'll see Orlando."

"Orlando?"

"Can you give him a message from me?"

Her confusion is plain. *"Sí, Enrique, claro.* I see him every day about this time. That boy loves to bring me peanuts."

"Please tell him I need his help."

"With what?"

Hank tells her about the lot and the wall that must be built.

"The boy can help with that?"

"I'm thinking of his father. You said he's a good worker?"

189

Josefina nods. "Used to be one of the best, and I hear that he's stopped drinking. Like you, Enrique, I think maybe Fidel just needs another chance."

"Well," says Hank, "looks like here it is."

He stalls outside the police station. Once, years ago, Hank passed out in the street and spent a night in its tiny cell. He walks up and opens the squeaky door.

An officer comes to the counter, one of those at the fire last night. "Can I help you, Señor?"

"Is Chief Aldamo here?"

"No." The man's unfriendliness is palpable. Must be familiar with Hank's bad reputation.

"Can you please tell me where to find him?"

"*El Jefe* is in Sololá."

"When will he be back?"

"I don't know."

"He took the drug dealer, Ernie, to be jailed?"

"Yes."

"Is there any possible way he could get out?"

The officer sighs, clearly suspicious of the poorly stated question. "Get out?" He seems offended. Or, at the very least, perturbed. "Absolutely not. The man has been charged with a serious crime. I assure you, Señor, he will remain in jail until his case is heard in court, which could take weeks."

Hank nods, unconvinced, and walks away feeling anxious.

He goes to the public deck at the bottom of Santander, stares out at the lake and tries, in vain, to calm himself.

Best to go home and take a nap. Maybe he's just tired.

Fiona is on the bed, reading. Does not give him the slightest glance. Wants her private time. Something about that unnerves him. He needs to talk about this, but can't. No, okay, he can't, and it's not her fault. Crazily energetic, he goes outside, moves the machete from behind the house into the shed, hides the damn thing within easy reach.

The thought of having to use it makes him shudder.

To settle his nervous stomach, Hank decides to work on the opening. *Sure, why not?* He grabs a hammer, a tape measure, a few sticks of blue chalk, and with Nunca at his side goes to the southern wall. First things first, he makes a blue mark a few feet to the left of the bougainvillea. To the left of that, every few inches on a horizontal plane, he taps lightly with the hammer, listening for differences of sound. He needs to figure out where the rebar is. That's what makes a block wall sturdy, and, unfortunately, also makes it difficult to break through. If he's lucky, this small area has none. That seems more likely as his taps continue to sound the same.

A few dogs on the other side begin to howl, must think the wall is theirs and should not be messed with. "Fuck you," says Hank, and chalks in the opening Fiona wants. He goes to the shed for his splitting maul. *A great big hammer, right?* Hank needs to show the dogs, and her, that he can do this. To even crack one block would be a positive start. Without another thought he hefts the maul above his head, swings with all his might in the center of the marked opening. *Pow!*

The jolt knocks him backwards, and its vibration, excruciatingly intense, sends a shock wave down his arms, from his shoulders to his wrists, that reverberates throughout his body. In dire pain he drops the maul, falls to his butt, then stretches out in the shade.

Nunca whines and lies next to him. "Stupid old man," Hank tells the dog. The time has come to be reasonable, make amends with the Garcías and, yes, ask again for help. It's not just this opening, there's also at least one wall to build on the other side.

"Are you hurt?" It's Fiona, running his way.

"No, honey, I'm all right."

"What happened?"

"Nothing. That's the problem."

She shows him a sad smile. "Maybe ain't *such a hero*, huh?"

"I guess not, no."

191

She sits and holds his hand. "Hey, you still are for me."

He closes his eyes, thankful for the sympathy but not finished feeling sorry for himself. A silent moment crawls by between them. Then comes a knock on the gate.

Nunca barks and runs to it.

Fiona says, "Expecting someone?"

She sits at the garden table as Hank goes and opens the gate. It's Orlando, who shows him a huge smile—a smile that shines with a prayer-like sense of hope. Next to the boy is a middle-aged man with a whiskered face, his eyes cast downward.

"Señor Enrique," says the boy, "I want you to meet my father, Fidel Oseo."

The man's shoulders are slumped, his eyes bloodshot. He's either sick, hungover, or very tired.

Hank shakes the father's hand, tries to disguise his disappointment. "Pleased to meet you, Señor Oseo."

Fidel blinks as if certain he's failed some test. He plainly does not want to be here, would likely run away were it not for his son and this *estranjero*—each in their own way holding onto him. Nevertheless, he smiles. A brief yet honest smile. "The pleasure is mine, Señor."

Hank is shocked they have come so fast. How does Josefina know where they live? *"Vengan adentro, amigos, vengan."* Regardless of his dismay, his sudden certainty that this will be a waste of time, he wants them to feel welcomed. "Fiona, some friends are here to visit."

She comes over and is her regular friendly self.

Meanwhile, Hank makes a more thorough assessment of Fidel. The man is short and muscular, dressed in western clothing from one of the town's many *PACAS:* stores full of clothes donated by first-world countries. He wears an old Detroit Tigers baseball cap, faded denim jeans and worn-out boots. Still, in spite of the western trappings, he is Maya through and through, with a thick arched nose, deep-set eyes, and a gentle spirit. He now straightens up and converses with Fiona. Her genuine kindness has won him over. No surprise in that. Fidel smiles when she bends down and introduces Nunca. Both he and Orlando pat the dog's head. Before long, though, there is nothing left to do or say. The Maya may be talkative among themselves, but are often shy with ladinos and foreigners. Predictable silence fills the air.

"I'm curious," Fiona says, "how do you know each other?"

"Another unwritten novel," jokes Hank.

"Ah, well," she says, because in Guatemala hospitality is expected, "I'm guessing this one is better than the others. I want to sit in the shade and hear it. Anyone hungry?"

The boy grins, reaches into his baggy pants and pulls out a plastic bag of peanuts. After a quick side glance at Hank he hands it to Fiona. "A gift for you, Señora."

"Thank you, Orlando. We should all share these."

They sit at the garden table. Hank goes into the house— twice—to bring out water, tortilla chips, salsa, and a large bunch of bananas. While thankful for Fiona's good manners, he also senses her discomfort. She has no idea why these strangers are here taking up her time. As Hank explains how he met Orlando, the boy tosses a stick for Nunca. They play for several minutes until even the dog looks bored.

Then Fidel says, "My son tells me you need a worker."

Fiona eyes Hank, obviously confused.

He avoids her stare and focuses on Fidel, who, she must be thinking, is certainly no García. What does Josefina know about good builders? This guy had been her customer, that's probably all she knows. A good person, yes, Hank feels sure that much is true, but a builder? "Have you ever worked on walls?"

Fidel nods, looks surprisingly confident. "Yes."

Could be he was a helper, dug ditches or mixed concrete. Not the kind of help that's needed. But Hank likes Fidel, feels calmed by his tranquil energy, and refuses to be rude. Fiona clears her throat, a hint they've been polite for long enough. And he agrees. Needing to be kind, yet direct, Hank walks to the southern wall and points at the chalked outline. "First I need to make a hole in this one."

"Oh," says Fidel, "that is something different."

It sounds like an admission, an excuse for why he cannot do the work. A way to save face with his young son. Hank takes a breath, relieved. Perhaps their awkward moment is almost over.

Fidel goes to the wall and explains the entire process, one step at a time. First, how to determine where the rebar is, and the tools they'll need to deal with it. The arch, he says, will be built later, after this section of wall is gone. "A lot of work, Señor, but you and I can do it."

Hank continues to feel skeptical, knowing foreigners must be wary. Guatemalans sometimes tell them only what they want to hear. "You have the tools?"

"No," says Fidel. "Just friends. Some tools they will loan me. Some we'll need to rent."

Hank looks at Fiona, who grins from ear to ear. A clear approval. That changes everything, gives permission to let go of his pernicious doubt, trust in his hopeful heart.

"Sounds good," he says, and nods to Fidel. "So, how soon can we get started?"

"Tomorrow morning?"

They smile and shake hands.

"I can help too," says Orlando.

"Of course you can," says Fiona. " You know what our biggest problem will be?" She points at Nunca, who is quick to Fiona's side, lolling his tongue and wagging his tail. "Think you can keep this guy out of trouble?"

Orlando gives a knowing smile and nods.

The next morning they show up, as agreed, at eight o'clock. Fidel has a bucket of tools in one hand, a circular saw in the other. Orlando lugs an extension cord. The saw and cord were rented from a friend for forty quetzales (about five bucks) a day. They carry the stuff to the southern wall. All business, Fidel asks Hank where he can find the closest electrical outlet.

"Not so fast!" calls Fiona from the porch. "Would you like a cup of coffee?"

"Oh, yes, please," says Fidel.

"What about you, Orlando? We've got some milk."

"Coffee, too. Please."

"Is that okay?" she says to his father.

Fidel nods. "We *Chapines* drink it weak."

Nunca growls, a stick already in his mouth. He shakes it back and forth, eyes riveted on Orlando.

The boy pats his head, a subterfuge, then grabs the stick and runs off, the dog in hot pursuit.

"Watch out for my flowers!" shouts Fiona.

Hank sees she's in some pain, which Fidel, fidgeting with his cap, must read as worry. "I'll keep an eye on them, Señora."

She smiles and goes into the house.

Hank unwinds the extension cord, plugs it into the nearest outlet. Fidel is over by the wall, unloading hand tools, when Fiona comes out and sets a platter on the garden table. Along with cups of coffee is a glass of milk, a bowl of sugar, and a stack of warm tortillas.

As they eat, Fidel says, "First, we'll scrape off plaster. Enough to see the concrete underneath. We have to start your opening at the space between two blocks."

Hank pictures them in his mind. "How long are they?"

"16 inches. Offset half that distance from row to row. We'll go two and a half blocks wide, or 40 inches."

"Which means," says Hank, "on every other row we'll have to cut through a block."

"Sí, Señor, exactly."

Fiona smiles. While maybe somewhat impressed with Hank's apparent know-how, she's mostly pleased at having Fidel here.

"Bueno," he says, and stands, *"ya vamos."*

His hurry seems to surprise her. "Would you like more coffee? More tortillas?"

"Thank you, Señora, no. I think we should get started." Fidel puts his cup on the platter and heads toward the wall. Orlando follows his father. Nunca is close behind.

Fiona turns to Hank. "I feel very lucky."

He sees she's feeling better. "Yeah, me too."

It takes half an hour of scraping to locate where the walkway must begin, two feet from the bougainvillea trunk. That established, Fidel locates the other line of blocks, forty inches to the left. He scribes a vertical line with an awl.

"Well," says Hank, pretending to be serious, "Can you think of any reason not to start?"

Fidel pretends a frown. "Not a good one." He picks up the saw and sets the masonry blade at a quarter inch. "This much with each pass. *Poco a poco.* Also, I'll need your help."

"With what?"

"The hose. If we don't keep the blade wet, the motor will burn out."

"Understood," says Hank.

Fidel puts in earplugs, then hands a pair to Hank. When both are ready, he gives a warning nod and turns on the saw—an instant assault on the tranquil morning. Even worse is when its blade hits block, the sound of a nearby songbird slaughtered by the god-awful high-pitched screech. Hank shudders, hates the hellish racket, but is determined to get this done. He twists the hose's nozzle open, squirts the spinning blade with a steady stream of water while Fidel grinds his way up the wall. A thick gray paste oozes from the cut.

It takes three hours to make use of the entire three-and-a-half-inch blade. Fidel sets down the saw, takes off his goggles, wipes the gray dust from his face. "Finished over here."

Hank points to the base of the wall. "Except down there."

"Yes." Because the blade could not reach the very bottom, they still have 6 inches of block to go. Fidel smiles, then digs out a hammer and cold chisel from his bucket. The remaining block must be pounded through by hand. The men trade off, chip away at the obstinate concrete, Hank in relief whenever Fidel looks spent. The blunt attack and stubborn resistance continues for more than an hour. Hank's hands are sore, his sweaty face also filmed by fine gray dust.

"Lunch time!" calls Fiona.

Ah, thank God! Hank checks his watch. Almost two o'clock.

The men clean up and go to the table. There, along with water, are plates of cheese enchiladas, beans, chips, and slices of apple. Fidel bows his head. "Muchas gracias, Señora."

"De nada, amigo. And please call me Fiona."

"Yes, of course. Fiona." He smiles, then glances around the yard. "Where is Orlando?"

"On my bed. Your son and our dog have been running around all day. Nunca needed a little nap. Orlando decided to help him out."

Fidel smiles. "I've never seen him so happy." He looks away, toward the wall. His face turns suddenly serious and he lets out a heavy sigh. An admission, perhaps, of how rarely he spends time with his son? The man seems deeply troubled.

Hank says, "Orlando is a fine boy."

Fidel nods, and sighs again, like he's had little to do with that.

Fiona leans toward him. "Are you okay?"

"Yes, I...I just realized, we are going to need a ladder."

"Oh," Fiona says, eyeing Hank with a sly grin, "a ladder."

"Yes," says Fidel, "I should have thought of this before."

"No problem," says Hank, "I've got an old wooden one in the shed."

The man at once looks hopeful. "Can I see?"

"Sure."

And they go examine it. "This should work," says Fidel with renewed confidence. "For us to get a clean break, I need to cut the wall on its other side."

Hank thinks of Señor Mocún, who must be outraged by their incessant noise. Oh well...*así es.*

They finish their meals, drink more coffee, then position the ladder. Fidel climbs up and straddles the wall. He takes the saw from Hank and lowers it by the cord to the vacant lot. Hank hands him a few feet of coiled hose, again thinks of Mocún, and then, far worse, the dogs.

"You, uh, see anything?"

Fidel looks around. "One large mango tree, a real beauty." He hoists up the wooden ladder, guides it over to the other side, and climbs down, out of sight. Hank breathes easier when he hears him scribing lines, then winces as Fidel starts to cut. Same horrific screech. His progress is much slower over there, since every few inches he must stop, grab the hose and soak the unquenchable concrete.

198

Finally, at the bottom of each line, he pounds away with the chisel, a disturbing clamor that goes on and on. It is nearly five o'clock. Poor guy must be worn out.

"Want some water?" calls Hank.

"No, I'm almost done."

"Hola," says Orlando. He and Nunca sit down by the wall.

Hank sighs, full of gratitude, and for a second feels at peace, certain the worst is over, when he hears howling from the other side of the wall.

Orlando cries, "Papa! Papa! Papa!"

Then, like magic, Fidel appears, leaps to the wall and straddles it like a cowboy on his horse. The hounds below him growl and bark. Though obviously shaken, he smiles down at his anxious son. "I'm all right."

Fiona comes hurrying from the porch.

Fidel sees her, and repeats in a calming voice, *"Todo está bién."*

"Did they bite you, Papa?"

"No, *mijo,* only tried. Must not like my work." He lifts the extension cord until able to grab the saw, lowers it to safety, then retrieves the ladder and swings it over the wall. Hank holds it steady while Fidel climbs down. The man shrugs and laughs. "Best we not open this up today."

"How many are there?"

"Maybe ten."

"You see why we need some outer walls?"

"Oh, yes," says Fidel, eyes opened wide, "I see."

27
Walls

The next morning comes fast. Fidel pounds away, several blows with the maul, and the massive white cut-out crashes into the empty lot like some giant broken tooth. It's a clean break at the bottom, and there's no rebar to deal with.

"You are lucky," says Fidel. "Whoever built this did not know what he was doing."

"Lucky us," says Hank, uncertain what that might mean for the remaining wall.

They step through the opening for a better look. Three street dogs scamper off down the driveway.

Orlando beams. "You showed them, Papa!"

"He sure did!" says Fiona.

Hank feels vulnerable with this new entrance to their property. It's like his mind has been opened up, and in flies fucking Ernie! He blinks him away, takes a breath, looks around at the other lots. All vacant. But close by, to his right, is a shallow ditch. Must be the start of their neighbor's wall, which will also serve as his. He looks at Fiona. "Have you heard anybody working over here?"

"Oh, yeah, the other day while you were swimming. Forgot to tell you."

"Well," he says, "looks like we only have one wall to build."

Fidel turns and smiles at Hank. "Ready?"

Hank nods, hopes to look more *macho* than he is. "Ready."

"Such big strong men," says Fiona. Sounds cheeky, but she actually seems to mean it.

The big strong men go for what they'll need: two picks and a square-edged shovel, all loaned by one of Fidel's friends. There is also a six-foot length of galvanized fence, delivered that morning by the local hardware store: soon to be a doggy barricade. They prop the metal grid next to the opening, will put it up after work.

First things first, Fidel wants to check the accuracy of the southern border line made of sticks. Based on dimensions included in Hank's deed, he measures along their eastern neighbor's wall and appears surprised. "Perfect." Fidel pounds in a wooden stake, then measures along the western ditch, right to its end. "Also perfect," he says, pounds in another stake, then runs a string between them. They grab their picks and start to dig, each at one end of the line. The ground is hard, the going slow, the sun already hot. Fiona brings them water from time to time, and for lunch a big plate of quesadillas.

Early in the afternoon, Señor Mocún comes around the corner of his house, stands and stares at them. Fidel, who had been warned, sets down his pick and gives the old man a friendly wave. *"Ütz awäch, Tata?" How are you today, sir?*

Mocún also speaks in Cakchiquel. The two carry on quite a conversation. As he digs, Hank hears them each say "gringo"

201

several times, the old man with predictable contempt. At last he shakes his head, scowls and walks back to his house.

"What did he say?"

"The Señor is not pleased about your wall."

"I'm not surprised."

"Says we cannot bring materials across his property."

"Yeah, he already told me."

"What bothers him most, I think, is you getting the mango tree. His father planted it sixty years ago, when he was a boy."

"Oh," Hank says, "I didn't know." He keeps digging, and feels bad. He would be angry too.

An hour later, three indigena men come up the subdivision driveway in a pickup. *"Fidel!"* the driver yells. He parks in the lot next door, close to the ditch, and they come over.

"Mis amigos," Fidel says to Hank, and introduces them: Pedro, Juan, Rolando.

Hank shakes their hands. *"Mucho gusto."*

These are some of the builders Fidel used to work with. After hearing of Hank's fraught relationship with Mocún, they offer, for a reasonable fee, to deliver the materials needed to build his wall. "The Señor will not like it," Rolando says, "but the property where we're working is not his. Or the driveway. So he can't stop us."

And from then on it's like a party. Rolando, the apparent leader of the group, cranks up their portable radio. Ranchero music fills the air. Though worried their frivolity might make things worse with Mocún, Hank feels indebted to these guys, does not want to upset their fun. He and Fidel help unload the pickup: numerous five-gallon buckets of a sand and gravel.

Pedro heads off for more supplies.

Rolando and Juan, like Fidel, are hard workers. Within an hour they finish the western ditch, then come help him and Fidel dig. Hank takes a break, drinks some water and lies on his back in the dirt. Though tired, it's been a long time since he's felt so capable and strong.

Pedro returns, the truck full of concrete blocks, rebar, bags of cement, and a wheelbarrow.

Orlando and Nunca play tag in the new lot. The boy, while dodging the dog, dances along to the music, which gets everybody laughing. For lunch, Fiona brings out a basket of hot tortillas. They all know who she is. There are few indigenous people in Pana who have not heard of "Seño Fiona." All of them hold her in high esteem.

A few hours later, as the sun begins to set, she brings out more tortillas.

"No gracias, Seño," says Rolando, "it's time for us to head home." Both ditches are filled with concrete, the rebar set, and a first row of block has been installed. "Nothing left to do until this hardens. See you Monday." Each of them shakes everyone else's hand. Their new friends wave good bye and drive off.

"Wow," says Hank, "it's suddenly so quiet."

"Not for long," says Fiona. "Best we leave, too, before the doggy brigade shows up."

"Good idea," says Fidel.

They go back to the garden, secure the metal barricade, and, sure enough, here come several mongrels to sniff around and piss on what used to be their domain. They charge the metal fence, snarl and bark at Nunca. The pup whines and starts to shiver. Orlando carries him away, accompanied by Fiona.

Hank also feels threatened, and thinks of Ernie. "Any chance those *monstros* can get in?"

Fidel shakes his head. "No, poor guys have no chance. That's why they're so mad!"

The men walk off, not wanting to incite any further rage, and soon the dogs are gone.

Fiona has made a stir-fry. She seems fine, must have taken something, maybe a Tramadol to augment her Oxycontin. The four of them sit around the kitchen table. It feels like family. She'd had her tuk-tuk driver, Gregorio, bring bottles of Coca Cola, which for Orlando is a treat.

They finish the meal and she pulls out ice-cream, also brought by Gregorio. "Anyone want dessert?"

"No, thank you," says Fidel. "We need to get home. Orlando's mother takes him to Bible class Saturday evenings."

The boy looks away from the ice-cream, his desire undeniable. *Hey*, thinks Hank, *it would just take a few more minutes.* But he won't push it. Truth is, he's impressed by this father's sense of duty.

"And tomorrow is Sunday," says Fidel, as if the meaning of that is clear.

He and Orlando leave. Nunca lies by the front gate, no doubt hoping his friend will soon be back. The pup stays put till the sky goes black, till the dogs return and start barking up a storm. He whines, rushes into the house, joins Fiona on her bed. She takes her Oxycontin a few hours early, puts in earplugs and tries to sleep. The curs fight among themselves, more furious than usual, perhaps aware that their old stomping grounds are about to be off limits.

On Monday the men get back to work. The walls get higher, though not enough to keep out dogs. Or, for that matter, people. Again Hank thinks of Ernie. He is relieved when, at the end of the day, their opening gets closed off by the metal fencing. Fidel and Orlando stay for dinner. Plus ice cream. Their company soothes him and he's sad to see them go.

Tuesday morning, like a blessing, the walls climb above four feet. Hank feels more at ease. And it is quiet, too! The others agreed with him to keep the radio off, at least till the afternoon. None of them want to provoke his neighbor, who in spite of a bad temper must be respected as a Maya elder. They work on in silence. A pickup full of blocks is passed over to the inner lot, exactly enough to finish Hank's wall. He is not surprised when, after lunch, the radio gets turned on. Or that Mocún then emerges to complain about the noise.

"Nothing he can do," Rolando whispers, noting it is common to have music at a worksite. The rest keep busy while he attends to the Señor, speaking in Cakchiquel, referring to him as *Tata* and using a kind, soft voice.

With no clue what Rolando says, Hank stops mixing mortar and watches the old man. His head is barely visible above the wall, his face pinched with righteous indignation. Mocún points at the mango tree and raises the volume of his disdain.

Fiona would be saddened by the old man's sense of loss. Good she and Orlando are in the house. "Señor," Hank says to Mocún, who turns to him and glowers. "I am truly sorry about your mango tree."

Everyone stops working. Someone turns off the music.

The Señor spits, looks more pissed-off than before. *"Truly sorry?"* he says in Spanish. His question sounds like an accusation.

Hank did not expect this would be easy. He's been playing it in his head for the last two days. "I have an offer."

"Offer?" the old man says with an enigmatic gape, perhaps unfamiliar with the word.

"Yes. If I could, I would give you back the tree."

Mocún explodes with contemptuous laughter. *"If you could?* Yes, *if you could,* I would take it!"

"So, because that is impossible, I *offer,* instead, the fruit."

The old man eyebrows wrinkle. *"Qué?"*

"From now on," says Hank, "when the mangos get ripe, all of them are yours."

Mocún's face goes blank. "Is this a trick?"

"No, Señor, you'll see I mean it."

"Pfff!" he sneers, spits again, throws up his hands and leaves.

By quitting time both walls have surpassed six feet. The workers cannot see each other over the top. They shout out, *"Buenas noches,"* and go their separate ways. Fidel and Orlando leave.

There is, of course, no longer any need to fence the opening. Not from dogs, anyhow. Hank dares not mention Ernie. *Oh, c'mon, there's nothing to worry about.* Truth is, he's too exhausted to think things through. Best to focus on Fiona, who happily wanders in her new space, Nunca by her side. Hank watches them awhile, then goes to his room. Though fighting a headache, and sore in every part of his body, he wants to trust that all is well. Within minutes is asleep.

On Wednesday morning, as the men work to finish off the walls, Orlando helps Fiona plot out her garden. They tap in little sticks and run strings between them, defining the narrow walkways between areas she'll plant. They laugh a lot, and take long breaks to play with Nunca—look like a mother and her loving son. The boy keeps her water bottle from going dry, seems to know when she gets tired and sits with her in the shade. Hank keeps a careful watch while busy busting up the section of fallen block. He uses the bigger chunks, at Fiona's direction, to mark the sides of each path. The remainder will get pounded into gravel.

By noon the walls have reached eight feet. Done. Fidel turns to his final job, the opening. He shapes the arch with wire and small lengths of bent rebar, now ready to be bonded with concrete. Tomorrow, however, he cannot come, needs a day off to work somewhere else.

On Thursday morning, early, Concepción comes to visit. Hank hasn't seen her since the fire. While Fiona is in the bathroom, perhaps taking an extra pain pill, he thanks their friend for all she and her brothers did to protect them. It's been a week now, and, aside from occasional lapses, Hank is beginning to believe their threat to Ernie worked.

"He won't come back," she says. "Don Julio heard he is locked up, somewhere in Canada."

"He's a Canadian?"

"That's the rumor."

"Rumor about what?" says Fiona, joining them.

"Ernie," says Concepción, "is gone forever."

The two of them believe it, and suddenly Hank feels hopeful, almost free of the vague worry that has plagued him. Their chat goes on and on at the garden table. Then Analu shows up.

Concepción knows of her estrangement from Fiona, says how happy she is to see that they've "healed their wounds."

The three friends walk around the new lot. To Hank it feels like the best of times, these women like loving sisters. They point at different areas and discuss the possibilities.

Excited, Fiona gets out her phone and calls Gregorio. Within minutes he arrives, and off they go to the local nursery.

Hank stays behind, astounded by Fiona's energy! "Big trouble for you though," he warns Nunca. "Soon as she can make it happen, there'll be no good place to shit."

The dog does not seem worried, curls up by the gate and waits for her return.

Hank has always been impressed by how fast dogs can relax, no matter where they are. So why not him? It's too dark in the house, and he likes having Nunca close. He finds a grassy spot by the nearby wall, stretches out in the shade, closes his eyes and quickly dozes off.

Friday morning comes, and Hank hears the expected knock. He's in the garden, drinking coffee. Fiona and Nunca barely beat him to the gate. Both must have been listening for that sound. She removes the lock, hooks it on the post's metal loop and opens the door. There stands Fidel. Alone.

Nunca whines, rushes outside to look around.

"No Orlando?" says Fiona.

"He wanted to come," Fidel says, "but his mother insisted he go to school."

"Oh," she says with barefaced disappointment. "Sure, okay."

"Going to school is good for him," says Fidel.

She nods. "Yes, yes, of course."

"Also good for me."

Hank is confused. "Why you?"

"When Orlando is at school my wife is happy, which can only happen if he does not need to go sell peanuts."

"And now," Hank says, "because you're working, he doesn't."

"Yes."

"Which means," Fiona says, suddenly aglow, "she's also happy with you!"

"Yes, and Orlando too, because her happiness makes him happy." A humble man by nature, Fidel appears embarrassed by his rightful pride. "Anyway, sorry, here I am by myself."

"Nunca will suffer," says Fiona, "but he'll survive. Come on, pup, come on."

The dog runs into the yard, races toward the new garden plot as if Orlando might be there hiding. Fidel and Fiona follow. Hank watches her, how carefree she is, how full of joy. And to his deep regret, he worries. *Too much joy,* it seems to him. *A tell,* he thinks, well-experienced with the look, afraid she's overdoing the Oxycontin.

That explains why Ernie, fucking Ernie, has popped into his head again, is making his stomach churn.

He closes the gate and locks it.

It took Fidel and Hank three days, with Sunday off for church, to plaster the garden's new four walls, and another to paint them. Fiona chose a pale yellow.

Orlando never showed. The boy's teacher, Fidel explained, said he must be more prepared at school, which meant spending his afternoons doing homework. "His mother helps the best she can. Mainly by keeping him at home."

Nunca took it hardest. Poor guy looked miserable, curled up in the shadows, moping beneath the mango tree. Seemed determined to suffer until his friend returned. Even Fiona could not distract him, a reluctant wag of the tail the most she ever got. By late Tuesday, however, he began to perk up, aided by the bones Analu dangled beneath his nose. She and Concepción had come to help break up the soil. Three García brothers arrived with a truckload of *abono*—*compost*—and worked it into the new beds.

On Wednesday morning Fiona begins to plant. Hank, still suspicious she might be abusing the Oxycontin, is glad to see her looking happy in a normal way.

Sheesh, a normal way? What the hell does that mean? He slaps his head. *Hey, asshole, unlike you, it's in her nature to be happy!*

After the self-critique, perhaps because he knows it's well-deserved, the following week passes calmly. Such a gift. Fiona spends a couple of hours every day in the new garden. He sits and watches her busy hands, digging in the loamy soil, caring for her plants. Each morning, before going to the lake, Hank patrols for doggy messes, then asks how else he can help. Will do whatever it takes to extend these happy times. She always smiles and shoos him off, but he's never gone for long. A short swim, a few glorious moments in the water, then he heads home.

Today, as he enters the garden, she's in a chair, Nunca at attention by her side.

"Go!" Fiona shouts, and the pup sprints toward Hank. "Quick, tell him to sit!"

"Sit!" orders Hank.

Nunca skids to a stop, then turns and runs back to Fiona, wags his tail and stares at her.

"Well," she says, patting his head, "not quite."

Hank walks over to the table. "You've been training him?"

"Trying. While you're down at the lake. I swear, he learned to sit for me! Every time! I wanted to surprise you."

"And, indeed, you have."

She takes hold of Nunca's head, brings her nose to his. "Ooh, such a clever boy!"

More days pass. It's another warm one. Maybe Monday, Hank isn't sure. Happy to have lost track. While Fiona naps, he weeds the seedlings by the new garden's southern wall, now referred to as "*La pared Mocún.*"

He takes a break, makes some tea, sits at the garden table and hears that familiar knock on the gate. Nunca charges from the porch, yapping with excitement. Hank hurries to let Orlando in.

Fiona rushes out of the house. "You're here!"

"My mother says I can come." He shows an impish grin. "After I do my homework."

"Yes, yes, *great!*" she says. *"For us!"*

And from then on, most every afternoon, the boy comes. He won't take money to play with Nunca, so Fiona finds other chores for him to do, mostly helping her in the garden, anything to have him near. Should she be feeling good, the daily sound of his arrival is enough to get her up.

But if there's pain she will linger in the house for several minutes. Afternoons are her hardest time, when the morning Oxycontin is wearing off.

Today, to his relief, the dog's joyful barking brings her quickly out into the sunshine. She has on a white summer dress, looks clear-eyed and gorgeous.

Hank opens the gate and lets the boy in.

"Amigo!" Fiona calls.

Orlando and Nunca go running to her. She hugs them both, then sits at the shaded table next to Hank, watches and laughs as "the kids" run around the yard. They might be at it for an hour. At some point Orlando will get bored, will want to be with Fiona, will tell her he's ready to work.

"So," she says to Hank, "how was the lake today?"

He knows she means its general health. And, in particular, if the level of cyanobacteria has increased. "Getting a bit worse."

"You're seeing *paxte?*"

Paxte (a Cakchiquel word) is a thick weedy vine that grows when the water has too much nitrogen—often the by-product of chemical fertilizers and other pollutants. It normally crawls along the bottom of the lake and is no problem. Should the water's natural alkalinity fail to mitigate the phosphates, however, the invasive plant proliferates and climbs. "In a few spots close to shore it's reached the surface. Last week a kid got stuck in it and drowned."

"Oh...oh, no."

Hank puts his arm around her.

Orlando and Nunca come running up. "I'm ready to work."

"Okay," she says, wiping at her eyes.

"Are you all right, Seño Fiona?"

"Better than all right," she says, managing a smile, "I am excited! Since Nunca already knows how to *sit*, he must now learn to *stay put* while we walk away."

"Really?" Orlando glances down at the panting pup. "I don't think he'll want to."

"We'll give him no other choice."

"I learned in a week," says Hank.

"Exactly," says Fiona. "And Nunca is *much* smarter."

Without further discussion, the rigorous job begins. By the time Orlando needs to leave, Nunca will sit still as everyone walks off, but will only "stay"—at most—for fifteen seconds. The pup cannot bear to be left alone for long.

Fiona laughs and throws up her hands. "Well, well, *oh well.*"

Orlando bends over, gently squeezes Nunca's ears and peers into his eyes. "I think tomorrow is your day."

He says the same for an entire week, until finally that day comes. The humans are able to walk off, turn and talk amongst each other, while the dog, leaning their direction, sits and watches, whining as he waits for someone, *any one,* to say "Come!" The magic word launches Nunca like a missile.

Today it's Fiona who gives the order. She rewards him with a treat. That's all he seems to need, right away eager to perform his trick again, again, and again.

"Wow," says Hank, "think he can learn to wash the dishes?"

"Oh, yes, Señor, no problem," says Orlando like a proud father, "and windows too."

"First," says Fiona, "he needs some extra training on how to avoid my flowers."

The boy happily volunteers. *"Pero despues de Navidad,"* he says, *"está bién?"*

"Christmas?" She looks at Hank, who has also forgotten.

"In two days. On Wednesday." Orlando looks confused. "You are joking," he says, "yes?"

"Yes," says Hank, the easiest answer he can give.

"Every year, starting tomorrow, my mother volunteers with the church. Me and Papa help her."

"Good for you," says Fiona.

Orlando smiles, always pleased to get her praise. "Can we start the training Friday?"

"Friday it is," she says.

The boy kneels down and looks into Nunca's eyes. "Oh, you are going to learn so fast!"

Christmas passes, unobserved by the unreligious gringos. Orlando comes Friday afternoon, as promised, the best gift they could get. He and Nunca stay near, yet clear of Fiona, who tends her flowers. Meanwhile, Hank continues to take care of domestic chores. His daily routine includes time down at the lake. He goes early, and occasionally brings Analu back with him to the house. Fiona is most sociable late morning, after her pain pill has taken affect and before her needed nap. While they drink tea, and chat, Hank occupies himself with something. Anything. He might call Aakesh, waste time engaging in aimless banter. Or whatever. Doesn't matter. He knows the women want these moments to themselves, and it's the same when Concepción comes by in the evenings.

Then, shortly after the new year has arrived, right when everything seems so good, it all changes.

Hank is about to leave for the lake when Fiona tells him, like she's given it lots of thought, "I need more peace and quiet."

The abrupt announcement is not really a huge surprise. On some unconscious level, he must have been expecting it.

"Yeah, okay."

"I mean no more visits." It's not the words but her tone that shocks him. She sounds defensive, almost angry. "It's just too much. I'm tired of having to think up things to say."

She's on her back in bed. Looks worn out. Sure, who wouldn't feel overwhelmed by the many days of constant attention she's been getting. But this seems like something else, something harder to explain. "They're your friends, Fiona. You can say, or not say, anything you want."

She closes her eyes. "You don't understand. I need a break, that's all."

He sighs, walks to the door and stops, afraid to ask. "You mean Orlando, too?"

"Yes. Just for awhile. I don't know how long."

Oh, shit. Her not wanting to see the boy is like hiding from the sun. "He'll be hurt by that."

"I'm sorry. I am. Right now I have to take care of myself."

"What about me?" he says, feeling oddly timid, afraid of what she might say but needing to know the truth. "Would it be best if I go somewhere for awhile?"

"No." She opens her eyes and looks at him. "No, Hank, I... you are the only one I really need." She offers a slight smile. "Go to the lake, enjoy your swim. Then please, honey, please come back."

Hank sits on the bed and holds her hand. "You sure?"

"I'm sure."

At the beach he explains things to Analu. She is upset, of course, but there's nothing he can do. They wish each other well and she gets into the water. Hank glances up into the cloudless sky. Its emptiness is no comfort. He gazes at the volcanos, which only make him feel small and insignificant, then scans the lake itself, hoping that might ease his troubled mind.

Until now, he had not seen Juan. The young fisherman waves. Hank swims out to say hello, thinks being in the water might do him good. It doesn't. "Any luck today?"

"Same as always," says Juan. "Fish are in no hurry."

Hank can't think of anything to say. He turns his head and takes in the beach. So far away. So empty. It seems crazy to try and fill this confusing time with empty words.

"I see you are sad," says Juan.

Hank looks at him and smiles. This day just keeps getting weirder. "How?"

"My grandfather, Mixoc, taught me. It's in your eyes, the way they look."

"How do they look?"

"Not out, but inward. To protect."

"Your grandfather must be very wise."

"Yes, he's...he's the wisest man I know." Juan laughs, apparently at himself, and shakes his head.

"What?"

"Sometimes, when he tells me things, I don't understand."

Hank smiles. "Sounds like my kind of guy."

"I don't know, but yes, I think so. I told him about you."

"Told him what?"

"You care about the lake. You worry it could die."

"I told you that?"

"No, but...I can see."

Hank sighs, blows out air, and drops straight down into the water, several feet, hoping to clear his mind. It would be wrong to show emotion in front of Juan. They would both feel uncomfortable. *So I won't,* he swears, *I won't!*

But when he comes up, to his astonishment, his normally reticent friend again looks deep into his eyes. Hank feels disturbed by the sudden openness. Juan is trying to be kind, *okay, yeah,* but they don't know each other well enough for this. "Good luck with the fish, amigo. I need to go."

"You should speak to my grandfather. I think he can help." The young man's eyes look certain. How could he possibly seem so certain? "What about tomorrow?"

Hank is surprised, and touched, by Juan's gracious persistence, something he would never have imagined. Then suddenly it hits him, like an unwanted premonition, that he should go, that he...he needs to go.

"So," says Juan, still looking in his eyes, "you will come?"

"Yes. Thank you. Only I...I don't know when."

"It's up to you, he never leaves our home."

"How do I find him?"

"Easy. Take the concrete path to the top of Santa Catarina. Ask for Tata Mixoc."

The word *Tata,* Hank knows, indicates a respected elder. Not a name one takes, but one that's given. "Your grandfather speaks Spanish?"

"No, only Cakchiquel, but I can translate. I'm always back from fishing by eleven."

Hank nods, says good bye, starts swimming, and for a moment feels relieved. Then that changes too.

What the hell? he thinks, almost wishing they hadn't talked at all. Though hoping this meeting with Mixoc will happen, he can't help being doubtful, like waking from a wonderful dream, one he doesn't want to end, and facing the real world. *Meeting with a Maya elder, sure.* Like some fucking fairytale. True, he feels hopeful, like this is one of those incredible, mysterious opportunities, somehow predetermined, somehow destined to occur. Then never does.

His spirit sinking, it's hard making it back to shore.

"Tata Mixoc" Hank repeats like a mantra as he heads home. A walking meditation. First steps, he imagines, to their actual meeting. Being doubtful it will ever happen cannot help. Fiona would want him to stay hopeful, so he will. Hell, he could use a bit of wisdom, that's or sure, so must summon the needed willpower, or whatever, to make this real.

He stops, watches an indigena woman and child splashing each other in the lake. He has observed this same kind of scene many times. There's something about the way they hug the shoreline that tells him neither knows how to swim. No surprise, since most Guatemalans don't. He senses their awareness of the potential danger, is fascinated by how joyful they are, how excitedly they play in spite of it.

Or perhaps because of it.

Their sweet, infectious energy holds him spellbound.

From that point on, Hank walks even slower, and stops often. The slightest thing might catch his eye. He spends several minutes considering the sign recently put up by the *Comité de Jucanya,* a group of local indigenous leaders, which warns to not cut trees or dump anything by the lake.

Amazing that people need to be told such things.

By the time he gets home it's a few minutes after noon. Fiona is deep asleep and snoring. Nunca, on the bed, wakes up, stretches and yawns. Not wanting Fiona disturbed, Hank picks him up, carries him outside. They sit in the shade at the garden table. There is no breeze. It's hot. The pale blue sky, empty of clouds, looks and feels heavy, closing in on him like a lid.

Hank shuts his eyes, exhausted. It's okay that he doesn't want to move. There is nothing he needs to do. *Tata Mixoc.* The name fills up his head.

Fiona comes out to the porch, and seems off-balance, holds onto one of the awning posts.

He calls to her, "You okay?"

She sees him at the table, does not answer.

He hurries over, helps her into the house and back to bed. "Is it the pain? You need a pill?"

"It's not that, it's…I can't describe it."

She is trembling. He pulls the covers to her chin. "I'm calling Doctor Palacio."

"No." She sounds adamant. "Call Vicente."

"But Fiona, I—"

"Please, all right? Before anyone else, I need to see Vicente."

It takes the shaman an hour, by bus and foot, to arrive from his village of San Jorge. Much faster than Hank expected. "She's in the house."

Hearing them enter, Fiona slowly scoots up to a sitting position, sighing with the effort.

Vicente lowers his pack to the ground, then turns to Hank. "We need some time alone."

"Sí. Claro."

He goes to the new garden, lies in the shade of *Pared Mocún.* Soon falls asleep. His dream is full of buildings, trees, and people, all inexplicably the same, bent over from a mighty wind. He opens his eyes, aware of having had this dream before. He looks up, watches as a band of clouds roll in, propelled by a sudden *Norte,* watches as they swallow the last trace of that heavy pale blue sky. He would check the time but can't find his phone, must have left it on the garden table.

Without warning, Nunca licks his face. "Whoa, where did you come from?"

Was here beside you all along, the dog says—or seems to say—with big solicitous brown eyes.

Hank wipes away the slobber, pulls the puppy to his side. Though sad and worried about Fiona, he smiles and gives Nunca a tender hug. "You and me, pal, you and me." Then he thinks of Orlando. "Didn't your friend come today?"

Nunca looks at him and sighs, for Hank a clear signal that the boy, for whatever reason, didn't. Strange to be so certain, he can hardly wait for this crazy day to end. At the moment, comforted by the steady, surrounding wind, he closes his eyes and again falls asleep.

When he wakes, the entire yard is in shadow. It feels ominous, way too quiet, like something terrible has happened.

Hank jumps to his feet, follows Nunca to the house, and through the window sees Vicente, standing at the foot of Fiona's bed, the room clouded with holy smoke. Hank sees the back of her head, watches as she keeps nodding. He steps back and sits at the garden table.

It's okay, he tells himself. *Everything is okay.*

Several more minutes pass. His phone says a quarter past five. This cleansing ritual has been going for three hours. He gets up and paces, then sits down. Paces again, then sits. It's almost six. The sun begins to set.

At last Vicente comes from the house and joins him. The two just sit there, a somber silence between them that confirms Hank's greatest fear. A truth he cannot fathom. Also, strange but true, he's learned over time to trust Vicente, his perception and straight-forward honesty, his genuine care for Fiona. Her ardent faith in the man has rubbed off. Hank patiently waits for whatever he will say.

The shaman turns to him. "You understand, she is dying."

Hank pauses, then says, "Yes."

Vicente nods and sighs. "Fiona feels death near. Her acceptance, her surrender, has helped to calm the pain. We can be glad for that."

Hank does not feel glad. "How...long? I mean, until she—"

"I can't be sure. Soon. No longer than a month. I will visit once a week, that is her wish. I will stay, do a ceremony, whenever the time comes."

"Bueno, amigo. Gracias."

Hank walks Vicente to the road, says good bye, then locks the gate. He picks up Nunca and they go to the house.

Fiona is sitting up in bed. She looks wide awake and in good spirits. Seeing Nunca, she holds out her arms to the squirming animal. "Come!"

He leaps onto the bed and charges.

Fiona covers her head with a pillow. "Ay-yi-yi!" she screams, clearly loving this wild moment, flailing her hands in a useless effort to control him. She drops the pillow, pulls the puppy close, rubs her face against his snout. "Ooh, you little thing!"

After Nunca has satisfied his burning need to be near her, he settles down.

Though obviously exhausted, she smiles tenderly at Hank. "You and Vicente talked?"

"Yes."

"So...you're okay with this?"

"I don't get a better choice?" That makes her laugh. He sits on the bed and they hold hands. "Sure, I'm okay, but...I really think we should see a doctor."

"We're way past doctors, Hank."

"How do you know?"

"Because I do. And when it's your turn, so will you."

Hank looks away, shaken by her resolve.

"Please," she says, "you need to trust me. My choice, okay?"

"Okay."

"Good." Fiona squeezes his hand. "Thanks."

Hank wonders why he let himself give in. His fear tells him to fight this, but he won't. Because he's learned to trust Fiona whenever she looks so certain. Her mind is made up, and to struggle against her wishes would only push them apart. That he can't allow. This is what she wants, what she has *chosen*, so the best he can do is help, give whatever it is she needs.

"No more food," Fiona says like ordering from a menu. "Only water. Maybe sometimes I'll need a pill. We'll see."

"All right."

"Vicente says it could take a month. I don't think so. Might just be a couple of weeks, and what I want most is for you to be around. A lot. Apart from your morning swim, that is."

"In other words, as usual."

"Yes," she says, "as usual." Then she starts to cry, a long and choppy swell of sobs that come from deep inside her. "Wow, I...I can't quite believe it."

Hank, too, has begun to cry. "Me either."

They squeeze their interlaced fingers tight together.

Fiona says, "I need you close."

Hank looks into her eyes, sees exactly what she means. Not sexual, but how they used to be when in love, when they loved just being together. He takes off his clothes and climbs in beside her. She snuggles into his arms. Neither says a thing as they lie there in the darkness.

She falls asleep, her head on his left bicep. After awhile it starts to throb, but he dares not move, will endure the slight discomfort for this closeness that feels so precious, that he's wanted for so long. Not till his arm goes numb does he slide her head onto the pillow. He gets up, goes to the bathroom, shakes away the pins and needles, goes back in bed. Though he gives her room to move, she snuggles with him again, this time makes sure that their feet are touching. It reminds Hank of when they first got together, and he feels happy. Truly happy. Not about the long gone past, not about some memory, but for now, this very moment.

Which startles him. How can he be happy? *How?* Here is Fiona, slowly dying by his side, the two of them trapped in a

221

dark truth they can't escape, and what he feels inside is a warming stillness, a calm contentment.

It must be because of her, that this is also what she's feeling.

Many hours pass. Hours he marks by every passing second. He hears *El Norte* rattle through the pines behind the house. On and on it blows, accompanied by a chorus of distant dogs. At some point, who knows when, they go mute, perhaps tired of their own complaints.

Then the wind halts, too, and time, as if it never had existed, seems to stop, frozen by this glacial flow of silence. His mind is imbued with wonder, like music from another world, in perfect tune with his soundless breath, in perfect harmony with his deep transcendent joy. There is nothing else. Nothing. Not the slightest murmur until dawn, when squirrels begin to scamper on the roof. Here comes another day of exquisite light, of birds filled up with song and the need to sing it!

Nunca runs to the door and whines. Probably needs to poop. "Poor baby," says Fiona.

Hank had no idea she was awake. He lets the dog out, then sits beside her on the bed.

She turns to him. "I've been thinking."

"Oh," he sighs, "not that again."

"Sorry," she smiles, "yes." Then also sighs. "Because before I wasn't thinking right, I really wasn't. I want friends with me while I'm dying. A small circle of the ones I truly love."

"The whole time?"

Fiona grimaces. "Oh gawd, no!" She scowls like a selfish child. "Only when I want them!"

He's going to miss her oddball jokes. "Ah."

"I just mean once in a while. If nothing else, to give me a break from you."

"Excellent idea."

"Yeah. So we need a meeting. With Vicente, for sure, and Concepción. And Analu. And you know who else?" Her face lights up, a look he associates with one very special person.

"Orlando."

Her glow suddenly disappears. She seems close to tears. "No, I...I think he's too young."

Hank can't imagine her final days without the boy. "It's okay, he'd be fine."

"I want him around, of course I do, like before, him and Nunca playing, but...but not when it gets hard. That would break my heart, it really would."

"I understand," he says, wiping at his eyes.

She nods, reaches out and holds his hand. "No, I mean María. To have María here would truly be a blessing. And Irma, too. I really want them with me at the end."

"They would both love that."

"Okay. So. Today is Monday, right?"

"Tuesday."

"Tuesday. And María still comes to town on Fridays?

"Right."

"You think we can we meet on Saturday, all of us sit around and talk this through?"

"Sure. What time?"

Fiona gives it a second's thought, then holds up her index finger. "How 'bout *high noon?*" she says with a western drawl, an unconvincing Annie Oakley. "I'll fix snacks. I'd love to make it like a party."

Party?

"Oh," she says, "and Aakesh! We'll need him here to keep things light."

Light? "Okay, sweetheart, I promise to make it happen."

Fiona beams as if she's won some sort of prize, as if nothing could be better. Then, perhaps aware of looking far too cheery, she shows a sympathetic frown and pats the bed beside her. "For now, my dear, I think you need more sleep."

Hank gets up at nine, dresses, drinks a cup of coffee, kisses Fiona and hurries to the lake. Analu has finished with her swim, is about to leave. She drops her pack as he walks up, seems to know it's not good news.

Hank searches for the words. His friend waits until he's ready. But he will never be ready, not for this. "Fiona's dying."

They sit down on the beach. The solemn message, now out of his head and into the open, makes the world feel less solid. Everything looks unreal. The earth seems to sink beneath him, like a slowly deepening hole. A hole he cannot get out of. And Hank accepts that. Yeah, sure, he's sad, but not afraid. Perhaps because of Fiona's bravery and sense of humor, he finds solace in his grief. "She wants a party."

Analu stares at him. He explains and she smiles. "Good for her. Please, amigo, let me do the planning."

A welcome consolation. "Yeah," he says, "okay."

"I'll tell Aakesh," she says. "If you can do the drinks, we'll take care of all the food."

"Thanks."

Analu hugs him, then picks up her pack. *Hasta pronto.*

"Hasta pronto," Hank calls out as she leaves.

He stands in the shallows, makes a slight but reverent bow and dives in, enlivened by the cold water. The cyanobacteria is there but does not upset him. He won't let it, will stay under as long as possible, because here, by some unknown magic, Hank Solter ceases to exist, becomes a part of this nameless miracle. Happens every time. Soon, however, his lungs in need of air, he surfaces, aware of being human, small and insignificant again. A tiny speck beneath the endless sky.

Hank closes his eyes, hears lanchas motoring their way to lakeside villages. And beyond the beach, above the whitewashed chalets, the twisty road to Santa Catarina rumbles with morning traffic. How different this place would be without the noise of people, with only music of the lake.

Again he ducks underwater. Again wishes he could stay. Again runs out of air.

Hank swims to shore, plops on his butt in the shallows and luxuriates for several minutes in the morning sunshine. He gets dressed and walks the half hour into town, straight to Irma's house. As with María, they kiss each other's cheeks. Then she holds his hands. "Something is wrong."

He nods.

Irma nods with him, as if instantly knowing the whole story. So many years with María has made her a wise woman too. "Dear Fiona."

At home he finds her sleeping. Nunca jumps from the bed and shoots out the door. Hank takes off his clothes, climbs in next to Fiona. She snuggles up without a word.

Later, he wakes up groggy, like he's been drugged. He hears barking, happy barking, which is soothing, like a thick, warm blanket, and seems to gently hold him down.

"Must be Orlando."

"What?" He opens his eyes, sees Fiona putting on her robe, heading for the door.

"You keep sleeping," she says. "The boy and I, we need some minutes to ourselves."

As if commanded, Hank drops back to sleep, like a great falling, deep and dark. Then something shakes him. Something in his mind, something he cannot see. He doesn't know what it is, only that he has to move, has to get up *now!*

He puts on his clothes, still barefoot, and goes outside. Fiona and Orlando are at the garden table. The boy is looking downward, a hand over his eyes, sobbing.

Hank looks at Fiona and whispers, "Anything I can do?"

"No, we're…it's okay." She reaches out and touches the boy's knee. "Not an easy thing to hear, that's all."

Orlando squeezes her hand tight. He won't let go, and can't stop crying.

Nothing more to say.

For the next two days, after a morning swim, Hank keeps the house clean but spends most of his time in the garden. Lots of weeding. Lots of picking up after Nunca. Fiona wants things nice for her "Death and Dying Party." By Saturday morning the whole place looks great. Vicente phones to say that he can't make it, needs to lead a Maya ceremony in the mountains. Fiona is not surprised, already knew he was very busy. But all the others on her list have said they'd come.

Aakesh called Hank yesterday—for them a typical phone conversation.

"Hey, man," said his old friend, "you okay?"

"Yeah."

"Yeah?"

"Yeah. You'll be here, right?"

"Of course *right*. Wouldn't miss it for the world."

"Love you."

"Love you too."

At a quarter till *high noon*, Concepción arrives with a gallon of Rosa de Jamaica. Pedro, her oldest brother, carries it from his truck into the house. He puts it on the kitchen counter, hugs Fiona, says he's *siempre disponible, always available,* should she ever need his help. He looks stricken.

Fiona rests her hands on his shoulders. "Pedro?"

"*Sí, amiga?*"

"Please don't worry. For me this is not so hard, but very private." Her voice is gentle, yet direct. "It may sound strange, but I want only the family and my closest friends to know. You must promise to keep this secret, all right?"

"Yes, all right, I promise."

She smiles, pats his chest, then turns to Concepción, who nods her understanding. Hank is relieved. Though Guatemalans love to gossip, same as most everyone else on the planet, when asked to keep something private, they do—their word to be taken seriously, like an oath.

Pedro leaves just as Analu shows up in a tuk-tuk. The driver, for the few quetzales she probably paid him, carries a large bowl of fruit salad toward the house. Concepción comes out and directs him to the garden table.

Fiona is right behind her, armed with a pile of plates. She looks good, almost like she's enjoying this, and turns to Hank with a playful scowl. "So, Señor, *where* do we sit?"

Sit? Oh, shit. "Sorry," he says, "I'm on it." He might have had the circle ready, has no idea why he didn't. Some part of him must be wishing that this day, this impossibly sad meeting, would not happen.

Hank hurries to the new garden, grabs the special lounge chair he'd bought Fiona and puts it by the fire pit. Then, as they'd discussed, he places the house's four table chairs—plus two folding chairs from the shed—around the shallow ash-filled hole. Seven seats. Just enough, since Vicente will not be here. With great care, he spaces them an equal distance from each other. *No, wait...*a few are directly in the sunlight. That won't be comfortable. He moves some back into the shade, adjusts the angle of others, away from the glaring light, then realizes, like a door slamming him in the face, that the sun does not stand still, that there is no way to evade it. *Idiot!* He moves the chairs back to how they'd been, sits in one and shakes his head.

"Looks like you need advice."

227

It's Aakesh, standing over by the gate. Seems he's been there awhile, maybe watching as Hank fussed around with the chairs. "Only if it's good."

"That's all I got," says his friend, who walks up and whispers in his ear: "Re…fucking…lax."

Hank sighs. "Yeah."

"Nothing you can do."

"I know."

Aakesh stands back and smiles. "Except, of course, whatever must be done, which is what?"

"That would be to *wait*," says Hank, "as wise men will, for women to decide."

"Exactly."

And right on cue here comes Analu. "Can you two *machos* lend a hand?"

"Absolutely," says Aakesh.

Fiona wants the fire pit covered, has decided to use her large round Maya symbol of The Jaguar, made of red clay, that hangs on the living room wall. This is a fragile piece of art and "must be handled," she says, "like your own beloved mother."

The two old men—neither of whom had beloved mothers—gawp at the obligation, then carry the thing outside. With utmost care they place it atop the bricks that surround the pit.

Chero, the forty-year-old restaurant owner who has known Fiona since he was a teenager, arrives on his motorcycle with a large bag of pupusas, a special order paid for by Aakesh. She comes from the house to thank him. He holds her hands and says a few quiet words. Chero has no idea what this party is about, is simply glad to see her. They kiss each other's cheeks and off he goes.

Then comes Irma and María through the open gateway. Irma has made custard with a topping of mangos. "This does not like the heat," she says, and hurries off to the fridge.

María holds her hands out for Fiona, and slowly, ceremoniously, kisses both her cheeks.

"Te extraño tanto," Fiona says. *I miss you so much.*

"Pues, querida," says María, *"ya estoy."* *Well, dear, here I am.*

Her words resonate like a promise, say far more than what is obvious. She is here, and always will be. Hank knows that's what she means. Fiona's tearful nod shows that she knows too.

Concepción brings out the Rosa de Jamaica, now in a glass container with lots of ice. Analu unwraps the pupusas. She puts them on a large central plate, along with the fermented cabbage, red sauce and chile garnishes.

"All right," Fiona says, "let's eat!"

After lunch, they sit in the circle around the Maya Jaguar. The sky has decided to cooperate, the sun's strong light blocked by thick white clouds, and Nunca helps out as well, lies under the garden table and is quiet.

"I thank you all for being here," says Fiona. She speaks in Spanish, slowly, so María feels included. "For quite awhile I have been sick with cancer. I tried hard to make it go away, I truly did, but it is time to let death take me. And I swear to you, I am not afraid. I don't know what is coming, but I…I trust that, like this wonderful life I've lived, it will be a great *adventure."*

She seems aware of how strange that must sound. Closes her eyes and takes some long deep breaths. Hank feels almost happy, soothed by the calmness in her face. He looks across at Concepción. Does this devout Christian woman ponder how her friend——in the grip of death, with no belief in God or heaven—can radiate such peace?

"I know we all think differently about life," Fiona says. "And, I admit, I don't know much. Only that…that I am lucky to know each of you." She smiles again. Everyone smiles with her, all choked up, but at the same time, Hank senses, relieved by this simple way to show their love. That's enough for now. Private words will be shared in private. "Bueno," says Fiona. "Now I need to ask a favor." Her eyes have lost their luster. She looks down at the Maya Jaguar. It signifies inner strength, which must be what she's hoping for right now.

She takes another breath, slumps forward, grips the sides of her lounge chair with both hands. Hank stiffens. Fiona glances at him, gives her head a slight shake and straightens up.

"Anything," says Concepción.

"Whatever you need," says Analu.

"At lunch," Fiona says, "I said I wasn't hungry. The thing is, I've stopped eating. And only drinking water. That will keep me going for awhile. There are still things I want to do." They all watch her closely, focused on every breath. "Vicente tells me this won't take long. A few weeks, more or less."

"We're here when you need us," says Irma.

"Thank you," says Fiona. "And especially to Enrique, for being with me every day."

Concepción stifles a rush of tears, looks down into her lap.

So does Irma.

Fiona laughs. "Come on, amigas, we can't let this get too heavy. It's only death, right Aakesh?"

He laughs with her. "Happens to the best of us."

"Right," she says, and opens her eyes wide. "Not my idea of fun, but hey, what's a girl to do?"

"You're doing good," says Aakesh.

She smiles, breaths, and waits some seconds for emotions to calm down. "What I want...what I need for my best good bye, is for all of us to be joyful!"

"*Sí,*" says María, "*todo tiempo es ahora.*" *All time is now.*

Fiona nods and looks at Concepción. "Okay?"

"*Sí...okay.*"

"Thank you," says Fiona, and retrieves a piece of paper from a pocket in her skirt. "I have a schedule—hours when I'm hoping to have time with each of you. If we need to change it, no problem. You tell me." She looks at the paper. "Most important is early morning, when Enrique is at the lake." Fiona leans forward in her chair. "Truth be told," she says, her voice low and conspiratorial, "he gets damn grouchy without a swim."

"Hah!" cries Aakesh, and the others all laugh with him.

230

She shakes her head like a disgruntled mother. "He'll also need a break in the early evening, before my pain pill, because I can get even grouchier."

There's a bit more laughter. Then it gets deathly silent. Nearly a minute passes.

"And times like this, of quiet, are also good. I mean it, just like this." Again the silence. Fiona looks at everyone in the circle, takes in every face. "I've learned to truly love it. No one has to entertain me. There's really not much to say, so I don't need to talk. I only want...just want you to be with me. That okay?" They all nod. "Good," she says. "Thank you. Now I... I have to rest."

She reaches out for Hank, who gets up and leads her back to bed. Now under the covers she signals him to get close. "I was wrong. Orlando should have been here."

"Yes."

"He needs to see, to...he doesn't have to be afraid."

Hank kisses her on the forehead. "No, he doesn't."

"Please, from now on, I want him close."

"Okay."

He goes to the garden table. The schedule has been filled out, everyone now packing up to leave. Still, they linger, in no hurry, and in hushed voices say to call if he ever needs them.

One by one they say goodbye and he's alone. Well, no, there is Nunca. Perhaps upset by being shut out of the house, away from Fiona, the dog heads for his spot out under the mango tree. Hank follows and lies down next to him.

The first few days are difficult for Fiona. Serious talks with Analu and Concepción, and perhaps too many kisses from María. Each wants to let her know how important she is in their lives. Most difficult of all is not seeing Orlando. She'd told him to visit anytime after Saturday, but he hasn't. She'd made him promise to keep her coming death a secret, except from his parents, and regrets how she'd handled that. Why else would he stay away? He'd cried hardest after promising, as if only then aware she would soon be gone.

This afternoon, following a tearful visit from Irma, Fiona turns to Hank with a wry grin. "An emotional rollercoaster," she says. "I must admit, I won't mind getting off."

Is he supposed to laugh at the gallows humor? Well, he won't. Changes the subject. These days are also difficult for him. Especially in the evenings when he's tired. As Fiona had requested, Analu has come at sunset to give Hank a break. The thing is, he doesn't want or need a break—only agreed because the two old friends also need time together. He's gone down to the promenade, sat on an empty bench and gazed out at the water—a forced meditation—until the allotted hour was up.

On the afternoon of day four, as Hank pulls weeds in a flower patch, Orlando shows up. Hank knows by the steady gentle knock. So does Nunca, napping on the porch, who now whines, perks up his ears and charges to the gate.

"Okay, fella, take it easy."

The dog sits, cannot stop squirming, and as the door swings open he bolts out through the opening, jumps against his friend's chest and knocks him to the ground. The two roll around in the dirt. Hank stands back and lets it happen. If only a few years younger, he'd be right down there with them.

They go into the garden, Hank closes the gate, and here comes Fiona. "Orlando!" After a long embrace, she stands back, hands on hips, and gives the boy a fake parental glare. "Okay, Señor, tell us where you have been?"

"I *have been* an excellent son."

"That I believe, but where?"

"At home."

"And what," she says, "made you so excellent?"

"After school I helped my papa work on our house. He's building us a new roof."

That news melts away her stern mask. Fiona glows. "Well, I bet your mother is very happy."

"Yes," Orlando says, *"very* happy. She and my papa both."

"The roof is finished?"

"Almost. He can do the rest himself, told me to come see if you might need some help."

Fiona lifts a joyful fist into the air. *"Yes!"*

Orlando's visits lift her spirits. Some days go by, and they spend lots of time together. Still, she often seems tired, and quite fragile, which might be something only Hank can see. Fiona tries not to show it, always says she's feeling fine.

Then one night she phones Irma. Hank stops reading his book and listens in. "I'm calling because you don't have to come tomorrow."

As she waits for a reply he feels himself starting to worry, figures this has to be bad news.

"No," Fiona tells her, "everything is good. I'll see you and María on Saturday."

When finished, she clicks off the phone and looks at him. He puts down his book. "What's up?"

"What's up," she says matter-of-factly, "is I won't need anyone here tomorrow morning."

He tries to not look upset, only confused. "Which means I won't be going to the lake?"

"No, of course you will! And—*surprise, surprise*—so will I!" Fiona lights up at his genuinely startled face and tells what she's been planning. She'd sent Gregorio on a hunt for one of those floaty rings that kids use when they're learning how to swim. Some friend got permission from his daughter to loan out hers. That was a few days ago. Since then, Fiona has gotten daily updates from Analu about the lake. "The last Norte, she told me, has made the water pristine and glassy."

"It's absolutely beautiful."

Fiona grins from ear to ear. *"Ya pues, Pancho,* a perfect time for me to make a splash!"

Hank smiles at her excitement. "Wow! Okay! Gregorio is coming to pick us up?"

"Will be here at eight."

Sounds like a wonderful plan to him. *"A sus órdenes, Señorita!"*

Gregorio is out front at eight sharp, complete with a beach umbrella and the floaty ring. Hank gets into the tuk-tuk first. He takes Fiona's hands and carefully guides her in. Then they're off. She requests that they take the roughest route, across the river shallows down by the shoreline, because she wants to see the lake right away. They turn onto the bumpy, pot-holed gravel road, the lake suddenly in view, spread out before them like the marvel that it is. "Oh, my god, so gorgeous," Fiona says between blissful sobs. "Oh my god." After crossing the river, its pungent stink a sobering interruption of her joy, they continue up to the wide pathway above the shore. She takes a deep breath, a look of ecstasy returning to her face. "It's like I've always been here."

Hank knows exactly what she means, the same feeling he gets every time he swims.

They pass the evangelicals, busy preparing for their daily prayer. Vendors put out their wares, the smell of frying corn tortillas fills the air, and Fiona, who misses nothing, smiles as if it's all been arranged for her. She asks Gregorio to slow down even more. They proceed at a walking pace and gaze out at the lake. Some people wave at her and she waves back. The sun has reached the water from over the eastern mountains, highlighting its glossy sheen. "Oh," says Fiona, "look!" She points to an egret on the bow of a lancha, the sleek white bird like a built-in mascot, an ideal image of purity and grace.

They park at the end of the narrow dirt roadway.

Hank helps Fiona out of the tuk-tuk, then puts on his pack. He gives Gregorio the umbrella and the floaty and puts his arm around her shoulder. "If you carry the toys, amigo, I'll manage the woman."

She laughs, shakes herself loose and takes off without him. "Don't worry, sonny boy, I'll make it on my own."

He expected that, and quickly catches up, Gregorio right behind them. She moves carefully, nice and slow. There are just a few places where she needs help. Gregorio then goes ahead, deposits the gear on the beach while Hank guides Fiona down the final short descent.

When at last on flat ground, and obviously taxed, she stops. "No one said life would be easy."

"Ah," says Gregorio, apparently familiar with the tired old phrase, and lifts a prophetic finger. "True," he says in English, "and we are...how you say it?...*blessed*, yes, very *blessed* to have this problem we cannot fix."

Hank smirks. "Yeah, says who?"

"*JESÚS!* That's why we need HIM, our holy father!" Gregorio juts out his chest like a proud, obedient son. He is the one Guatemalan they know who loves to make fun of Christianity. "The pastor tells us, over and over, that this life might not be so hard if we do everything HE orders."

Fiona chortles, waves off the silly joke and walks with stiff determination to the lake. She hesitates at the shoreline, then

235

flops down on her butt like a little kid, removes her sandals, scoots forward and sticks her feet in the water. "Whoa is me!"

"Is cold," says Gregorio, "yes?"

"Oh yes, very cold." She turns to him. "This will take some time, amigo. Can you please come back and get us in an hour?"

"I see you then," he says, and leaves.

Now the place is theirs, that's how it feels. Fiona strips to her bathing suit, Hank to his skivvies, and they sit shoulder to shoulder, gazing at the sparkling water. She spots Analu swimming, already a hundred yards from shore. "It must feel great to be way out there."

"Hey," says Hank, "this water right here is every bit as great."

"Ya think?"

"I know."

"Bueno, let's get in it!"

Hank stands and holds out both hands. She takes them, rises slowly to her feet, then steps into the shallows, up to her knees, and waits as he retrieves the floaty, slides it over her head and shoulders, down to her waist. "Okay, girl, you ready?"

He assumes, as in the past, this will begin her lengthy ritual of resistance. Fiona has an intense aversion to cold water, cannot bear it without a big dose of persuasion. So he's shocked when she doesn't hesitate for a second, lunges out into the lake with a high-pitched squeal, flops down with a buoyant bounce. *"Oh, fuck me, it's freezing!"*

Hank dives in. From beneath he gives her ass a pinch. When he comes up she splashes him squarely in the face. A direct hit. The water shot into his nose and down his throat. He takes hold of the floaty, tries to blow and cough the liquid out.

"Oh, geez, I'm sorry," Fiona says, her hand on his. "Honey, are you okay? Hank?"

At last he gets a decent breath. "Could not be better." He sees that she is shivering. "Too cold, huh?"

"No, it's…exactly what I want, but I can't stay in for long."

"Amazing you're in at all."

"Yeah," she says," so here's the deal. You stay here and hold the ring while I go under."

"What?"

"Just for a sec."

"No, no, wait, I—"

Then she's gone. He twists to his right, looks down and finds her, follows her descent—not far away, but for more seconds than he'd expect. It's plain how much she loves the water. Same as him, won't come up till she has to. *Oh no, oh shit.* Hank holds his breath, at once bewildered, afraid that Fiona might have planned this, too. She doesn't want to die in a house over the course of weeks or months, does not want her life sung out like some sad dirge. No, hell no, she'd much rather it be today—right here, right now—in this glorious water! His heart has begun to pound. Then she pops up on the other side of the ring, grabs hold of it and hollers, *"Increíble!"*

Hank exhales.

Fiona blinks and looks him in the eye. "What, you were thinking I might stay under?"

"The thought did cross my mind."

"I wouldn't do that to you, Hank. Sure, this is where I'd choose to be, but I know that can't happen."

He's relieved to hear her say it, and also sees she's tired. "Should we go in?"

"Yeah, I've had enough."

"Okay." He paddles them to shore, gets their towels out of his pack. They lie down in the sun, and, as is usual for him, time ceases to exist. There is only this warm and hypnotic air, the sublime feel of it drying his chilled skin.

Sometime later—perhaps ten minutes but who knows?—she sits up, reaches over and holds his hand. He sits up too. Her eyes have waited for his to find them. "Want to hear a story?"

"I don't know," he says, "am I going to like it?"

"I think you might love it."

"Well, then, darlin', I'm all ears."

"It's kind of like your novels, Hank. Never to be finished."

"My favorite kind, does it have a name?"

"Yes. 'Air.' Best name I can think of."

"Okay, I'm ready, tell me."

She smiles and lets go of his hand. Closes her eyes. A few seconds later they open, their blue brilliance cranked way up, and he feels pulled into her vision, could not turn away even if he wanted to. "In this story," Fiona says, "I am living my final day. And know it. Though aware that death was close I'm now astounded it's really here."

She takes a long deep breath and he breathes with her.

"My mind, once so dependable, now does whatever it wants. There are piles of mixed-up memories everywhere I look. And I'm fine with that. It's kind of fun to see what childish mess I'll be finding next, because none of it matters, does not affect me in the least. I now see life as an adventure. Each moment comes, stays, seems to last forever, then is gone, replaced by something else. And all of it is amazing. I feel no pain or fear, feel thankful for every moment, and very lucky." She playfully bats her eyelids and throws her hands into the air. "Good story, right, if that's the way it goes?"

"I love you, Fiona."

"I love you, too. And, before my mind goes off too far, you need to know how much."

He nods. "I know."

"Good." She pauses for a second, seems to be thinking, trying to relocate where she was. "Okay, let me finish. What happens is, *poco a poco,* I lose track of myself, of who I am." She laughs. "Because everything is way more interesting than me!" She grabs his hands and squeezes them. "What I love most is to feel air against my face. Ah, the amazing air, and the things it touches, everywhere around me. Even things I can't see. And the sounds I could not hear without it. The constant music. When I listen closely, very closely, that's all there is. Music. I breathe it in. I breathe it out. The world and I have joined together, and we're moving, like on a journey to some place I've never been."

She lets go of his hands, closes her eyes, seems to go way inside. Hank can feel it. Something important—essential—has changed, and he knows to hold the silence.

"Then, all of a sudden, I have no body, and I'm aware of that. Somehow observing that. Aware there is no longer any *me*. Whatever I was keeps changing, almost timelessly transforming. Like each and every thing that dies, I'm now slowly turning into dust, smaller and smaller bits of dust, at last a dust so fine that I pass through the world unnoticed, the wind picking me up and whisking me around until finally I have no form at all, I'm only air. Just lovely, eternal, air."

Fiona opens her eyes and looks at Hank.

Mesmerized, it takes a second before he's able to respond. "Is that the end?"

"No, silly." She smiles. "Because, same as in your stories, there is no end."

"Sounds like a dream."

"Yep, that's how I see it. A wonderful dream, and endless, which is why I'm in no hurry."

Hank is relieved by her humor and obvious sense of peace, which must mean death still feels far away. "Good."

"No hurry, I mean, in becoming air. That will take many years. First, of course, comes dirt."

Hank blinks, confused. "I'm sorry, I...you lost me."

"We've always agreed on cremation."

He nods.

"Sorry, I've changed my mind. I don't know, maybe being burned reminds me too much of the Christian Hell." Fiona titters like an anxious child and waves away the vision. "Ugh, no. What I want, truly want, is to be buried in the ground."

"Oh."

She reaches over, holds his trembling hands, gives them a soothing squeeze. "You okay?"

"Yeah."

"Not easy to hear."

He shakes his head. "No."

"Or to say. But I need you to understand."

He doesn't, and cannot pretend. *What is she thinking?* Sad, but true, no one gets buried anymore in Pana. There's no room left in the tiny cemetery, she knows that. These days, to conserve space, the dead get put in coffins and stacked, one atop the other, in concrete tombs. "Buried where?"

"In our garden."

"What?"

Again Fiona squeezes his hands and smiles. "Yeah, I know, it's illegal." Her face turns serious. "But you could do it."

"Yes, I, I guess I could, but—"

"Please, Hank." Her eyes are clear, her voice gentle and calm. "Please, that's where I want to be."

It's like their entire life together was lived for this very second. "You sure?"

"I'm sure." She shows her impish grin. "First I'll feed the worms and nurture flowers. In time, who cares how much, I'll get to the air through them."

32

New Flowers

For another week everything went fine. Irma and María came in the mornings, Orlando and Concepción in the afternoons, Analu and/or Aakesh in the early evenings. The rest of the time it was Hank and Fiona by themselves, which for him felt like a living dream. They spent many hours cuddled up in bed, sometimes talking and sometimes quiet, either awake or asleep together, side by side.

Then, within a couple of days, she slowly began to slip away, showed no real interest in conversation, or anything else, including her garden.

"My mind is fading," she said one morning.

"Fading how?" said Hank. Though a well-intentioned question, a chance to reconnect, it made her cry. "No, please, never mind," he said, and held her close, gently rocked her until she fell asleep. From that moment on he would not leave.

A few nights ago Fiona turned to him and whispered, "It's like my story. Remember, Hank? My story?"

"Sure, honey, I remember."

As Fiona gets weaker, now mostly unaware of their comings and goings, her circle of friends gather more often at the house. Except at night, there is always at least one other person along with Hank, who stays patiently by her side, his heart yearning for any word.

And at times she seems to summon his attention. She might stare at him, as if the look alone should say what he needs to hear. But when it doesn't, and he must try, with his sad eyes, to say he's sorry, say he does not understand, Fiona goes back into her own world.

This morning Hank feels distracted—at odds with himself, does not know why—and keeps pacing between the living room and the kitchen. It's ten o'clock. Irma and María have been here for two hours, and seem rattled by his chaotic, hovering energy. They urge him to go take a swim. Just a short break for his own well-being. He refuses, stays fixated on Fiona, on full alert, determined to be near in case he's needed.

Sitting against the bed's backrest, she looks at him and sighs. Then, with obvious effort, she leans forward from her pillow, an unmistakable sign that she wants to speak.

He gets close and bends toward her. "Yes, I'm listening."

Fiona whispers something he cannot understand, her eyebrows pinched and her voice strained. Then, slowly but quite clearly, she says, "the...lake."

María, standing behind him, taps his shoulder. "She knows."

Hank stays with Fiona's eyes. "You mean I should go?"

She blinks, then leans back and shuts her eyes.

"Yeah," he says, "okay."

The lake still has its early morning sheen. Hank crosses the river to Jucanyá. He hurries past the throng of evangelicals, does not give them a single thought, and soon is on his beloved beach. Goes to the exact spot where Fiona had told her story about air. Remembers almost every word. It's as if she's right there with him, telling it again.

He dives in, swims down and comes close to a patch of paxte. A large black bass, not common this close to shore, emerges from the vine. It sees him, then retreats into the gnarly plant. Paxte, for the fish, is not a deathtrap but a sanctuary. The only scary thing is this old man. Hank smiles and feels himself relax, had not realized how tense he was.

He glides up to the surface, swims to shore, sits on his butt in the shallows and looks at the bright blue sky. Savors every second. Fiona would love to be here, right where air and water meet. He imagines her beside him. Feels her close.

Okay, time to go.

The thought comes like a stern command.

Hank gets home a few minutes before noon, refreshed and excited to be back. When he enters the garden, however, something feels off-kilter. Ahead, Nunca whines and scratches at the front door. Does not even look his way. He closes the gate and locks it. Leans against the wall. Above, the sun suddenly disappears, enveloped by a churning bank of clouds.

Hank walks with trepidation to the house.

Inside, on the couch, are María, Irma, and Concepción. They all look stunned, their teary eyes focused on Fiona.

"She won't wake up," says Irma.

Nunca jumps on the bed, bounds to Fiona and licks her face. Hank grabs the pup, puts him outside and shuts the door, then sits next to her. She has a pulse, but does not respond to his words or touch. He sees she is nearly gone.

"Please, we need to be alone."

He doesn't care if his words sound selfish or insensitive. Should she regain consciousness, even for an instant, he needs that time just for them, wants nothing to distract from their final moments together.

Concepción says they should call a doctor.

Hank shakes his head. "No."

María smiles at him and turns to Irma. *"Vámonos."*

They stand. Irma follows the old woman out the door.

Concepción stays put. "Can we talk?"

"Not now, amiga. Please."

She wipes at her wet eyes. Without another word she leaves, and closes the door behind her. Nunca scratches it and whines.

After a minute, Hank goes outside, leans down and caresses the puppy's head. "It's okay, bud, it's okay." He fills his bowls with food and water. The dog plows in, perhaps hasn't eaten since last night. Hank goes back into the house, leaves the door open, gets on the bed and cuddles up to Fiona. He lays his head over her heart, its beat far too quiet and irregular.

Later, who knows when, he hears that familiar soft knock on the gate. Orlando. Such a patient knock. Or maybe it's just a dream, because Nunca doesn't bark.

Hank opens his eyes, sees he's lying on his back between Fiona and the dog. Damn, he thinks, I fell asleep! How could I fall asleep? Again he lays his head onto her chest, relieved that she's still with him, and he's determined to stay awake. He breathes with her, slowly, in and out, treasuring every second, right until those final, harsh, involuntary gasps.

Her chest quivers as she passes, as she joins her blessed air.

Hank lets his tears come. For a long time. After they stop, he smiles and kisses her on the lips. "Good for you, sweetheart. Good for you."

Nunca jumps from the bed and runs out the door. The sudden action surprises Hank, and somehow helps him breathe, and think, and realize what must be done. He kisses Fiona's forehead and gets his phone. It's five o'clock. He calls Concepción, who says she will call the others.

Within an hour they are gathered in the garden. All except Vicente and Orlando. The shaman is on his way from some village in the mountains. Irma, who knows where Orlando lives, heads off to fetch him. Hank says to also bring Fidel. And his shovel. He takes the rest of them into the new garden, to the spot, in the shade of Señor Mocún's mango tree, where Fiona wants to be.

"What a beautiful way to remember her beauty," says Aakesh.

María kneels down, bends over and kisses the earth, then murmurs something in Cakchiquel.

Analu joins the old woman on the ground. "I will feel happy, every day, thinking of her here."

Concepción crouches next to them, closes her eyes and intones, with great solemnity, some Christian prayer. Though she is not in favor of this burial in the garden, mainly because it is illegal, Hank feels her genuine support. She prays for several minutes. He lays his hands on her trembling shoulders and gently comforts her while she sobs.

Irma arrives with Orlando and Fidel. The boy goes straight to Hank, throws his arms around him.

The whole group circles and is silent, holding hands. The sun, which has found a crack in the blackened clouds, balances a few more seconds above the western wall and then, like a heavy stone, drops out of sight.

The Xocomil suddenly grows stronger, charges haphazardly through the trees, shakes their branches, flaps their leaves, chatters like a mischievous child who cannot be controlled. The wind's disruptive nature, especially at such a somber moment, strikes Hank as ironic. He can see Fiona smiling.

"Bueno," he says. "All that happens, including things we do not understand, is in honor of our dear friend."

Everyone nods, then moves. The women go in unison to the house. They will wash Fiona's body, massage it with fragrant oils and clothe it in her beloved Guatemalan *corte*—handmade fabric she has treasured for many years—now laid aside to be her burial gown. The men will prepare the grave. That includes Orlando, who wants to help any way he can. His main job, of course, is to keep Nunca occupied and out of trouble.

Fiona chose a spot far enough from the mango tree to avoid its roots. The area must first be cleared of the flowers she'd seeded a month ago, a few days before deciding this as her resting place. The tender plants are carefully removed and put in separate pots. Orlando gives each a splash of water.

Hank marks out the exact dimension of the hole: three feet wide by eight feet long.

"*Listo?*" asks Fidel, who has stood patiently to the side while Hank made sure of what he wanted.

"*Sí, amigo, listo.*"

Fidel digs in the center of the marked-off space. Hank, with the hoe, makes a clean-line ditch to define its perimeter.

The excavated dirt goes in the wheelbarrow and Aakesh dumps it about ten feet off to the side. An hour later Vicente arrives, takes over for whoever needs a break. Dusk slowly settles in. From time to time they all pause to rest, sit on the ground and gulp down water. At some point Irma brings out a bowl of guacamole and a basket of hot tortillas.

Night washes over them as they work. Orlando aims the flashlight as directed, until the hole reaches six feet deep. "Good enough," says Hank—one of Fiona's favorite sayings. He sets down his shovel and starts for the house, followed by the others.

Inside, lying on the bed, her lower body is wrapped in layers of corte. Above it, she has on her most cherished *huipil,* from Nebaj. Fiona's head, as she'd requested, is uncovered, her face like a porcelain vase, its features painted by a steady, loving hand.

Hank glances at Orlando, who seems fine. The boy looks at him with a sad smile.

Vicente, speaking Cakchiquel, imparts a traditional Maya prayer. He finishes, nods, and the women lead the way, each with a candle. Following them, the men carry Fiona—Hank and Fidel on one side, Vicente and Aakesh on the other. Orlando shines the flashlight from behind. Nunca stays with him.

Everyone stops by the mango tree. The women set down their candles and cover the grave with a large piece of corte—four smaller pieces sewn into one—that extends out from its center and onto the ground, at least three feet in all directions. Then they make space for the men, who kneel onto the fabric and lay Fiona directly above the grave. The weight of her body makes the corte dip, but the men's collective bulk easily supports it. Carefully they inch backwards, allowing her to slowly sink beneath the surface. Once she's down a couple of feet they take hold of the corte and manage the final descent. The remaining fabric settles on top of her like a veil.

Concepción and Analu sit cross-legged at one end of the grave, María and Irma at the other. The men light candles of their own and sit on either side of its length. Orlando joins them, Nunca calm in his loving grasp.

Then, as Fiona had wished, Vicente offers her most adored Maya blessing: "Please accept me, sacred beings, who live forever in my new home. Let us be in harmony together."

After a moment of silence, Concepción clears her throat. "Amigos," she says, then again goes silent, needs a few seconds to recover. "Amigos," she repeats, her voice still shaky, "you must know that none of us can speak of this." She is looking down into the grave. "Not to anyone outside this circle. *Anyone.* To protect Fiona, and Enrique, this has to remain our secret. Please say *yes* if you agree."

Everyone nods and earnestly says yes.

Hank feels their attention turn to him.

"I am thankful," he says, "to all of you for…for being here, with me, to see our dear friend off on her new journey. Each of you is aware, because you feel her, that Fiona is here with us. Always will be, that was her promise. A blessing we all share." He pauses. Breathes. "She told me there is no end. She was certain, and I believe it."

He takes a handful of dirt and sprinkles it down on top of her. The rest do the same, and then each helps to fill the hole. They make it slightly mounded on top—as she would like—and the same flowers are planted again, like new.

33
Locked In

Everyone is exhausted. They wish Hank a good night and go home. Missing Fiona, he lies on the bed, head on her pillow. With Nunca beside him he falls asleep. She and the dog wander through his many dreams. He wakes to a bright blue morning, his mind clouded by a sense of doom, random memories and half-baked thoughts, a haunted cosmos he wants no part of.

He can't believe she's gone.

Gone? Some part of his mind insists she is, that he is now alone, must live in the world without her. Ideas that deeply trouble him. *As they should!* says Fiona. She feels close, just out of sight, and for the moment is upset with his hopeless thinking.

Hank falls asleep again, sometime later opening his eyes to a darkened room. And no Nunca.

It's four p.m. He gets up, yawns, then goes outside.

The dog charges him from the new garden, snout caked with dirt, does his silly little shimmy, then runs back toward the mango tree. *Oh shit.* Hank hurries to catch up.

Plants are strewn around, and there is Nunca on the grave, digging away like some demonic excavation tool. Hank lunges, grabs hold of the pliant skin at the back of the puppy's neck, yanks with both hands and heaves him off to the side. Nunca hits the ground with a painful yelp. He scrambles to his feet, tail tucked between his legs, and stares at Hank.

"No! You hear me! No!"

How the hell to handle this? There must be some fucking manual! Should he rub the dog's snout in the dirt and slap it? He doesn't think that's right, but isn't sure. So, not being sure, and overwhelmingly frustrated by his confusion, he steps toward him, perhaps a bit too aggressively, raises his fists and *screams,* tears pouring down his face.

Nunca whines, turns and races for the house.

That's okay with Hank, who is relieved to be alone. He needs to reconstitute the grave, save some of the injured plants, which takes almost an hour. By the time he's finished it all looks fine. At least that's what Fiona tells him.

He lies on his back and gazes into the gray sky. Suddenly, out of nowhere, Nunca licks his face. Hank takes the pup into his arms. "Sorry, pal, not your fault, I understand why you did it." He carries him to the shed, puts him down and retrieves the metal fencing—the same used to keep stray dogs out of their yard before the new walls were built. He blocks off the archway, makes sure Nunca can't get past it, then goes into the house and lies down on the bed.

Nunca jumps up with him. He should clean off those dirty paws, that dirty snout, but doesn't.

In the morning Hank removes the barricade. Then, as if instructed by Fiona, he unwinds the hose and waters her many flowers. It feels like a sacred ritual. He senses her with him, teaching about the garden. Some plants are fragile, she says, and need extra care. He pays close attention, loves learning the little secrets, and does his best, cultivating and mulching, weeding the patches left untended since she became deathly ill. Somewhere inside him, Fiona smiles at his heartfelt effort.

"I understand," Hank says, suddenly emotional, "I really do."

By late that afternoon he and Nunca both need a rest. They lie in the shade of La Pared Mocún, quiet as can be, when the phone starts ringing. Such an obnoxious noise. He pays no attention, and...at last...it stops.

249

Grateful for the reprieve, Hank turns to his side, begins to gently fade, when the phone again starts ringing. This time won't stop. Like some unwanted stranger making havoc in the house. He grumbles, gets up, goes and finds it in the kitchen.

"Hola."

"Enrique, *estás bién?"* It's Concepción. When he does not immediately respond, she repeats the question, now using the English word "okay." Is he *okay?*

Wow, such a vacuous, silly word! He struggles against his mounting irritation.

"Enrique?"

"Yes," he says, "I am."

"Is there anything you need?"

"Nothing I can think of."

"Please, can I come see you?"

Hank senses her deep concern, and just can't face it. There's no room for that right now, no space for other people—only him, Fiona and Nunca. "No, not yet."

She sighs. "What about tomorrow, can I—"

"No, amiga, I'll let you know."

"I worry about you, Enrique."

"I'm doing good, I truly am. And, please, tell the others not to call. Can you do that for me?"

He imagines her rolling eyes, her shaking head. "Yes."

"Gracias, Concepción. Espero que todo esté bién contigo también."

I hope all is good with you also.

"Sí, Enrique, sí."

Hank says good-bye and goes back to the garden, back to his needed silence. Thankful for the locked gate, that no one can disturb him, he lies next to Nunca, and begins to fall asleep, when the phone goes off again, sounds like some screaming banshee. He runs back into the house, wants to smash it with a hammer. Then, as if actually feeling threatened, it stops ringing. *Yeah, uh-huh, all right, but I'm not doing this anymore.* He's so tired of the world's senseless noise!

Besides, he tells himself, there's no longer any reason to have a phone. Someday, maybe, but at least not now. He could turn it off, but can't stand the thought of even having it in the house, like some sort of spy. Yeah, sounds crazy. Hank doesn't care. He puts it in a plastic bag and takes it outside. For later, should the damn thing ever actually be needed, he buries it behind the shed and immediately feels better. Feels safe.

For several days he hardly eats, and almost never speaks. Though at times he thinks of Orlando, wonders how the boy is doing, those kinds of thoughts don't last long. He's too occupied with Nunca. Never leaving each other's side, they communicate by the simplest of means—feelings, movements, gestures—and rarely disagree.

There is no need for words.

Fiona, of course, is with them, always with them, and smiles along with Hank at all the good things he is learning. The dog teaches him a lot, such as to eat only when he's hungry. That ends up one of the easier lessons. More difficult is how to sense the tiny changes happening all around him. While his mind sometimes feels clouded, cannot focus, Nunca seems perpetually aware. His ears perk up at any new sight or smell or sound.

That's how Hank wants to be, for him like a different way of living, where passing thoughts must be ignored, where nothing matters except what happens in the moment. All of it is real, and all worthy of his attention.

He follows the dog around on his hands and knees, doesn't want to miss a thing, and they go slowly around the garden, sniffing whatever attracts their interest. Some odors are so intriguing that both of them take a taste. Hank's limit, where he must draw the line, is with dead animals—sometimes a bird, sometimes a rat.

"Nope," he says to Nunca, one of the few times he ever speaks. "Can't go there, pal. Not yet."

But in the coming days he does go further. The dog has a lot to show him. Is Hank aware that this isn't normal? Oh yeah, for sure, but he's not worried in the least. It feels like he's being guided, by Fiona and Nunca both.

They spend many hours in the garden, usually on the ground. Hank smells every flower, and also the earth itself, the myriad bits of everything it contains. While dead animals continue to repel him, he finds lots of stuff to nibble on: grasses, seeds, twigs and leaves. Strange that he's so happy here, doesn't miss the lake at all. It's as if, like Nunca, like Fiona and her air, the water is always with him.

They sleep outside at night, under the stars. In the daytime, should there be no garden work to do, they play. A favorite game is tag. The dog, much faster and more agile, must slow down and let the old man catch him. Hank sometimes pretends he can't, which is hilarious for Fiona. When *IT,* Nunca acts confounded by Hank's feeble faints and dodges, but does eventually smack him with a paw.

Hank had tried to teach his friend hide and seek. Nunca would lie down, presumably not watching as Hank hid behind the house, or a bush, or tree. The man then clapped and the dog came running, never had a problem finding him, always loved it, but refused—when his turn came—to hide. He always wanted Hank in view and easily within reach.

It took awhile to realize that time does not, in any important way, exist. At least not for Hank. To honor how good he feels, and hoping the goodness never ends, he unplugs the house clock. Ah, how simple, and what a blessing, to be timeless!

Not just that, but to be fine with whatever happens. Even when uncertain what it is! Life plays out, one beat mixing with the next, a melodic oscillation between cloudiness and clarity. Now you see or hear it, now you don't. That's the way it goes.

And more days pass. Hank sleeps a lot, has many dreams, no longer always certain what is real.

Real? That's another word, like *okay,* whose meaning makes him wonder. Wondering about such things is always good, the one type of thought that seems truly honest, that keeps him from pretending he has anything figured out.

His mind has changed. Changed completely. The way he now sees life, it just happens, an ongoing mystery, in and out of dreams. For Hank, all of it is real. One state of consciousness blends into the other. Everything overlaps. Though he has always believed this to be true, it's suddenly undeniable—and while sometimes confused which state he's in, there is no questioning its reality or his need to take careful notice.

Like the other day, when a bird he'd never seen before landed on his garden table. It had a dark shiny crimson body, bright blue feathers and a yellow beak. Was he dreaming or only seeing it for the first time? How could he be sure?

And, more importantly, did it matter?

No. Either way, for him, the beautiful bird was *there*, a true marvel and a gift.

Hank thinks of last night, when he noticed something hover above the house, impossible to describe because it kept spinning around, kept changing shape: a swirling light in the black star-dotted sky. He had not known if it was "actually" there, yet felt certain he had seen it. Even if a figment of his imagination, it was real, some kind of supernatural visitation.

And today, this very minute, in his dream Hank senses another coming. He and Nunca are asleep under the mango tree, with Fiona, when an odd scraping sound wakes him up. It comes from somewhere out in the front yard—not loud, but a most unpleasant noise, more odious than even a ringing phone. *What the hell?* Weird that Nunca does not react, is snoring to beat the band. This must be meant for Hank alone.

Still groggy from his nap, he goes to check it out, is by the house when something drops down from the northern wall. Like a huge cat, Ernie lands upright, in perfect balance, smiles and says, "Guess who?"

Though nothing could be stranger or less believable, Hank is no longer surprised by anything. Mostly, he just feels curious. "Ever since you left I've been expecting that you'd come back."

"Yeah," says Ernie, "because you owe me and have to pay."

"You want money? I don't have much."

"I'll take whatever you got."

"Bueno," says Hank, who, for whatever reason, does not feel the least bit frightened. On the contrary, it seems good to at last take care of this lingering problem. He was, after all, somewhat responsible for Ernie's sad demise, so why not help him if he can? To give a bit of money would be an easy way to handle the situation. He goes into the house, finds almost a hundred dollars worth of quetzales hidden in the secret pouch beneath his rug, comes back outside and hands it over.

Ernie stares at the thin stack of bills, unimpressed. "You're shitting me, right?"

Then Nunca charges them, honed in on their intruder, barking up a storm.

Somehow knowing Ernie has a gun, Hank gives the dog a stern look and lowers both his hands—a gesture Nunca understands. He slides to a hasty halt, sits on his haunches and awaits further instructions.

"Smart animal," says Ernie. "Would be a damn shame if I have to kill him."

The dog growls.

"Please," says Hank, "take the money and leave us alone."

"Well, no, not so fast," says Ernie. "Truth is, after pondering our issue for the past month, I've come to a startling conclusion! It's not your money I want, it's to fuck your life up the way you fucked up mine."

"I don't understand."

"Well, old man, you will." He points toward the new garden. "Turns out, as you well know, it's illegal to bury your girlfriend wherever the hell you want. Soon as I find a way to tell Aldamo, he'll come and find out where you're hiding her."

Hank wonders how Ernie could know about Fiona, but there's no time to think it through. Nor any need. "Why risk trying to fuck me up? I'm really not worth the trouble."

"No?" Ernie smirks. "Why not?"

"Because I don't care what happens. I'm not afraid of you anymore. Neither is Fiona."

Ernie grins. "We'll see about that, you crazy fucker."

Nunca leans his way, teeth bared.

Ernie pulls a pistol from his jacket. "All right, asshole," he says to Hank, "time you let me out. "

"Sure, no problem." Hank reaches into his pants pocket and grabs the key. "Come on, pal," he says to Nunca.

Ernie follows a few paces behind, waits for Hank to remove the lock and open the gate. "Okay," he says, "if you don't want me to shoot the pooch, tell him to back off."

Seeing he means it, Hank points toward the house. "Go on, boy, go!" Nunca whines. Obviously displeased, he reluctantly backs away several steps.

Ernie pushes Hank out onto the callejón, slams the gate closed behind him, looks immediately at ease. Even somewhat friendly. "Come to think of it, pal, I do have advice for you."

Though knowing not to trust anything this guy says, Hank feels relaxed. Nunca is safe, so let him say whatever he wants.

"Advice?"

"Yeah." Smiling, Ernie grabs hold of his shirt. "You really *should* care what happens."

"Why?"

"Because it's going to hurt, old man, a whole lot worse than this." And with the side of his gun he smashes Hank in the forehead.

Hank wakes to Nunca whining, then feels the dog's snout nudge his shoulder. He remembers the searing pain when Ernie hit him, and his fall out on the callejón, but not how he made it back into the yard. His face is smeared with blood. So is the front porch beneath his head. A bit woozy, he makes it to the bathroom, accompanied by Nunca, and washes up. There's a dark crimson bruise above his left eye. He puts his largest bandage over its oozing slit. Then, as if confused by what had happened, Hank feels drawn to revisit the scene and finds the lock missing from the gate. What, did Ernie take it? Why?

He searches the alley, and the yard. Can't find it anywhere.

He goes and sits on the porch, looks at the spot of bloody concrete, has a vague memory of falling there. That must have happened after Ernie left. A reasonable explanation, so why doesn't he believe it? Hank closes his eyes and replays the whole thing in his mind. Though much of it is a blur, specific images come through, like a big dark cat dropping down from the northern wall. *A cat?* Yeah, that's what he'd first imagined. But it was windy, there were lots of shadows, he hadn't gotten a good look, and then suddenly saw Ernie. Hank opens his eyes and blinks, can still picture the guy standing there, staring at him, smiling like a…a wax museum figure come to life.

Oh, fuck, no, could I have dreamt the whole damn thing?

Well, yeah, he must admit it's possible. But even if just a dream, that doesn't mean it wasn't real. If only in some inner dimension of his mind, his enemy was here.

Still, Hank wants to know the *actual* truth of it. He goes and checks under his rug. The secret pouch has been opened and his entire stash is gone, which infers it went to Ernie. But how can he be sure? He hasn't needed money in several days, since before Fiona's death. A lot was spent for food, drink, and other things during her final weeks. Could be that's where it went.

He returns to the porch, cleans the bloody spot, then sits on the stoop and mulls it over. Of only one thing is he certain: in some meaningful form, actual or ethereal, Ernie came yesterday to frighten him. And failed. Hank had been completely honest, that he's not concerned with his own safety. Nor does he care about what is or is not "legal." Fiona is not afraid, is beyond fear, so why let Ernie worry them in the least?

Nunca drops a stick at his feet, then backs up, doesn't look worried either, just wants to play. An excellent sign for Hank, who suddenly feels at ease. He throws the stick over the dog's head. Nunca leaps up and catches it in his mouth.

Absolutely amazing!

And on that happy note, excited for whatever next comes his way, Hank gets a huge surprise: Analu pushes open the gate and walks toward him. "Ah," he says, "how wonderful to see you!"

"What happened to your head?"

He laughs and gives it a little shake. "Good question!"

"You don't know?"

Best not confuse her with too much truth. "I fell."

She hugs him, holds on for a long time and whispers in his ear, "We need to talk." Analu grips him by the shoulders, looks him in the eye. "You've been here way too long."

Here? She must mean at the house, though Hank's first thought is *in this crazy world.* "Yeah."

"What would Fiona want you to do?"

Oh, of that there is no doubt. "Only what I love."

Analu pauses, perhaps had not expected such an emotional response. "Yes, and…and what is it you love the most? Where did you use to go, every day, to find some peace?"

He smiles, pleased by so many easy questions. "To the lake."

She exhales her held breath, lets go of his shoulders, noticeably relieved. "Exactly."

"But I don't need to anymore. It's right here with me."

Analu sighs, frowns, goes and sits at the garden table.

"I mean I feel it," he says, "I really do." He sits with her. Nunca lies down at their feet. "I'm simply happy staying home, just me and this little guy."

She leans over and gives the dog a friendly pat. "Or maybe you're just hiding." Her voice, while serious, is very soft and caring. She points above the wall. "Is there something out there you're afraid of?"

Yeah, fair question, he thinks, determined to be completely truthful. *Out There* has certainly been confusing at times and caused him a lot of trouble. But after his recent ordeal with Ernie, it's undeniable that life is also confusing here. Either way, in or out, none of it frightens him anymore. He's not who he used to be, and confusion now seems quite normal, nothing to shy away from, so why not welcome it as he would any other friend? He thinks of Rumi. As the poet noted, not every friend is easy to get along with. Some, like Analu or Aakesh, can be a real pain in the ass. Luckily, he's learned that the difficult ones are, in essential ways, the most endearing. Analu is one of those, and he loves her deeply. "No, I'm not afraid. It may be true, however, that I've been here too long."

"I think so," she says. "Come on, let's go see the lake."

The image of it glistens in his mind. "Yes, all right." He goes into the house and grabs his pack. Nunca is with him all the way. Hank checks the small zippered pocket in front, sees he has a few ten quetzal bills and a bunch of coins. Good, because being *Out There* sometimes requires money.

As they approach Analu, standing by the gate, she frowns and says, "Maybe we should leave the puppy home."

Hank had not considered that possibility, had fully expected to bring his friend along. But she's right, no one can assume to know the needs of someone else. He kneels down and faces Nunca. "Well, pal, what do you say?"

The dog whines, runs to the porch and lies down. An apparent warning that *Out There* is not a safe place to be. Not surprising, really, given how hard it must have been for him in the world alone. The hunger and constant sense of danger. This home, guarded by these walls, is the only safe place he's ever known.

"I understand," Hank calls. "Don't worry, I'll be back soon."

Analu laughs as if he's joking. *"Pues, amigo, ya nos vamos."*

They move through the series of callejones, emerge on the bumpy river road. Lake Atitlán stretches out before them.

"Look," Analu says, as though perhaps he might not have noticed. "How beautiful is that?"

Hank hears in the question her expectation of an answer.

"Inexplicable," he says for lack of a better word. Beautiful, yes, but for him it is so much more, and impossible to describe.

Atitlán—for those interested in such things—has a jaw-dropping geological history. Born eighty-five thousand years ago, the product of a volcanic explosion that killed every living thing for hundreds of miles, it is by far the deepest lake in Central America.

Impressive, absolutely, though none of that is relevant to Hank. What matters is his sense of belonging here, a profoundly intimate connection with the water and everything that surrounds it. For him this is home and family: the eleven Maya villages, the boats that motor back and forth between them, the sibling volcanos and their adjoining mountains, the endless sky above and invisible depths below. The entirety of this place, in some way he cannot comprehend, is him. He does not exist without it—without all of it, good and bad. He feels bonded to the lake, and also to the tainted river that flows into it, the human waste, the gas and oil leaks left by its many boats, the malignant cyanobacteria and strangling paxte. While simply one of many people in Atitlán, he is different than most, who think their existence is somehow separate. They are wrong. This place is also them. Birds sing, dogs bark, a helicopter lands thundering in the distance as someone zooms by on a shiny motorcycle, spewing out toxic smoke. It all plays out through each person here, like a living dream.

As they get near the lake, Hank sees the many buses parked along the road. "It must be Sunday." Wow, what an overly obvious thing to say. That's what his Uncle Abe would think.

Analu eyes him, thinking more or less the same. Why would he voice something so damned *indubitable,* something any local child would know? "When's the last time you ate?"

He doesn't remember. "Last time I was hungry."

"Well," she says, "should we get you a couple of tacos?"

"No, amiga, gracias, I'm fine."

They get to the flat area down by the river. There's some sort of festival happening, a great deal of commotion, and vendors trying to sell their stuff to Guatemalan tourists—most of whom, as usual, ignore it. But a local entrepreneur has come up with something new! For five quetzales (60 U.S. cents) parents can buy their young child a thrill: one time around a short dirt track on a miniature, fully-motorized, four-wheeler.

"God," says Analu, "how obnoxious!"

Hank agrees, but it also strikes him as funny. "Kinda cute."

"Cute?"

"You know, in an obnoxious sort of way."

They walk beyond the flat, cross over the stinking river and up to the lakeside path, into the throng of devout, enraptured evangelicals. Analu, with a stealthy sneer, calls them "Holy Rollers." There are more than Hank has ever seen, and today audaciously showy: several dramatic sermons in apparent competition, each with a band, music filling the air with deafening amplification.

"The louder we sing out truth," a pastor once told him, "the better to wake up sinners." He was a small man with a deeply resonant voice. "This is our Dear Lord's Message. For a few HE need only whisper, but for most HE has to shout."

The unpleasant racket, as with everything else, also includes Hank—an echo of the noise that sometimes muddles up his mind. It is a sad sound, a desperate sound, a scream of inner fear. And, at the same time, as he knows well, a prayer for the fear to end. "Damn fanatics," says Analu.

Hank says nothing, feels no anger toward these people or any need to change them. Well, to be completely honest, he wishes they would turn their sad noise down.

Ten minutes later comes the beach. They walk to his favorite rock. "It's getting hot," Analu says, and checks her watch. "Almost eleven. By this time I would normally be gone." She removes her dress, unveils the bathing suit underneath, dives into the lake and glances back, expecting him to follow.

Hank waves her on, sits on his rock. With a great sigh of relief he tosses away his flip-flops, dangles his feel in the water, and feels settled. Yes, he needs to come here every day.

He's still on the rock when Analu returns a half hour later. "You're not going to swim?"

"Not yet. I'm in no hurry."

"The Xocomil is coming."

"Fine with me."

She dries off, then hides her body within the towel while changing out of the wet bathing suit and, with incredible deftness, back into her dress. Hank does not usually watch this private act. Today, however, everything enthralls him and he can't pull his eyes away.

Analu seems a bit suspicious. "Sure you're all right?"

"Even better," he says—Fiona's stock joke whenever asked that question, which always made him laugh. He laughs now, too. Does not bother to explain. Analu sighs, a clear sign of exasperation, so Hank puts on his most serious face. "Thank you for bringing me here, my dear, and please don't worry, I remember my way home."

She smiles, as he'd intended, reaches out and musses with his hair…finds a couple of twigs embedded in the long white flow of wiry tangles.

"Hey," he says, "good thing it's not spiders."

"Maybe you should cut this mop."

"Yeah, maybe."

"And get rid of that straggly beard."

He purses his lips and scratches his fuzzy chin, only now aware of the weeks its been since he shaved.

Analu frowns. "You won't."

"No, most likely not."

She laughs. "Oh, oh, Enrique."

Hank also laughs, glad to see she's given up, is now looking a bit more relaxed.

She points at his forehead. "I think, at least, you should change the bandage."

"That, *at least*, I will."

"And please," she says with emphasis, "*please* promise me you will come for a swim tomorrow."

"Consider yourself promised."

Analu grins at his wise-guy sass. "Good!"

She hugs him and hurries off.

Good, yes. Oh so good. Hank steps out into the water, deep enough to dunk himself, and lies face down in the shallows.

The goodness he is feeling, is this what it's like for the faithful when they get baptized? He smiles, to his amazement thinking fondly of evangelicals, who deep within their spiritual selves believe the lake can heal. Yes, on that much he agrees, an agreement to be nurtured because it makes him feel good, and opened wide, and without a trace of fear.

It comes to him, like a message, that this feeling can be shared with others. Just simple goodness. And with that peaceful thought he comes up for needed air.

35
Good News

Hank wanders back and forth along the shoreline. He's been here for many hours, has watched jet skis come and go, people come and go. It's late in the afternoon, the wind is picking up, but he keeps walking, does not want to leave, has no idea what time it is and wouldn't care except for Nunca, who might be getting anxious. Or hungry. *Okay, pal, I'm coming.*

His intention is to go directly home, but he's in no hurry, does not want to miss a thing. He is conscious of each step and feels the goodness everywhere around him, a vast surrounding harmony of all he hears and sees.

Well, except for trash. Everything but that.

What is it with human beings, how mindless they can be? How did this unwanted stuff somehow evade the many garbage cans? He stops several times to pick it up.

The most egregious area is where evangelicals had been praying to be saved. The worshippers are finished now, getting ready to leave on the rented buses, return home to distant villages with a renewed faith in their Lord. Left behind, as Hank could have predicted from years of observation, are candy wrappers, plastic water bottles, spoons and forks and plates. This is typical of the lakeside gatherings, the garbage ignored until local residents (*El comité de Jucanya*) come to deal with it. Many members of the *comité* are lakeside vendors. Though presumably not pleased to also be trash collectors, what choice do they have? They can't afford to insult the religious tourists. A shame that their God-fearing patrons, focused only on self-salvation, could not care less about such a sinful mess.

For Hank, however, this is not about insulting anyone, it's about doing what is right.

So, with goodness in his heart, he goes down by the lake and gathers up bits of litter. Sure, he knows this is not normal, not a thing most foreigners ever do, and he watches as the news quickly spreads.

GOOD NEWS Hank would hope, but that's not how it feels.

People stop what they are doing, turn and stare. An old woman in the distance points and laughs. Some seem suspicious, might think he's trying to shame them. Others look bewildered, and sympathetic, perhaps believe that he's gone nuts. Could be they recognize him because of Fiona, still honored by so many, and feel sorry for her old disheveled mate. One or two offer a tepid smile—vendors, perhaps, who do not mind him doing what they'd otherwise have to do themselves.

Hank returns to the path and dumps the debris into a well-marked garbage can. In spite of those awkward moments on the beach, he feels surprisingly good. And hopeful. He's done his small part, which is enough, and now there's more to do. Things in his own life also need cleaning up. To begin with, he has to make sure Orlando is okay.

Hang on, Nunca, just a while longer.

He crosses the stinking river, then the dusty flat, and up past the tourist restaurants, offers a fond *"Buenas Tardes"* to whoever might glance his way. He enters Josefina's stall and raises his hands. "I feel so lucky to have found this wonderful place!"

A couple of men at a nearby table give him a strange look. He smiles at them, very friendly.

Josefina, though busy at the grill, takes a second to shake Hank's hand. Her sparkling eyes show that she has missed him. "It's good to see you again, Enrique!"

"Good to see you, too!"

"What happened to your head?"

"Good question!" He laughs, feeling slightly giddy, like telling some stupid worn-out joke. "I fell."

"Oh." Josefina winces at the wound, perhaps accepting his frivolous answer because there's no time to ask for details. She turns back to the grill, flips a chunk of chicken and stirs a pot of beans. Then gives him another look. Why, she seems to ask herself, is he still there, standing right beside her? She is obviously not at ease with his attentive gaze. Why this intimate hovering as if they're best of friends?

That's how Hank reads her shy grin, and he walks off, finds a table and sits down. Suddenly feels like an old fool.

After taking care of her other customers, she comes over, clearly intent on getting past their brief discomfort. "Orlando said you and Fidel are working on a new wall."

That was many weeks ago. *Time, the great illusion.* He sees she does not know about Fiona, which means Orlando has kept their secret. "We're all finished."

A man and woman come into the stall. Josefina eyes them, nods and smiles, points to an open table. "So," she says to Hank, "you can finally come and eat!"

He is relieved by her jesting tone. "I can!"

"Good. And I suppose you want *The Same?*"

Though he had not planned to stay, the thought of her food makes his stomach growl. "Well," he says, and as usual pretends to struggle with the decision, "yeah, okay, why not?"

That brings a smile. She nods and hurries off.

The men at the other table are giving him furtive glances. Hank doesn't care. He gazes out at the lake, covered by whitecaps, the oddly patterned movement of wind across the water. Patterned, but at the same time wild and indistinct, it is a language impossible to decipher, and strangely musical, cacophonous yet also somehow melodic. He blurs his vision, mesmerized by the elusive rhythm.

Sometime later he must blink to end the spell. Sees his plate of food waiting on the table. Wow, when did that show up?

Again he feels emotional, grateful for life's magic, its wonderful little gifts. And now Josefina brings him more: a basket of hot tortillas, a bowl of jalapeño peppers.

Hank looks up into her smiling eyes. "Gracias, amiga." Then, though aware she might feel embarrassed, he says he's missed her. Because it's true. Because he needs to tell the truth, especially if it might make someone feel good, and in spite of her girlish blush he sees it does. That accomplished, his attention shifts to why he really came. "I also miss Orlando."

"Yes," Josefina says, "me too."

"You don't see him anymore?"

"I do, almost every day as he goes by with his peanuts. But that boy has changed."

"How?"

"Not the little joker he used to be. Always in a hurry. I'm lucky to get a wave."

"He's a hard worker, like his father."

"Yes," she says, "I suppose that's it."

"Can you give him a message from me?"

"Of course, Enrique, what?"

"Please tell him to come by the house. I have some work."

"You can tell him yourself." Josefina points off to the side.

Orlando is walking along the path below, lugging his bag of peanuts. Hank calls out, smiles and waves. The boy comes into the stall and to his table. They shake hands.

Hank appreciates the faux formality. Orlando shows a polite smile, but not a trace of true emotion—understands that their sadness about Fiona must be kept secret.

"You see," says Josefina, "see how serious?"

She means it to be funny, so Hank laughs. "Because Orlando is a very busy guy, the same as me. Even on a Sunday there's no time to goof around." He gestures him to sit. "And now, *por favor,* we busy guys could use a Coca Cola."

Josefina goes off to get the drinks.

"I see you're back to selling peanuts."

"Just after school. Papa's working, but we owe someone money. I don't know who, or how much. Mama says I need to help. I'm trying, but..." He looks away, out at the lake.

Between this and losing Fiona, life is clearly hard right now, but the kid will not complain. Hank respects that, but also wants to help. He looks at him straight on, mirrors his stoic face. "Are you hungry?"

Orlando shakes his head, seems determined not to cry.

"Good, because I'm not going to feed you."

Orlando grins at the dumb joke, an obvious relief, then sniffs back his unstoppable grief.

"And," says Hank, "you know what else is good?"

The boy looks baffled.

"Nunca really wants you to come visit."

His eyes fill with tears. "It's all right with you, Enrique?"

"I would love it, amigo. Tomorrow, if you want."

"Sí, Señor, I want."

On his way home, walking up Rancho Grande, Hank continues to take his time, has stopped thinking about Nunca, knows his friend will understand. People watch as he approaches. Some look alarmed, perhaps by his long white hair and frowsy beard. Or it could be the large bandage on his forehead.

Analu's right, it probably should be changed.

267

A delivery van sits idling on the street, thick black smoke streaming from its exhaust pipe. A middle-aged man is closing its rear doors. Hank points at the pollution. "That's not good."

The man nods. "No" he says, "not good. But I can't afford to fix it. Maybe you can pay the bill?"

Hank hears the playful sarcasm, does not take offense. "Well, yes, maybe I can. How much?"

"Way more than it's worth," says the man, and laughs.

"To me it's worth a lot," says Hank. "Find out what it costs, amigo. I'll go to the bank tomorrow. How will I find you?"

The man knits his brow, looks suddenly put out, does not know what to make of this old gringo. "I think you mean it."

"Yes, I do."

"No, amigo, no, I..." He shakes Hank's hand. "But I appreciate the offer. *Yo soy Adolfo.*"

"*Enrique.*"

"*Mucho gusto, Enrique.*" Adolfo climbs up into the driver's seat and points down at Hank's forehead. "You really need to change that bandage."

Hank smiles and waves good bye as Adolfo pulls away, then keeps walking up Rancho Grande. *You see,* he tells himself, aware that he has never quite believed it, *if given a chance, all people can get along, can do what's right. And anything—yes, anything—is possible.*

He hears the brazen, repulsive roar of a coming motorcycle. Sees it a couple of blocks away, carelessly speeding his direction. *Anything.*

With that in mind, Hank steps out into street, gets down on his hands and knees as if perhaps he's lost something of great value. People on the sidewalk gasp. The motorcycle honks, then swerves to miss him and powers on.

Someone hollers, "Get out of the road, you fucking idiot!"

Hank looks up and sees Bret, his old nemesis from the Circus Bar, on the sidewalk. An indigenous woman, standing next to him, seems perplexed by Bret's English words, and why he's yelling at the old man. She comes and kneels down by Hank. "Do you need help, Señor?"

"Gracias, amiga, sí." He lets her guide him to his feet.

"Careful," Bret calls out to her Spanish, "that guy is *loco.*"

The woman frowns at the harsh word. She walks with Hank to the other side of the street, then looks at him with questioning eyes. "I was watching, I...I saw you get in the way of that motorcycle on purpose. Why?"

"Well, I was hoping it might slow him down."

"Really?"

He laughs at his misguided innocence. "Yeah, really."

"Would be easier to stop a shooting star."

"Probably true."

She reaches out, gives his elbow a gentle squeeze. "Please, Señor, promise you'll be more careful."

"Okay, I promise."

She gives his elbow another squeeze, then leaves.

Be careful? Hank chuckles at how hard that is to do. *Hah, perhaps I should not have promised!* He smiles to himself, closes his eyes and takes a long deep breath, intending to try his best.

"Well I'll be fucked!" It's Bret, standing a few feet away, pointing at Hank's head. "Old brain finally leakin' out, huh?"

People are watching. Lots of people watching. It's rare to ever see an argument on the street.

"Go home, old man!" shouts Bret. He grins, baiting him, expecting some kind of retaliation.

But Hank feels no anger, only sadness for this fool's ugly rage. He turns away, starts walking.

"And stay there!"

Hank quickens his step, can hear Bret laughing behind him.

News of their clash has reverberated up the street. Several people move when he gets near.

To his relief, a small boy waves from his mother's arms.

Hank waves back, consciously slows down, quiets his troubled heart and eventually makes it home to Nunca's ecstatic greeting. He drops to the ground and snuggles the pup, accepts several licks to his face.

"Yeah, I know, damn hard to live without me!"

He goes to the bathroom and changes the bandage. A bit bloody, but not so bad.

The next morning he changes it again. This one is smaller, flesh-colored, hardly noticeable. He fills Nunca's bowls and waits till his friend has finished eating. "Hey, pal, time we get our asses to the lake!" The dog lets out a mighty sigh and flops down in the dirt. "Yeah, all right, whatever you want, no worries." Nunca does not budge. "Okay, later."

By the time he gets to the beach the sun has covered the sandy shoreline. Analu and Ingrid are already swimming. Hank watches them for a minute, but feels antsy, does not really want to be here. He walks directly to the bank and collects his one thousand dollars. After paying bills and putting money aside for Eduardo, there will still be a few hundred. Far more than he needs. Adolfo, his new friend, will be surprised.

He goes to *El Mercado* for fresh vegetables and fruit, then to Chalos for rice and beans—enough, in all, to last him for a week. Back at home he joins Nunca for a nap.

Orlando shows up in the late afternoon. The dog goes nuts. Howls and shimmies around in circles, then goes running off with the boy into the new garden. Hank heads for the house, gets a sheet of paper, a pen, and sits at the garden table. In large bold letters he writes the same thing five times in Spanish, with big spaces in between.

GOOD NEWS!
We can all slow down and enjoy each other's company.
There is no need to hurry.
Whatever has to happen will.

Hank squeezes his eyes shut and groans. Another bout of foolish innocence. He'd had this silly whim, what just minutes ago seemed like a great idea: to make twenty copies, which he would cut into a hundred little flyers, then hire Orlando to spread them around town. And he had other *great ideas* too, was planning to make lots of **GOOD NEWS!** pronouncements. For instance, how people should not need holy guidance to know what is right and wrong.

Wow, he thinks, *before long I'll be down preaching at the lake! What the hell is wrong with me?*

Nothing, says Abe, *but it's time to quit fooling around. You know what needs to happen.*

His uncle's voice was clear and forceful. Not to be ignored.

Orlando and Nunca come to the table. The boy sits next to Hank, sees the piece of paper in his hand. "What's that?"

"Nothing," he says, and crumples it up.

"Are you sad, Enrique?"

"Not sad, just a little tired."

"You want me to go?"

"No, no, please stay." He rests his hands on the boy's shoulders. "I have to ask a favor."

"Of course, Enrique, anything."

"I really need your help, and I can pay you."

"To do what?"

Hank points at Nunca. "I'm going to be very busy. He'll need to be taken care of."

Orlando smiles. "Yes, I...if you want, I can be here every day from three till six. And weekends too."

"Sí, Señor, I want."

"Starting tomorrow?"

"Perfect. Thank you."

Hank feels so grateful that this kid is in his life. That he also has Fiona and Uncle Abe. He can feel them urging him on. Okay, no more stalling, it's time to write his novel.

36
Mixoc

The next morning passes slowly. Hank, lingering under the mango tree since dawn, knows what his novel will be about *(the meaning of life, of course, what else!)* but has no clue how to start. And is getting nowhere. He goes to the house, grabs his pack and fills his water bottle. After checking in with Nunca, who still chooses to stay home, he heads off for the lake. Better late than not at all. Hopes a swim might inspire him.

Not far from the beach Hank stops. *Mixoc.*

The name spins through his mind like a whirling dervish and he fees driven to go see this village elder, *a trusted wise man.* Yeah, exactly what is needed!

He hurries up past the graveyard, then walks the quarter mile of Calle Cementerio to the road that leads to Santa Catarina.

Shortly, as expected, an old pickup truck (a *"flete,"* the cheap shuttle service around the lake) pulls over to let Hank on. He takes off his pack, holds it to his chest and squeezes in, stands by the tailgate, grabs the metal railing for support. The bed of the truck has two low wooden benches packed with locals wearing traje.

He sees from the sun it must be almost noon. By now, Juan should be home.

Just before the road dips down to the lakeside village, Hank bangs on the side of the truck, which pulls over and stops. He pays the driver, then starts up the nearby concrete steps. This pathway was constructed several years ago. It traverses the hill and enters the village from the north, about halfway to the top, where Juan said he and Mixoc live.

It's quite a climb, and in this heat isn't easy. At last he reaches the first houses. A scrubby pine tree offers a bit of shade. He drinks from his water bottle, then goes on for a while longer. Suddenly spent, he stops to rest, leans back against a stone wall and looks out on the lake: a million-dollar view if these dirt-poor people could figure out how to sell it. For the most part they are here, in the same ramshackle huts where they were born and raised, because there is no other option. Few have toilets or electricity. Hank has always marveled at how they tolerate, with good humor, such deplorable conditions.

No, that's wrong. *Deplorable* is far too harsh a word. His word, not theirs. This is their life, that's all, and he doesn't really know how they feel about it.

A middle-aged man rounds the corner from above, bent over from a heavy load of firewood on his back. He glances at Hank and mumbles, *"Buenos días."*

Though most people here speak little or no Spanish, that is a common welcome they use with foreigners.

"Buenos días," he responds as the man shuffles by, and at once Hank feels stronger, determined to keep going. Perhaps a bit too determined. Farther along the concrete path is another set of rising steps, where again he must stop to catch his breath.

A woman comes out of a concrete hut—perhaps had watched him pass by—and seems genuinely concerned.

"Adonde va, Señor?"

She probably thinks he's lost. Not many foreigners ever come way up here, especially old ones. Most are only interested in the tourist shops by the lake. Sensing she speaks good Spanish, Hank throws up his hands and sighs. He glances around as if truly befuddled. "This is not New York, right?"

She makes a funny face. "No, you did not go far enough."

Hank clenches his fists and shows a scowl of disappointment. "Well then, amiga, I could use some help." He calms his voice. "Do you know Tata Mixoc?"

She blinks, seems either confused or worried. "Yes, but…but he does not speak Spanish. Only Cakchiquel."

Hank smiles, hopes to convince her he's not crazy. "His grandson, Juan, said he could translate."

"Ah." She nods approval. Must know Juan. "Bueno, Señor, it's not far, I'll show you."

She seems in something of a hurry, is simply trying to be polite. They don't bother exchanging names. The woman leads him up a series of narrow concrete walkways. Dogs growl or snarl at his unexpected, unwanted presence. She shushes them and they back off. The walkway turns to dirt, at last reaching the upper hillside, *los tablones,* where farmers grow flowers. Across from the terraced slopes is an old adobe hut.

The woman goes to the door and knocks. *"Oye, Tata, ajaf riyin ntintinel."* A couple of minutes pass and then she knocks again. *"Oye, Tata?"*

The door suddenly opens. An extremely short old man, with a hunched back, comes out to the stoop. Hank notices his dark, leathery feet. He is dressed in Santa Catarina traje: multi-colored knee-length pants, a red and gray striped shirt, a similarly striped scarf wrapped around his head. His face is crosshatched by deep wrinkles. His eyes have a milky glaze.

The woman points at Hank and continues in Cakchiquel, perhaps explaining where she found the gringo.

Hank says, "Could you please ask if Juan is here."

She does.

Mixoc waves his palm down at the ground and shuffles off the stoop.

"Tata says to go with him."

"Gracias, amiga," says Hank.

"De nada."

The woman starts down the hill. Hank follows Mixoc to a small fire pit behind the hut. They sit across from each other on small flat boulders. Chickens run about the yard. In one corner, ears of corn are drying on a tattered plastic tarp.

The old man grunts, gets Hank's attention, reaches up and taps the top of his head. "Mixoc."

Hank taps on his. "Enrique."

Mixoc puts a hand over his heart. "Tata."

Because *Tata* identifies him as a respected elder, Hank decides to say what an honor it is to be here. He knows to keep the Spanish simple, and to speak slowly. *"Me gusta estár con usted."*

Mixoc aims his milky gaze away, and sighs, perhaps did not understand. Then he gets up, walks over and puts Hank's right hand on his heart—on Hank's own heart—and holds it there with an impressive amount of force. "Tata." He lets go, steps back, makes sure that Hank leaves his hand where he'd put it, then returns to sit on the boulder. Again he covers his heart. Taps it. "Tata!" he repeats with emphasis, his eyes intense, a sharp demand for Hank's agreement.

This must be a tradition, for them to each be honored as wise old men. *Sure, why not?* Hank smiles, encouraged, hopeful that this strange journey might soon make some sense. He taps his chest. "Tata."

Mixoc nods and shuts his eyes. Several seconds pass. Maybe Hank is also expected to shut his? He does, and immediately feels at peace, a sense of inner calm only before experienced while in the lake. It's as if he were there, immersed deep beneath the surface like a timeless, effortless sinking, until at last he hears a sound, a long melodic note followed by another, and another. His mind floats on the bright harmonic tones. His eyelids flutter. Then, like a passing wind, the notes slowly begin to fade, grow fainter and fainter, now indistinguishable from the silence, a music he intuits but cannot hear.

"Enrique?" Hank opens his eyes. Across from him sits Mixoc, who smiles from ear to ear, and behind the old man stands Juan. "Sorry I am late."

"No problem," says Hank. He gazes back at the beaming elder, befuddled by what just happened.

Juan sits on the dirt next to his grandfather. "Tata is amazed that you are here." He looks up at Mixoc, who gestures toward Hank, eyebrows pinched, says a few words to his grandson in Cakchiquel and gives his head a little wobble. "He says you did not need to come so far."

Huh? What did I miss? Hank feels frustrated, and struggles not to show it. He's here because Juan invited him. Here because the fisherman said his grandfather, *the wisest man he's ever known*, wanted him to come. "I don't understand."

Mixoc purses his lips and shows a clownish pout. It seems a mild rebuke of Hank's obvious consternation. The old man waves a hand in the air, brings it to his mouth and mumbles into his palm, like telling himself a secret.

"Tata says you need to see inside your eyes." Juan gives an embarrassed laugh. "Sorry, I don't know what that means."

Hank takes a breath of air, then blows it out. Is this wise man always so damn cryptic? He wants to understand, but how? "Have I come at a bad time?"

"No." The young man seems truly apologetic, and equally perplexed. "Tata is pleased you're here. I think. Sometimes, to be honest, I'm not sure what to think."

"Can you please ask what he means about my eyes?"

Juan shows a diplomatic grin. "My grandfather does not give explanations, would say you either understand or don't."

"I don't."

Mixoc laughs, points up at the sky, waves his hand around and again goes silent.

Why had Hank believed, with such certainty, that this old indigenous man would have something crucial to tell him, something to inspire him, get him writing? He feels lost. *Why the hell would I come out of my way for this?* He thinks of Orlando, needs to get home before the boy arrives, nods at Mixoc and says in Spanish, "Thank you, Tata, for seeing me. I feel honored to have met you."

Not really true, but he wants to be respectful.

Juan translates. The old man stares down at his feet.

As Hank stands to leave, Mixoc groans. A guttural rumbling from deep inside him. Again his eyes are closed. Again he lifts his hands into the air. His head moves back and forth, trance-like, then he speaks some solemn, somber words—all carefully chosen, it seems, for this particular moment. Perhaps an ageless Maya saying. The old man opens his eyes, stares ahead, and slowly repeats the words to Hank, who somehow knows he's come for this, to hear what has just been said. And there will be no explanation. He knows that, too. Some truths, as Fiona said, are like air, can be felt yet never fully understood. This is one of those, and Hank feels certain he won't like it.

Juan looks stunned. "Tata says we have gone too far."

We? Though Hank might easily be confused, he isn't. *Humans. He means humans.*

The young man seems strangely anxious. "*Mam,* Tata says, has come to take us back."

Hank knows that *Mam* is the principle Maya god, but has never given *HIM* much thought. The name itself sounds feminine, like *Mama.* Though this Maya god is probably fierce and unyielding, as most gods are, he would rather imagine *HIM* as somewhat motherly—a kind nurturer, and forgiving.

He takes a needed breath, ready to hear the wise man's truth. "Back where?"

"I don't know. *Mam* cannot be known, that's what Tata always tells me."

Mixoc holds out his palm like a stop sign, makes a short and earnest statement, then again shuts his eyes.

Juan sighs, as if reluctant to deliver the old man's final words. "You must go home, Tata says. Says you have things to see. Says you know what to do."

37

A Most Critical Concern

I know what to do? Hank has no idea what that means. Nearly three weeks pass, and each day leaves him more in doubt. Every morning he tries to write, long anxious hours, a waste of time, then tries coaxing Nunca to the lake. Today, as usual, the dog refuses. Hank laughs. "You just ain't no normal pooch!"

Face it, says Fiona, *lately you ain't been no fun.*

True.

Don't worry, honey, it'll be okay.

He thanks her for the hopeful thought and leaves, these days taking a different path to the lake, a longer route through Jucanya to avoid the evangelicals. His other new habit, after swimming, is to move away from the shoreline, away from people, up under the shady caña, alone, to think. He's obsessed with what Mixoc said, that humans "have gone too far" and will be "taken back." Those haunting words clench his heart.

Taken Back. Good title for a novel, though not the one he's been pondering.

Each day Analu waves as she passes, keeps her distance, uneasy with how he's changed since Fiona's death—his hair and beard perhaps too straggly, his ways too unpredictable.

Yeah, Hank understands. For now he's better off by himself.

Paying close attention to the sun, he always makes it home before Orlando comes. Nunca is often dozing, bored stiff until that happens. Today, however, waiting just inside the gate, the pup whines and races to his bowls, which Hank sees are empty. Must have forgotten to top them off before he left.

"Sorry, pal, I've been fucking up."

Hank fills them. Then, upset with himself, he goes and sits under the mango tree. Feels trapped inside his thoughts. *A Most Critical Concern.* That would be the title of the novel he wants to write: an absurdist tale which questions why human beings, in spite of their essential goodness, regard the planet as a possession—as some material thing they own, can treat any damn way that suits them!

In his story, the greatest minds of the world are determined to understand this age-old problem. To ensure an objective approach, they isolate from each other in separate ivory towers and do years of private research and serious contemplation, at last emerging with theories and counter-theories, a battle of well-intentioned philosophies about the causes and cures of human selfishness.

In other words, none of them agree. And each is quite defensive of his or her opinion. All think they alone have found the answer. So many different answers, and none of these proud experts will back down from their professed certainty!

Hank is stuck right there, trying to find a funny way to show why people, even when inspired to work for the common good, so often feel driven—as if by inner demons—to be seen as somehow special.

Orlando arrives and takes charge of Nunca. Hank goes off by himself for a lot more thinking. He can sense, like Mixoc said, there is something he needs to see. Yes, all right, but what? *What?* It's like trying to thread a needle in the dark.

Uncle Abe once said, "The truth is near when you can't quite find it. And if found there'll be no question (nor any real interest) because most people won't want to hear it."

Nunca runs up, Orlando close behind. "I have to go."

"Already?"

The boy points to the sun, now dropping behind the western wall. *"Hasta mañana,"* he says, and hurries out the gate.

Hank tries to interest Nunca in a game of tag. The pup, obviously worn out by Orlando, stares at him like he's gone bonkers, then leads them into the house and jumps up on the bed. "Yeah, okay." Hank goes to the kitchen, makes a sandwich, sits at the desk and stares at his still-blank pad of paper. Can't even bear to touch it.

No worries, whispers Uncle Abe. *Like it or not, and you probably won't, the truth is sure to come.*

In the morning, to his surprise, Hank wakes up feeling good! Truly good! Fiona had been with him throughout the night in every dream. And Nunca too. Abe showed up at some point and the four of them were laughing.

The dog races to his bowls. Time to get on with the day, which for him means food!

Hank takes care of his buddy. Feels good about that also. He puts on his shorts, fills his water bottle and grabs a bag of peanuts—a gift from Orlando. "Beautiful day for a swim," he says to Nunca, "you're gonna love it!" The dog seems unconvinced. "Hey, I tell you what. After the lake, amigo, for a bit of extra fun, we'll go to Aakesh's house and you can shit all over his garden."

Nunca wags his tail, follows him until they reach the gate, then runs back to the porch.

Hank makes an exaggerated pout. "Really?"

Nunca whines.

Strange, but there's nothing to be done. "Okay, pal, your loss." He waves good bye and heads off on his own.

After swimming, Hank switches back to his old routine, sitting on the rock and letting his feet dangle in the lake. It must be another weekend because families begin to gather along the shore. Their dogs come by to give him a quick sniff, and he's fine with that, pets each of them, says a few friendly words. Then they're off to the races, playing with one another, kicking up water while they run by in front of him, again and again.

Hank takes his pack and moves up to his favorite stand of caña. From here he's free of the frenzied animals while also getting a better view of the families. A pure delight! He loves watching the small children, accompanied by a parent, as they splash around in the shallows. Hank laughs at their boundless joy, has never forgotten how wonderful it was to be a child, how everything astounded him—and right now, at this moment, it seems his life is heading that way again, to an unknown place where everything is new. So new it defies description, *cannot be written about,* will always be a mystery. And that's right where he wants to be. Wants to be and wants to stay!

Abe and Fiona must have known, from the beginning, that it's best for him to not actually write a novel. Not now, not ever! Maybe this is the "truth" that Abe was saying he'd "not quite found." He can almost see his uncle smiling.

Yes, all right, no more of that, it's over. Enough of his silly pondering. All he needs to do is live and openly welcome life.

The lake has regained its glassy sheen. A slight breeze cools his warm skin and Hank feels oh so very good! Analu, whom he'd not noticed until now, walks up toward him from the shore. Must have something on her mind. "Hola amiga!"

"*Hola, amigo,*" she calls out, "*como estás?*"

Hank hears worry in her voice. "Better, I'd say, than ever!"

"Yes?" She laughs like he must be joking. "I ask because… because of what I hear, what some people are saying."

Hank is not surprised to know there's talk behind his back. Nothing new in that. It hasn't bothered him for years, and since Fiona's death he simply doesn't care. "Some people, as you have often heard, are always saying something."

She laughs again, perhaps relieved to see he still has a sense of humor. "So you're not crazy, right?"

"Not yet."

Analu kneels down, kisses his forehead and whispers, "You know I love you, yes?"

"Yes."

"And would do anything to help you?"

"Yes, of course, I know."

"Which might include giving you a haircut."

Hank takes both hands and flips up the sides of his curly mop. "Who knows," he says, "someday it might happen."

"What, you going crazy or the haircut?"

"Both."

She smiles for an instant, then turns serious. "We'll talk more later, okay?"

A tried-and-true exit line, a fast escape from this difficult moment. "Yeah, okay."

Analu gives him a quick hug and is off. *Bueno.* Hank is glad to be by himself. By now on a weekend he would also want to leave, but today has fallen in love with these families—far enough away yet warmly present. Five separate groups are spread out along the beach, each equally wonderful to watch. There's nowhere he'd rather be.

Yet only moments later a fancy powerboat motors in and glides up to the sand. The children look spellbound by this unusual intrusion. Their parents, the way Hank sees it, are, like him, not pleased by the sudden change.

A young man jumps from the boat into the knee-high water. He gets to the beach, grabs the rope thrown his way by the captain, and holds it steady, like a human anchor. A ladder is then lowered from the bow.

Two ladino adults, a middle-aged man and woman, climb down into the shallows. Hank assumes they are rich ladinos, probably from the city, because of the fancy boat and fawning attention of its crew. Most Maya people could never afford such a luxury. The captain lowers a cooler, a big umbrella, and a radio. Once his passengers are on shore and his assistant back aboard, he motors off.

The ladina woman strips out of a loose-fitting dress, reveals a pink bikini that barely contains her bulbous ass and bulging breasts. The staring children are called away by their parents, who themselves—especially the fathers—keep on looking.

Good time to take a nap, Hank decides, receding into the caña's welcome shade. He hopes that a brief closing of the eyes, and a few deep breaths, will ease his irritation with these invaders of his simple, idyllic world.

Ah, there he goes again. *Thinking.* Way too damn much thinking! Nunca would not approve. *C'mon, man, forget it!*

He smiles to himself, slowly breathes the blessed air, in and out, comforted by Fiona's loving energy. Time gently passes, his mind relaxes. He's about to fall asleep when the music starts.

Oh, no.

Hank rolls to his side, tries to ignore the loud, misplaced urban salsa. Can't. He sits up and looks down at the ladino couple, sees the busty woman sway her curvaceous hips to the lusty beat. The indigenous families pretend, as perhaps they must, to not be the least bit bothered. Or, for all Hank knows, some of them like the gaudy spectacle, the raucous party spirit these wealthy strangers have provided.

Knowing his opinion does not matter, it's time to leave. While packing up his things he sees the ladina woman open the cooler and bend over in search of something.

Then, as if aware that Hank is watching, she looks up at him. Their eyes lock. Though boiling inside, he simpers, feeling a touch of pity for this selfish person, who, even on an unconscious level, has no clue of his frustration with her obnoxious noise. Or, if she does, does not care. But should. Yes, of course she should! So why not let her know?

With both hands flattened out, palms down, Hank steadily lowers them: a gentle hint, a bit of friendly advice, that for a change she might think of others.

Please, could you drop the volume just a little?

The woman glances down at her breasts, apparently assumes *(Oh no!)* he's asking to see more. She pulls up the sagging top and flashes him a dirty look.

No, no, no. He tries to wave off the innocent mistake, but it's too late. She's turned and is talking to the ladino man, who's lying on a towel. The man jumps to his feet and glares at Hank. With a violent upward sweep of his hands, he sends a message that can't be missed. *What the hell, you asshole creep!* That, at least, is the gist of it, and must not be ignored.

Seeing no future in sign language, Hank grabs his pack and walks down to the couple. "I am sorry," he says in Spanish, "there has been a misunderstanding."

"What don't you understand?" says the ladino man, puffing up his chest while the radio spins out a sprightly guitar riff. "Maybe you need my wife to slap your face?"

Hank takes a breath and looks at the woman. "I did not mean what you thought."

She stiffens, blinks, clearly does not believe him. "Oh?"

He makes the same gesture with his hands. "I was hoping you might turn the music down."

"Really?" sneers the man.

"Yes," says Hank, beginning to get pissed, believing he's been extremely diplomatic, unwilling to compromise his feelings any further, "really."

"You think that is better?" The man grunts out an angry sigh. "Think you have the right to tell us what to do?"

"No, I...I was only—"

"No," the man says, "no right at all. Because, as you should know, this is not your country."

Oh no, not that stale old line!

This guy thinks that being a rich ladino allows him do whatever the hell he wants. "Not your country either," Hank says, and sweeps his hand from side to side, indicating the indigena families along the shore, each of them paying close attention. "If anyone's, it's theirs."

The man seems shocked to have been confronted. "What is your name?"

In days gone by, Hank might have punched this asshole in the face. Instead he just walks off.

"I'll find out!" the man shouts.

Hank shrugs and keeps on moving, up and away from his beloved beach. Outrage, like a thick dark cloud, envelops him. His hands are trembling.

Some minutes later, upset by the deep, still bubbling anger, he forgets to take the alternate route back home, passes by the throng of evangelicals, and at once remembers yesterday's episode with the garbage. Again he notices what seem like suspicious looks. Or maybe not, he can't be sure. Right now Hank is unsure of everything, himself included.

Could it be true, do these people think I'm crazy?

He keeps moving, tries to get free of that bothersome thought, but it follows him, taunts him like some evil spirit.

After crossing the river and moving along the flat, Hank comes upon the same white female dog he's passed dozens of times before. An unexpected gift! For years he's known this dog, who never shows him the slightest bit of attention. At the moment that's precisely what he needs, to be ignored.

She had been pregnant. The big belly is now gone and her breasts are full of milk. *Ah, the babies have arrived! Qué milagro!*

The sight of her lessened load makes him happy again. His pent-up tension quickly dissipates. A tiny pup scrambles out of the bushes and wobbles toward its mother. Hank slows and for a moment stops, his heart captured by the precious little thing.

Unfortunately, the mother must have misread his hesitation, must see it as a threat, because she barks and charges him, hackles high.

Hank pulls back, tries to show with raised hands he meant no harm. But she keeps coming. Oh shit, what can he do? He freezes, considers picking up a rock to scare her off, when one whizzes by him and barely misses the furious dog.

"No, Blanca, no!" A small girl, maybe ten years old, runs past Hank, already throwing another rock. It also misses Blanca, who stops barking and retreats several steps.

The girl gets close to the grouchy beast and shakes her finger. *"No, mamita, me entiendes?"*

Yes, Blanca seems to understand. Tail between her legs, she shambles over to the pup, noses it back toward the bushes.

"Sorry, Tata," the girl says, her brown eyes opened wide, her voice sweet and caring, "are you all right?"

He is struck by her angelic beauty. Also surprised that she called him Tata. "Yes, dear, thanks to you."

Hank offers his hand, expecting her to shake it. Instead she holds it. Kisses it. Does not let go.

"Come," the girl says, and leads him past the dog. "Blanca is not so friendly since her babies came."

"A good mother," says Hank.

She gives his hand a tender squeeze, an obvious agreement.

38
Dire Warnings

The next morning, for no apparent reason, Nunca waits for him at the gate, then rushes out to the callejón. It's like he thinks Hank might be in trouble, somehow knows how bad things were yesterday at the lake. "Hey, pal, don't go on my account." But the dog seems duty-bound to be his escort, and does so with great trepidation, stopping to flinch at any noise. Hank keeps moving. "It's all good," he calls back with a gentle voice, and his friend hurries to catch up.

Several mongrels along the way come to check Nunca out, give thorough and intimate sniffs in all the regular places. Perhaps because he stands very still, shows not a glimmer of opposition, they find no need to cause a ruckus.

At the beach, while Hank seems purposefully avoided, Nunca has numerous friendly encounters with humans and dogs alike. And there's no doubt that he loves the water. His obvious joy makes Hank joyous too. He's so glad to have given up on the novel, and to let go of yesterday's hideous incident with the ladinos. What a pleasure to reconnect with this magical place he loves so much.

True, there's cyanobacteria, but with Fiona's help he has learned to acknowledge it, and grieve for the lake, without feeling bad. Since there is nothing he can do, why feel bad?

For lunch they go to Josefina's. She welcomes Nunca with a glowing smile, a bowl of water and a bone. Hank, as usual, has *The Same,* and basks in the sunny afternoon. The lake mirrors the bright blue sky, a light breeze blows in, and he feels Fiona all around him. Life could not be any better.

For three consecutive mornings that's how it goes. Nunca hurries them to the lake, and each day is equally perfect. Time goes by so swimmingly well that this afternoon, on their way home, Hank imagines always being happy. The idea seems far-fetched yet vaguely possible. He rounds the final corner and sees Concepción at his gate, her anxious face like a loud rebuttal.

"Hola, amiga," he says, *"qué pasa?"*

She shows a troubled smile. "Can we go inside?"

"Yes, yes, of course."

They sit at the garden table. Concepción lets out a deep dramatic sigh, then gazes around at the various flower patches and seems confounded. "Everything looks so…so nice."

Hank smiles. "Sure, because Fiona shows me what to do, won't let me miss a single plant."

That only makes her look more troubled.

He reaches over and puts his hand on hers. "Please, dear, is there something you want to tell me?"

She frowns, on the verge of tears. "I don't know, Enrique. I worry about you."

"Why?"

She sighs. "People say you are causing problems."

"Problems?"

"Say you bothered the mayor's brother's wife at the beach."

"That was the mayor's brother's wife?"

She seems shocked. "You mean you did?"

"No, not really, no."

288

Concepción gasps and squeezes his hand. "Oh, Enrique, this is bad! What did you do?"

"Nothing. At least nothing meant to bother her. The woman misunderstood me."

"How?"

"It's a long story, Concepción." He gently pulls away his hand. "Too hard to explain."

"Well, that's not the only thing."

"What else?"

"Someone said you tried to cause a wreck the other day on Rancho Grande."

"You mean the motorcycle?"

She widens her eyes, incredulous. "Enrique!"

"Another misunderstanding."

"Sounds like a lot of misunderstandings."

Hank can't help laughing, in absolute agreement and resignation. Why do people get so upset by misunderstandings? Why not admit how little they know about other people? Or, for that matter, about themselves! About anything!

She scowls. "You think this is funny?"

"No."

"No, I'm afraid it's not. It could be dangerous, all right, so maybe you should stop."

"Stop what?"

"These things that people do not understand!"

Hank holds back a full-on chortle. Since he disagrees with much of what goes on in this town, including how she and others gossip, it seems wrong to say nothing in response. But that is what he'll force himself to do. Best to avoid any more misunderstandings.

Concepción's shoulders slump. She leans in with frightened eyes. "Please, Enrique, I...there is talk of some strange sickness in the world. No one knows what it is or where it comes from. Lots of people are dying. And now I hear all this! So I worry, yes, I worry. Are you sure things are okay?"

There's that silly word again. *Okay?*

No, there are plenty of things definitely *not okay*. Not in the world at large, and certainly not in Pana. Tempted to mention details, he's on the verge of a useless rant when Nunca comes to the rescue, nudges Hank's knee with his snout.

Thanks, pal. "Ah, the pooch is thirsty."

"Listen," says Concepción. Her face turns grim. "I'm coming back tomorrow so we can talk about what to do."

"Do about what?"

"I don't know, Enrique, I really don't." She looks at a total loss. "That's why we need to talk."

Hank is sadly shocked at how quickly rumors and innuendo whisper their way through town. He loves Concepción, but the last thing he needs is another talk like that. *Oh never mind*, why get bothered by well-intended paranoia. Smiling to himself, sensing Fiona near and also humored, some peaceful moments pass as he gazes around the garden, listens to wind rustling through the pines. He has regained his cherished serenity, again without a care, when the gate creaks open. It's Aakesh. His bald head shines, backlit by the sun. He peeks into the garden and sees Hank. "Where the hell is your lock?"

It sounds like an accusation. "Wish I'd found it before you showed up."

His friend lets out a groan, closes the gate and walks to the table. "What happened to your head?"

"Another good question! Never mind, it's okay."

"I'm not so sure. Why don't you ever answer your phone?"

Though tempted to admit he buried the damn thing, it's plain that Aakesh would not appreciate his reasoning. "Truth is, pal, I got better things to do."

"Yeah?"

"Yeah."

"So tell me, please, what the fuck is wrong with you?"

"Depends on who you ask."

His friend sits down. "Okay, listen to me."

"I'm listening."

Aakesh slams his palms down on the table. "For fucksakes, man, Analu is all freaked out! Some damn thing about you and the mayor's wife."

"Mayor's brother's wife."

"Huh?"

"It was the mayor's brother's wife."

Aakesh gapes. "You mean it's true, you were nasty to her?"

"You need to listen," says Hank in a slow, condescending voice. "Are you listening? Are...you...sure?"

"Yeah...ass...hole...I'm...sure."

So Hank describes, in great detail, how his idyllic scene at the beach had been rudely interrupted by rich ladinos, a pink bikini, and loud music. He gets to where he's lowering his hands, at which point his friend cracks up.

"Oh no, oh shit!" Aakesh cups both hands beneath his chest to suggest the woman's bulging breasts, then mimes looking down at them. "Yeah?"

"Yeah."

"Okay, okay, then what?"

Once Hank has told the rest they start guffawing like young boys. Soon as one is finished, the other props up his imagined bikini top, looks down with a throaty gasp, and off they go again, tears pouring down their faces.

At last Aakesh holds up his hands. "Hey, enough, this isn't funny, you could be in real trouble!"

"Me?" Hank assumes his friend is joking.

"Damn it, man, I'm serious."

"Why?"

"Because that woman is a blabber mouth. What's worse, because she's well-connected, people listen to the lies she's spreading all over town. Bitch wrote an 'official complaint' to the police chief."

Hank has stopped laughing. "You gotta be shitting me."

"I shit you not. And her story, from what I hear, lacks your sense of humor."

"Wow."

"Yeah," says Aakesh, eyes opened wide, *"Wow!"* He chews a second on his lower lip. "Analu thinks you may not be allowed."

"Allowed?"

"At your swimming beach."

"What? No, they can't stop me from going to the lake."

Aakesh sighs. "I wouldn't be so sure. The chief might think you're drinking again, getting into fights. Or maybe crazy. Word has it you started trouble with some tourist on the street."

"Huh? You mean Bret?"

"Who?"

Hank tells the entire motorcycle story.

By the end, Aakesh has closed his eyes. Again he pounds the table. "I don't believe this!" He looks away for an instant, then back at Hank. "No, I fucking do, I believe it, I just don't want to! I mean c'mon, man, what the hell? No, no, never mind, I don't have time, I gotta go. Only came to say you should be more fucking careful. Around here, as you should know, there's no telling what might happen!"

Yeah, he's right. How did things get so bad so fast? Hank has no idea what to do.

Aakesh puts a hand on his shoulder. "Look, it'll probably be okay. We've both seen how things play out in Pana. For awhile you'll be the story, the whole shebang. Then, as usual, forgotten. People will find something else to fill their mouths with. Just don't go to the lake for a week or so."

Those words give Hank a chill.

Aakesh shrugs at his obvious resistance. "I don't mean just because of that. People are weird right now, freaked out by all of the scary news."

"What news?"

"C'mon, caveman, you kidding me?"

"I don't have time for such crap."

"Well, my friend, you may have no choice. To be brief, it turns out there's a pandemic going on. You understand, amigo, know what that word, *pandemic,* means?"

Hank lets out a sarcastic sigh. "Yes," he says, not really sure, "some kind of worldwide sickness."

"Genius!" Aakesh snoots, not pleased at having to explain. "Started in China, they think. No one really knows. A virus, I can't remember what they call it. Has spread through Europe and last week hit the United States. The only thing for sure is that it's killing a lot of people."

"But it's not here, right?"

"Not yet, no, and maybe never, but that won't stop the gossip. Rumor mongers swear it's coming, and some locals think it's us foreigners who are spreading it. So maybe, like me, you should also stay out of town."

Hank looks down and groans, loath to be controlled by other people's fears.

Aakesh pats him on the shoulder. "I can see that my good advice is wasted."

"Hey, since when do I do what I'm supposed to?"

His friend smiles. "So there's no reason for me to talk more common sense, right?"

Hank smiles with him. "Right."

"Okay, well, I promised Analu I'd try."

"Which you did."

"Which I certainly did. And now, thank God, that's over."

"Yeah, thank God."

For a moment they sit quietly, each in his own thoughts. Nothing more to say. They've been here often over the years, a safe and silent place, a sanctuary of their own making. Neither has any clue what will happen next. Or cares. The moment lingers on, as if it might never end. There is no putting this wondrous emptiness into words. The two men smile at each other and stay quiet.

"You know," Aakesh says at last, "I suspect there is a reason."

"Reason?"

"One of those cryptic cosmic reasons why some people, like that ladina woman, are prone to assume the worst."

"More than *some*," says Hank. "It's the modern sickness, like a worldwide pandemic. All comes down to time."

"Time?"

"Yeah. When old guys like us weren't looking, time sped up." Hank twirls his index finger round and round. "Sped up like a spinning top as humans all went crazy chasing after it."

Aakesh knits his brow. "Ooh," he says, and stands. "Sounds like you've given this far too much thought."

"Yeah." Hank also stands. "I once started a novel about—"

"Please," Aakesh says, "spare me. I don't wanta hear it!"

Hank feigns disappointment. "It would've been quite short."

"Which would be way too long for me."

Nunca rushes out of the new garden, perhaps thinks they're about to leave and doesn't want to get left behind. He sits at their feet and waits. Each leans over to pet him.

Aakesh checks his watch. "Oh no, fucking time!" he shouts. Then turns serious. "It's after four, the bank closes in fifty minutes, and I need money. Tomorrow I'm off to the city. Old brain needs another check. My doctor says I'm doing good but advises me to take it easy, avoid all stressful situations. Such as, for instance, hearing about any of your unfinished novels. Would probably say to ignore you altogether."

Hank nods. "Excellent advice."

"Yeah. So. Can you stay out of trouble till I get back?"

Hank bites his lip, scratches his chin.

Aakesh bends down to Nunca, takes hold of his head with both hands and looks him in the eye. "Well, fella, seems like it's up to you. Gotta keep this asshole in plain sight."

The pup wags his tail and whines.

After Aakesh is gone, Hank lies next to Nunca in the shade. And, with a sense of sweet nostalgia, he remembers that novel he never wrote, about the moment when time ended.

This would happen in the spring of 2050.

Quite a change from the first third of the twenty-first century, when time seemed in short supply—when people used far too much of it for things they thought needed to be done, leaving little for the more pleasurable ways they'd otherwise choose to live. Indeed, throughout the world, human existence had become unbearably stressful.

Then, from about 2030 till 2050, came what was eventually termed "The Bad Old Days." The time when technology took over. Like a promised antidote to the global anxiety, it just kept progressing, but could not solve many social problems. People continued to cause each other grief, got into petty fights and even major wars. Nor could it halt the looming ecological cataclysm. Numerous coastal cities were already underwater.

However, for those not immediately threatened with some catastrophe, life appeared to be improving. By 2048, technological innovation had evolved to the point where anything seemed possible. Directed by artificial intelligence, incrementally-better quality products—for whatever need—were invented on a daily basis. Expectations rose, and continued to rise, until all but the poorest people (nearly half of the global population, who never have any say in how things work) demanded supreme excellence on each and every front.

By the dawn of 2050, even after premature deaths from the world's ongoing wars and climate disasters were factored in, the average lifespan surpassed 100 years for those who could afford the expensive new drugs and treatments. There seemed no end to the miraculous feats achievable by modern science. It was confidently predicted that most diseases—and perhaps natural death itself—would soon be conquered.

Thus marked the proverbial moment when (sorry, Nietzsche) God truly died—and, both inexplicably and simultaneously, time came to a crashing halt.

No more past or future. No more *was* or *will be*, only *is*.

39
Taken Back

On that oddly reverberating note, Hank floats through the remainder of his day, and tonight sleeps on the bed for the first time in a several weeks. But he can't nod off. Keeps wondering how that "timeless" story of his ends. Many hours later, after a long and restless night, somewhere close to dawn, he thinks of Mixoc and suddenly understands what was meant by "we have gone too far." What the old man had not said, perhaps did not realize, is that most people—at least unconsciously—know it.

Yes, human beings have gone too far, have gotten lost, and want to get back home. His "timeless" story does not end, it just begins when we are taken back.

It's dark outside. A rooster crows. He tosses away the covers, rolls out of bed, goes to his desk and picks up a pen. The empty pad of paper waits as it has for weeks.

Somewhere behind his eyes, or maybe from *inside them*, Abe is frowning. "C'mon, buddy, please," his uncle whispers, "for your own sake, put that damn thing down." It's as if the ballpoint pen were a loaded gun. "Please?"

But Hank can't stop himself, writing until the sun comes up, then pacing around the room. He's got the basic idea figured out: Not just time, but also science, and all forms of human progress, have come to a crashing halt. That's the premise.

A good start, but not much else. It's like an outline, a stack of random notes, that's all he's really got.

Now the hardest work begins, when he must create believable characters to inhabit this new world. Who actually lives there? Who are these transformed people, and how might they disagree on what, if anything, should happen? He can't figure out where to begin. Only one thing is for certain: that humans will not *devolve* as wisely as Hank would like.

He feels stuck, should maybe go take a swim, but doesn't. Sits back at the tiny desk, exhausted. *What is it I'm missing?*

Then, out of the blue, he recalls an argument with Bret. It was about this same basic thing, about the need for people to simplify their lives. Oh…oh yeah…it was a night at the Circus Bar when their normal animosity, before only verbal, almost became a fight. This happened long before their clash five years ago, when things got even worse. Hank had made the observation—a passage from one of his silly unfinished novels —that cows, who exist in such a peaceful way, deserve more respect than many human beings.

Bret, as usual drunk, laughed like a damn hyena. "Well, there you have it! So fucking simple, huh?"

"I think it could be, yeah."

"I mean c'mon, for chrissakes, what the hell does that mean, we should all live like cows?"

"No," Hank said, "just less stupidly than some people."

"Then quit saying such stupid shit!"

"What I said is not the problem, Bret. It's how stupidly you heard it."

"Oh yeah?"

"Yeah."

Bret lumbered to the stage, all riled up, got face to face with Hank, and their angry words came close to blows. No, not a pretty scene. On the other hand, it showed without any doubt what a problem humanoids can be, and made the disgusted crowd think more fondly, perhaps, of cows.

Hank smiles, feels inspired. Yes, of course, *CONFLICT:* the proven ploy of focusing attention! That's what his novel needs, a bit of conflict! There could be some character, a head-strong jerk like Bret (or, even better, Ernie) who fights to keep time going—hold back humanity's needed metamorphosis.

In Hank's story, of course, this character will get nowhere. The transformed people are sympathetic, patiently try to calm him down, explain that "nowhere" is a wonderful place to be, like being everywhere at once.

Poor Nunca, disturbed all night by Hank's sleeplessness, his constant twists and turns, his often incoherent mumbles, whines at him from the bed. He jumps to the floor, runs out the door and barks. Hank goes to see what's up. The dog is at the gate, pawing and whining, a clear demand that they both leave.

Hank sits on the edge of the porch. "Wow, pal, you've certainly changed your tune!"

Nunca keeps barking, keeps scratching at the gate.

"Sorry, it's too early for a swim."

He races to Hank and doggedly, insistently, noses his knee.

"Okay, okay, listen…let me take a nap, then we'll go. *Maybe.*" He laughs at what has become his favorite word. Feeling tired, slightly off balance, he goes into the house, stretches out on the bed and closes his eyes, but his mind will not quit working, anxious to plot out where his novel needs to go. Eventually to *nowhere*, that's the plan. Pure existence in its simplest form. Yeah, yeah, yeah, so how does he get there?

He thinks of a way to show it, like with a small boy walking slowly, by himself, down a long dirt road. Maybe he picks up a blade of grass and chews it. Has nothing else to do. The boy sits down to take a rest, then lies on his back and looks up at the sky, sees a flock of honking geese, tries to count them but they're too quickly gone, disappearing into a bank clouds.

Hank opens his eyes and stares up at the ceiling, for a second has no idea where he is.

"Enrique?"

Nunca jumps onto the bed and licks his face.

"Okay, okay, back off." He pushes him away, then spots someone standing by the door. Orlando. *"Hola, amigo,"* Hank says, *"que pasa?"*

The boy comes closer. "Are you all right?"

Hank gets to a sitting position, leans back against the wall, wipes at his tired eyes. "Yes, I'm fine." But he does feel strange, and senses something might be wrong. "Why are you here?"

"Because it's three o'clock."

Huh? Really? Hank looks out the window at the sun-lit gate. "Oh." He sighs, relieved he's wrong, that there is no problem. "Okay, good. Guess I fell asleep."

"You can sleep some more. I'll be outside with Nunca." Orlando takes the dog and shuts the door behind them.

Hank lies back down, closes his eyes, and soon is aware he's dreaming, dark disturbing shapes moving through his mind. He shakes himself awake, crawls out of bed, goes to the desk and reads over what he's written. Still mostly just random notes. The word CONFLICT is scribbled in big bold letters. Up in one corner, the names Bret and Ernie have been circled.

Hank groans and shakes his head.

See what I mean, says Uncle Abe.

The front door opens and in comes Concepción. Her troubled face jolts him from his seat. He holds her hands, looks into her frightened eyes. "What is it?"

"I don't know, Enrique. Something very bad."

The words "very bad" make him think of Ernie. So damn weird. She had insisted the guy was gone, gone forever, so why does he keep sneaking through Hank's mind? Oh shit, oh hell, could he be back, could he have hurt one of her brothers?

Concepción blocks a rush of tears. "People say a lot of things, but no one…no one really…"

She seems confused, at a loss for words. "Please, amiga, tell me what you—"

"I shouldn't be here. It's dangerous to be outside, that's all they say." Orlando and Nunca come into the house. She tells the boy he must go home. "Your parents will be worried."

The boy looks panicked. "Why?"

"There is some kind of sickness in the air. Police have ordered everyone off the streets."

Sickness in the air?

Sounds almost comical. Are these Aakesh's mentioned rumors gone out of control, gone crazy? What is it with people, especially in this town, always needing something to talk about? But Hank knows his curt skepticism is not fair. It might be better, at times like these, to question *himself*, ask why he never wants to listen? What is it that he doesn't want to hear? He sees that Orlando paid close attention and believed her. The boy hugs him and Nunca good-bye, then runs off. Hank turns to Concepción. "I don't understand, what is this sickness?"

"I don't know, I…I came to warn you, that's all, but I have to go. I can't find Lydia, I have to go find…please, Enrique, please stay here. When I hear more I will tell you." She hurries from the house, rushes out the gate and slams it closed.

He knows how emotional his friend can get. Sometimes without reason. This, however, feels different, probably based on something real.

The "pandemic" Aakesh told him about, is that what this is?

Hank is not worried, only curious what's going on. He takes the dog out to the callejón. Seeing no one to ask, they keep walking, get to Calle Frutal. It must be about five o'clock, the busiest time of day, but there is no traffic—none—and not a

300

single person. *Huh?* They walk the half block to Rancho Grande, look up and down the wide empty street.

Nothing but ghostly silence.

Nunca whines, squirms, takes a few steps back toward the house. "No," says Hank, "not yet, we need to make sure María is okay." They cross the street, go through the series of narrow alleys to the soccer field. Strange that no kids are out there playing. *Relax*, he tells himself, then kneels next to Nunca and softly rubs the puppy's ears. "I promise, we'll go back soon."

They get past the field and turn left on the callejón that leads to Santander.

"You can't be here, Tata. Police say not to be outside."

He looks up, sees a boy watching them from a nearby balcony. "Do you know why?"

The boy shakes his head, looks very scared.

"It's okay," says Hank, "we're on our way home right now."

Calle Santander is also empty, except for a group of people, ten or so, gathered around María, who sits on her sidewalk stoop. The scene looks solemn, like some kind of vigil. Hank picks Nunca up and goes across the street. A teenage Maya boy is kneeling, looking up into María's eyes. He speaks quietly in Cakchiquel. Like a confession. He kisses her hand. She leans forward, gently grips his shoulders, kisses the crown of his head and whispers something.

"What did Nan say?" a ladina woman calls out in Spanish.

"Nan says you should all go home." It's Irma, on the other side of María.

Hank looks around at the frightened faces, for the first time feels some fear himself.

Someone says, "Please, Nan, tell us what is happening!"

The ladina woman wails, then gets on her knees and shouts up at the sky, "Is this the end of the world?"

Irma stands. "Calm down," she says with obvious irritation.

María wants to know what the ladina said. When Irma tells her, the old woman just shrugs, which causes more frightened grumbling in the crowd. Then, as if resigned, she gets to her feet and speaks, for less than a minute, very slowly, in Caqchikel. Everyone is hushed. The few ladinos have no idea what she's saying. When finished, she lets out a mighty sigh, waves a hand in the air, sits and closes her eyes.

Hank is reminded of Mixoc, who had ended his talk with the same dismissive gesture. He considers repeating what Aakesh had said, that this might be some strange illness that has spread around the planet. Then decides against it. No one would understand. These people might think he's crazy, which would only make matters worse.

"Nan is right," Irma says to the stunned crowd, "the world will never end. You must get ready for what is coming. Because we refuse to change, Mam will now change us."

The ladina woman again begins to wail, and others keep asking questions, getting louder and more frantic, but María's eyes stay closed.

"Enough!" shouts Irma, her angry face a warning. "All of you go home! That's all Nan has to say! Prepare yourselves before it is too late!"

With that command the crowd disperses, further encouraged by the approach of a policeman in a face mask. Some run to him, hoping he will have answers. The wailing woman is bent over, face to the ground. Irma squats and kindly pats her back.

"Hola, María," says Hank.

The old woman's eyes flash open and see him. She looks instantly at peace. "Ah, Enrique!" Her calmness makes him calm too. He sits next to her. They kiss each other's cheeks, then María points at Nunca. *"Tu chucho?"*

"Yes, my dog."

"Bueno," she says, and cuddles her face into the silky fur, giggles when Nunca licks her forehead.

Hank holds her hand. *"Estás bien?"*

María leans her forehead into his. *"Sí, Enrique, todo está bién."* *Everything is fine.* Same as Fiona tells him all the time.

But it's not, of that much he is certain.

The masked policeman walks up to Hank. "You have to get off the street."

"Why?"

"There is a sickness going around. Something dangerous."

"A virus?"

The policeman blinks at him and rolls his eyes, seems both angry and painfully distressed. "I don't know! I only know what *El Presidente* orders us to do! Now move!"

"Yes, all right, we're going," says Irma. She leans down and lifts María to her feet.

The policeman reaches out to take Hank's elbow, apparently to guide him. He evades it. "I don't need your help," Hank says, and starts toward the callejón. *"Hasta pronto,"* he calls back to his friends.

Irma looks terrified. María, however, looks at him and smiles, as if certain that all is well, and waves good bye.

Nunca scoots down the alley, in a hurry, and leads them directly home. Hank lets him inside the gate and closes it. "I'll be back soon." He walks to the river road and down toward the lake. Just above the large flat, a yellow ribbon is stretched between two metal posts. In front of it is this sign:

LAKE ACCESS PROHIBITED
UNTIL FURTHER NOTICE

There are policemen down on the flat, all wearing face masks. One of them holds up a hand and walks his way. "Excuse me, Señor, you should not be here."

"Can you please tell me why?"

"We don't know. Some kind of health issue. Something dangerous and contagious. Presidente Giammattei will be on television tomorrow morning. He will explain."

"But I'm sure it's not coming from the lake," says Hank. "I won't bother anyone, will only sit a few minutes by the water."

"Sorry, that's not allowed. There is a curfew all over town. Anywhere people might gather. Everything is closed off, including the lake. You need to stay in your house."

Hank understands he's being warned and must comply, returns up the hill and down the series of callejónes to his gate.

Nunca is waiting inside. He twists around in circles, then bolts toward his bowls. Though they're still half full, Hank tops them off—a sign of normalcy which calms his friend, a sign he desperately seems to need. And Hank needs one too. For him, though, it's not so easy. He sits on the porch, then leans back onto his elbows. The clouds are turning from pink to gray. The sun has set, dusk coming on. In an hour it will be dark.

No, of course the world is not ending, but he feels deeply worried. How long can they stop him from going to the lake? What if this sickness, whatever it is, keeps getting worse?

He goes into the house, takes the blanket from the bed and stuffs it in his pack. He gathers a few carrots from the kitchen, some tortillas, the last of Orlando's peanuts, and fills his water bottle. He changes from shorts to pants, pulls a hoodie over his tee-shirt, puts on socks and sneakers. Thinking of Nunca, he tops off the pack with a small plastic bag of dog food. The pooch has watched all this closely, aware that something is going on, and whines. Does not look pleased.

"Do what you want," says Hank, "I'm going to the lake." He leaves the house, walks through the garden, pauses at the gate. "Last chance," he says, and his friend comes running. "Yeah, good choice."

40
Going Home

As they get to the river road Hank hears a vehicle. "Sit," he says to Nunca. The dog does as he's told, looks proud to have remembered, his eyes opened wide, his ears perked up. "Good boy," says Hank, and peeks around the corner toward the lake. Two police cars are coming. He picks up Nunca, hides behind a bush, watches as they go by. Yep, just as Hank expected: *Quitting Time!* The police assume that no one would go to the lake at night, so there's no reason to stand guard.

He waits a few more minutes, then they hurry down the dirt road to its end, past the yellow ribbon and across the flat. Though the sky is getting dark, Hank has no problem seeing. Good that he knows this path so well. And there is no one else, not even dogs.

At the beach, they go to his regular stand of caña. He gazes at the water, now barely distinguishable from the volcanos or the sky, all fading fast into one dark shade of gray. He puts down his pack and sits, Nunca right beside him.

Strange that, in spite of the supposed danger, he's never felt more safe or more at peace. It's as if something has truly changed, as if the world, instead of ending, has started over!

Taken Back.

Oh, if only such a thing could happen! Not going back in time, Hank has no romantic notions about primitive existence. He would not have enjoyed the daily struggle to survive, hunt and gather enough to eat while probably coerced into toiling, year after year, to shape and move gigantic stones—build temples in fearful reverence to the gods.

No, not the simple life Hank would hope for, like when he was a child, when everything was a mystery and, while often confusing, made him curious, not afraid.

Once, at about age four, he asked Abe, "Why are we alive?"

His uncle laughed. "I got no clue. But that's a darn good thing to wonder about each day."

The boy, who preferred straight-forward answers, heard his question being dodged. "Huh?"

"The answer is in the asking, Henry. If you don't wonder, there's no chance you'll ever know."

Hank had taken that to heart. Still does.

He turns his attention to the lake and lets the wonder come, it's depth and stillness settling into him, his mind opening to its silence. He lies back and looks up into the darkness, watches as the gray turns black, watches as the first stars emerge, watches them fill the sky. Yes, of course, this is why primitive people observed the heavens, why they followed the constellations, the sun, and phases of the moon. This is why they built the temples. Not out of fear, but homage. Tributes to the unknown. Nothing romantic in that, just true. Hank imagines that ancient time when humans did not exist as a bunch of selfish "I's." Life on Earth was once a collective "we," which included every living thing.

And, true, some of those things would kill and eat you. Were people at times afraid? Yes, and maybe often, but living each day as part of nature's mystery they felt a need to express their wonder. He thinks of the great pyramids, and other temples around the world. How paltry compared to the planet's massive mountain ranges, its deep canyons and mighty rivers, unfathomable oceans and endless sky.

And this place where he is right now, this incredible lake, born of a volcanic explosion eighty thousand years ago! How fucking awesome, how inconceivable is that?

It was nature the ancients revered, not some created deity. If only we were so wise today. But no more temples are required. No churches or any kind of god. All nature needs is to be honored, taken care of, its soil and water and air kept clean.

Hank closes his eyes and falls asleep, journeys in and out of dreams, then wakes to see the moon, nearly full, rise over the eastern mountains, lighting up the darkness. He sits up. The shining lake is irresistible. He takes off his clothes and goes down to the water, Nunca by his side. They walk slowly along the shoreline, in the shallows, the man wet to his knees, the dog up to his chest. Hank considers that soaked fur, thinks of the problem it will be, sometime later, when his friend wants to snuggle up. He laughs. *Ah, yes, some time later.* He thinks of his latest unfinished novel. *A time that might never come!*

They get to the far point, climb onto a large concrete slab lying on the sand. Once the main support of a chalet dock, it is now just a worthless chunk of man-made stone.

Nunca shakes, his body rippling and water flying. "Okay, okay, enough!" Hank moves to the top of the slab, lays on his back and looks up at the moon and stars. He smiles at his simple pleasure, would stay right here all night, but after half an hour he feels stiff, the surface far too hard, its coldness wicking into his bones. "That's it, pal, let's go."

They return along the high path, away from the water, which gives Nunca more time to dry.

At their camp, Hank grabs the towel and rubs his buddy down. He then pulls his pack farther into the caña—a bit more protection should the wind pick up. For the time being it is warm, the air still, but there's a lot of night to come. He wipes the sand from his feet, puts on his pants, his socks, his sweatshirt, lies back and wraps himself in the blanket.

Nunca, as expected, cuddles close.

The next day comes tenderly, soundlessly, first as a soft gray veil, then a pale blue sky surrounding white puffy clouds. The sun lights the tops of all three volcanos. The lake spreads out before them. Nunca is already out there, belly-deep in the water, watching a group of ducks by the shoreline reeds.

Hank frees himself from the blanket, stands and stretches, lift his hands into the sky. "Good morning!"

Nunca comes running.

"Hello, hello, hello!" says Hank, kneading the puppy's ears. "Want some breakfast?" He opens his pack and pulls out the bag of dog food. Having no better choice, he pours it into his shoe. Nunca, fine with that, even gobbles a second helping before returning to the lake.

Hank eats a carrot, a handful of peanuts, drinks some water and goes to his special rock. It's about the same time that he's usually here. By now, Analu and Ingrid would be out swimming. Their absence confirms they won't be coming. Not them or anyone else. Indeed, beach access has been prohibited. And not a single boat on the water! *Increíble!*

It's like his early days in San Marcos, forty years ago, when he might have an entire morning without other people, only him and the ducks and egrets. This chance may never come again.

He strips and dives in. Few sensations are more sublime than swimming naked, even in water as cold as this. Enlivened and enchanted, Hank savors every stroke. It seems there's less cyanobacteria, as if this temporary pause from human use has begun to heal the lake.

Inspired by that hopeful thought he keeps going, and going, until he's breathing hard. He stops and pants for air, sees Nunca watching from the distant shore.

Yeah, uh-huh, what the hell am I doing, right?

To his surprise, Hank suddenly feels weak. And kind of spooked. Though his body is not tired, his mind—like a separate being—brings on a wave of intense jitters, his body trembling. *So, uh, maybe you've overdone it?*

He's heard that voice before, felt this panic that sometimes comes when he's out so far, with so much water underneath him, like he's trespassed beyond a sacred boundary, has taken the lake for granted, is out of balance with its nature, and in danger.

To counter a growing sense of peril, he must change this negative story in his head, *must change it now*—must accept and welcome the wonder of where he is.

Focus.

All that matters is the blessed air. In and out. In…and…out.

With every breath he thinks of Fiona, which helps to slow his pounding heart. *It's all right.* That's all she says, and all he needs to hear, over and over for several minutes, as she comforts him, then brings sunlight to warm his spirit.

The fear, like a forgotten thought, is gone. The lake is smooth and soothing and Hank again feels strong.

He could easily swim in, but won't, knows that Fiona wants him to stay. It's like she's trying to send a message, saying, over and over, there's something to learn out here. Something he needs to understand. Or maybe not, he isn't sure, maybe only to love this moment, to not be in any hurry.

He spots Nunca, there in the exact same spot, still watching. The pup must be confused. Is Hank ever coming back?

Yeah, good question!

He smiles to himself. *Wow, maybe not, huh? Maybe this is it.*

The thought echoes inside him like a long harmonic note, a reverberating tone, not coming from his mind but from the lake. He knows this music well and listens closely, feels Fiona with him and knows she hears it too.

Hank remembers her last swim, how frightened he was when she went underwater, afraid she might intentionally be drowning. He remembers his great relief when she finally surfaced, remembers her seeing his fear, remembers what she said.

"Sure, the lake is where I'd choose to be, but I know that can't happen."

She'd meant because of him, because he could not have handled being left alone. But so much has changed since then. He's not alone, Hank knows that now. Knows there's nothing to be afraid of.

Wherever you are, it's home. That's Fiona deep inside him.

He wipes clear his tearful eyes, refocuses on the beach. It looks like there are people next to Nunca. Hank squints to be sure that's what he's seeing. Wow, yes, two police officers, one of them with long black hair. A woman. He's seen her before in town. She kneels and pets the pup, who must be whining, must be terrified, has no idea what is happening, why his friend is so far away.

It's all right, pal, it's all right.

Hank takes another breath, feels grateful to still be breathing, and wonders what might come next.

Oh yes, a curious little thing.

The male officer sees him looking, lifts both hands out his way and, like a cop directing traffic, waves him in.

Hank smiles. Like in any good novel, it's a sign that can't be missed. So, with a sense of unsinkable joy, he starts swimming.